W9-CLJ-360

# CHARLES DICKENS

PROFOUND COGITATION OF CAPTAIN CUTTLE.

# *CHARLES DICKENS*

# DOMBEY AND SON

## VOLUME I

WITH ILLUSTRATIONS BY

HABLÔT KNIGHT BROWNE ('PHIZ')

*WALTER J. BLACK, INC.*

NEW YORK

PRINTED IN THE UNITED STATES OF AMERICA

# CONTENTS

# ILLUSTRATIONS

# DOMBEY AND SON

# DOMBEY AND SON

## CHAPTER I

### DOMBEY AND SON

DOMBEY sat in the corner of the darkened room in the great arm-chair by the bedside, and Son lay tucked up warm in a little basket bedstead, carefully disposed on a low settee immediately in front of the fire and close to it, as if his constitution were analogous to that of a muffin, and it was essential to toast him brown while he was very new.

Dombey was about eight-and-forty years of age. Son about eight-and-forty minutes. Dombey was rather bald, rather red, and though a handsome well-made man, too stern and pompous in appearance to be prepossessing. Son was very bald, and very red, and though (of course) an undeniably fine infant, somewhat crushed and spotty in his general effect, as yet. On the brow of Dombey, Time and his brother Care had set some marks, as on a tree that was to come down in good time—remorseless twins they are for striding through their human forests, notching as they go—while the countenance of Son was crossed and recrossed with a thousand little creases, which the same deceitful Time would take delight in smoothing out and wearing away with the flat part of his scythe, as a preparation of the surface for his deeper operations.

Dombey, exulting in the long-looked-for event, jingled and jingled the heavy gold watch-chain that depended from below his trim blue coat, whereof the buttons sparkled phosphorescently in the feeble rays of the distant fire. Son, with his little fists curled up and clenched, seemed, in his feeble way, to be squaring at existence for having come upon him so unexpectedly.

'The house will once again, Mrs. Dombey,' said Mr. Dombey, 'be not only in name but in fact Dombey and Son; Dom-bey and Son!'

The words had such a softening influence, that he appended a term of endearment to Mrs. Dombey's name (though not without some hesitation, as being a man but little used to that form of address): and said, 'Mrs. Dombey, my—my dear.'

A transient flush of faint surprise overspread the sick lady's face as she raised her eyes towards him.

'He will be christened Paul, my—Mrs. Dombey—of course.'

She feebly echoed, 'Of course,' or rather expressed it by the motion of her lips, and closed her eyes again.

'His father's name, Mrs. Dombey, and his grandfather's! I wish his grandfather was alive this day!' And again he said 'Dom-bey and Son,' in exactly the same tone as before.

Those three words conveyed the one idea of Mr. Dombey's life. The earth was made for Dombey and Son to trade in, and the sun and moon were made to give them light. Rivers and seas were formed to float their ships; rainbows gave them promise of fair weather; winds blew for or against their enterprises; stars and planets circled in their orbits, to preserve inviolate a system of which they were the centre. Common abbreviations took new meanings in his eyes, and had sole reference to them: A. D. had no concern with anno Domini, but stood for anno Dombei—and Son.

He had risen, as his father had before him, in the course of life and death, from Son to Dombey, and for nearly twenty years had been the sole representative of the firm. Of those years he had been married, ten—married, as some said, to a lady with no heart to give him; whose happiness was in the past, and who was content to bind her broken spirit to the dutiful and meek endurance of the present. Such idle talk was little likely to reach the ears of Mr. Dombey, whom it nearly concerned; and probably no one in the world would have received it with such utter incredulity as he, if it had reached him. Dombey and Son had often dealt in hides, but never in hearts. They left that fancy ware to boys and girls, and boarding-schools and books. Mr. Dombey would have reasoned: That a matrimonial alliance with himself *must,* in the nature of things, be gratifying and honourable to any woman of common sense. That the hope of giving birth to a new partner in such a house, could not fail to awaken a glorious and stirring ambition in the breast of the least ambitious of her sex. That Mrs. Dombey had entered on that social contract of matrimony: almost necessarily part of a genteel and wealthy station, even without reference to the perpetuation of family firms: with her eyes fully open to these advantages. That Mrs. Dombey had had daily practical knowledge of his position in society. That Mrs. Dombey had always sat at the head of his table, and done the honours of his house in a remarkably lady-like and becoming manner. That Mrs. Dombey must have been happy. That she couldn't help it.

Or, at all events, with one drawback. Yes. That he would have allowed. With only one; but that one certainly involving much. They had been married ten years, and until this present day on which Mr. Dombey sat jingling and jingling his heavy gold watch-chain in the great arm-chair by the side of the bed, had had no issue.

—To speak of; none worth mentioning. There had been a girl some six years before, and the child, who had stolen into the chamber unobserved, was now crouching timidly, in a corner whence she could see her mother's face. But what was a girl to Dombey and Son! In the capital of the House's name and dignity, such a child was merely a piece of base coin that couldn't be invested—a bad Boy—nothing more.

Mr. Dombey's cup of satisfaction was so full at this moment, however, that he felt he could afford a drop or two of its contents, even to sprinkle on the dust in the by-path of his little daughter.

So he said, 'Florence, you may go and look at your pretty brother, if you like, I dare say. Don't touch him!'

The child glanced keenly at the blue coat and stiff white cravat, which, with a pair of creaking boots and a very loud ticking watch, embodied her idea of a father; but her eyes returned to her mother's face immediately, and she neither moved nor answered.

Next moment, the lady had opened her eyes and seen the child; and the child had run towards her; and, standing on tiptoe, the better to hide her face in her embrace, had clung about her with a desperate affection very much at variance with her years.

'Oh Lord bless me!' said Mr. Dombey, rising testily. 'A very ill-advised and feverish proceeding this, I am sure. I had better ask Doctor Peps if he 'll have the goodness to step upstairs again perhaps. I 'll go down. I'll go down. I needn't beg you, ' he added, pausing for a moment at the settee before the fire, 'to take particular care of this young gentleman, Mrs.——'

'Blockitt, sir?' suggested the nurse, a simpering piece of faded gentility, who did not presume to state her name as a fact, but merely offered it as a mild suggestion.

'Of this young gentleman, Mrs. Blockitt.'

'No, sir, indeed. I remember when Miss Florence was born——'

'Ay, ay, ay,' said Mr. Dombey, bending over the basket bedstead, and slightly bending his brows at the same time. 'Miss Florence was all very well, but this is another matter. This young gentleman has to accomplish a destiny. A destiny, little fellow!' As he thus apostrophised the infant he raised one of his hands to his lips, and kissed it; then, seeming to fear that the action involved some compromise of his dignity, went, awkwardly enough, away.

Doctor Parker Peps, one of the Court Physicians, and a man of immense reputation for assisting at the increase of great families, was walking up and down the drawing-room with his hands behind him, to the unspeakable admiration of the family surgeon, who had regularly puffed the case for the last six weeks, among all his patients, friends, and acquaintances, as one to which he was in hourly expectation day and night of being summoned, in conjunction with Doctor Parker Peps.

'Well, sir,' said Doctor Parker Peps in a round, deep, sonorous voice, muffled for the occasion, like the knocker; 'do you find that your dear lady is at all roused by your visit?'

'Stimulated as it were?' said the family practitioner faintly: bowing at the same time to the Doctor, as much as to say, 'Excuse my putting in a word, but this is a valuable connection.'

Mr. Dombey was quite discomfited by the question. He had thought so little of the patient, that he was not in a condition to answer it. He said that it would be a satisfaction to him, if Doctor Parker Peps would walk upstairs again.

'Good! We must not disguise from you, sir,' said Doctor Parker Peps, 'that there is a want of power in Her Grace the Duchess—I beg your pardon; I confound names; I should say, in your amiable lady. That there is a certain degree of languor, and a general absence of elasticity, which we would rather—not—'

'See,' interposed the family practitioner with another inclination of the head.

'Quite so,' said Doctor Parker Peps, 'which we would rather not see. It would appear that the system of Lady Cankaby—excuse me: I should say of Mrs. Dombey: I confuse the names of cases—'

'So very numerous,' murmured the family practitioner—'can't be expected I 'm sure—quite wonderful if otherwise—Doctor Parker Peps's West End practice—'

'Thank you,' said the Doctor, 'quite so. It would appear, I was observing, that the system of our patient has sustained a shock, from which it can only hope to rally by a great and strong—'

'And vigorous,' murmured the family practitioner.

'Quite so,' assented the Doctor—'and vigorous effort. Mr. Pilkins here, who from his position of medical adviser in this family—no one better qualified to fill that position, I am sure.'

'Oh!' murmured the family practitioner. ' "Praise from Sir Hubert Stanley!" '

'You are good enough,' returned Doctor Parker Peps, 'to say so. Mr. Pilkins who, from his position, is best acquainted with the patient's constitution in its normal state (an acquaintance very valuable to us in forming our opinions on these occasions), is of opinion, with me, that Nature must be called upon to make a vigorous effort in this instance; and that if our interesting friend the Countess of Dombey—I *beg* your pardon; Mrs. Dombey—should not be—'

'Able,' said the family practitioner.

'To make that effort successfully,' said Doctor Parker Peps, 'then a crisis might arise, which we should both sincerely deplore.'

With that, they stood for a few seconds looking at the ground. Then, on the motion—made in dumb show—of Doctor Parker Peps, they went upstairs; the family practitioner opening the room-door for that distinguished professional, and following him out, with most obsequious politeness.

To record of Mr. Dombey that he was not in his way affected by this intelligence, would be to do him an injustice. He was not a man of whom it could properly be said that he was ever startled or shocked; but he certainly had a sense within him, that if his wife should sicken and decay, he would be very sorry, and that he would find a something gone from among his plate and furniture, and other household possessions, which was well worth the having, and could not be lost without sincere regret. Though it would be a cool, business-like, gentlemanly, self-possessed regret, no doubt.

His meditations on the subject were soon interrupted, first by the rustling of garments on the staircase, and then by the sudden whisking into the room of a lady rather past the middle age than otherwise, but dressed in a very juvenile manner, particularly as to the tightness of her bodice, who, running up to him with a kind of screw in her face and carriage, expressive of suppressed emotion, flung her arms round his neck, and said in a choking voice—

'My dear Paul! He 's quite a Dombey!'

'Well, well!' returned her brother—for Mr. Dombey was her brother—'I think he *is* like the family. Don't agitate yourself, Louisa.'

'It 's very foolish of me,' said Louisa, sitting down, and taking out her pocket-handkerchief, 'but he 's—he 's such a perfect Dombey! *I* never saw anything like it in my life!'

'But what is this about Fanny, herself?' said Mr. Dombey. 'How is Fanny?'

'My dear Paul,' returned Louisa, 'it 's nothing whatever. Take my word, it 's nothing whatever. There is exhaustion, certainly, but nothing like what I underwent myself, either with George or Frederick. An effort is necessary. That 's all. If dear Fanny were a Dombey!—But I dare say she 'll make it; I have no doubt she 'll make it. Knowing it to be required of her, as a duty, of course she 'll make it. My dear Paul, it 's very weak and silly of me, I know, to be so trembly and shaky from head to foot; but I am so very queer that I must ask you for a glass of wine and a morsel of that cake. I thought I should have fallen out of the staircase window as I came down from seeing dear Fanny, and that tiddy ickle sing.' These last words originated in a sudden vivid reminiscence of the baby.

They were succeeded by a gentle tap at the door.

'Mrs. Chick,' said a very bland female voice outside, 'how are you now, my dear friend?'

'My dear Paul,' said Louisa in a low voice, as she rose from her seat, 'it 's Miss Tox. The kindest creature! I never could have got here without her!

Miss Tox, my brother Mr. Dombey. Paul, my dear, my very particular friend Miss Tox.'

The lady thus specially presented, was a long lean figure, wearing such a faded air that she seemed not to have been made in what linen-drapers call 'fast colours' originally, and to have, by little and little, washed out. But for this she might have been described as the very pink of general propitiation and politeness. From a long habit of listening admirably to everything that was said in her presence, and looking at the speakers as if she were mentally engaged in taking off impressions of their images upon her soul, never to part with the same but with life, her head had quite settled on one side. Her hands had contracted a spasmodic habit of raising themselves of their own accord as in involuntary admiration. Her eyes were liable to a similar affection. She had the softest voice that ever was heard; and her nose, stupendously aquiline, had a little knob in the very centre or key-stone of the bridge, whence it tended downwards towards her face, as in an invincible determination never to turn up at anything.

Miss Tox's dress, though perfectly genteel and good, had a certain character of angularity and scantiness. She was accustomed to wear odd weedy little flowers in her bonnets and caps. Strange grasses were sometimes perceived in her hair; and it was observed by the curious, of all her collars, frills, tuckers, wristbands, and other gossamer articles—indeed of everything she wore which had two ends to it intended to unite—that the two ends were never on good terms, and wouldn't quite meet without a struggle. She had furry articles for winter wear, as tippets, boas, and muffs, which stood up on end in a rampant manner, and were not at all sleek. She was much given to the carrying about of small bags with snaps to them, that went off like little pistols when they were shut up; and when full-dressed, she wore round her neck the barrenest of lockets, representing a fishy old eye, with no approach to speculation in it. These and other appearances of a similar nature, had served to propagate the opinion, that Miss Tox was a lady of what is called a limited independence, which she turned to the best account. Possibly her mincing gait encouraged the belief, and suggested that her clipping a step of ordinary compass into two or three, originated in her habit of making the most of everything.'

'I am sure,' said Miss Tox, with a prodigious curtsey, 'that to have the honour of being presented to Mr. Dombey is a distinction which I have long sought, but very little expected at the present moment. My dear Mrs. Chick—may I say Louisa!'

Mrs. Chick took Miss Tox's hand in hers, rested the foot of her wine-glass upon it, repressed a tear, and said in a low voice 'Bless you!'

'My dear Louisa then,' said Miss Tox, 'my sweet friend, how are you now?'

'Better,' Mrs. Chick returned. 'Take some wine. You have been almost as anxious as I have been, and must want it, I am sure.'

Mr. Dombey of course officiated.

'Miss Tox, Paul,' pursued Mrs. Chick, still retaining her hand, 'knowing how much I have been interested in the anticipation of the event of to-day, has been working at a little gift for Fanny, which I promised to present. It is only a pin-cushion for the toilette table, Paul, but I do say, and will say, and must say, that Miss Tox has very prettily adapted the sentiment to the occasion. I call "Welcome little Dombey" poetry, myself!'

'Is that the device?' inquired her brother.

'That is the device,' returned Louisa.

'But do me the justice to remember, my dear Louisa,' said Miss Tox in a tone of low and earnest entreaty, 'that nothing but the—I have some difficulty in expressing myself—the dubiousness of the result would have induced me to take so great a liberty: "Welcome, Master Dombey," would have been much more congenial to my feelings, as I am sure you know. But the uncertainty attendant on angelic strangers, will, I hope, excuse what must otherwise appear an unwarrantable familiarity.' Miss Tox made a graceful bend as she spoke, in favour of Mr. Dombey, which that gentleman graciously acknowledged. Even the sort of recognition of Dombey and Son, conveyed in the foregoing conversation, was so palatable to him, that his sister, Mrs. Chick—though he affected to consider her a weak good-natured person—had perhaps more influence over him than anybody else.

'Well!' said Mrs. Chick, with a sweet smile, 'after this, I forgive Fanny everything!'

It was a declaration in a Christian spirit, and Mrs. Chick felt that it did her good. Not that she had anything particular to forgive in her sister-in-law, nor indeed anything at all, except her having married her brother—in itself a species of audacity—and her having, in the course of events, given birth to a girl instead of a boy: which, as Mrs. Chick had frequently observed, was not quite what she had expected of her, and was not a pleasant return for all the attention and distinction she had met with.

Mr. Dombey being hastily summoned out of the room at this moment, the two ladies were left alone together. Miss Tox immediately became spasmodic.

'I knew you would admire my brother. I told you so beforehand, my dear,' said Louisa.

Miss Tox's hands and eyes expressed how much.

'And as to his property, my dear!'

'Ah!' said Miss Tox, with deep feeling.

'Im—mense!'

'But his deportment, my dear Louisa!' said Miss Tox. 'His presence! His dignity! No portrait that I have ever seen of any one has been half so replete with those qualities. Something so stately, you know: so uncompromising: so very wide across the chest: so upright! A pecuniary Duke of York, my love, and nothing short of it!' said Miss Tox. 'That 's what *I* should designate him.'

'Why, my dear Paul!' exclaimed his sister, as he returned, 'you look quite pale! There 's nothing the matter?'

'I am sorry to say, Louisa, that they tell me that Fanny—'

'Now, my dear Paul,' returned his sister, rising, 'don't believe it. If you have any reliance on my experience, Paul, you may rest assured that there is nothing wanting but an effort on Fanny's part. And that effort,' she continued, taking off her bonnet, and adjusting her cap and gloves, in a business-like manner, 'she must be encouraged, and really, if necessary, urged to make. Now, my dear Paul, come upstairs with me.'

Mr. Dombey, who, besides being generally influenced by his sister for the reason already mentioned, had really faith in her as an experienced and bustling matron, acquiesced: and followed her, at once, to the sick chamber.

The lady lay upon her bed as he had left her, clasping her little daughter to her breast. The child clung close about her, with the same intensity as before, and never raised her head, or moved her soft cheek from her mother's face, or looked on those who stood around, or spoke, or moved, or shed a tear.

'Restless without the little girl,' the Doctor whispered to Mr. Dombey. 'We found it best to have her in again.'

There was such a solemn stillness round the bed; and the two medical attendants seemed to look on the impassive form with so much compassion and so little hope, that Mrs. Chick was for the moment diverted from her purpose. But presently summoning courage and what she called presence of mind, she sat down by the bedside, and said in the low precise tone of one who endeavours to awaken a sleeper—

'Fanny! Fanny!'

There was no sound in answer but the loud ticking of Mr. Dombey's watch and Doctor Parker Peps's watch, which seemed in the silence to be running a race.

'Fanny, my dear,' said Mrs. Chick, with assumed lightness, 'here 's Mr. Dombey come to see you. Won't you speak to him? They want to lay your little boy—the baby, Fanny, you know; you have hardly seen him yet, I think—in bed; but they can't till you rouse yourself a little. Don't you think it 's time you roused yourself a little? Eh?'

She bent her ear to the bed, and listened: at the same time looking round at the bystanders, and holding up her finger.

'Eh?' she repeated, 'what was it you said, Fanny? I didn't hear you.'

No word or sound in answer. Mr. Dombey's watch and Dr. Parker Peps's watch seemed to be racing faster.

'Now, really Fanny, my dear,' said the sister-in-law, altering her position, and speaking less confidently, and more earnestly, in spite of herself, 'I shall have to be quite cross with you, if you don't rouse yourself. It 's necessary for you to make an effort, and perhaps a very great and painful effort which you are not disposed to make: but this is a world of effort you know, Fanny, and we must never yield, when so much depends upon us. Come! Try! I must really scold you if you don't!'

The race in the ensuing pause was fierce and furious. The watches semed to jostle, and to trip each other up.

'Fanny!' said Louisa, glancing round, with a gathering alarm. 'Only look at me. Only open your eyes to show me that you hear and understand me; will you? Good Heaven, gentlemen, what is to be done!'

The two medical attendants exchanged a look across the bed; and the physician, stooping down, whispered in the child's ear. Not having understood the purport of his whisper, the little creature turned her perfectly colourless face, and deep dark eyes towards him; but without loosening her hold in the least.

The whisper was repeated.

'Mamma!' said the child.

The little voice, familiar and dearly loved, awakened some show of consciousness, even at that ebb. For a moment, the closed eye-lids trembled, and the nostril quivered, and the faintest shadow of a smile was seen.

'Mamma!' cried the child, sobbing aloud. 'Oh dear mamma! oh dear mamma!'

The Doctor gently brushed the scattered ringlets of the child, aside from the face and mouth of the mother. Alas how calm they lay there; how little breath there was to stir them!

Thus, clinging fast to that slight spar within her

arms, the mother drifted out upon the dark and unknown sea that rolls round all the world.

## CHAPTER II

### IN WHICH TIMELY PROVISION IS MADE FOR AN EMERGENCY THAT WILL SOMETIMES ARISE IN THE BEST-REGULATED FAMILIES

'I SHALL never cease to congratulate myself,' said Mrs. Chick, 'on having said, when I little thought what was in store for us,—really as if I was inspired by something,—that I forgave poor dear Fanny everything. Whatever happens, that must always be a comfort to me!'

Mrs. Chick made this impressive observation in the drawing-room, after having descended thither from the inspection of the mantua-makers upstairs, who were busy on the family mourning. She delivered it for the behoof of Mr. Chick, who was a stout bald gentleman, with a very large face, and his hands continually in his pockets, and who had a tendency in his nature to whistle and hum tunes, which, sensible of the indecorum of such sounds in a house of grief, he was at some pains to repress at present.

'Don't you over-exert yourself, Loo,' said Mr. Chick, 'or you 'll be laid up with spasms, I see. Right tol loor rul! Bless my soul, I forgot! We 're here one day and gone the next!'

Mrs. Chick contented herself with a glance of reproof, and then proceeded with the thread of her discourse.

'I am sure,' she said, 'I hope this heart-rending occurrence will be a warning to all of us, to accustom ourselves to rouse ourselves, and to make efforts in time where they 're required of us. There 's a moral in everything, if we would only avail ourselves of it. It will be our own faults if we lose sight of this one.'

Mr. Chick invaded the grave silence which ensued on this remark with the singularly inappropriate air of 'A cobbler there was'; and checking himself, in some confusion, observed, that it was undoubtedly our own faults if we didn't improve such melancholy occasions as the present.

'Which might be better improved, I should think, Mr. C.,' retorted his helpmate, after a short pause, 'than by the introduction, either of the College Hornpipe, or the equally unmeaning and unfeeling remark of rump-te-iddity, bow-wow-wow!'—which Mr. Chick had indeed indulged in, under his breath, and which Mrs. Chick repeated in a tone of withering scorn.

'Merely habit, my dear,' pleaded Mr. Chick.

'Nonsense! Habit!' returned his wife. 'If you 're a rational being, don't make such ridiculous excuses. Habit! If I was to get a habit (as you call it) of walking on the ceiling, like the flies, I should hear enough of it, I dare say.'

It appeared so probable that such a habit might be attended with some degree of notoriety, that Mr. Chick didn't venture to dispute the position.

'How 's the baby, Loo?' asked Mr. Chick: to change the subject.

'What baby do you mean?' answered Mrs. Chick. 'I am sure the morning I have had, with that dining-room downstairs one mass of babies, no one in their senses would believe.'

'One mass of babies!' repeated Mr. Chick, staring with an alarmed expression about him.

'It would have occurred to most men,' said Mrs. Chick, 'that poor dear Fanny being no more, it becomes necessary to provide a nurse.'

'Oh! Ah!' said Mr. Chick. 'Toor-rul—such is life, I mean. I hope you are suited, my dear.'

'Indeed I am not,' said Mrs. Chick; 'nor likely to be, so far as I can see. Meanwhile, of course, the child is—'

'Going to the very deuce,' said Mr. Chick, thoughtfully, 'to be sure.'

Admonished, however, that he had committed himself, by the indignation expressed in Mrs. Chick's countenance at the idea of a Dombey going there; and thinking to atone for his misconduct by a bright suggestion, he added—

'Couldn't something temporary be done with a teapot?'

If he had meant to bring the subject prematurely to a close, he could not have done it more effectually. After looking at him for some moments in silent resignation, Mrs. Chick walked majestically to the window and peeped through the blind, attracted by the sound of wheels. Mr. Chick, finding that his destiny was, for the time, against him, said no more, and walked off. But it was not always thus with Mr. Chick. He was often in the ascendant himself, and at those times punished Louisa roundly. In their matrimonial bickerings they were, upon the whole, a well-matched, fairly-balanced, give-and-take couple. It would have been, generally speaking, very difficult to have betted on the winner. Often when Mr. Chick seemed beaten, he would suddenly make a start, turn the tables, clatter them about the ears of Mrs. Chick, and carry all before him. Being liable himself to similar unlooked-for checks from Mrs. Chick, their little contests usually possessed a character of uncertainty that was very animating.

Miss Tox had arrived on the wheels just now

alluded to, and came running into the room in a breathless condition.

'My dear Louisa,' said Miss Tox, 'is the vacancy still unsupplied?'

'You good soul, yes,' said Mrs. Chick.

'Then, my dear Louisa,' returned Miss Tox, 'I hope and believe—but in one moment, my dear, I 'll introduce the party.'

Running downstairs again as fast as she had run up, Miss Tox got the party out of the hackney-coach, and soon returned with it under convoy.

It then appeared that she had used the word, not in its legal or business acceptation, when it merely expresses an individual, but as a noun of multitude, or signifying many: for Miss Tox escorted a plump rosy-cheeked wholesome apple-faced young woman, with an infant in her arms; a younger woman not so plump, but apple-faced also, who led a plump and apple-faced child in each hand; another plump and also apple-faced boy who walked by himself; and finally, a plump and apple-faced man, who carried in his arms another plump and apple-faced boy, whom he stood down on the floor, and admonished, in a husky whisper, to 'kitch hold of his brother Johnny.'

'My dear Louisa,' said Miss Tox, 'knowing your great anxiety, and wishing to relieve it, I posted off myself to the Queen Charlotte's Royal Married Females, which you had forgot, and put the question, Was there anybody there that they thought would suit? No, they said there was not. When they gave me that answer, I do assure you, my dear, I was almost driven to despair on your account. But it did so happen, that one of the Royal Married Females, hearing the inquiry, reminded the matron of another who had gone to her own home, and who, she said, would in all likelihood be most satisfactory. The moment I heard this, and had it corroborated by the matron—excellent references and unimpeachable character—I got the address, my dear, and posted off again.'

'Like the dear good Tox, you are!' said Louisa.

'Not at all,' returned Miss Tox. 'Don't say so. Arriving at the house (the cleanest place, my dear! You might eat your dinner off the floor), I found the whole family sitting at table; and feeling that no account of them could be half so comfortable to you and Mr. Dombey as the sight of them all together, I brought them all away. This gentleman,' said Miss Tox, pointing out the apple-faced man, 'is the father. Will you have the goodness to come a little forward, sir?'

The apple-faced man having sheepishly complied with this request, stood chuckling and grinning in a front row.

'This is his wife, of course,' said Miss Tox, singling out the young woman with the baby. 'How do you do, Polly?'

'I 'm pretty well, I thank you, ma'am,' said Polly.

By way of bringing her out dexterously, Miss Tox had made the inquiry as in condescension to an old acquaintance whom she hadn't seen for a fortnight or so.

'I 'm glad to hear it,' said Miss Tox. 'The other young woman is her unmarried sister who lives with them, and would take care of her children. Her name 's Jemima. How do you do, Jemima?'

'I 'm pretty well, I thank you, ma'am,' returned Jemima.

'I 'm very glad indeed to hear it,' said Miss Tox. 'I hope you 'll keep so. Five children. Youngest six weeks. The fine little boy with a blister on his nose is the eldest. The blister, I believe,' said Miss Tox, looking round upon the family, 'is not constitutional, but accidental?'

The apple-faced man was understood to growl, 'Flat iron.'

'I beg your pardon, sir,' said Miss Tox, 'did you—'

'Flat iron,' he repeated.

'Oh yes,' said Miss Tox. 'Yes! quite true. I forgot. The little creature, in his mother's absence, smelt a warm flat iron. You 're quite right, sir. You were going to have the goodness to inform me, when we arrived at the door, that you were by trade, a—'

'Stoker,' said the man.

'A choker!' said Miss Tox, quite aghast.

'Stoker,' said the man. 'Steam ingine.'

'Oh-h! Yes!' returned Miss Tox, looking thoughtfully at him, and seeming still to have but a very imperfect understanding of his meaning. 'And how do you like it, sir?'

'Which, mum?' said the man.

'That,' replied Miss Tox. 'Your trade.'

'Oh! Pretty well, mum. The ashes sometimes gets in here'; touching his chest: 'and makes a man speak gruff, as at the present time. But it *is* ashes, mum, not crustiness.'

Miss Tox seemed to be so little enlightened by this reply, as to find a difficulty in pursuing the subject. But Mrs. Chick relieved her, by entering into a close private examination of Polly, her children, her marriage certificate, testimonials, and so forth. Polly coming out unscathed from this ordeal, Mrs. Chick withdrew with her report to her brother's room, and as an emphatic comment on it, and corroboration of it, carried the two rosiest little Toodles with her, Toodle being the family name of the apple-faced family.

Mr. Dombey had remained in his own apartment

since the death of his wife, absorbed in visions of the youth, education, and destination of his baby son. Something lay at the bottom of his cool heart, colder and heavier than its ordinary load; but it was more a sense of the child's loss than his own, awakening within him an almost angry sorrow. That the life and progress on which he built such hopes, should be endangered in the outset by so mean a want; that Dombey and Son should be tottering for a nurse, was a sore humiliation. And yet in his pride and jealousy, he viewed with so much bitterness the thought of being dependent for the very first step towards the accomplishment of his soul's desire, on a hired serving-woman who would be to the child, for the time, all that even *his* alliance could have made his own wife, that in every new rejection of a candidate he felt a secret pleasure. The time had now come, however, when he could no longer be divided between these two sets of feelings. The less so, as there seemed to be no flaw in the title of Polly Toodle after his sister had set it forth, with many commendations on the indefatigable friendship of Miss Tox.

'These children look healthy,' said Mr. Dombey. 'But to think of their some day claiming a sort of relationship to Paul! Take them away, Louisa! Let me see this woman and her husband.'

Mrs. Chick bore off the tender pair of Toodles, and presently returned with that tougher couple whose presence her brother had commanded.

'My good woman,' said Mr. Dombey, turning round in his easy chair, as one piece, and not as a man with limbs and joints, 'I understand you are poor, and wish to earn money by nursing the little boy, my son, who has been so prematurely deprived of what can never be replaced. I have no objection to your adding to the comforts of your family by that means.

So far as I can tell, you seem to be a deserving object. But I must impose one or two conditions on you, before you enter my house in that capacity. While you are here, I must stipulate that you are always known as—say as Richards—an ordinary name, and convenient. Have you any objection to be known as Richards? You had better consult your husband.'

As the husband did nothing but chuckle and grin, and continually draw his right hand across his mouth, moistening the palm, Mrs. Toodle, after nudging him twice or thrice in vain, dropped a curtsey and replied 'that perhaps if she was to be called out of her name, it would be considered in the wages.'

'Oh, of course,' said Mr. Dombey. 'I desire to make it a question of wages, altogether. Now, Richards, if you nurse my bereaved child, I wish you to remember this always. You will receive a liberal stipend in return for the discharge of certain duties, in the performance of which, I wish you to see as little of your family as possible. When those duties cease to be required and rendered, and the stipend ceases to be paid, there is an end of all relations between us. Do you understand me?'

Mrs. Toodle seemed doubtful about it; and as to Toodle himself, he had evidently no doubt whatever, that he was all abroad.

'You have children of your own,' said Mr. Dombey. 'It is not at all in this bargain that you need become attached to my child, or that my child need become attached to you. I don't expect or desire anything of the kind. Quite the reverse. When you go away from here, you will have concluded what is a mere matter of bargain and sale, hiring and letting: and will stay away. The child will cease to remember you; and you will cease, if you please, to remember the child.'

Mrs. Toodle, with a little more colour in her cheeks than she had had before, said 'she hoped she knew her place.'

'I hope you do, Richards,' said Mr. Dombey. 'I have no doubt you know it very well. Indeed it is so plain and obvious that it could hardly be otherwise. Louisa, my dear, arrange with Richards about money, and let her have it when and how she pleases. Mr. what 's-your-name, a word with you, if you please!'

Thus arrested on the threshold as he was following his wife out of the room, Toodle returned and confronted Mr. Dombey alone. He was a strong, loose, round-shouldered, shuffling, shaggy fellow, on whom his clothes sat negligently: with a good deal of hair and whisker, deepened in its natural tint, perhaps by smoke and coal-dust: hard knotty hands: and a square forehead, as coarse in grain as the bark of an oak. A thorough contrast in all respects to Mr. Dombey, who was one of those close-shaved close-cut moneyed gentlemen who are glossy and crisp like new bank-notes, and who seem to be artificially braced and tightened as by the stimulating action of golden shower-baths.

'You have a son, I believe?' said Mr. Dombey.

'Four on 'em, sir. Four hims and a her. All alive!'

'Why, it 's as much as you can afford to keep them!' said Mr. Dombey.

'I couldn't hardly afford but one thing in the world less, sir.'

'What is that?'

'To lose 'em, sir.'

'Can you read?' asked Mr. Dombey.

'Why, not partik'ler, sir.'

'Write?'

'With chalk, sir?'

'With anything?'

'I could make shift to chalk a little bit, I think, if I was put to it,' said Toodle after some reflection.

'And yet,' said Mr. Dombey, 'you are two or three and thirty, I suppose?'

'Thereabouts, I suppose, sir,' answered Toodle, after more reflection.

'Then why don't you learn?' asked Mr. Dombey.

'So I'm a going to, sir. One of my little boys is a going to learn me, when he's old enough, and been to school himself.'

'Well!' said Mr. Dombey, after looking at him attentively, and with no great favour, as he stood gazing round the room (principally round the ceiling) and still drawing his hand across and across his mouth. 'You heard what I said to your wife just now?'

'Polly heerd it,' said Toodle, jerking his hat over his shoulder in the direction of the door, with an air of perfect confidence in his better half. 'It's all right.'

'As you appear to leave everything to her,' said Mr. Dombey, frustrated in his intention of impressing his vews still more distinctly on the husband, as the stronger character, 'I suppose it is of no use my saying anything to you.'

'Not a bit,' said Toodle. 'Polly heerd it. *She's* awake, sir.'

'I won't detain you any longer then,' returned Mr. Dombey disappointed. 'Where have you worked all your life?'

'Mostly underground, sir, till I got married. I come to the level then. I'm a going on one of these here railroads when they comes into full play.'

As the last straw breaks the laden camel's back, this piece of underground information crushed the sinking spirits of Mr. Dombey. He motioned his child's foster-father to the door, who departed by no means unwillingly: and then turning the key, paced up and down the room in solitary wretchedness. For all his starched, impenetrable dignity and composure, he wiped blinding tears from his eyes as he did so; and often said, with an emotion of which he would not, for the world, have had a witness, 'Poor little fellow!'

It may have been characteristic of Mr. Dombey's pride, that he pitied himself through the child. Not poor me. Not poor widower, confiding by constraint in the wife of an ignorant hind who has been working 'mostly underground' all his life, and yet at whose door Death had never knocked, and at whose poor table four sons daily sit—but poor little fellow!

Those words being on his lips, it occurred to him—and it is an instance of the strong attraction with which his hopes and fears and all his thoughts were tending to one centre—that a great temptation was being placed in this woman's way. Her infant was a boy too. Now, would it be possible for her to change them?

Though he was soon satisfied that he had dismissed the idea as romantic and unlikely—though possible, there was no denying—he could not help pursuing it so far as to entertain within himself a picture of what his condition would be, if he should discover such an imposture when he was grown old. Whether a man so situated, would be able to pluck away the result of so many years of usage, confidence, and belief, from the impostor, and endow a stranger with it?

As his unusual emotion subsided, these misgivings gradually melted away, though so much of their shadow remained behind, that he was constant in his resolution to look closely after Richards himself, without appearing to do so. Being now in an easier frame of mind, he regarded the woman's station as rather an advantageous circumstance than otherwise, by placing, in itself, a broad distance between her and the child, and rendering their separation easy and natural.

Meanwhile terms were ratified and agreed upon between Mrs. Chick and Richards, with the assistance of Miss Tox; and Richards being with much ceremony invested with the Dombey baby, as if it were an Order, resigned her own, with many tears and kisses, to Jemima. Glasses of wine were then produced, to sustain the drooping spirits of the family.

'You 'll take a glass yourself, sir, won't you?' said Miss Tox, as Toodle appeared.

'Thankee, mum,' said Toodle, 'since you *are* suppressing.'

'And you 're very glad to leave your dear good wife in such a comfortable home, ain't you, sir?' said Miss Tox, nodding and winking at him stealthily.

'No, mum,' said Toodle. 'Here 's wishing of her back agin.'

Polly cried more than ever at this. So Mrs. Chick, who had her matronly apprehensions that this indulgence in grief might be prejudicial to the little Dombey ('acid, indeed,' she whispered Miss Tox), hastened to the rescue.

'Your little child will thrive charmingly with your sister Jemima, Richards,' said Mrs. Chick; 'and you have only to make an effort—this is a world of effort, you know, Richards—to be very happy indeed. You have been already measured for your mourning, haven't you, Richards?'

'Ye—es, ma'am,' sobbed Polly.

'And it 'll fit beautifully, I know,' said Mrs. Chick, 'for the same young person has made me many dresses. The very best materials, too!'

'Lor, you 'll be so smart,' said Miss Tox, 'that your husband won't know you; will you, sir?'

'I should know her,' said Toodle, gruffly, 'anyhows and anywheres.'

Toodle was evidently not to be bought over.

'As to living, Richards, you know,' pursued Mrs. Chick, 'why the very best of everything will be at your disposal. You will order your little dinner every day; and anything you take a fancy to, I 'm sure will be as readily provided as if you were a lady.'

'Yes, to be sure!' said Miss Tox, keeping up the ball with great sympathy. 'And as to porter!—quite unlimited, will it not, Louisa?'

'Oh, certainly!' returned Mrs. Chick in the same tone. 'With a little abstinence, you know, my dear, in point of vegetables.'

'And pickles, perhaps,' suggested Miss Tox.

'With such exceptions,' said Louisa, 'she 'll consult her choice entirely, and be under no restraint at all, my love.'

'And then, of course, you know,' said Miss Tox, 'however fond she is of her own dear little child—and I 'm sure, Louisa, *you* don't blame her for being fond of it?'

'Oh no!' cried Mrs. Chick, benignantly.

'Still,' resumed Miss Tox, 'she naturally must be interested in her young charge, and must consider it a privilege to see a little cherub closely connected with the superior classes, gradually unfolding itself from day to day at one common fountain. Is it not so, Louisa?'

'Most undoubtedly!' said Mrs. Chick. 'You see, my love, she 's already quite contented and comfortable, and means to say good-bye to her sister Jemima and her little pets, and her good honest husband, with a light heart and a smile; don't she, my dear!'

'Oh yes!' cried Miss Tox. 'To be sure she does!'

Notwithstanding which, however, poor Polly embraced them all round in great distress, and finally ran away to avoid any more particular leave-taking between herself and the children. But the stratagem hardly succeeded as well as it deserved; for the smallest boy but one divining her intent, immediately began swarming upstairs after her—if that word of doubtful etymology be admissible—on his arms and legs; while the eldest (known in the family by the name of Biler, in remembrance of the steam engine) beat a demoniacal tattoo with his boots, expressive of grief; in which he was joined by the rest of the family.

A quantity of oranges and halfpence thrust indiscriminately on each young Toodle, checked the first violence of their regret, and the family were speedily transported to their own home, by means of the hackney-coach kept in waiting for that purpose. The children, under the guardianship of Jemima, blocked up the window, and dropped out oranges and halfpence all the way along. Mr. Toodle himself preferred to ride behind among the spikes, as being the mode of conveyance to which he was best accustomed.

## CHAPTER III

### IN WHICH MR. DOMBEY, AS A MAN AND A FATHER, IS SEEN AT THE HEAD OF THE HOME DEPARTMENT

THE funeral of the deceased lady having been 'performed' to the entire satisfaction of the undertaker as well as of the neighbourhood at large, which is generally disposed to be captious on such a point, and is prone to take offence at any omissions or shortcomings in the ceremonies, the various members of Mr. Dombey's household subsided into their several places in the domestic system. That small world, like the great one out of doors, had the capacity of easily forgetting its dead; and when the cook had said she was a quiet-tempered lady, and the housekeeper had said it was the common lot, and the butler had said who 'd have thought it, and the housemaid had said she couldn't hardly believe it, and the footman had said it seemed exactly like a dream, they had quite worn the subject out, and began to think their mourning was wearing rusty too.

On Richards, who was established upstairs in a state of honourable captivity, the dawn of her new life seemed to break cold and grey. Mr. Dombey's house was a large one, on the shady side of a tall, dark, dreadfully genteel street in the region between Portland Place and Bryanstone Square. It was a corner house, with great wide areas containing cellars frowned upon by barred windows, and leered at by crooked-eyed doors leading to dustbins. It was a house of dismal state, with a circular back to it, containing a whole suit of drawing-rooms looking upon a gravelled yard, where two gaunt trees, with blackened trunks and branches, rattled rather than rustled, their leaves were so smoke-dried. The summer sun was never on the street, but in the morning about breakfast-time, when it came with the water-carts and the old clothes-men, and the people with geraniums, and the umbrella-mender, and the man who trilled the little bell of the Dutch clock as he went along. It was soon gone again to return no more that day; and the bands of music and the straggling Punch's shows going after it, left it a pray to the most dismal of organs, and white mice; with now and then a porcupine, to vary the entertainments; until the butlers whose families were dining out, began to stand at the house-doors in the twilight, and the lamplighter made his nightly failure in attempting to brighten up the street with gas.

It was as black a house inside as outside. When the funeral was over, Mr. Dombey ordered the furniture to be covered up—perhaps to preserve it for the son with whom his plans were all associated —and the rooms to be ungarnished, saving such as he retained for himself on the ground floor. Accordingly, mysterious shapes were made of tables and chairs, heaped together in the middle of rooms, and covered over with great winding-sheets. Bell-handles, window-blinds, and looking-glasses, being papered up in journals, daily and weekly, obtruded fragmentary accounts of deaths and dreadful murders. Every chandelier or lustre, muffled in holland, looked like a monstrous tear depending from the ceiling's eye. Odours, as from vaults and damp places, came out of the chimneys. The dead and buried lady was awful in a picture-frame of ghastly bandages. Every gust of wind that rose, brought eddying round the corner from the neighbouring mews, some fragments of the straw that had been strewn before the house when she was ill, mildewed remains of which were still cleaving to the neighbourhood; and these, being always drawn by some invisible attraction to the threshold of the dirty house to let immediately opposite, addressed a dismal eloquence to Mr. Dombey's windows.

The apartments which Mr. Dombey reserved for his own inhabiting, were attainable from the hall, and consisted of a sitting-room; a library, which was in fact a dressing-room, so that the smell of hot-pressed paper, vellum, morocco, and Russia leather, contended in it with the smell of divers pairs of boots; and a kind of conservatory or little glass breakfast-room beyond, commanding a prospect of the trees before mentioned, and, generally speaking, of a few prowling cats. These three rooms opened upon one another. In the morning, when Mr. Dombey was at his breakfast in one or other of the two first-mentioned of them, as well as in the afternoon when he came home to dinner, a bell was rung for Richards to repair to this glass chamber, and there walk to and fro with her young charge. From the glimpses she caught of Mr. Dombey at these times, sitting in the dark distance, looking out towards the infant from among the dark heavy furniture—the house had been inhabited for years by his father, and in many of its appointments was old-fashioned and grim—she began to entertain ideas of him in his solitary state, as if he were a lone prisoner in a cell, or a strange apparition that was not to be accosted or understood.

Little Paul Dombey's foster-mother had led this life herself, and had carried little Paul through it for some weeks; and had returned upstairs one day from a melancholy saunter through the dreary rooms of state (she never went out without Mrs. Chick, who called on fine mornings, usually accompanied by Miss Tox, to take her and Baby for an airing—or in other words, to march them gravely up and down the pavement; like a walking funeral); when, as she was sitting in her own room, the door was slowly and quietly opened, and a dark-eyed little girl looked in.

'It's Miss Florence come home from her aunt's, no doubt,' thought Richards, who had never seen the child before. 'Hope I see you well, miss.'

'Is that my brother?' asked the child, pointing to the baby.

'Yes, my pretty,' answered Richards. 'Come and kiss him.'

But the child, instead of advancing, looked her earnestly in the face and said—

'What have you done with my mamma?'

'Lord bless the little creeter!' cried Richards, 'what a sad question! I done? Nothing, miss.'

'What have *they* done with my mamma?' inquired the child.

'I never saw such a melting thing in all my life!' said Richards, who naturally substituted for this child one of her own, inquiring for herself in like circumstances. 'Come nearer here, my dear miss! Don't be afraid of me.'

'I am not afraid of you,' said the child, drawing nearer. 'But I want to know what they have done with my mamma.'

'My darling,' said Richards, 'you wear that pretty black frock in remembrance of your mamma.'

'I can remember my mamma,' returned the child, with tears springing to her eyes, 'in any frock.'

'But people put on black, to remember people when they 're gone.

'Where gone?' asked the child.

'Come and sit down by me,' said Richards, 'and I 'll tell you a story.'

With a quick perception that it was intended to relate to what she had asked, little Florence laid aside the bonnet she had held in her hand until now, and sat down on a stool at the nurse's feet, looking up into her face.

'Once upon a time,' said Richards, 'there was a lady—a very good lady, and her little daughter dearly loved her.'

'A very good lady and her little daughter dearly loved her,' repeated the child.

'Who, when God thought it right that it should be so, was taken ill and died.'

The child shuddered.

'Died, never to be seen again by any one on earth, and was buried in the ground where the trees grow.'

'The cold ground?' said the child, shuddering again.

'No! The warm ground,' returned Polly, seizing her advantage, 'where the ugly little seeds turn into beautiful flowers, and into grass, and corn, and I don't know what all besides. Where good people turn into bright angels, and fly away to Heaven!'

The child, who had drooped her head, raised it again, and sat looking at her intently.

'So; let me see,' said Polly, not a little flurried between this earnest scrutiny, her desire to comfort the child, her sudden success, and her very slight confidence in her own powers. 'So, when this lady died, wherever they took her, or wherever they put her, she went to God! and she prayed to Him, this lady did,' said Polly, affecting herself beyond measure; being heartily in earnest, 'to teach her little daughter to be sure of that in her heart: and to know that she was happy there and loved her still: and to hope and try—Oh, all her life—to meet her there one day, never, never, never to part any more.'

'It was my mamma!' exclaimed the child, springing up, and clasping her round the neck.

'And the child's heart,' said Polly, drawing her to her breast: 'the little daughter's heart was so full of the truth of this, that even when she heard it from a strange nurse that couldn't tell it right, but was a poor mother herself and that was all, she found a comfort in it—didn't feel so lonely—sobbed and cried upon her bosom—took kindly to the baby lying in her lap—and—there, there, there!' said Polly, smoothing the child's curls and dropping tears upon them. 'There, poor dear!'

'Oh well, Miss Floy! And won't your pa be angry neither!' cried a quick voice at the door, proceeding from a short, brown, womanly girl of fourteen, with a little snub nose, and black eyes like jet beads. 'When it was 'tickerleyly given out that you wasn't to go and worrit the wet nurse.'

'She don't worry me,' was the surprised rejoinder of Polly. 'I am very fond of children.'

'Oh! but begging your pardon, Mrs. Richards, that don't matter, you know,' returned the black-eyed girl, who was so desperately sharp and biting that she seemed to make one's eyes water. 'I may be very fond of pennywinkles, Mrs. Richards, but it don't follow that I 'm to have 'em for tea.'

'Well, it don't matter,' said Polly.

'Oh, thank'e, Mrs. Richards, don't it!' returned the sharp girl. 'Remembering, however, if you 'll be so good, that Miss Floy 's under my charge, and Master Paul 's under your'n.'

'But still we needn't quarrel,' said Polly.

'Oh no, Mrs. Richards,' rejoined Spitfire. 'Not at all, I don't wish it, we needn't stand upon that footing, Miss Floy being a permanency, Master Paul a temporary.' Spitfire made use of none but comma pauses; shooting out whatever she had to say in one sentence, and in one breath, if possible.

'Miss Florence has just come home, hasn't she?' asked Polly.

'Yes, Mrs. Richards, just come, and here, Miss Floy, before you 've been in the house a quarter of an hour, you go a smearing your wet face against the expensive mourning that Mrs. Richards is a wearing for your ma!' With this remonstrance, young Spitfire, whose real name was Susan Nipper, detached the child from her new friend by a wrench —as if she were a tooth. But she seemed to do it, more in the excessively sharp exercise of her official functions, than with any deliberate unkindness.

'She 'll be quite happy, now she has come home again,' said Polly, nodding to her with an encouraging smile upon her wholesome face, 'and will be so pleased to see her dear papa to-night.'

'Lork, Mrs. Richards!' cried Miss Nipper, taking up her words with a jerk. 'Don't. See her dear papa indeed! I should like to see her do it!'

'Won't she then?' asked Polly.

'Lork, Mrs. Richards, no, her pa 's a deal too wrapped up in somebody else, and before there was somebody else to be wrapped up in she never was a favourite, girls are thrown away in this house, Mrs. Richards, *I* assure you.'

The child looked quickly from one nurse to the other, as if she understood and felt what was said.

'You surprise me!' cried Polly. 'Hasn't Mr. Dombey seen her since—'

'No,' interrupted Susan Nipper. 'Not once since, and he hadn't hardly set his eyes upon her before that for months and months, and I don't think he 'd have known her for his own child if he had met her in the streets, or would know her for his own child if he was to meet her in the streets to-morrow, Mrs. Richards, as to *me*,' said Spitfire, with a giggle, 'I doubt if he 's aweer of my existence.'

'Pretty dear!' said Richards; meaning, not Miss Nipper, but the little Florence.

'Oh! there 's a Tartar within a hundred miles of where we 're now in conversation, I can tell you, Mrs. Richards, present company always excepted too,' said Susan Nipper; 'wish you good morning, Mrs. Richards, now Miss Floy, you come along with me, and don't go hanging back like a naughty wicked child that judgments is no example to, don't.'

In spite of being thus adjured, and in spite also of some hauling an the part of Susan Nipper, tending towards the dislocation of her right shoulder, little Florence broke away, and kissed her new friend, affectionately.

'Good-bye!' said the child. 'God bless you! I shall come to see you again soon, and you 'll come to see me? Susan will let us. Won't you, Susan?'

Spitfire seemed to be in the main a good-natured little body, although a disciple of that school of trainers of the young idea which holds that childhood, like money, must be shaken and rattled and jostled about a good deal to keep it bright. For, being thus appealed to with some endearing gestures and caresses, she folded her small arms and shook her head, and conveyed a relenting expression into her very-wide-open black eyes.

'It ain't right of you to ask it, Miss Floy, for you know I can't refuse you, but Mrs. Richards and me will see what can be done, if Mrs. Richards likes, I may wish, you see, to take a voyage to Chaney, Mrs. Richards, but I mayn't know how to leave the London Docks.'

Richards assented to the proposition.

'This house ain't so exactly ringing with merry-making,' said Miss Nipper, 'that one need be lonelier than one must be. Your Toxes and your Chickses may draw out my two front double teeth, Mrs. Richards, but that 's no reason why I need offer 'em the whole set.'

This proposition was also assented to by Richards, as an obvious one.

THE DOMBEY FAMILY.

'So I 'm agreeable, I 'm sure,' said Susan Nipper, 'to live friendly, Mrs. Richards, while Master Paul continues a permanency, if the means can be planned out without going openly against orders, but goodness gracious ME, Miss Floy, you haven't got your things off yet, you naughty child, you haven't, come along!'

With these words, Susan Nipper, in a transport of coercion, made a charge at her young ward, and swept her out of the room.

The child, in her grief and neglect, was so gentle, so quiet, and uncomplaining; was possessed of so much affection that no one seemed to care to have, and so much sorrowful intelligence that no one seemed to mind or think about the wounding of; that Polly's heart was sore when she was left alone again. In the simple passage that had taken place between herself and the motherless little girl, her own motherly heart had been touched no less than the child's; and she felt, as the child did, that there was something of confidence and interest between them from that moment.

Notwithstanding Mr. Toodle's great reliance on Polly, she was perhaps in point of artificial accomplishments very little his superior. But she was a good plain sample of a nature that is ever, in the mass, better, truer, higher, nobler, quicker to feel, and much more constant to retain, all tenderness and pity, self-denial and devotion, than the nature of men. And, perhaps, unlearned as she was, she could have brought a dawning knowledge home to Mr. Dombey at that early day, which would not then have struck him in the end like lightning.

But this is from the purpose. Polly only thought, at that time, of improving on her successful propitiation of Miss Nipper, and devising some means of having little Florence beside her, lawfully, and without rebellion. An opening happened to present itself that very night.

She had been rung down into the glass room as usual, and had walked about and about it a long time, with the baby in her arms, when, to her great surprise and dismay, Mr. Dombey came out, suddenly, and stopped before her.

'Good evening, Richards.'

Just the same austere, stiff gentleman, as he had appeared to her on that first day. Such a hard-looking gentleman, that she involuntarily dropped her eyes and her curtsey at the same time.

'How is Master Paul, Richards?'

'Quite thriving, sir, and well.'

'He looks so,' said Mr. Dombey, glancing with great interest at the tiny face she uncovered for his observation, and yet affecting to be half careless of it. 'They give you everything you want, I hope?'

'Oh yes, thank you, sir.'

She suddenly appended such an obvious hesitation to this reply, however, that Mr. Dombey, who had turned away, stopped, and turned round again, inquiringly.

'I believe nothing is so good for making children lively and cheerful, sir, as seeing other children playing about 'em,' observed Polly, taking courage.

'I think I mentioned to you, Richards, when you came here,' said Mr. Dombey, with a frown, 'that I wished you to see as little of your family as possible. You can continue your walk if you please.'

With that, he disappeared into his inner room; and Polly had the satisfaction of feeling that he had thoroughly misunderstood her object, and that she had fallen into disgrace without the least advancement of her purpose.

Next night, she found him walking about the conservatory when she came down. As she stopped at the door, checked by this unusual sight, and uncertain whether to advance or retreat, he called her in.

'If you really think that sort of society is good for the child,' he said sharply, as if there had been no interval since she proposed it, 'where's Miss Florence?'

'Nothing could be better than Miss Florence, sir,' said Polly eagerly, 'but I understood from her little maid that they were not to—'

Mr. Dombey rang the bell, and walked till it was answered.

'Tell them always to let Miss Florence be with Richards when she chooses, and go out with her, and so forth. Tell them to let the children be together, when Richards wishes it.'

The iron was now hot, and Richards striking on it boldly—it was a good cause and she was bold in it, though instinctively afraid of Mr. Dombey—requested that Miss Florence might be sent down then and there, to make friends with her little brother.

She feigned to be dandling the child as the servant retired on this errand, but she thought that she saw Mr. Dombey's colour changed; that the expression of his face quite altered; that he turned, hurriedly, as if to gainsay what he had said, or she had said, or both, and was only deterred by very shame.

And she was right. The last time he had seen his slighted child, there had been that in the sad embrace between her and her dying mother, which was at once a revelation and a reproach to him. Let him be absorbed as he would in the Son on whom he built such high hopes, he could not forget that closing scene. He could not forget that he had had no part in it. That, at the bottom of its clear depths of tenderness and truth, lay those two figures clasped in each other's arms, while he stood on the bank above them, looking down a mere spectator—not a sharer with them—quite shut out.

Unable to exclude these things from his remembrance, or to keep his mind free from such imperfect shapes of the meaning with which they were fraught, as were able to make themselves visible to him through the mist of his pride, his previous feelings of indifference towards little Florence changed into an uneasiness of an extraordinary kind. He almost felt as if she watched and distrusted him. As if she held the clue to something secret in his breast, of the nature of which he was hardly informed himself. As if she had an innate knowledge of one jarring and discordant string within him, and her very breath could sound it.

His feeling about the child had been negative from her birth. He had never conceived an aversion to her: it had not been worth his while or in his humour. She had never been a positively disagreeable object to him. But now he was ill at ease about her. She troubled his peace. He would have preferred to put her idea aside altogether, if he had known how. Perhaps—who shall decide on such mysteries!—he was afraid that he might come to hate her.

When little Florence timidly presented herself, Mr. Dombey stopped in his pacing up and down and looked towards her. Had he looked with greater interest and with a father's eye, he might have read in her keen glance the impulses and fears that made her waver; the passionate desire to run clinging to him, crying, as she hid her face in his embrace, 'Oh, father, try to love me! there 's no one else!' the dread of a repulse; the fear of being too bold, and of offending him; the pitiable need in which she stood of some assurance and encouragement; and how her overcharged young heart was wandering to find some natural resting-place, for its sorrow and affection.

But he saw nothing of this. He saw her pause irresolutely at the door and look towards him; and he saw no more.

'Come in,' he said, 'come in: what is the child afraid of?'

She came in; and after glancing round her for a moment with an uncertain air, stood pressing her small hands hard together, close within the door.

'Come here, Florence,' said her father, coldly. 'Do you know who I am?'

'Yes, papa.'

'Have you nothing to say to me?'

The tears that stood in her eyes as she raised them quickly to his face, were frozen by the expression it wore. She looked down again, and put out her trembling hand.

Mr. Dombey took it loosely in his own, and stood looking down upon her for a moment, as if he knew as little as the child, what to say or do.

'There! Be a good girl,' he said, patting her on the head, and regarding her as it were by stealth with a disturbed and doubtful look. 'Go to Richards! Go!'

His little daughter hesitated for another instant as though she would have clung about him still, or had some lingering hope that he might raise her in his arms and kiss her. She looked up in his face once more. He thought how like her expression was then, to what it had been when she looked round at the Doctor—that night—and instinctively dropped her hand and turned away.

It was not difficult to perceive that Florence was at a great disadvantage in her father's presence. It was not only a constraint upon the child's mind, but even upon the natural grace and freedom of her actions. Still Polly persevered with all the better heart for seeing this; and, judging of Mr. Dombey by herself, had great confidence in the mute appeal of poor little Florence's mourning dress. 'It 's hard indeed,' thought Polly, 'if he takes only to one little motherless child, when he has another, and that a girl, before his eyes.'

So, Polly kept her before his eyes, as long as she could, and managed so well with little Paul, as to make it very plain that he was all the livelier for his sister's company. When it was time to withdraw upstairs again, she would have sent Florence into the inner room to say good-night to her father, but the child was timid and drew back: and when she urged her again, said, spreading her hands before her eyes, as if to shut out her own unworthiness, 'Oh no, no! He don't want me. He don't want me!'

The little altercation between them had attracted the notice of Mr. Dombey, who inquired from the table where he was sitting at his wine, what the matter was.

'Miss Florence was afraid of interrupting, sir, if she came in to say good-night,' said Richards.

'It doesn't matter,' returned Mr. Dombey. 'You can let her come and go without regarding me.'

The child shrunk as she listened—and was gone, before her humble friend looked round again.

However, Polly triumphed not a little in the success of her well-intentioned scheme, and in the address with which she had brought it to bear: whereof she made a full disclosure to Spitfire when she was once more safely intrenched upstairs. Miss Nipper received that proof of her confidence, as well as the prospect of their free association for the future, rather coldly, and was anything but enthusiastic in her demonstrations of joy.

'I thought you would have been pleased,' said Polly.

'Oh yes, Mrs. Richards, I 'm very well pleased, thank you,' returned Susan, who had suddenly become so very upright that she seemed to have put an additional bone in her stays.

'You don't show it,' said Polly.

'Oh! Being only a permanency I couldn't be expected to show it like a temporary,' said Susan Nipper. 'Temporaries carries it all before 'em here, I find, but though there 's a excellent party-wall between this house and the next, I mayn't exactly like to go to it, Mrs. Richards, notwithstanding!'

## CHAPTER IV

### IN WHICH SOME MORE FIRST APPEARANCES ARE MADE ON THE STAGE OF THESE ADVENTURES

THOUGH the offices of Dombey and Son were within the liberties of the City of London, and within hearing of Bow Bells, when their clashing voices were not drowned by the uproar in the streets, yet were there hints of adventurous and romantic story to be observed in some of the adjacent objects. Gog and Magog held their state within ten minutes' walk; the Royal Exchange was close at hand; the Bank of England, with its vaults of gold and silver 'down among the dead men' underground, was their magnificent neighbour. Just round the corner stood the rich East India House, teeming with suggestions of precious stuffs and stones, tigers, elephants, howdahs, hookahs, umbrellas, palm trees, palanquins, and gorgeous princes of a brown complexion sitting on carpets, with their slippers very much turned up at the toes. Anywhere in the immediate vicinity there might be seen pictures of ships speeding away full sail to all parts of the world; outfitting warehouses ready to pack off anybody anywhere, fully equipped in half an hour; and little timber midshipmen in obsolete naval uniforms, eternally employed outside the shopdoors of nautical instrument-makers in taking observations of the hackney coaches.

Sole master and proprietor of one of these effigies —of that which might be called, familiarly, the woodenest—of that which thrust itself out above the pavement, right leg foremost, with a suavity the least endurable, and had the shoe buckles and flapped waistcoat the least reconcilable to human reason, and bore at its right eye the most offensively disproportionate piece of machinery—sole master and proprietor of that midshipman, and proud of him too, an elderly gentleman in a Welsh wig had paid house-rent, taxes, and dues, for more years than many a full-grown midshipman of flesh and blood has numbered in his life; and midshipmen who have attained a pretty green old age, have not been wanting in the English navy.

The stock in trade of this old gentleman comprised chronometers, barometers, telescopes, compasses, charts, maps, sextants, quadrants, and specimens of every kind of instrument used in the working of a ship's course, or the keeping of a ship's reckoning, or the prosecuting of a ship's discoveries. Objects in brass and glass were in his drawers and on his shelves, which none but the initiated could have found the top of, or guessed the use of, or having once examined, could have ever got back again into their mahogany nests without assistance. Everything was jammed into the tightest cases, fitted into the narrowest corners, fenced up behind the most impertinent cushions, and screwed into the acutest angles, to prevent its philosophical composure from being disturbed by the rolling of the sea. Such extraordinary precautions were taken in every instance to save room, and keep the thing compact; and so much practical navigation was fitted, and cushioned, and screwed into every box (whether the box was a mere slab, as some were, or something between a cocked hat and a star-fish, as others were, and those quite mild and modest boxes as compared with others); that the shop itself, partaking of the general infection, seemed almost to become a snug, sea-going, ship-shape concern, wanting only good sea-room, in the event of an unexpected launch, to work its way securely to any desert island in the world.

Many minor incidents in the household life of the ship's instrument-maker who was proud of his little midshipman, assisted and bore out this fancy. His acquaintance lying chiefly among ship-chandlers and so forth, he had always plenty of the veritable ships' biscuit on his table. It was familiar with dried meats and tongues, possessing an extraordinary flavour of rope yarn. Pickles were produced upon it, in great wholesale jars, with 'dealer in all kinds of Ships' Provisions' on the label; spirits were set forth in case bottles with no throats. Old prints of ships with alphabetical references to their various mysteries, hung in frames upon the walls; the Tartar Frigate under weigh, was on the plates; outlandish shells, seaweeds, and mosses, decorated the chimney-piece; the little wainscoted back-parlour was lighted by a sky-light, like a cabin.

Here he lived too, in skipper-like state, all alone with his nephew Walter: a boy of fourteen who looked quite enough like a midshipman, to carry out the prevailing idea. But there it ended, for Solomon Gills himself (more generally called old Sol) was far from having a maritime appearance. To say nothing of his Welsh wig, which was as plain and stubborn a Welsh wig as ever was worn, and in which he looked like anything but a Rover, he was a slow, quiet-spoken, thoughtful old fellow, with eyes as red as if they had been small suns looking at you through a fog; and a newly-awakened manner, such as he might have acquired by having stared for three or four days successively through every optical instrument in his shop, and suddenly came back to the world again, to find it green. The only change ever known in his outward man, was from a complete suit of coffee-colour cut very square, and ornamented with glaring buttons, to the same suit of coffee-colour minus the inexpressibles, which were then of a pale nankeen. He wore a very precise shirt-frill, and carried a pair of first-rate spectacles on his forehead, and a tremendous chronometer in his fob, rather than doubt which precious possession, he would have believed in a conspiracy against it on the part of all the clocks and watches in the City, and even of the very sun itself. Such as he was, such he had been in the shop and parlour behind the little midshipman, for years upon years; going regularly aloft to bed every night in a howling garret remote from the lodgers, where, when gentlemen of England who lived below at ease had little or no idea of the state of the weather, it often blew great guns.

It is half-past five o'clock, and an autumn afternoon, when the reader and Solomon Gills become acquainted. Solomon Gills is in the act of seeing what time it is by the unimpeachable chronometer. The usual daily clearance has been making in the City for an hour or more; and the human tide is still rolling westward. 'The streets have thinned,' as Mr. Gills says, 'very much.' It threatens to be wet to-night. All the weather-glasses in the shop are in low spirits, and the rain already shines upon the cocked hat of the wooden midshipman.

'Where 's Walter, I wonder!' said Solomon Gills, after he had carefully put up the chronometer again. 'Here 's dinner been ready, half an hour, and no Walter!'

Turning round upon his stool behind the counter, Mr. Gills looked out among the instruments in the window, to see if his nephew might be crossing the road. No. He was not among the bobbing umbrellas, and he certainly was not the newspaper boy in the oilskin cap who was slowly working his way along the piece of brass outside, writing his name over Mr. Gills's name with his forefinger.

'If I didn't know he was too fond of me to make a run of it, and go and enter himself aboard ship against my wishes, I should begin to be fidgety,' said Mr. Gills, tapping two or three weather-glasses with his knuckles. 'I really should. All in the Downs, eh! Lots of moisture! Well! It 's wanted.

'I believe,' said Mr. Gills, blowing the dust off the glass top of a compass case, 'that you don't point more direct and due to the back-parlour than the boy's inclination does after all. And the parlour couldn't bear straighter either. Due north. Not the twentieth part of a point either way.'

'Halloa, uncle Sol!'

'Halloa, my boy!' cried the instrument-maker, turning briskly round. 'What! you are here, are you?'

A cheerful-looking, merry boy, fresh with running home in the rain; fair-faced, bright-eyed, and curly-haired.

'Well, uncle, how have you got on without me all day! Is dinner ready? I'm so hungry.'

'As to getting on,' said Solomon good-naturedly, 'it would be odd if I couldn't get on without a young dog like you a great deal better than with you. As to dinner being ready, it 's been ready this half-hour and waiting for you. As to being hungry, *I* am!'

'Come along then, uncle!' cried the boy. 'Hurrah for the admiral!'

'Confound the admiral!' returned Solomon Gills. 'You mean the Lord Mayor.'

'No I don't!' cried the boy. 'Hurrah for the admiral. Hurrah for the admiral! For—ward!'

At this word of command, the Welsh wig and its wearer were borne without resistance into the back-parlour, as at the head of a boarding party of five hundred men; and uncle Sol and his nephew were speedily engaged on a fried sole with a prospect of steak to follow.

'The Lord Mayor, Wally,' said Solomon, 'for ever! No more admirals. The Lord Mayor 's *your* admiral.'

'Oh, is he though!' said the boy, shaking his head. 'Why, the Sword Bearer 's better than him. He draws *his* sword sometimes.'

'And a pretty figure he cuts with it for his pains,' returned the uncle. 'Listen to me, Wally, listen to me. Look on the mantelshelf.'

'Why who has cocked my silver mug up there, on a nail!' exclaimed the boy.

'I have,' said his uncle. 'No more mugs now. We must begin to drink out of glasses to-day, Walter. We are men of business. We belong to the City. We started in life this morning.'

'Well, uncle,' said the boy, 'I 'll drink out of anything you like, so long as I can drink to you. Here 's to you, uncle Sol, and hurrah for the—'

'Lord Mayor,' interrupted the old man.

'For the Lord Mayor, Sheriffs, Common Council, and Livery,' said the boy. 'Long life to 'em!'

The uncle nodded his head with great satisfaction. 'And now,' he said, 'let 's hear something about the firm.'

'Oh! there 's not much to be told about the firm, uncle,' said the boy, plying his knife and fork. 'It 's a precious dark set of offices, and in the room where I sit, there 's a high fender, and an iron safe, and some cards about ships that are going to sail, and an almanack and some desks and stools, and an inkbottle, and some books, and some boxes, and a lot of cobwebs, and in one of 'em, just over my head, a shrivelled-up blue bottle that looks as if it had hung there ever so long.'

'Nothing else?' said the uncle.

'No, nothing else, except an old bird-cage (I wonder how *that* ever came there!) and a coal-scuttle.'

'No bankers' books, or cheque books, or bills, or such tokens of wealth rolling in from day to day?' said old Sol, looking wistfully at his nephew out of the fog that always seemed to hang about him, and laying an unctuous emphasis upon the words.

'Oh yes, plenty of that I suppose,' returned his nephew carelessly; 'but all that sort of thing 's in Mr. Carker's room, or Mr. Morfin's, or Mr. Dombey's.'

'Has Mr. Dombey been there to-day?' inquired the uncle.

'Oh yes! In and out all day.'

'He didn't take any notice of you, I suppose?'

'Yes he did. He walked up to my seat,—I wish he wasn't so solemn and stiff, uncle, and said "Oh! you are the son of Mr. Gills the ships' instrument-maker." "Nephew, sir," I said. "I said nephew, boy," said he. But I could take my oath he said son, uncle.'

'You 're mistaken, I dare say. It 's no matter.'

'No, it 's no matter, but he needn't have been so sharp, I thought. There was no harm in it though he did say son. Then he told me that you had spoken to him about me, and that he had found me employment in the House accordingly, and that I was expected to be attentive and punctual, and then he went away. I thought he didn't seem to like me much.'

'You mean, I suppose,' observed the instrument-maker, 'that you didn't seem to like him much.'

'Well, uncle,' returned the boy, laughing. 'Perhaps so; I never thought of that.'

Solomon looked a little graver as he finished his dinner, and glanced from time to time at the boy's bright face. When dinner was done, and the cloth was cleared away (the entertainment had been brought from a neighbouring eating-house), he lighted a candle, and went down below into a little cellar, while his nephew, standing on the mouldy staircase, dutifully held the light. After a moment's groping here and there, he presently returned with a very ancient-looking bottle, covered with dust and dirt.

'Why, uncle Sol!' said the boy, 'what are you about! that 's the wonderful Madeira!—there 's only one more bottle!'

Uncle Sol nodded his head, implying that he knew very well what he was about; and having drawn the cork in solemn silence, filled two glasses and set the bottle and a third clean glass on the table.

'You shall drink the other bottle, Wally,' he said, 'when you come to good fortune; when you are a thriving, respected, happy man; when the start in life you have made to-day shall have brought you, as I pray Heaven it may!—to a smooth part of the course you have to run, my child. My love to you!'

Some of the fog that hung about old Sol seemed to have got into his throat; for he spoke huskily. His hand shook too, as he clinked his glass against his nephew's. But having once got the wine to his lips, he tossed it off like a man, and smacked them afterwards.

'Dear uncle,' said the boy, affecting to make light of it, while the tears stood in his eyes, 'for the honour you have done me, et cetera, et cetera. I shall now beg to propose Mr. Solomon Gills with three times three and one cheer more. Hurrah! and you 'll return thanks, uncle, when we drink the last bottle together; won't you?'

They clinked their glasses again; and Walter, who was hoarding his wine, took a sip of it, and held the glass up to his eye with as critical an air as he could possibly assume.

His uncle sat looking at him for some time in silence. When their eyes at last met, he began at once to pursue the theme that had occupied his thoughts, aloud, as if he had been speaking all the while.

'You see, Walter,' he said, 'in truth this business is merely a habit with me. I am so accustomed to the habit that I could hardly live if I relinquished it: but there 's nothing doing, nothing doing. When that uniform was worn,' pointing out towards the little midshipman, 'then indeed, fortunes were to be made, and were made. But competition, competition—new invention, new invention—alteration, alteration—the world 's gone past me. I hardly know where I am myself; much less where my customers are.'

'Never mind 'em, uncle!'

'Since you came home from weekly boarding-school at Peckham, for instance—and that 's ten days,' said Solomon, 'I don't remember more than one person that has come into the shop.'

'Two, uncle, don't you recollect? There was the man who came to ask for change for a sovereign—'

'That 's the one,' said Solomon.

'Why, uncle! don't you call the woman anybody, who came to ask the way to Mile-End Turnpike?'

'Oh! it 's true,' said Solomon, 'I forgot her. Two persons.'

'To be sure, they didn't buy anything,' cried the boy.

'No. They didn't buy anything,' said Solomon, quietly.

'Nor want anything,' cried the boy.

'No. If they had, they 'd gone to another shop,' said Solomon, in the same tone.

'But there were two of 'em, uncle,' cried the boy, as if that were a great triumph. 'You said only one.'

'Well, Wally,' resumed the old man, after a short pause: 'not being like the savages who came on Robinson Crusoe's Island, we can't live on a man who asks for change for a sovereign, and a woman who inquires the way to Mile-End Turnpike. As I said just now, the world has gone past me. I don't blame it; but I no longer understand it. Tradesmen are not the same as they used to be, apprentices are not the same, business is not the same, business commodities are not the same. Seven-eighths of my stock is old-fashioned. I am an old-fashioned man in an old-fashioned shop, in a street that is not the same as I remember it. I have fallen behind the time, and am too old to catch it again. Even the noise it makes a long way ahead, confuses me.'

Walter was going to speak, but his uncle held up his hand.

'Therefore, Wally—therefore it is that I am anxious you should be early in the busy world, and on the world's track. I am only the ghost of this business—its substance vanished long ago; and when I die, its ghost will be laid. As it is clearly no inheritance for you then, I have thought it best to use for your advantage, almost the only fragment of the old connection that stands by me, through long habit. Some people suppose me to be wealthy. I wish for your sake they were right. But whatever I leave behind me, or whatever I can give you, you in such a house as Dombey's are in the road to use well and make the most of. Be diligent, try to like it, my dear boy, work for a steady independence, and be happy!'

'I 'll do everything I can, uncle, to deserve your affection. Indeed I will,' said the boy, earnestly.

'I know it,' said Solomon. 'I am sure of it,' and he applied himself to a second glass of the old Madeira, with increased relish. 'As to the sea,' he pursued, 'that 's well enough in fiction, Wally, but it won't do in fact: it won't do at all. It 's natural enough that you should think about it, associating it with all these familiar things; but it won't do, it won't do.'

Solomon Gills rubbed his hands with an air of stealthy enjoyment, as he talked of the sea, though; and looked on the seafaring objects about him with inexpressible complacency.

'Think of this wine for instance,' said old Sol, 'which has been to the East Indies and back, I 'm not able to say how often, and has been once round the world. Think of the pitch-dark nights, the roaring winds, and rolling seas!'

'The thunder, lightning, rain, hail, storm of all kinds,' said the boy.

'To be sure,' said Solomon,—'that this wine has passed through. Think what a straining and creaking of timbers and masts: what a whistling and howling of the gale through ropes and rigging!'

'What a clambering aloft of men, vying with each other who shall lie out first upon the yards to furl the icy sails, while the ship rolls and pitches, like mad!' cried his nephew.

'Exactly so,' said Solomon: 'has gone on, over the old cask that held this wine. Why, when the Charming Sally went down in the—'

'In the Baltic Sea, in the dead of the night; five-and-twenty minutes past twelve when the captain's watch stopped in his pocket; he lying dead against the main-mast—on the fourteenth of February, seventeen forty-nine!' cried Walter, with great animation.

'Ay, to be sure!' cried old Sol, 'quite right! Then, there were five hundred casks of such wine aboard; and all hands (except the first mate, first lieutenant, two seamen, and a lady, in a leaky boat) going to work to stave the casks, got drunk and died drunk, singing, "Rule Britannia," when she settled and went down, and ending with one awful scream in chorus.'

'But when the George the Second drove ashore, uncle, on the coast of Cornwall, in a dismal gale, two hours before daybreak, on the fourth of March, 'seventy-one, she had near two hundred horses aboard; and the horses breaking loose down below, early in the gale, and tearing to and fro, and trampling each other to death, made such noises, and set up such human cries, that the crew believing the ship to be full of devils, some of the best men, losing heart and head, went overboard in despair, and only two were left alive, at last, to tell the tale.'

'And when,' said old Sol, 'when the Polyphemus—'

'Private West India trader, burden three hundred and fifty tons, Captain, John Brown of Deptford. Owners, Wiggs and Co.,' cried Walter.

'The same,' said Sol; 'when she took fire, four days' sail with a fair wind out of Jamaica Harbour, in the night—'

'There were two brothers on board,' interposed his nephew, speaking very fast and loud, 'and there not being room for both of them in the only boat that wasn't swamped, neither of them would consent to go, until the elder took the younger by the waist and flung him in. And then the younger rising in the boat, cried out, "Dear Edward, think of your promised wife at home. I 'm only a boy. No one waits at home for me. Leap down into my place!" and flung himself in the sea!'

The kindling eye and heightened colour of the boy, who had risen from his seat in the earnestness of what he said and felt, seemed to remind old Sol of something he had forgotten, or that his encircling mist had hitherto shut out. Instead of proceeding with any more anecdotes, as he had evidently intended but a moment before, he gave a short dry cough, and said, 'Well! suppose we change the subject.'

The truth was, that the simple-minded uncle in his secret attraction towards the marvellous and adventurous—of which he was, in some sort, a distant relation, by his trade—had greatly encouraged the same attraction in the nephew; and that everything that had ever been put before the boy to deter him from a life of adventure, had had the usual unaccountable effect of sharpening his taste for it. This is invariable. It would seem as if there never was a book written, or a story told, expressly with the object of keeping boys on shore, which did not lure and charm them to the ocean, as a matter of course.

But an addition to the little party now made its appearance, in the shape of a gentleman in a wide suit of blue, with a hook instead of a hand attached to his right wrist; very bushy black eyebrows; and a thick stick in his left hand, covered all over (like his nose) with knobs. He wore a loose black silk handkerchief round his neck, and such a very large coarse shirt collar, that it looked like a small sail. He was evidently the person for whom the spare wine-glass was intended, and evidently knew it; for having taken off his rough outer coat and hung up, on a particular peg behind the door, such a hard glazed hat as a sympathetic person's head might ache at the sight of, and which left a red rim round his own forehead as if he had been wearing a tight basin, he brought a chair to where the clean glass was, and sat himself down behind it. He was usually addressed as Captain, this visitor; and had been a pilot, or a skipper, or a privateer's-man, or all three perhaps; and was a very salt-looking man indeed.

His face, remarkable for a brown solidity, brightened as he shook hands with uncle and nephew; but he seemed to be of a laconic disposition, and merely said—

'How goes it?'

'All well,' said Mr. Gills, pushing the bottle towards him.

He took it up, and having surveyed and smelt it, said with extraordinary expression—

*'The?'*

*'The,'* returned the instrument-maker.

Upon that he whistled as he filled his glass, and seemed to think they were making holiday indeed.

'Wal'r!' he said, arranging his hair (which was

OLD SOL AND CAPTAIN CUTTLE.

thin) with his hook, and then pointing it at the instrument-maker, 'look at him! Love! Honour! And Obey! Overhaul your catechism till you find that passage, and when found turn the leaf down. Success, my boy!'

He was so perfectly satisfied both with his quotation and his reference to it, that he could not help repeating the words again in a low voice, and saying he had forgotten 'em these forty year.

'But I never wanted two or three words in my life that I didn't know where to lay my hand upon 'em, Gills,' he observed. 'It comes of not wasting language as some do.'

The reflection perhaps reminded him that he had better, like young Norval's father, 'increase his store.' At any rate he became silent, and remained so, until old Sol went out into the shop to light it up, when he turned to Walter, and said, without any introductory remark—

'I suppose he could make a clock if he tried?'

'I shouldn't wonder, Captain Cuttle,' returned the boy.

'And it would go!' said Captain Cuttle, making a species of serpent in the air with his hook. 'Lord, how that clock would go!'

For a moment or two he seemed quite lost in contemplating the pace of this ideal timepiece, and sat looking at the boy as if his face were the dial.

'But he 's chock-full of science,' he observed, waving his hook towards the stock-in-trade. 'Look ye here! Here 's a collection of 'em. Earth, air, or water. It 's all one. Only say where you 'll have it. Up in a balloon? There you are. Down in a bell? There you are. D' ye want to put the North Star in a pair of scales and weigh it? He 'll do it for you.'

It may be gathered from these remarks that Captain Cuttle's reverence for the stock of instruments was profound, and that his philosophy knew little or no distinction between trading in it and inventing it.

'Ah!' he said, with a sigh, 'it 's a fine thing to understand 'em. And yet it 's a fine thing not to understand 'em. I hardly know which is best. It 's so comfortable to sit here and feel that you might be weighed, measured, magnified, electrified, polarised, played the very devil with: and never know how.'

Nothing short of the wonderful Madeira, combined with the occasion (which rendered it desirable to improve and expand Walter's mind), could have ever loosened his tongue to the extent of giving utterance to this prodigious oration. He seemed quite amazed himself at the manner in which it opened up to view the sources of the taciturn delight he had had in eating Sunday dinners in that parlour for ten years. Becoming a sadder and a wiser man, he mused and held his peace.

'Come!' cried the subject of his admiration, returning. 'Before you have your glass of grog, Ned, we must finish the bottle.'

'Stand by!' said Ned, filling his glass. 'Give the boy some more.'

'No more, thank 'e, uncle!'

'Yes, yes,' said Sol, 'a little more. We 'll finish the bottle, to the House, Ned—Walter's house. Why it may be his house one of these days, in part. Who knows? Sir Richard Whittington married his master's daughter.'

'"Turn again Whittington, Lord Mayor of London, and when you are old you will never depart from it,"' interposed the captain. 'Wal'r! Overhaul the book, my lad.'

'And although Mr. Dombey hasn't a daughter,' Sol began.

'Yes, yes, he has, uncle,' said the boy, reddening and laughing.

'Has he?' cried the old man. 'Indeed I think he has too.'

'Oh! I know he has,' said the boy. 'Some of 'em were talking about it in the office to-day. And they do say, uncle and Captain Cuttle,' lowering his voice, 'that he 's taken a dislike to her, and that she 's left, unnoticed, among the servants, and that his mind 's so set all the while upon having his son in the House, that although he 's only a baby now, he is going to have balances struck oftener than formerly, and the books kept closer than they used to be, and has even been seen (when he thought he wasn't) walking in the Docks, looking at his ships and property and all that, as if he was exulting like, over what he and his son will possess together. That 's what they say. Of course *I* don't know.'

'He knows all about her already, you see,' said the instrument-maker.

'Nonsense, uncle,' cried the boy, still reddening and laughing, boy-like. 'How can I help hearing what they tell me?'

'The son 's a little in our way at present, I 'm afraid, Ned,' said the old man, humouring the joke.

'Very much,' said the captain.

'Nevertheless, we 'll drink him,' pursued Sol. 'So, here 's to Dombey and Son.'

'Oh, very well, uncle,' said the boy, merrily. 'Since you have introduced the mention of her, and have connected me with her, and have said that I know all about her, I shall make bold to amend the toast. So here 's to Dombey—and Son—and Daughter!'

## CHAPTER V

### PAUL'S PROGRESS AND CHRISTENING

Little Paul suffering no contamination, from the blood of the Toodles, grew stouter and stronger every day. Every day, too, he was more and more ardently cherished by Miss Tox, whose devotion was so far appreciated by Mr. Dombey that he began to regard her as a woman of great natural good sense, whose feelings did her credit and deserved encouragement. He was so lavish of this condescension, that he not only bowed to her, in a particular manner, on several occasions, but even entrusted such stately recognitions of her to his sister as 'pray tell your friend, Louisa, that she is very good,' or 'mention to Miss Tox, Louisa, that I am obliged to her'; specialities which made a deep impression on the lady thus distinguished.

Miss Tox was often in the habit of assuring Mrs. Chick, that 'nothing could exceed her interest in all connected with the development of that sweet child'; and an observer of Miss Tox's proceedings might have inferred so much without declaratory confirmation. She would preside over the innocent repasts of the young heir, with ineffable satisfaction, almost with an air of joint proprietorship with Richards in the entertainment. At the little ceremonies of the bath and toilette, she assisted with enthusiasm. The administration of infantine doses of physic awakened all the active sympathy of her character; and being on one occasion secreted in a cupboard (whither she had fled in modesty), when Mr. Dombey was introduced into the nursery by his sister, to behold his son in the course of preparation for bed, taking a short walk uphill over Richards's gown, in a short and airy linen jacket, Miss Tox was so transported beyond the ignorant present as to be unable to refrain from crying out, 'Is he not beautiful, Mr. Dombey? Is he not a Cupid, sir?' and then almost sinking behind the closet door with confusion and blushes.

'Louisa,' said Mr. Dombey, one day, to his sister, 'I really think I must present your friend with some little token, on the occasion of Paul's christening. She has exerted herself so warmly in the child's behalf from the first, and seems to understand her position so thoroughly (a very rare merit in this world, I am sorry to say), that it would really be agreeable to me to notice her.'

Let it be no detraction from the merits of Miss Tox, to hint that in Mr. Dombey's eyes, as in some others that occasionally see the light, they only achieved that mighty piece of knowledge, the understanding of their own position, who showed a fitting reverence for his. It was not so much their merit that they knew themselves, as that they knew him, and bowed low before him.

'My dear Paul,' returned his sister, 'you do Miss Tox but justice, as a man of your penetration was sure, I knew, to do. I believe if there are three words in the English language for which she has a respect amounting almost to veneration, those words are, Dombey and Son.'

'Well,' said Mr. Dombey, 'I believe it. It does Miss Tox credit.'

'And as to anything in the shape of a token, my dear Paul,' pursued his sister, 'all I can say is that anything you give Miss Tox will be hoarded and prized, I am sure, like a relic. But there *is* a way, my dear Paul, of showing your sense of Miss Tox's friendliness in a still more flattering and acceptable manner, if you should be so inclined.'

'How is that?' asked Mr. Dombey.

'Godfathers, of course,' continued Mrs. Chick, 'are important in point of connection and influence.'

'I don't know why they should be, to my son,' said Mr. Dombey, coldly.

'Very true, my dear Paul,' retorted Mrs. Chick, with an extraordinary show of animation, to cover the suddenness of her conversion; 'and spoken like yourself. I might have expected nothing else from you. I might have known that such would have been your opinion. Perhaps'; here Mrs. Chick flattered again, as not quite comfortably feeling her way; 'perhaps that is a reason why you might have the less objection to allowing Miss Tox to be godmother to the dear thing, if it were only as deputy and proxy for some one else. That it would be received as a great honour and distinction, Paul, I need not say.'

'Louisa,' said Mr. Dombey, after a short pause, 'it is not to be supposed—'

'Certainly not,' cried Mrs. Chick, hastening to anticipate a refusal, 'I never thought it was.'

Mr. Dombey looked at her impatiently.

'Don't flurry me, my dear Paul,' said his sister; 'for that destroys me. I am far from strong. I have not been quite myself, since poor dear Fanny departed.'

Mr. Dombey glanced at the pocket-handkerchief which his sister applied to her eyes, and resumed—

'It is not to be supposed, I say—'

'And I say,' murmured Mrs. Chick, 'that I never thought it was.'

'Good Heaven, Louisa!' said Mr. Dombey.

'No, my dear Paul,' she remonstrated with tearful dignity, 'I must really be allowed to speak. I am not so clever, or so reasoning, or so eloquent, or so anything, as you are. I know that very well. So much the worse for me. But if they were the last words

I had to utter—and last words should be very solemn to you and me, Paul, after poor dear Fanny—I should still say I never thought it was. And what is more,' added Mrs. Chick with increased dignity, as if she had withheld her crushing argument until now, 'I never *did* think it was.'

Mr. Dombey walked to the window and back again.

'It is not to be supposed, Louisa,' he said (Mrs. Chick had nailed her colours to the mast, and repeated 'I know it isn't,' but he took no notice of it), 'but that there are many persons who, supposing that I recognised any claim at all in such a case, have a claim upon me superior to Miss Tox's. But I do not. I recognise no such thing. Paul and myself will be able, when the time comes, to hold our own—the House, in other words, will be able to hold its own, and maintain its own, and hand down its own of itself, and without any such commonplace aids. The kind of foreign help which people usually seek for their children, I can afford to despise; being above it, I hope. So that Paul's infancy and childhood pass away well, and I see him becoming qualified without waste of time for the career on which he is destined to enter, I am satisfied. He will make what powerful friends he pleases in after-life, when he is actively maintaining—and extending, if that is possible—the dignity and credit of the firm. Until then, I am enough for him, perhaps, and all in all. I have no wish that people should step in between us. I would much rather show my sense of the obliging conduct of a deserving person like your friend. Therefore let it be so; and your husband and myself will do well enough for the other sponsors, I dare say.'

In the course of these remarks, delivered with great majesty and grandeur, Mr. Dombey had truly revealed the secret feelings of his breast. An indescribable distrust of anybody stepping in between himself and his son; a haughty dread of having any rival or partner in the boy's respect and deference; a sharp misgiving, recently acquired, that he was not infallible in his power of bending and binding human wills; as sharp a jealousy of any second check or cross; these were, at that time, the master-keys of his soul. In all his life, he had never made a friend. His cold and distant nature had neither sought one, nor found one. And now when that nature concentrated its whole force so strongly on a partial scheme of parental interest and ambition, it seemed as if its icy current, instead of being released by this influence, and running clear and free, had thawed for but an instant to admit its burden, and then frozen with it into one unyielding block.

Elevated thus to the godmothership of little Paul, in virtue of her insignificance, Miss Tox was from that hour chosen and appointed to office; and Mr. Dombey further signified his pleasure that the ceremony, already long delayed, should take place without further postponement. His sister, who had been far from anticipating so signal a success, withdrew as soon as she could, to communicate it to her best of friends; and Mr. Dombey was left alone in his library.

There was anything but solitude in the nursery; for there, Mrs. Chick and Miss Tox were enjoying a social evening, so much to the disgust of Miss Susan Nipper, that that young lady embraced every opportunity of making wry faces behind the door. Her feelings were so much excited on the occasion, that she found it indispensable to afford them this relief, even without having the comfort of any audience or sympathy whatever. As the knight-errants of old relieved their minds by carving their mistress's names in deserts, and wildernesses, and other savage places where there was no probability of there ever being anybody to read them, so did Miss Susan Nipper curl her snub-nose into drawers and wardrobes, put away winks of disparagement in cupboards, shed derisive squints into stone pitchers, and contradict and call names out in the passage.

The two interlopers, however, blissfully unconscious of the young lady's sentiments, saw little Paul safe through all the stages of undressing, airy exercise, supper, and bed; and then sat down to tea before the fire. The two children now lay, through the good offices of Polly, in one room; and it was not until the ladies were established at their tea-table that, happening to look towards the little beds, they thought of Florence.

'How sound she sleeps!' said Miss Tox.

'Why, you know, my dear, she takes a great deal of exercise in the course of the day,' returned Mrs. Chick, 'playing about little Paul so much.'

'She is a curious child,' said Miss Tox.

'My dear,' retorted Mrs. Chick, in a low voice: 'her mamma, all over!'

'Indeed!' said Miss Tox. 'Ah dear me!'

A tone of most extraordinary compassion Miss Tox said it in, though she had no distinct idea why, except that it was expected of her.

'Florence will never, never, never, be a Dombey,' said Mrs. Chick, 'not if she lives to be a thousand years old.'

Miss Tox elevated her eyebrows and was again full of commiseration.

'I quite fret and worry myself about her,' said Mrs. Chick, with a sigh of modest merit. 'I really don't see what is to become of her when she grows older, or what position she is to take. She don't gain on her papa, in the least. How can one expect she should, when she is so very unlike a Dombey?'

Miss Tox looked as if she saw no way out of such a cogent argument as that, at all.

'And the child, you see,' said Mrs. Chick, in deep confidence, 'has poor Fanny's nature. She 'll never make an effort in after-life, I 'll venture to say. Never! She 'll never wind and twine herself about her papa's heart like—'

'Like the ivy?' suggested Miss Tox.

'Like the ivy,' Mrs. Chick assented. 'Never! She 'll never glide and nestle into the bosom of her papa's affections like—the—'

'Startled fawn?' suggested Miss Tox.

'Like the startled fawn,' said Mrs. Chick. 'Never! Poor Fanny! Yet, how I loved her!'

'You must not distress yourself, my dear,' said Miss Tox, in a soothing voice. 'Now really! You have too much feeling.'

'We have all our faults,' said Mrs. Chick, weeping and shaking her head. 'I dare say we have. I never was blind to hers. I never said I was. Far from it. Yet how I loved her!'

What a satisfaction it was to Mrs. Chick—a commonplace piece of folly enough, compared with whom her sister-in-law had been a very angel of womanly intelligence and gentleness—to patronise and be tender to the memory of that lady: in exact pursuance of her conduct to her in her lifetime: and to thoroughly believe herself, and take herself in, and make herself uncommonly comfortable on the strength of her toleration! What a mighty pleasant virtue toleration should be when we are right, to be so very pleasant when we are wrong, and quite unable to demonstrate how we come to be invested with the privilege of exercising it!

Mrs. Chick was yet drying her eyes and shaking her head, when Richards made bold to caution her that Miss Florence was awake and sitting in her bed. She had risen, as the nurse said, and the lashes of her eyes were wet with tears. But no one saw them glistening save Polly. No one else leant over her, and whispered soothing words to her, or was near enough to hear the flutter of her beating heart.

'Oh! dear nurse!' said the child, looking earnestly up in her face, 'let me lie by my brother!'

'Why, my pet?' said Richards.

'Oh! I think he loves me,' cried the child wildly. 'Let me lie by him. Pray do!'

Mrs. Chick interposed with some motherly words about going to sleep like a dear, but Florence repeated her supplication, with a frightened look, and in a voice broken by sobs and tears.

'I 'll not wake him,' she said, covering her face and hanging down her head. 'I 'll only touch him with my hand, and go to sleep. Oh, pray, pray, let me lie by my brother to-night, for I believe he 's fond of me!'

Richards took her without a word, and carrying her to the little bed in which the infant was sleeping laid her down by his side. She crept as near him as she could without disturbing his rest; and stretching out one arm so that it timidly embraced his neck, and hiding her face on the other, over which her damp and scattered hair fell loose, lay motionless.

'Poor little thing,' said Miss Tox; 'she has been dreaming, I dare say.'

This trivial incident had so interrupted the current of conversation, that it was difficult of resumption;

and Mrs. Chick moreover had been so affected by the contemplation of her own tolerant nature, that she was not in spirits. The two friends accordingly soon made an end of their tea, and a servant was despatched to fetch a hackney cabriolet for Miss Tox. Miss Tox had great experience in hackney cabs, and her starting in one was generally a work of time, as she was systematic in the preparatory arrangements.

'Have the goodness, if you please, Towlinson,' said Miss Tox, 'first of all, to carry out a pen and ink and take his number legibly.'

'Yes, miss,' said Towlinson.

'Then, if you please, Towlinson,' said Miss Tox, 'have the goodness to turn the cushion. Which,' said Miss Tox apart to Mrs. Chick, 'is generally damp, my dear.'

'Yes, miss,' said Towlinson.

'I 'll trouble you also, if you please,' said Miss Tox, 'with this card and this shilling. He 's to drive to the card, and is to understand that he will not on any account have more than the shilling.'

'No, miss,' said Towlinson.

'And—I 'm sorry to give you so much trouble, Towlinson,' said Miss Tox, looking at him pensively.

'Not at all, miss,' said Towlinson.

'Mention to the man, then, if you please, Towlinson,' said Miss Tox, 'that the lady's uncle is a magistrate, and that if he gives her any of his impertinence he will be punished terribly. You can pretend to say that, if you please, Towlinson, in a friendly way, and because you know it was done to another man, who died.'

'Certainly, miss,' said Towlinson.

'And now good night to my sweet, sweet, sweet, godson,' said Miss Tox, with a soft shower of kisses at each repetition of the adjective; 'and Louisa, my dear friend, promise me to take a little something warm before you go to bed, and not to distress yourself.'

It was with extreme difficulty that Nipper, the black-eyed, who looked on steadfastly, contained herself at this crisis, and, until the subsequent departure of Mrs. Chick. But the nursery being at length free of visitors, she made herself some recompense for her late restraint.

'You might keep me in a strait-waistcoat for six weeks,' said Nipper, 'and when I got it off I 'd only be more aggravated, who ever heard the like of them two griffins, Mrs. Richards?'

'And then to talk of having been dreaming, poor dear!' said Polly.

'Oh you beauties!' cried Susan Nipper, affecting to salute the door by which the ladies had departed. 'Never be a Dombey won't she? It 's to be hoped she won't, we don't want any more such, one 's enough.'

'Don't wake the children, Susan dear,' said Polly.

'I 'm very much beholden to you, Mrs. Richards,' said Susan, who was not by any means discriminating in her wrath, 'and really feel it as a honour to receive your commands, being a black slave and a mulotter. Mrs. Richards, if there 's any other orders you can give me, pray mention 'em.'

'Nonsense; orders,' said Polly.

'Oh! bless your heart, Mrs. Richards,' cried Susan, 'temporaries always orders permanencies here, didn't you know that, why wherever was you born, Mrs. Richards? But wherever you was born, Mrs. Richards,' pursued Spitfire, shaking her head resolutely, 'and whenever, and however (which is best known to yourself), you may bear in mind, please, that it 's one thing to give orders, and quite another thing to take 'em. A person may tell a person to dive off a bridge head foremost into five-and-forty feet of water, Mrs. Richards, but a person may be very far from diving.'

'There now,' said Polly, 'you 're angry because you 're a good little thing, and fond of Miss Florence; and yet you turn round on me, because there 's nobody else.'

'It 's very easy for some to keep their tempers, and be soft-spoken, Mrs. Richards,' returned Susan, slightly mollified, 'when their child 's made as much of as a prince, and is petted and patted till it wishes its friends further, but when a sweet young pretty innocent, that never ought to have a cross word spoken to or of it, is run down, the case is very different indeed. My goodness gracious me, Miss Floy, you naughty, sinful child, if you don't shut your eyes this minute, I 'll call in them hobgoblins that lives in the cock-loft to come and eat you up alive!'

Here Miss Nipper made a horrible lowing, supposed to issue from a conscientious goblin of the bull species, impatient to discharge the severe duty of his position. Having further composed her young charge by covering her head with the bed-clothes, and making three or four angry dabs at the pillow, she folded her arms, and screwed up her mouth, and sat looking at the fire for the rest of the evening.

Though little Paul was said, in nursery phrase, 'to take a deal of notice for his age,' he took as little notice of all this as of the preparations for his christening on the next day but one; which nevertheless went on about him, as to his personal apparel, and that of his sister and the two nurses, with great activity. Neither did he, on the arrival of the appointed morning, show any sense of its importance; being, on the contrary, unusually inclined to sleep, and unusually inclined to take it ill in his attendants that they dressed him to go out.

It happened to be an iron-grey autumnal day, with a shrewd east wind blowing—a day in keeping with the proceedings. Mr. Dombey represented in himself the wind, the shade, and the autumn of the christening. He stood in his library to receive the company, as hard and cold as the weather; and when he looked out through the glass room, at the trees in the little garden, their brown and yellow leaves came fluttering down, as if he blighted them.

Ugh! They were black, cold rooms; and seemed to be in mourning, like the inmates of the house. The books precisely matched as to size, and drawn up in line, like soldiers, looked in their cold, hard, slippery uniforms, as if they had but one idea among them, and that was a freezer. The bookcase, glazed and locked, repudiated all familiarities. Mr. Pitt, in bronze on the top, with no trace of his celestial origin about him, guarded the unattainable treasure like an enchanted Moor. A dusty urn at each high corner, dug up from an ancient tomb, preached desolation and decay, as from two pulpits; and the chimney-glass, reflecting Mr. Dombey and his portrait at one blow, seemed fraught with melancholy meditations.

The stiff and stark fire-irons appeared to claim a nearer relationship than anything else there to Mr. Dombey, with his buttoned coat, his white cravat, his heavy gold watch-chain, and his creaking boots. But this was before the arrival of Mr. and Mrs. Chick, his lawful relatives, who soon presented themselves.

'My dear Paul,' Mrs. Chick murmured, as she embraced him, 'the beginning, I hope, of many joyful days!'

'Thank you, Louisa,' said Mr. Dombey, grimly. 'How do you do, Mr. John?'

'How do you do, sir?' said Chick.

He gave Mr. Dombey his hand, as if he feared it

might electrify him. Mr. Dombey took it as if it were a fish, or seaweed, or some such clammy substance, and immediately returned it to him with exalted politeness.

'Perhaps, Louisa,' said Mr. Dombey, slightly turning his head in his cravat, as if it were a socket, 'you would have preferred a fire?'

'Oh, my dear Paul, no,' said Mrs. Chick, who had much ado to keep her teeth from chattering; 'not for me.'

'Mr. John,' said Mr. Dombey, 'you are not sensible of any chill?'

Mr. John, who had already got both his hands in his pockets over the wrists, and was on the very threshold of that same canine chorus which had given Mrs. Chick so much offence on a former occasion, protested that he was perfectly comfortable.

He added in a low voice, 'With my tiddle tol toor rul'—when he was providentially stopped by Towlinson, who announced—

'Miss Tox!'

And enter that fair enslaver, with a blue nose and indescribably frosty face, referable to her being very thinly clad in a maze of fluttering odds and ends, to do honour to the ceremony.

'How do you do, Miss Tox?' said Mr. Dombey.

Miss Tox, in the midst of her spreading gauzes, went down altogether like an opera-glass shutting-up; she curtsied so low, in acknowledgment of Mr. Dombey's advancing a step or two to meet her.

'I can never forget this occasion, sir,' said Miss Tox, softly. ''Tis impossible. My dear Louisa, I can hardly believe the evidence of my senses.'

If Miss Tox could believe the evidence of one of her senses, it was a very cold day. That was quite clear. She took an early opportunity of promoting the circulation in the tip of her nose by secretly chafing it with her pocket-handkerchief, lest, by its very low temperature, it should disagreeably astonish the baby when she came to kiss it.

The baby soon appeared, carried in great glory by Richards; while Florence, in custody of that active young constable, Susan Nipper, brought up the rear. Though the whole nursery party were dressed by this time in lighter mourning than at first, there was enough in the appearance of the bereaved children to make the day no brighter. The baby too—it might have been Miss Tox's nose—began to cry. Thereby, as it happened, preventing Mr. Chick from the awkward fulfilment of a very honest purpose he had; which was, to make much of Florence. For this gentleman, insensible to the superior claims of a perfect Dombey (perhaps on account of having the honour to be united to a Dombey himself, and being familiar with excellence), really liked her, and showed that he liked her, and was about to show it in his own way now, when Paul cried, and his helpmate stopped him short.

'Now, Florence, child!' said her aunt, briskly, 'what are you doing, love? Show yourself to him. Engage his attention, my dear!'

The atmosphere became or might have become colder and colder, when Mr. Dombey stood frigidly watching his little daughter, who, clapping her hands, and standing on tiptoe before the throne of his son and heir, lured him to bend down from his high estate, and look at her. Some honest act of Richards's may have aided the effect, but he did look down, and held his peace. As his sister hid behind her nurse, he followed her with his eyes; and when she peeped out with a merry cry to him, he sprang up and crowed lustily—laughing outright when she ran in upon him;

and seeming to fondle her curls with his tiny hands, while she smothered him with kisses.

Was Mr. Dombey pleased to see this? He testified no pleasure by the relaxation of a nerve; but outward tokens of any kind of feeling were unusual with him. If any sunbeam stole into the room to light the children at their play, it never reached his face. He looked on so fixedly and coldly, that the warm light vanished even from the laughing eyes of little Florence, when, at last, they happened to meet his.

It was a dull, grey, autumn day indeed, and in a minute's pause and silence that took place, the leaves fell sorrowfully.

'Mr. John,' said Mr. Dombey, referring to his watch, and assuming his hat and gloves. 'Take my sister, if you please: my arm to-day is Miss Tox's. You had better go first with Master Paul, Richards. Be very careful.'

In Mr. Dombey's carriage, Dombey and Son, Miss Tox, Mrs. Chick, Richards, and Florence. In a little carriage following it, Susan Nipper and the owner Mr. Chick. Susan looking out of window, without intermission, as a relief from the embarrassment of confronting the large face of that gentleman, and thinking whenever anything rattled that he was putting up in paper an appropriate pecuniary compliment for herself.

Once upon the road to church, Mr. Dombey clapped his hands for the amusement of his son. At which instance of parental enthusiasm Miss Tox was enchanted. But exclusive of this incident, the chief difference between the christening party and a party in a mourning coach, consisted in the colours of the carriage and horses.

Arrived at the church steps, they were received by a portentous beadle. Mr. Dombey dismounting first to help the ladies out, and standing near him at the church door, looked like another beadle. A beadle less gorgeous but more dreadful; the beadle of private life; the beadle of our business and our bosoms.

Miss Tox's hand trembled as she slipped it through Mr. Dombey's arm, and felt herself escorted up the steps, preceded by a cocked hat and a Babylonian collar. It seemed for a moment like that other solemn institution, 'Wilt thou have this man, Lucretia?' 'Yes, I will.'

'Please to bring the child in quick out of the air there,' whispered the beadle, holding open the inner door of the church.

Little Paul might have asked with Hamlet 'into my grave?' so chill and earthy was the place. The tall shrouded pulpit and reading-desk; the dreary perspective of empty pews stretching away under the galleries, and empty benches mounting to the roof and lost in the shadow of the great grim organ; the dusty matting and cold stone slabs; the grisly free seats in the aisles; and the damp corner by the bell-rope, where the black tressels used for funerals were stowed away, along with some shovels and baskets, and a coil or two of deadly-looking rope; the strange, unusual, uncomfortable smell, and the cadaverous light; were all in unison. It was a cold and dismal scene.

'There 's a wedding just on, sir,' said the beadle, 'but it 'll be over directly, if you 'll walk into the westry here.'

Before he turned again to lead the way, he gave Mr. Dombey a bow and a half-smile of recognition, importing that he (the beadle) remembered to have had the pleasure of attending on him when he buried his wife, and hoped he had enjoyed himself since.

The very wedding looked dismal as they passed

in front of the altar. The bride was too old and the bridegroom too young, and a superannuated beau with one eye and an eye-glass stuck in its blank companion, was giving away the lady, while the friends were shivering. In the vestry the fire was smoking; and an over-aged, and over-worked and under-paid attorney's clerk, 'making a search,' was running his forefinger down the parchment pages of an immense register (one of a long series of similar volumes) gorged with burials. Over the fireplace was a ground-plan of the vaults underneath the church; and Mr. Chick, skimming the literary portion of it aloud, by way of enlivening the company, read the reference to Mrs. Dombey's tomb in full, before he could stop himself.

After another cold interval, a wheezy little pew-opener, afflicted with an asthma, appropriate to the churchyard, if not to the church, summoned them to the font. Here they waited some little time while the marriage party enrolled themselves; and meanwhile the wheezy little pew-opener—partly in consequence of her infirmity, and partly that the marriage party might not forget her—went about the building coughing like a grampus.

Presently the clerk (the only cheerful-looking object there, and *he* was an undertaker) came up with a jug of warm water, and said something, as he poured it into the font, about taking the chill off; which millions of gallons boiling hot could not have done for the occasion. Then the clergyman, an amiable and mild-looking young curate but obviously afraid of the baby, appeared like the principal character in a ghost-story, 'a tall figure all in white'; at sight of whom Paul rent the air with his cries, and never left off again till he was taken out black in the face.

Even when that event had happened, to the great

relief of everybody, he was heard under the portico, during the rest of the ceremony, now fainter, now louder, now hushed, now bursting forth again with an irrepressible sense of his wrongs. This so distracted the attention of the two ladies, that Mrs. Chick was constantly deploying into the centre aisle, to send out messages by the pew-opener, while Miss Tox kept her Prayer-book open at the Gunpowder Plot, and occasionally read responses from that service.

During the whole of these proceedings, Mr. Dombey remained as impassive and gentlemanly as ever, and perhaps assisted in making it so cold, that the young curate smoked at the mouth as he read. The only time that he unbent his visage in the least, was when the clergyman, in delivering (very unaffectedly and simply) the closing exhortation, relative to the future examination of the child by the sponsors, happened to rest his eye on Mr. Chick; and then Mr. Dombey might have been seen to express by a majestic look, that he would like to catch him at it.

It might have been well for Mr. Dombey, if he had thought of his own dignity a little less; and had thought of the great origin and purpose of the ceremony in which he took so formal and so stiff a part, a little more. His arrogance contrasted strangely with its history.

When it was all over, he again gave his arm to Miss Tox, and conducted her to the vestry, where he informed the clergyman how much pleasure it would have given him to have solicited the honour of his company at dinner, but for the unfortunate state of his household affairs. The register signed, and the fees paid, and the pew-opener (whose cough was very bad again) remembered, and the beadle gratified, and the sexton (who was accidentally on the door-steps, looking with great interest at the weather) not forgotten, they got into the carriage again, and drove home in the same bleak fellowship.

There they found Mr. Pitt turning up his nose at a cold collation, set forth in a cold pomp of glass and silver, and looking more like a dead dinner lying in state than a social refreshment. On their arrival, Miss Tox produced a mug for her godson, and Mr. Chick a knife and fork and spoon in a case. Mr. Dombey also produced a bracelet for Miss Tox; and, on the receipt of this token, Miss Tox was tenderly affected.

'Mr. John,' said Mr. Dombey, 'will you take the bottom of the table, if you please. What have you got there, Mr. John?'

'I have got a cold fillet of veal here, sir,' replied Mr. Chick, rubbing his numbed hands hard together. 'What have *you* got there, sir?'

'This,' returned Mr. Dombey, 'is some cold preparation of calf's head, I think. I see cold fowls—ham—patties—salad—lobster. Miss Tox will do me the honour of taking some wine? Champagne to Miss Tox.'

There was a toothache in everything. The wine was so bitter cold that it forced a little scream from Miss Tox, which she had great difficulty in turning into a 'Hem!' The veal had come from such an airy pantry, that the first taste of it had struck a sensation as of cold lead to Mr. Chick's extremities. Mr. Dombey alone remained unmoved. He might have been hung up for sale at a Russian fair as a specimen of a frozen gentleman.

The prevailing influence was too much even for his sister. She made no effort at flattery or small talk, and directed all her efforts to looking as warm as she could.

'Well, sir,' said Mr. Chick, making a desperate plunge, after a long silence, and filling a glass of sherry; 'I shall drink this, if you 'll allow me, sir, to little Paul.'

'Bless him!' murmured Miss Tox, taking a sip of wine.

'Dear little Dombey!' murmured Mrs. Chick.

'Mr. John,' said Mr. Dombey, with severe gravity, 'my son would feel and express himself obliged tc you, I have no doubt, if he could appreciate the favour you have done him. He will prove, in time to come, I trust, equal to any responsibility that the obliging disposition of his relations and friends, in private, or the onerous nature of our position, in public, may impose upon him.'

The tone in which this was said admitting of nothing more, Mr. Chick relapsed into low spirits and silence. Not so Miss Tox, who, having listened to Mr. Dombey with even a more emphatic attention than usual, and with a more expressive tendency of her head to one side, now leant across the table, and said to Mrs. Chick softly—

'Louisa!'

'My dear,' said Mrs. Chick.

'Onerous nature of our position in public may—I have forgotten the exact term.'

'Expose him to,' said Mrs. Chick.

'Pardon me, my dear,' returned Miss Tox, 'I think not. It was more rounded and flowing. Obliging disposition of relations and friends, in private, or onerous nature of position in public—may—impose upon him!'

'Impose upon him, to be sure,' said Mrs. Chick.

Miss Tox struck her delicate hands together lightly, in triumph; and added, casting up her eyes, 'eloquence indeed!'

Mr. Dombey, in the meanwhile, had issued orders for the attendance of Richards, who now entered curtseying, but without the baby; Paul being asleep after the fatigues of the morning. Mr. Dombey, having delivered a glass of wine to this vassal, addressed her in the following words: Miss Tox previously settling her head on one side, and making other little arrangements for engraving them on her heart.

'During the six months or so, Richards, which have seen you an inmate of this house, you have done your duty. Desiring to connect some little service to you with this occasion, I considered how I could best effect that object, and I also advised with my sister, Mrs.—

'Chick,' interposed the gentleman of that name.

'Oh, hush if you *please*!' said Miss Tox.

'I was about to say to you, Richards,' resumed Mr. Dombey with an appalling glance at Mr. John, 'that I was further assisted in my decision, by the recollection of a conversation I held with your husband in this room, on the occasion of your being hired, when he disclosed to me the melancholy fact that your family, himself at the head, were sunk and steeped in ignorance.'

Richards quailed under the magnificence of the reproof.

'I am far from being friendly,' pursued Mr. Dombey, 'to what is called by persons of levelling sentiments, general education. But it is necessary that the inferior classes should continue to be taught to know their position, and to conduct themselves properly. So far I approve of schools. Having the power of nominating a child on the foundation of an ancient establishment, called (from a worshipful company) the Charitable Grinders; where not only is a wholesome education bestowed upon the scholars, but where a dress and badge is likewise provided for them;

I have (first communicating, through Mrs. Chick, with your family) nominated your eldest son to an existing vacancy; and he has this day, I am informed, assumed the habit. The number of her son, I believe,' said Mr. Dombey, turning to his sister and speaking of the child as if he were a hackney-coach, 'is one hundred and forty-seven. Louisa, you can tell her.'

'One hundred and forty-seven,' said Mrs. Chick. 'The dress, Richards, is a nice, warm, blue baize tailed coat and cap, turned up with orange-coloured binding; red worsted stockings; and very strong leather small-clothes. One might wear the articles one's-self,' said Mrs. Chick, with enthusiasm, 'and be grateful.'

'There, Richards!' said Miss Tox. 'Now, indeed, you *may* be proud. The Charitable Grinders!'

'I am sure I am very much obliged, sir,' returned Richards faintly, 'and take it very kind that you should remember my little ones.' At the same time a vision of Biler as a Charitable Grinder, with his very small legs encased in the serviceable clothing described by Mrs. Chick, swam before Richards's eyes, and made them water.

'I am very glad to see you have so much feeling, Richards,' said Miss Tox.

'It makes one almost hope, it really does,' said Mrs. Chick, who prided herself on taking trustful views of human nature, 'that there may yet be some faint spark of gratitude and right feeling in the world.'

Richards deferred to these compliments by curtseying and murmuring her thanks; but finding it quite impossible to recover her spirits from the disorder into which they had been thrown by the image of her son in his precocious nether garments, she gradually approached the door and was heartily relieved to escape by it.

Such temporary indications of a partial thaw that

had appeared with her, vanished with her; and the frost set in again, as cold and hard as ever. Mr. Chick was twice heard to hum a tune at the bottom of the table, but on both occasions it was a fragment of the Dead March in Saul. The party seemed to get colder and colder, and to be gradually resolving itself into a congealed and solid state, like the collation round which it was assembled. At length Mrs. Chick looked at Miss Tox, and Miss Tox returned the look, and they both rose and said it was really time to go. Mr. Dombey receiving this announcement with perfect equanimity, they took leave of that gentleman, and presently departed under the protection of Mr. Chick; who, when they had turned their backs upon the house and left its master in his usual solitary state, put his hands in his pockets, threw himself back in the carriage, and whistled 'With a hey ho chevy!' all through; conveying into his face as he did so, an expression of such gloomy and terrible defiance, that Mrs. Chick dared not protest, or in any way molest him.

Richards, though she had little Paul on her lap, could not forget her own first-born. She felt it was ungrateful; but the influence of the day fell even on the Charitable Grinders, and she could hardly help regarding his pewter badge, number one hundred and forty-seven, as, somehow, a part of its formality and sternness. She spoke, too, in the nursery, of his 'blessed legs,' and was again troubled by his spectre in uniform.

'I don't know what I wouldn't give,' said Polly, 'to see the poor little dear before he gets used to 'em.'

'Why, then, I tell you what, Mrs. Richards,' retorted Nipper, who had been admitted to her confidence, 'see him and make your mind easy.'

'Mr. Dombey wouldn't like it,' said Polly.

'Oh wouldn't he, Mrs. Richards!' retorted Nipper, 'he 'd like it very much, I think, when he was asked.'

'You wouldn't ask him, I suppose, at all?' said Polly.

'No, Mrs. Richards, quite contrairy,' returned Susan, 'and them two inspectors Tox and Chick, not intending to be on duty to-morrow, as I heard 'em say, me and Miss Floy will go along with you to-morrow morning, and welcome, Mrs. Richards, if you like, for we may as well walk there, as up and down a street, and better too.'

Polly rejected the idea pretty stoutly at first; but by little and little she began to entertain it, as she entertained more and more distinctly the forbidden pictures of her children, and her own home. At length, arguing that there could be no great harm in calling for a moment at the door, she yielded to the Nipper proposition.

The matter being settled thus, little Paul began to cry most piteously, as if he had a foreboding that no good would come of it.

'What 's the matter with the child?' asked Susan.

'He 's cold, I think,' said Polly, walking with him to and fro, and hushing him.

It was a bleak autumnal afternoon indeed; and as she walked, and hushed, and, glancing through the dreary windows, pressed the little fellow closer to her breast, the withered leaves came showering down.

## CHAPTER VI

### PAUL'S SECOND DEPRIVATION

Polly was beset by so many misgivings in the morning, that but for the incessant promptings of her black-eyed companion, she would have abandoned all thoughts of the expedition, and formally petitioned for leave to see number one hundred and forty-seven, under the awful shadow of Mr. Dombey's roof. But Susan who was personally disposed in favour of the excursion, and who (like Tony Lumpkin), if she could bear the disappointments of other people with tolerable fortitude, could not abide to disappoint herself, threw so many ingenious doubts in the way of this second thought, and stimulated the original intention with so many ingenious arguments, that almost as soon as Mr. Dombey's stately back was turned, and that gentleman was pursuing his daily road towards the City, his unconscious son was on his way to Staggs's Gardens.

This euphonious locality was situated in a suburb, known by the inhabitants of Staggs's Gardens by the name of Camberling Town; a designation which the Strangers' Map of London, as printed (with a view to pleasant and commodious reference) on pocket-handkerchiefs, condenses, with some show of reason, into Camden Town. Hither the two nurses bent their steps, accompanied by their charges; Richards carrying Paul, of course, and Susan leading little Florence by the hand, and giving her such jerks and pokes from time to time, as she considered it wholesome to administer.

The first shock of a great earthquake had, just at that period, rent the whole neighbourhood to its centre. Traces of its course were visible on every side. Houses were knocked down; streets broken through and stopped; deep pits and trenches dug in the ground; enormous heaps of earth and clay thrown up; buildings that were undermined and shaking, propped by great beams of wood. Here, a chaos of carts, overthrown and jumbled together, lay topsy-turvy at the bottom of a steep unnatural hill; there, confused treasures of iron soaked and rusted in something that had accidentally become a pond. Everywhere were bridges that led nowhere; thoroughfares that were wholly impassable; Babel towers of chimneys, wanting half their height; temporary wooden houses and enclosures, in the most unlikely situations; carcases of ragged tenements, and fragments of unfinished walls and arches, and piles of scaffolding, and wildernesses of bricks, and giant forms of cranes, and tripods straddling above nothing. There were a hundred thousand shapes and substances of incompleteness, wildly mingled out of their places, upside down, burrowing in the earth, aspiring in the air, mouldering in the water, and unintelligible as any dream. Hot springs and fiery eruptions, the usual attendants upon earthquakes, lent their contributions of confusion to the scene. Boiling water hissed and heaved within dilapidated walls; whence, also, the glare and roar of flames came issuing forth; and mounds of ashes blocked up rights of way, and wholly changed the law and custom of the neighbourhood.

In short, the yet unfinished and unopened railroad was in progress; and, from the very core of all this dire disorder, trailed smoothly away, upon its mighty course of civilisation and improvement.

But as yet, the neighbourhood was shy to own the railroad. One or two bold speculators had projected streets; and one had built a little, but had stopped among the mud and ashes to consider farther of it. A bran-new tavern, redolent of fresh mortar and size, and fronting nothing at all, had taken for its sign The Railway Arms; but that might be rash enterprise—and then it hoped to sell drink to the workmen. So, the Excavators' House of Call had sprung up from a beer shop; and the old-established ham and beef shop had become the Railway Eating House, with a roast leg of pork daily, through interested motives of a similar immediate and popular description. Lodging-house keepers were favourable in like manner; and for the like reasons were not to be trusted. The general belief was very slow. There were frowzy fields, and cow-houses, and dunghills, and dustheaps, and ditches, and gardens, and summer-houses, and carpet-beating grounds, at the very door of the railway. Little tumuli of oyster shells in the oyster season, and of lobster shells in the lobster season, and of broken crockery and faded cabbage leaves in all seasons, encroached upon its high places. Posts, and rails, and old cautions to trespassers, and backs of mean houses, and patches of wretched vegetation, stared it out of countenance. Nothing was the better for it, or thought of being so. If the miserable waste ground lying near it could have laughed, it would have laughed it to scorn, like many of the miserable neighbours.

Staggs's Gardens was uncommonly incredulous. It was a little row of houses, with little squalid patches of ground before them, fenced off with old doors, barrel staves, scraps of tarpaulin, and dead bushes; with bottomless tin kettles and exhausted iron fenders, thrust into the gaps. Here, the Staggs's Gardeners trained scarlet beans, kept fowls and rabbits, erected rotten summer-houses (one was an old boat), dried clothes, and smoked pipes. Some were of opinion that Staggs's Gardens derived its name from a deceased capitalist, one Mr. Staggs, who had built it for his delectation. Others, who had a natural taste for the country, held that it dated from those rural times when the antlered herd, under the familiar denominations of Staggses, had resorted to its shady precincts. Be this as it may, Staggs's Gardens was regarded by its population as a sacred grove not to be withered by railroads: and so confident were they generally of its long outliving any such ridiculous inventions, that the master chimney-sweeper at the corner, who was understood to take the lead in the local politics of the Gardens, had publicly declared that on the occasion of the railroad opening, if ever it did open, two of his boys should ascend the flues of his dwelling, with instructions to hail the failure with derisive jeers from the chimney-pots.

To this unhallowed spot, the very name of which had hitherto been carefully concealed from Mr. Dombey by his sister, was little Paul now borne by Fate and Richards.

'That 's my house, Susan,' said Polly, pointing it out.

'Is it, indeed, Mrs. Richards?' said Susan, condescendingly.

'And there 's my sister Jemima at the door, I do declare!' cried Polly, 'with my own sweet precious baby in her arms!'

The sight added such an extensive pair of wings to Polly's impatience, that she set off down the Gardens at a run, and bouncing on Jemima, changed babies with her in a twinkling; to the utter astonishment of that young damsel, on whom the heir of the Dombeys seemed to have fallen from the clouds.

'Why, Polly!' cried Jemima. 'You! what a turn you *have* given me! who 'd have thought it! come along in Polly! How well you do look to be sure! The children will go half wild to see you Polly, that they will.'

That they did, if one might judge from the noise they made, and the way in which they dashed at Polly and dragged her to a low chair in the chimney corner, where her own honest apple face became immediately the centre of a bunch of smaller pippins, all laying their rosy cheeks close to it, and all evidently the growth of the same tree. As to Polly, she was full as noisy and vehement as the children; and it was not until she was quite out of breath, and her hair was hanging all about her flushed face, and her new christening attire was very much dishevelled, that any pause took place in the confusion. Even then, the smallest Toodle but one remained in her lap, holding on tight with both arms round her neck; while the smallest Toodle but two mounted on the back of the chair, and made desperate efforts, with one leg in the air, to kiss her round the corner.

'Look! there 's a pretty little lady come to see you,' said Polly; 'and see how quiet *she* is! what a beautiful little lady, ain't she?'

This reference to Florence, who had been standing by the door not unobservant of what passed, directed the attention of the younger branches towards her; and had likewise the happy effect of leading to the formal recognition of Miss Nipper, who was not quite free from a misgiving that she had been already slighted.

'Oh do come in and sit down a minute, Susan, please,' said Polly. 'This is my sister Jemima, this is. Jemima, I don't know what I should ever do with myself, if it wasn't for Susan Nipper; I shouldn't be here now but for her.'

'Oh do sit down, Miss Nipper, if you please,' quoth Jemima.

Susan took the extreme corner of a chair, with a stately and ceremonious aspect.

'I never was so glad to see anybody in all my life; now really I never was, Miss Nipper,' said Jemima.

Susan relaxing, took a little more of the chair, and smiled graciously.

'Do untie your bonnet-strings, and make yourself at home, Miss Nipper, please,' entreated Jemima. 'I am afraid it 's a poorer place than you 're used to; but you 'll make allowances, I 'm sure.'

The black-eyed was so softened by this deferential behaviour, that she caught up little Miss Toodle who was running past, and took her to Banbury Cross immediately.

'But where 's my pretty boy?' said Polly. 'My poor fellow? I came all this way to see him in his new clothes.'

'Ah what a pity!' cried Jemima. 'He 'll break his heart, when he hears his mother has been here. He 's at school, Polly.'

'Gone already!'

'Yes. He went for the first time yesterday, for fear he should lose any learning. But it 's half-holiday, Polly: if you could only stop till he comes home—you and Miss Nipper, leastways,' said Jemima, mindful in good time of the dignity of the black-eyed.

'And how does he look, Jemima? bless him!' faltered Polly.

'Well, really he don't look so bad as you 'd suppose,' returned Jemima.

'Ah!' said Polly, with emotion, 'I knew his legs must be too short.'

'His legs *is* short,' returned Jemima; 'especially behind; but they 'll get longer, Polly, every day.'

It was a slow, prospective kind of consolation; but the cheerfulness and good nature with which it was administered, gave it a value it did not intrinsically possess. After a moment's silence, Polly asked, in a more sprightly manner—

'And where 's father, Jemima dear?'—for by that patriarchal appellation, Mr. Toodle was generally known in the family.

'There again!' said Jemima. 'What a pity! Father took his dinner with him this morning, and isn't coming home till night. But he 's always talking of you, Polly, and telling the children about you; and is the peaceablest, patientest, best temperedst soul in the world, as he always was and will be!'

'Thankee, Jemima,' cried the simple Polly; delighted by the speech, and disappointed by the absence.

'Oh you needn't thank me, Polly,' said her sister, giving her a sound kiss upon the cheek, and then dancing little Paul cheerfully. 'I say the same of you sometimes, and think it too.'

In spite of the double disappointment, it was impossible to regard in the light of a failure a visit which was greeted with such a reception; so the sisters talked hopefully about family matters, and about Biler, and about all his brothers and sisters: while the black-eyed, having performed several journeys to Banbury Cross and back, took sharp note of the furniture, the Dutch clock, the cupboard, the castle on the mantel-piece with red and green windows in it, susceptible of illumination by a candle-end within; and the pair of small black velvet kittens, each with a lady's reticule in its mouth; regarded by the Staggs's Gardeners as prodigies of imitative art. The conversation soon becoming general lest the black-eyed should go off at score and turn sarcastic, that young lady related to Jemima a summary of everything she knew concerning Mr. Dombey, his prospects, family, pursuits, and character. Also an exact inventory of her personal wardrobe, and some account of her principal relations and friends. Having relieved her mind of these disclosures, she partook of shrimps and porter, and evinced a disposition to swear eternal friendship.

Little Florence herself was not behindhand in improving the occasion: for, being conducted forth by the young Toodles to inspect some toadstools and other curiosities of the Gardens, she entered with them, heart and soul, on the formation of a temporary breakwater across a small green pool that had collected in a corner. She was still busily engaged in that labour, when sought and found by Susan; who, such was her sense of duty, even under the humanising influence of shrimps, delivered a moral address to her (punctuated with thumps) on her degenerate nature, while washing her face and hands; and predicted that she would bring the grey hairs of her family in general, with sorrow to the grave. After some delay, occasioned by a pretty long confidential interview above-stairs on pecuniary subjects, between Polly and Jemima, an interchange of babies was again effected —for Polly had all this time retained her own child, and Jemima little Paul—and the visitors took leave.

But first the young Toodles, victims of a pious fraud, were deluded into repairing in a body to a chandler's shop in the neighbourhood, for the ostensible purpose of spending a penny; and when the coast was quite clear, Polly fled: Jemima calling after her that if they could only go round towards the City Road on their way back, they would be sure to meet little Biler coming from school.

'Do you think that we might make time to go a little round in that direction, Susan?' inquired Polly, when they halted to take breath.

'Why not, Mrs. Richards?' returned Susan.

'It 's getting on towards our dinner-time you know,' said Polly.

But lunch had rendered her companion more than indifferent to this grave consideration, so she allowed no weight to it, and they resolved to go 'a little round.'

Now, it happened that poor Biler's life had been,

since yesterday morning, rendered weary by the costume of the Charitable Grinders. The youth of the streets could not endure it. No young vagabond could be brought to bear its contemplation for a moment, without throwing himself upon the unoffending wearer, and doing him a mischief. His social existence had been more like that of an early Christian, than an innocent child of the nineteenth century. He had been stoned in the streets. He had been overthrown into gutters; bespattered with mud; violently flattened against posts. Entire strangers to his person had lifted his yellow cap off his head and cast it to the winds. His legs had not only undergone verbal criticisms and revilings, but had been handled and pinched. That very morning, he had received a perfectly unsolicited black eye on his way to the Grinders' establishment, and had been punished for it by the master: a superannuated old Grinder of savage disposition who had been appointed schoolmaster because he didn't know anything, and wasn't fit for anything, and for whose cruel cane all chubby little boys had a perfect fascination.

Thus it fell out that Biler, on his way home, sought unfrequented paths; and slunk along by narrow passages and back streets, to avoid his tormenters. Being compelled to emerge into the main road, his ill-fortune brought him at last where a small party of boys, headed by a ferocious young butcher, were lying in wait for any means of pleasurable excitement that might happen. These, finding a Charitable Grinder in the midst of them—unaccountably delivered over, as it were, into their hands—set up a general yell and rushed upon him.

But it so fell out likewise, that, at the same time, Polly, looking hopelessly along the road before her, after a good hour's walk, had said it was no use going any further, when suddenly she saw this sight. She no sooner saw it than, uttering a hasty exclamation, and giving Master Dombey to the black-eyed, she started to the rescue of her unhappy little son.

Surprises, like misfortunes, rarely come alone. The astonished Susan Nipper and her two young charges were rescued by the bystanders from under the very wheels of a passing carriage before they knew what had happened; and at that moment (it was market day) a thundering alarm of 'Mad bull!' was raised.

With a wild confusion before her, of people running up and down, and shouting, and wheels running over them and boys fighting, and mad bulls coming up, and the nurse in the midst of all these dangers being torn to pieces, Florence screamed and ran. She ran till she was exhausted, urging Susan to do the same; and then, stopping and wringing her hands as she remembered they had left the other nurse behind, found, with a sensation of terror not to be described, that she was quite alone.

'Susan! Susan!' cried Florence, clapping her hands in the very ecstasy of her alarm. 'Oh, where are they? where are they?'

'Where are they?' said an old woman, coming hobbling across as fast as she could from the opposite side of the way. 'Why did you run away from 'em?'

'I was frightened,' answered Florence. 'I didn't know what I did. I thought they were with me. Where are they?'

The old woman took her by the wrist, and said, 'I 'll show you.'

She was a very ugly old woman, with red rims round her eyes, and a mouth that mumbled and chattered of itself when she was not speaking. She was miserably dressed, and carried some skins over her arm. She seemed to have followed Florence some little way at all events, for she had lost her breath; and this made her uglier still, as she stood trying to regain it: working her shrivelled yellow face and throat into all sorts of contortions.

Florence was afraid of her, and looked, hesitating, up the street, of which she had almost reached the bottom. It was a solitary place—more a back-road than a street—and there was no one in it but herself and the old woman.

'You needn't be frightened now,' said the old woman, still holding her tight. 'Come along with me.'

'I—I don't know you. What 's your name?' asked Florence.

'Mrs. Brown,' said the old woman. 'Good Mrs. Brown.'

'Are they near here?' asked Florence, beginning to be led away.

'Susan an't far off,' said Good Mrs. Brown; 'and the others are close to her.'

'Is anybody hurt?' cried Florence.

'Not a bit of it,' said Good Mrs. Brown.

The child shed tears of delight on hearing this, and accompanied the old woman willingly; though she could not help glancing at her face as they went along—particularly at that industrious mouth—and wondering whether Bad Mrs. Brown, if there were such a person, was at all like her.

They had not gone far, but had gone by some very uncomfortable places, such as brick-fields and tile-yards, when the old woman turned down a dirty lane, where the mud lay in deep black ruts in the middle of the road. She stopped before a shabby little house, as closely shut up as a house that was full of cracks and crevices could be. Opening the door with a key she took out of her bonnet, she pushed the child before her into a back-room, where there was a great heap of rags of different colours lying on the floor; a heap of bones, and a heap of sifted dust or cinders; but there was no furniture at all, and the walls and ceilings were quite black.

The child became so terrified that she was stricken speechless, and looked as though about to swoon.

'Now don't be a young mule,' said Good Mrs. Brown, reviving her with a shake. 'I 'm not a going to hurt you. Sit upon the rags.'

Florence obeyed her, holding out her folded hands, in mute supplication.

'I 'm not a going to keep you, even, above an hour,' said Mrs. Brown. 'D' ye understand what I say?'

The child answered with great difficulty, 'Yes.'

'Then,' said Good Mrs. Brown, taking her own seat on the bones, 'don't vex me. If you don't, I tell you I won't hurt you. But if you do, I 'll kill you. I could have you killed at any time—even if you was in your own bed at home. Now let 's know who you are, and what you are, and all about it.'

The old woman's threats and promises; the dread of giving her offence; and the habit, unusual to a child, but almost natural to Florence now, of being quiet, and repressing what she felt, and feared, and hoped; enabled her to do this bidding, and to tell her little history, or what she knew of it. Mrs. Brown listened attentively, until she had finished.

'So your name 's Dombey, eh?' said Mrs. Brown.

'Yes, ma'am.'

'I want that pretty frock, Miss Dombey,' said Good Mrs. Brown, 'and that little bonnet, and a petticoat or two, and anything else you can spare. Come! Take 'em off.'

Florence obeyed, as fast as her trembling hands would allow; keeping, all the while, a frightened eye on Mrs. Brown. When she had divested herself of all the articles of apparel mentioned by that lady, Mrs. B. examined them at leisure, and seemed tolerably well satisfied with their quality and value.

'Humph!' she said, running her eyes over the child's slight figure, 'I don't see anything else—except the shoes. I must have the shoes, Miss Dombey.'

Poor little Florence took them off with equal alacrity, only too glad to have any more means of conciliation about her. The old woman then produced some wretched substitutes from the bottom of the heap of rags, which she turned up for that purpose; together with a girl's cloak, quite worn out and very old; and the crushed remains of a bonnet that had probably been picked up from some ditch or dunghill. In this dainty raiment, she instructed Florence to dress herself; and as such preparation seemed a prelude to her release, the child complied with increased readiness, if possible.

In hurriedly putting on the bonnet, if that may be called a bonnet which was more like a pad to carry loads on, she caught it in her hair which grew luxuriantly, and could not immediately disentangle it. Good Mrs. Brown whipped out a large pair of scissors, and fell into an unaccountable state of excitement.

'Why couldn't you let me be,' said Mrs. Brown, 'when I was contented? You little fool!'

'I beg your pardon. I don't know what I have done,' panted Florence. 'I couldn't help it.'

'Couldn't help it!' cried Mrs. Brown. 'How do you expect I can help it? Why, Lord!' said the old woman, ruffling her curls with a furious pleasure, 'anybody but me would have had 'em off first of all.'

Florence was so relieved to find that it was only

her hair and not her head which Mrs. Brown coveted, that she offered no resistance or entreaty, and merely raised her mild eyes towards the face of that good soul.

'If I hadn't once had a gal of my own—beyond seas now—that was proud of her hair,' said Mrs. Brown, 'I'd have had every lock of it. She's far away, she's far away! Oho! Oho!'

Mrs. Brown's was not a melodious cry, but, accompanied with a wild tossing up of her lean arms, it was full of passionate grief, and thrilled to the heart of Florence, whom it frightened more than ever. It had its part, perhaps, in saving her curls; for Mrs. Brown, after hovering about her with the scissors for some moments, like a new kind of butterfly; bade her hide them under the bonnet and let no trace of them escape to tempt her. Having accomplished this victory over herself, Mrs. Brown resumed her seat on the bones, and smoked a very short black pipe, mowing and mumbling all the time, as if she were eating the stem.

When the pipe was smoked out, she gave the child a rabbit-skin to carry, that she might appear the more like her ordinary companion, and told her that she was now going to lead her to a public street whence she could inquire her way to her friends. But she cautioned her, with threats of summary and deadly vengeance in case of disobedience, not to talk to strangers, nor to repair to her own home (which may have been too near for Mrs. Brown's convenience), but to her father's office in the City; also to wait at the street corner where she would be left, until the clock struck three. These directions Mrs. Brown enforced with assurances that there would be potent eyes and ears in her employment cognisant of all she did; and these directions Florence promised faithfully and earnestly to observe.

At length, Mrs. Brown, issuing forth, conducted her changed and ragged little friend through a labyrinth of narrow streets and lanes and alleys, which emerged, after a long time, upon a stable yard, with a gateway at the end, whence the roar of a great thoroughfare made itself audible. Pointing out this gateway, and informing Florence that when the clocks struck three she was to go to the left, Mrs. Brown, after making a parting grasp at her hair which seemed involuntary and quite beyond her own control, told her she knew what to do, and bade her go and do it: remembering that she was watched.

With a lighter heart, but still sore afraid, Florence felt herself released, and tripped off to the corner. When she reached it, she looked back and saw the head of Good Mrs. Brown peeping out of the low wooden passage, where she had issued her parting injunctions; likewise the fist of Good Mrs. Brown shaking towards her. But though she often looked back afterwards—every minute, at least, in her nervous recollection of the old woman—she could not see her again.

Florence remained there, looking at the bustle in the street, and more and more bewildered by it; and in the meanwhile the clocks appeared to have made up their minds never to strike three any more. At last the steeples rang out three o'clock; there was one close by, so she couldn't be mistaken; and—after often looking over her shoulder, and often going a little way, and as often coming back again, lest the all-powerful spies of Mrs. Brown should take offence, she hurried off, as fast as she could in her slipshod shoes, holding the rabbit-skin tight in her hand.

All she knew of her father's offices was that they belonged to Dombey and Son, and that that was a great power belonging to the City. So she could only ask the way to Dombey and Son's in the City; and as she generally made inquiry of children—being afraid to ask grown people—she got very little satisfaction indeed. But by dint of asking her way to the City after a while, and dropping the rest of her inquiry for the present, she really did advance, by slow degrees, towards the heart of that great region which is governed by the terrible Lord Mayor.

Tired of walking, repulsed and pushed about, stunned by the noise and confusion, anxious for her brother and the nurses, terrified by what she had undergone, and the prospect of encountering her angry father in such an altered state; perplexed and frightened alike by what had passed, and what was passing, and what was yet before her; Florence went upon her weary way with tearful eyes, and once or twice could not help stopping to ease her bursting heart by crying bitterly. But few people noticed her at those times, in the garb she wore; or if they did, believed that she was tutored to excite compassion, and passed on. Florence, too, called to her aid all the firmness and self-reliance of a character that her sad experience had prematurely formed and tried; and keeping the end she had in view, steadily before her, steadily pursued it.

It was full two hours later in the afternoon than when she had started on this strange adventure, when, escaping from the clash and clangour of a narrow street full of carts and waggons, she peeped into a kind of wharf or landing-place upon the riverside, where there were a great many packages, casks, and boxes, strew about; a large pair of wooden scales; and a little wooden house on wheels, outside of which, looking at the neighbouring masts and boats, a stout man stood whistling, with his pen behind his ear, and his hands in his pockets, as if his day's work were nearly done.

'Now then!' said this man, happening to turn round. 'We haven't got anything for you, little girl. Be off!'

'If you please, is this the City?' asked the trembling daughter of the Dombeys.

'Ah! it 's the City. You know that well enough, I dare say. Be off! We haven't got anything for you.'

'I don't want anything! thank you,' was the timid answer. 'Except to know the way to Dombey and Son's.'

The man who had been strolling carelessly towards her, seemed surprised by this reply, and looking attentively in her face, rejoined—

'Why, what can *you* want with Dombey and Son's?'

'To know the way there, if you please.'

The man looked at her yet more curiously, and rubbed the back of his head so hard in his wonderment that he knocked his own hat off.

'Joe!' he called to another man—a labourer—as he picked it up and put it on again.

'Joe it is!' said Joe.

'Where 's that young spark of Dombey's who 's been watching the shipment of them goods?'

'Just gone, by the t'other gate,' said Joe.

'Call him back a minute.'

Joe ran up an archway, bawling as he went, and very soon returned with a blithe-looking boy.

'You 're Dombey's jockey, an't you?' said the first man.

'I 'm in Dombey's house, Mr. Clark,' returned the boy.

'Look ye here, then,' said Mr. Clark.

Obedient to the indication of Mr. Clark's hand,

the boy approached towards Florence, wondering, as well he might, what he had to do with her. But she, who had heard what passed, and who, besides the relief of so suddenly considering herself safe at her journey's end, felt reassured beyond all measure by his lively youthful face and manner, ran eagerly up to him, leaving one of the slipshod shoes upon the ground and caught his hand in both of hers.

'I am lost, if you please!' said Florence.

'Lost!' cried the boy.

'Yes, I was lost this morning, a long way from here—and I have had my clothes taken away, since—and I am not dressed in my own now—and my name is Florence Dombey, my little brother's only sister—and, oh dear, dear, take care of me, if you please!' sobbed Florence, giving full vent to the childish feelings she had so long suppressed, and bursting into tears. At the same time her miserable bonnet falling off, her hair came tumbling down about her face: moving to speechless admiration and commiseration, young Walter, nephew of Solomon Gills, ships' instrument-maker in general.

Mr. Clark stood rapt in amazement: observing under his breath, *I* never saw such a start on *this* wharf before. Walter picked up the shoe, and put it on the little foot as the Prince in the story might have fitted Cinderella's slipper on. He hung the rabbit-skin over his left arm; gave the right to Florence; and felt, not to say like Richard Whittington—that is a tame comparison—but like Saint George of England, with the dragon lying dead before him.

'Don't cry, Miss Dombey,' said Walter, in a transport of enthusiasm. 'What a wonderful thing for me that I am here. You are as safe now as if you were guarded by a whole boat's crew of picked men from a man-of-war. Oh, don't cry.'

'I won't cry any more,' said Florence. 'I am only crying for joy.'

'Crying for joy!' thought Walter, 'and I 'm the cause of it! Come along, Miss Dombey. There 's the other shoe off now! Take mine, Miss Dombey.'

'No, no, no,' said Florence, checking him in the act of impetuously pulling off his own. 'These do better. These do very well.'

'Why, to be sure,' said Walter, glancing at her foot, 'mine are a mile too large. What am I thinking about! You never could walk in *mine*! Come along, Miss Dombey. Let me see the villain who will dare molest you now.'

So Walter, looking immensely fierce, led off Florence, looking very happy; and they went arm-in-arm along the streets, perfectly indifferent to any astonishment that their appearance might or did excite by the way.

It was growing dark and foggy, and beginning to rain too; but they cared nothing for this: being both wholly absorbed in the late adventures of Florence, which she related with the innocent good faith and confidence of her years, while Walter listened as if, far from the mud and grease of Thames Street, they were rambling alone among the broad leaves and tall trees of some desert island in the tropics—as he very likely fancied, for the time, they were.

'Have we far to go?' asked Florence at last, lifting up her eyes to her companion's face.

'Ah! By the bye,' said Walter stopping, 'let me see; where are we? Oh! I know. But the offices are shut up now, Miss Dombey. There 's nobody there. Mr. Dombey has gone home long ago. I suppose we must go home too? or, stay. Suppose I take you to my uncle's, where I live—it 's very near here—and go to your house in a coach to tell them you are safe, and bring you back some clothes. Won't that be best?'

'I think so,' answered Florence. 'Don't you? What do you think?'

As they stood deliberating in the street, a man passed them, who glanced quickly at Walter as he went by, as if he recognised him; but seeming to correct that first impression, he passed on without stopping.

'Why, I think it's Mr. Carker,' said Walter. 'Carker in our House. Not Carker our manager, Miss Dombey—the other Carker; the junior—Halloa! Mr. Carker!'

'Is that Walter Gay?' said the other, stopping and returning. 'I couldn't believe it with such a strange companion.'

As he stood near a lamp, listening with surprise to Walter's hurried explanation, he presented a remarkable contrast to the two youthful figures arm-in-arm before him. He was not old, but his hair was white; his body was bent, or bowed as if by the weight of some great trouble: and there were deep lines in his worn and melancholy face. The fire of his eyes, the expression of his features, the very voice in which he spoke, were all subdued and quenched, as if the spirit within him lay in ashes. He was respectably, though very plainly dressed, in black; but his clothes, moulded to the general character of his figure, seemed to shrink and abase themselves upon him, and to join in the sorrowful solicitation which the whole man from head to foot expressed, to be left unnoticed, and alone in his humility.

And yet his interest in youth and hopefulness was not extinguished with the other embers of his soul, for he watched the boy's earnest countenance as he spoke with unusual sympathy, though with an inexplicable show of trouble and compassion, which escaped into his looks, however hard he strove to hold it prisoner. When Walter, in conclusion, put to him the question he had put to Florence, he still stood glancing at him with the same expression, as if he read some fate upon his face, mournfully at variance with its present brightness.

'What do you advise, Mr. Carker?' said Walter, smiling. 'You always give me good advice, you know, when you *do* speak to me. That 's not often, though.'

'I think your own idea is the best,' he answered: looking from Florence to Walter, and back again.

'Mr. Carker,' said Walter, brightening with a generous thought, 'Come! Here 's a chance for you. Go you to Mr. Dombey's and be the messenger of good news. It may do you some good, sir. I'll remain at home. You shall go.'

'I!' returned the other.

'Yes. Why not, Mr. Carker?' said the boy.

He merely shook him by the hand in answer; he seemed in a manner ashamed and afraid even to do that; and bidding him good night, and advising him to make haste, turned away.

'Come, Miss Dombey,' said Walter, looking after him as they turned away also, 'we 'll go to my uncle's as quick as we can. Did you ever hear Mr. Dombey speak of Mr. Carker the junior, Miss Florence?'

'No,' returned the child, mildly, 'I don't often hear papa speak.'

'Ah! true! more shame for him,' thought Walter. After a minute's pause, during which he had been looking down upon the gentle patient little face moving on at his side, he bestirred himself with his accustomed boyish animation and restlessness to change the subject; and one of the unfortunate shoes coming off again opportunely, proposed to carry Florence to his uncle's in his arms. Florence, though very tired, laughingly declined the proposal, lest he should let her fall; and as they were already near the wooden midshipman, and as Walter went on to cite various precedents, from shipwrecks and other moving accidents, where younger boys than he had triumphantly rescued and carried off older girls than Florence, they were still in full conversation about it when they arrived at the instrument-maker's door.

'Holloa, uncle Sol!' cried Walter, bursting into the shop, and speaking incoherently and out of breath, from that time forth, for the rest of the evening. 'Here 's a wonderful adventure! Here 's Mr. Dombey's daughter lost in the streets, and robbed of her clothes by an old witch of a woman—found by me—brought home to our parlour to rest—look here!'

'Good Heaven!' said uncle Sol, starting back against his favourite compass-case. 'It can't be! Well, I—'

'No, nor anybody else,' said Walter, anticipating the rest. 'Nobody would, nobody could, you know. Here! just help me lift the little sofa near the fire, will you, uncle Sol—take care of the plates—cut some dinner for her, will you, uncle—throw those shoes under the grate. Miss Florence—put your feet on the fender to dry—how damp they are—here 's an adventure, uncle, eh?—God bless my soul, how hot I am!'

Solomon Gills was quite as hot, by sympathy, and in excessive bewilderment. He patted Florence's head, pressed her to eat, pressed her to drink, rubbed the soles of her feet with his pocket-handkerchief heated at the fire, followed his locomotive nephew with his eyes, and ears, and had no clear perception of anything except that he was being constantly knocked against and tumbled over by that excited young gentleman, as he darted about the room attempting to accomplish twenty things at once, and doing nothing at all.

'Here, wait a minute, uncle,' he continued, catching up a candle, 'till I run upstairs, and get another jacket on, and then I 'll be off. I say, uncle, isn't this an adventure?'

'My dear boy,' said Solomon, who, with his spectacles on his forehead and the great chronometer in his pocket, was incessantly oscillating between Florence on the sofa and his nephew in all parts of the parlour, 'it 's the most extraordinary—'

'No, but do, uncle, please—do, Miss Florence—dinner, you know, uncle.'

'Yes, yes, yes,' cried Solomon, cutting instantly into a leg of mutton, as if he were catering for a giant. 'I 'll take care of her, Wally! I understand. Pretty dear! Famished, of course. You go and get ready. Lord bless me! Sir Richard Whittington thrice Lord Mayor of London.'

Walter was not very long in mounting to his lofty garret and descending from it, but in the meantime Florence, overcome by fatigue, had sunk into a doze before the fire. The short interval of quiet, though only a few minutes in duration, enabled Solomon Gills so far to collect his wits as to make some little arrangements for her comfort, and to darken the room, and to screen her from the blaze. Thus, when the boy returned, she was sleeping peacefully.

'That 's capital!' he whispered, giving Solomon such a hug that it squeezed a new expression into his face. 'Now I 'm off. I 'll just take a crust of bread with me, for I 'm very hungry—and—don't wake her, uncle Sol.'

'No, no,' said Solomon. 'Pretty child.'

'Pretty, indeed!' cried Walter. '*I* never saw such a face, uncle Sol. Now I 'm off.'

'That 's right,' said Solomon, greatly relieved.

'I say, uncle Sol,' cried Walter, putting his face in at the door.

'Here he is again,' said Solomon.

'How does she look now?'

'Quite happy,' said Solomon.

'That 's famous! now I 'm off.'

'I hope you are,' said Solomon to himself.

'I say, uncle Sol,' cried Walter, reappearing at the door.

'Here he is again!' said Solomon.

'We met Mr. Carker the junior in the street, queerer than ever. He bade me good-bye, but came behind us here—there 's an odd thing!—for when we reached the shop door, I looked round, and saw him going quietly away, like a servant who had seen me home, or a faithful dog. How does she look now, uncle?'

'Pretty much the same as before, Wally,' replied uncle Sol.

'That 's right. Now I *am* off!'

And this time he really was: and Solomon Gills, with no appetite for dinner, sat on the opposite side of the fire, watching Florence in her slumber, building a great many airy castles of the most fantastic architecture; and looking, in the dim shade, and in the close vicinity of all the instruments, like a magician disguised in a Welsh wig and a suit of coffee colour, who held the child in an enchanted sleep.

In the meantime, Walter proceeded towards Mr. Dombey's house at a pace seldom achieved by a hack horse from the stand; and yet with his head out of window every two or three minutes, in impatient remonstrance with the driver. Arriving at his journey's end, he leaped out, and breathlessly announcing his errand to the servant, followed him straight into the library, where there was a great confusion of tongues, and where Mr. Dombey, his sister, and Miss Tox, Richards, and Nipper, were all congregated together.

'Oh! I beg your pardon, sir,' said Walter, rushing up to him, 'but I 'm happy to say it 's all right, sir. Miss Dombey 's found!'

The boy with his open face, and flowing hair, and sparkling eyes, panting with pleasure and excitement, was wonderfully opposed to Mr. Dombey, as he sat confronting him in his library chair.

'I told you, Louisa, that she would certainly be found,' said Mr. Dombey, looking slightly over his shoulder at that lady, who wept in company with Miss Tox. 'Let the servants know that no further steps are necessary. This boy who brings the information, is young Gay, from the office. How was my daughter found, sir? I know how she was lost.' Here he looked majestically at Richards. 'But how was she found? Who found her?'

'Why, I believe *I* found Miss Dombey, sir,' said Walter modestly; 'at least I don't know that I can claim the merit of having exactly found her, sir, but I was the fortunate instrument of—'

'What do you mean, sir,' interrupted Mr. Dombey, regarding the boy's evident pride and pleasure in his share of the transaction with an instinctive dislike, 'by not having exactly found my daughter, and by being a fortunate instrument? Be plain and coherent, if you please.'

It was quite out of Walter's power to be coherent; but he rendered himself as explanatory as he could, in his breathless state, and stated why he had come alone.

'You hear this, girl?' said Mr. Dombey sternly to the black-eyed. 'Take what is necessary, and return immediately with this young man to fetch Miss Florence home. Gay, you will be rewarded to-morrow.'

'Oh! thank you, sir,' said Walter. 'You are very kind. I 'm sure I was not thinking of any reward, sir.'

'You are a boy,' said Dombey, suddenly and almost fiercely; 'and what you think of, or affect to think of, is of little consequence. You have done well, sir. Don't undo it. Louisa, please to give the lad some wine.'

Mr. Dombey's glance followed Walter Gay with sharp disfavour, as he left the room under the pilotage of Mrs. Chick; and it may be that his mind's eye followed him with no greater relish, as he rode back to his uncle's with Miss Susan Nipper.

There they found that Florence, much refreshed by sleep, had dined, and greatly improved the acquaintance of Solomon Gills, with whom she was on terms of perfect confidence and ease. The black-eyed (who had cried so much that she might now be called the red-eyed, and who was very silent and depressed) caught her in her arms without a word of contradiction or reproach, and made a very hysterical meeting of it. Then converting the parlour, for the nonce, into a private tiring room, she dressed her, with great care, in proper clothes; and presently led her forth, as like a Dombey as her natural disqualifications admitted of her being made.

'Good-night!' said Florence, running up to Solomon. 'You have been very good to me.'

Old Sol was quite delighted, and kissed her like her grandfather.

'Good-night, Walter! Good-bye!' said Florence.

'Good-bye!' said Walter, giving both his hands.

'I 'll never forget you,' pursued Florence. 'No! indeed I never will. Good-bye, Walter!'

In the innocence of her grateful heart, the child lifted up her face to his. Walter, bending down his own, raised it again, all red and burning; and looked at uncle Sol, quite sheepishly.

'Where 's Walter?' 'Good-night, Walter!' 'Good-bye, Walter!' 'Shake hands once more, Walter!' This was still Florence's cry, after she was shut up with her little maid, in the coach. And when the coach at length moved off, Walter on the door-step gaily returned the waving of her handkerchief, while the wooden midshipman behind him seemed, like himself, intent upon that coach alone, excluding all the other passing coaches from his observation.

In good time Mr. Dombey's mansion was gained again, and again there was a noise of tongues in the library. Again, too, the coach was ordered to wait—'for Mrs. Richards,' one of Susan's fellow-servants ominously whispered, as she passed with Florence.

The entrance of the lost child made a slight sensation, but not much. Mr. Dombey, who had never found her, kissed her once upon the forehead, and cautioned her not to run away again, or wander anywhere with treacherous attendants. Mrs. Chick stopped in her lamentations on the corruption of human nature, even when beckoned to the paths of virtue by a Charitable Grinder; and received her with a welcome something short of the reception due to none but perfect Dombeys. Miss Tox regulated her feelings by the models before her. Richards, the culprit Richards, alone poured out her heart in broken words of welcome, and bowed herself over the little wandering head as if she really loved it.

'Ah, Richards!' said Mrs. Chick, with a sigh. 'It

would have been much more satisfactory to those who wish to think well of their fellow-creatures, and much more becoming in you, if you had shown some proper feeling, in time, for the little child that is now going to be prematurely deprived of its natural nourishment.'

'Cut off,' said Miss Tox, in a plaintive whisper, 'from one common fountain!'

'If it was *my* ungrateful case,' said Mrs. Chick, solemnly, 'and I had *your* reflections, Richards, I should feel as if the Charitable Grinders' dress would blight my child, and the education choke him.'

For the matter of that—but Mrs. Chick didn't know it—he had been pretty well blighted by the dress already; and as to the education, even its retributive effect might be produced in time, for it was a storm of sobs and blows.

'Louisa!' said Mr. Dombey. 'It is not necessary to prolong these observations. The woman is discharged and paid. You leave this house, Richards, for taking my son—my son,' said Mr. Dombey, emphatically repeating these two words, 'into haunts and into society which are not to be thought of without a shudder. As to the accident which befell Miss Florence this morning, I regard that as, in one great sense, a happy and fortunate circumstance; inasmuch as, but for that occurrence, I never could have known—and from your own lips too—of what you had been guilty. I think, Louisa, the other nurse, the young person,' here Miss Nipper sobbed aloud, 'being so much younger, and necessarily influenced by Paul's nurse, may remain. Have the goodness to direct that this woman's coach is paid to—' Mr. Dombey stopped and winced—'to Staggs's Gardens.'

Polly moved towards the door, with Florence holding to her dress, and crying to her in the most pathetic manner not to go away. It was a dagger in the haughty father's heart, an arrow in his brain, to see how the flesh and blood he could not disown, clung to this obscure stranger, and he sitting by. Not that he cared to whom his daughter turned, or from whom turned away. The swift sharp agony struck through him, as he thought of what his son might do.

His son cried lustily that night, at all events. Sooth to say, poor Paul had better reason for his tears than sons of that age often have, for he had lost his second mother—his first, so far as he knew —by a stroke as sudden as that natural affliction which had darkened the beginning of his life. At the same blow, his sister too, who cried herself to sleep so mournfully, had lost as good and true a friend. But that is quite beside the question. Let us waste no words about it.

## CHAPTER VII

### A BIRD'S-EYE GLIMPSE OF MISS TOX'S DWELLING-PLACE; ALSO OF THE STATE OF MISS TOX'S AFFECTIONS

MISS TOX inhabited a dark little house that had been squeezed, at some remote period of English history, into a fashionable neighbourhood at the west end of the town, where it stood in the shade like a poor relation of the great street round the corner, coldly looked down upon by mighty mansions. It was not exactly in a court, and it was not exactly in a yard; but it was in the dullest of No-Thoroughfares, rendered anxious and haggard by distant double knocks. The name of this retirement, where grass grew between the chinks in the stone pavement, was Princess's Place; and in Princess's Place was Princess's Chapel, with a tinkling bell, where sometimes as many as five-and-twenty people attended service on a Sunday. The Princess's Arms was also there, and much resorted to by splendid footmen. A sedan chair was kept inside the railing before the Princess's Arms, but it had never come out within the memory of man; and on fine mornings, the top of every rail (there were eight-and-forty, as Miss Tox had often counted) was decorated with a pewter-pot.

There was another private house besides Miss Tox's in Princess's Place: not to mention an immense pair of gates, with an immense pair of lion-headed knockers on them, which were never opened by any chance, and were supposed to constitute a disused entrance to somebody's stables. Indeed, there was a smack of stabling in the air of Princess's Place; and Miss Tox's bedroom (which was at the back) commanded a vista of mews, where hostlers, at whatever sort of work engaged, were continually accompanying themselves with effervescent noises; and where the most domestic and confidential garments of coachmen and their wives and families, usually hung, like Macbeth's banners, on the outward walls.

At this other private house in Princess's Place tenanted by a retired butler who had married a housekeeper, apartments were let furnished, to a single gentleman: to wit, a wooden-featured, blue-faced major, with his eyes starting out of his head, in whom Miss Tox recognised, as she herself expressed it, 'something so truly military'; and between whom and herself, an occasional interchange of newspapers and pamphlets, and such Platonic dalliance, was effected through the medium of a dark servant of the major's, who Miss Tox was quite content to classify as a 'native,' without connecting him with any geographical idea whatever.

Perhaps there never was a smaller entry and staircase, than the entry and staircase of Miss Tox's house. Perhaps, taken altogether, from top to bottom, it was the most inconvenient little house in England, and the crookedest; but then, Miss Tox said, what a situation! There was very little daylight to be got there in the winter: no sun at the best of times: air was out of the question, and traffic was walled out. Still Miss Tox said, think of the situation! So said the blue-faced major, whose eyes were starting out of his head: who gloried in Princess's Place: and who delighted to turn the conversation at his club, whenever he could, to something connected with some of the great people in the great street round the corner, that he might have the satisfaction of saying they were his neighbours.

The dingy tenement inhabited by Miss Tox was her own; having been devised and bequeathed to her by the deceased owner of the fishy eye in the locket, of whom a miniature portrait, with a powdered head and a pigtail, balanced the kettle-holder on opposite sides of the parlour fireplace. The greater part of the furniture was of the powdered-head and pigtail period: comprising a plate-warmer, always languishing and sprawling its four attenuated bow-legs in somebody's way; and an obsolete harpsichord, illuminated round the maker's name with a painted garland of sweet peas.

Although Major Bagstock had arrived at what is called in polite literature, the grand meridian of life, and was proceeding on his journey downhill with hardly any throat, and a very rigid pair of jaw-bones, and long-flapped elephantine ears, and his eyes and complexion in the state of artificial excitement already mentioned, he was mightily proud of awakening an interest in Miss Tox, and tickled his vanity with the fiction that she was a splendid woman, who had her eye on him. This he had several times hinted at the club: in connection with little jocularities, of which old Joe Bagstock, old Joey Bagstock, old J. Bagstock, old Josh Bagstock, or so forth, was the perpetual theme: it being, as it were, the major's stronghold and donjon-keep of light humour, to be on the most familiar terms with his own name.

'Joey B., sir,' the major would say, with a flourish of his walking-stick, 'is worth a dozen of you. If you had a few more of the Bagstock breed among you, sir, you'd be none the worse for it. Old Joe, sir, needn't look far for a wife even now, if he was on the look-out; but he's hard-hearted, sir, is Joe—he's tough, sir, tough, and de-vilish sly!' After such a declaration wheezing sounds would be heard; and the major's blue would deepen into purple, while his eyes strained and started convulsively.

Notwithstanding his very liberal laudation of himself, however, the major was selfish. It may be doubted whether there ever was a more entirely selfish person at heart; or at stomach is perhaps a better expression, seeing that he was more decidedly endowed with that latter organ than with the former. He had no idea of being overlooked or slighted by anybody; least of all, had he the remotest comprehension of being overlooked and slighted by Miss Tox.

And yet, Miss Tox, as it appeared, forgot him—gradually forgot him. She began to forget him soon after her discovery of the Toodle family. She continued to forget him up to the time of the christening. She went on forgetting him with compound interest after that. Something or somebody had superseded him as a source of interest.

'Good morning, ma'am,' said the major, meeting Miss Tox in Princess's Place, some weeks after the changes chronicled in the last chapter.

'Good morning, sir,' said Miss Tox; very coldly.

'Joe Bagstock, ma'am,' observed the major, with his usual gallantry, 'has not had the happiness of bowing to you at your window, for a considerable period. Joe has been hardly used, ma'am. His sun has been behind a cloud.'

Miss Tox inclined her head; but very coldly indeed.

'Joe's luminary has been out of town, ma'am, perhaps,' inquired the major.

'I? out of town? oh no, I have not been out of town,' said Miss Tox. 'I have been much engaged lately. My time is nearly all devoted to some very intimate friends. I am afraid I have none to spare, even now. Good morning, sir!'

As Miss Tox, with her most fascinating step and carriage, disappeared from Princess's Place, the major stood looking after her with a bluer face than ever: muttering and growling some not at all complimentary remarks.

'Why, damme, sir,' said the major, rolling his lobster eyes round and round Princess's Place, and apostrophising its fragrant air, 'six months ago, the woman loved the ground Josh Bagstock walked on. What 's the meaning of it?'

The major decided, after some consideration, that it meant man-traps; that it meant plotting and snaring; that Miss Tox was digging pitfalls. 'But you won't catch Joe, ma'am,' said the major. 'He 's tough, ma'am, tough, is J. B. Tough, and de-vilish sly!' over which reflection he chuckled for the rest of the day.

But still, when that day and many other days were gone and past, it seemed that Miss Tox took no heed whatever of the major, and thought nothing at all about him. She had been wont, once upon a time, to look out at one of her little dark windows by accident, and blushingly return the major's greeting; but now, she never gave the major a chance, and cared nothing at all whether he looked over the way or not. Other changes had come to pass too. The major, standing in the shade of his own apartment, could make out that an air of greater smartness had recently come over Miss Tox's house; that a new cage with gilded wires had been provided for the ancient little canary bird; that divers ornaments, cut out of coloured cardboards and paper, seemed to decorate the chimney-piece and tables; that a plant or two had suddenly sprung up in the windows; that Miss Tox occasionally practised on the harpsichord, whose garland of sweet peas was always displayed ostentatiously, crowned with the Copenhagen and Bird Waltzes in a music book of Miss Tox's own copying.

Over and above all this, Miss Tox had long been dressed with uncommon care and elegance in slight mourning. But this helped the major out of his difficulty; and he determined within himself that she had come into a small legacy, and grown proud.

It was on the very next day after he had eased his mind by arriving at this decision, that the major, sitting at his breakfast, saw an apparition so tremendous and wonderful in Miss Tox's little drawing-room, that he remained for some time rooted to his chair; then, rushing into the next room, returned with a double-barrelled opera-glass, through which he surveyed it intently for some minutes.

'It 's a baby, sir,' said the major, shutting up the glass again, 'for fifty thousand pounds!'

The major couldn't forget it. He could do nothing but whistle, and stare to that extent, that his eyes compared with what they now became, had been in former times quite cavernous and sunken. Day after day, two, three, four times a week, this baby reappeared. The major continued to stare and whistle. To all other intents and purposes he was alone in Princess's Place. Miss Tox had ceased to mind what he did. He might have been black as well as blue, and it would have been of no consequence to her.

The perseverance with which she walked out of Princess's Place to fetch this baby and its nurse, and walked back with them, and walked home with them again, and continually mounted guard over them; and the perseverance with which she nursed it herself, and fed it, and played with it, and froze its young blood with airs upon the harpsichord; was extraordinary. At about this same period too, she was seized with a passion for looking at a certain bracelet; also with a passion for looking at the moon, of which she would take long observations from her chamber window. But whatever she looked at; sun, moon, stars, or bracelets; she looked no more at the major. And the major whistled, and stared, and wondered, and dodged about his room, and could make nothing of it.

'You 'll quite win my brother Paul's heart, and that 's the truth, my dear,' said Mrs. Chick, one day.

Miss Tox turned pale.

'He grows more like Paul every day,' said Mrs. Chick.

Miss Tox returned no other reply than by taking the little Paul in her arms, and making his cockade perfectly flat and limp with her caresses.

'His mother, my dear,' said Miss Tox, 'whose acquaintance I was to have made through you, does he at all resemble her?'

'Not at all,' returned Louisa.

'She was—she was pretty, I believe?' faltered Miss Tox.

'Why, poor dear Fanny was interesting,' said Mrs. Chick, after some judicial consideration. 'Certainly interesting. She had not that air of commanding superiority which one would somehow expect, almost as a matter of course, to find in my brother's wife; nor had she that strength and vigour of mind which such a man requires.'

Miss Tox heaved a deep sigh.

'But she was pleasing,' said Mrs. Chick: 'extremely so. And she meant!—oh, dear, how well poor Fanny meant!'

'You angel!' cried Miss Tox to little Paul. 'You picture of your own papa!'

If the major could have known how many hopes and ventures, what a multitude of plans and speculations, rested on that baby head; and could have seen them hovering, in all their heterogeneous confusion and disorder, round the puckered cap of the unconscious little Paul; he might have stared indeed. Then would he have recognised, among the crowd, some few ambitious motes and beams belonging to Miss Tox; then would he perhaps have understood the nature of that lady's faltering investment in the Dombey firm.

If the child himself could have awakened in the night, and seen, gathered about his cradle-curtains, faint reflections of the dreams that other people had of him, they might have scared him, with good reason. But he slumbered on, alike unconscious of the kind intentions of Miss Tox, the wonder of the major, the early sorrows of his sister, and the stern visions of his father; and innocent that any spot of earth contained a Dombey or a Son.

## CHAPTER VIII

### PAUL'S FURTHER PROGRESS, GROWTH, AND CHARACTER

Beneath the watching and attentive eyes of Time—so far another major—Paul's slumbers gradually changed. More and more light broke in upon them; distincter and distincter dreams disturbed them; an accumulating crowd of objects and impressions swarmed about his rest, and so he passed from babyhood to childhood, and became a talking, walking, wondering Dombey.

On the downfall and banishment of Richards, the nursery may be said to have been put into commission: as a public department is sometimes, when no individual Atlas can be found to support it. The Commissioners were, of course, Mrs. Chick and Miss Tox: who devoted themselves to their duties with such astonishing ardour that Major Bagstock had every day some new reminder of his being forsaken, while Mr. Chick, bereft of domestic supervision, cast himself upon the gay world, dined at clubs and coffee-houses, smelt of smoke on three distinct occasions, went to the play by himself, and in short, loosened (as Mrs. Chick once told him) every social bond, and moral obligation.

Yet, in spite of his early promise, all this vigilance and care could not make little Paul a thriving boy. Naturally delicate, perhaps, he pined and wasted after the dismissal of his nurse, and, for a long time, seemed but to wait his opportunity of gliding through their hands, and seeking his lost mother. This dangerous ground in his steeplechase towards manhood passed, he still found it very rough riding, and was grievously beset by all the obstacles in his course. Every tooth was a break-neck fence, and every pimple in the measles a stone wall to him. He was down in every fit of the hooping-cough, and rolled upon and crushed by a whole field of small diseases, that came trooping on each other's heels to prevent his getting up again. Some bird of prey got into his throat instead of the thrush; and the very chickens turning ferocious—if they have anything to do with that infant malady to which they lend their name—worried him like tiger-cats.

The chill of Paul's christening had struck home, perhaps to some sensitive part of his nature, which could not recover itself in the cold shade of his father; but he was an unfortunate child from that day. Mrs. Wickam often said she never see a dear so put upon.

Mrs. Wickam was a waiter's wife—which would seem equivalent to being any other man's widow—whose application for an engagement in Mr. Dombey's service had been favourably considered, on account of the apparent impossibility of her having any followers, or any one to follow; and who, from within a day or two of Paul's sharp weaning, had been engaged as his nurse. Mrs. Wickam was a meek woman, of a fair complexion, with her eyebrows always elevated, and her head always drooping; who was always ready to pity herself, or to be pitied, or to pity anybody else; and who had a surprising natural gift of viewing all subjects in an utterly forlorn and pitiable light, and bringing dreadful precedents to bear upon them, and deriving the greatest consolation from the exercise of that talent.

It is hardly necessary to observe, that no touch of this quality ever reached the magnificent knowledge of Mr. Dombey. It would have been remarkable, indeed, if any had; when no one in the house—not even Mrs. Chick or Miss Tox—dared ever whisper to him that there had, on any one occasion, been the least reason for uneasiness in reference to little Paul. He had settled, within himself, that the child must necessarily pass through a certain routine of minor maladies, and that the sooner he did so the better. If he could have bought him off, or provided a substitute, as in the case of an unlucky drawing for the militia, he would have been glad to do so on liberal terms. But as this was not feasible, he merely wondered, in his haughty manner, now and then, what Nature meant by it; and comforted himself with the reflection that there was another milestone passed upon the road, and that the great end of the journey lay so much the nearer. For the feeling uppermost in his mind, now and constantly intensifying, and increasing in it as Paul grew older, was impatience. Impatience for the time to come, when his visions of their united consequence and grandeur would be triumphantly realised.

Some philosophers tell us that selfishness is at the root of our best loves and affections. Mr. Dombey's young child was, from the beginning, so distinctly important to him as a part of his own greatness, or (which is the same thing) of the greatness of Dombey and Son, that there is no doubt his parental affection might have been easily traced, like many a goodly superstructure of fair fame, to a very low foundation. But he loved his son with all the love he had. If there were a warm place in his frosty heart, his son occupied it; if its very hard surface could receive the impression of any image, the image of that son was there; though not so much as an infant, or as a boy, but as a grown man—the 'Son' of the Firm. Therefore he was impatient to advance into the future, and to hurry over the intervening passages of his history. Therefore he had little or no anxiety about them, in spite of his love; feeling as if the boy had a charmed life, and *must* become the man with whom he held such constant communication in his thoughts, and for whom he planned and projected, as for an existing reality, every day.

Thus Paul grew to be nearly five years old. He was a pretty little fellow; though there was something wan and wistful in his small face, that gave occasion to many significant shakes of Mrs. Wickam's head, and many long-drawn inspirations of Mrs. Wickam's breath. His temper gave abundant promise of being imperious in after-life; and he had as hopeful an apprehension of his own importance, and the rightful subservience of all other things and persons to it, as heart could desire. He was childish and sportive enough at times, and not of a sullen disposition; but he had a strange, old-fashioned, thoughtful way, at other times, of sitting brooding in his miniature arm-chair, when he looked (and talked) like one of those terrible little beings in the fairy tales, who, at a hundred and fifty or two hundred years of age, fantastically represent the children for whom they have been substituted. He would frequently be stricken with this precocious mood upstairs in the nursery; and would sometimes lapse into it suddenly, exclaiming that he was tired: even while playing with Florence, or driving Miss Tox in single harness. But at no time did he fall into it so surely, as when, his little chair being carried down into his father's room, he sat there with him after dinner, by the fire. They were the strangest pair at such a time that ever fire-light shone upon. Mr. Dombey so erect and solemn, gazing at the blaze; his little image, with an old, old face, peering into the red perspective with the fixed and rapt attention of a sage. Mr. Dombey entertaining complicated worldly schemes and plans; the little image entertaining Heaven knows what wild fancies, half-formed thoughts, and wandering speculations. Mr. Dombey stiff with starch and arrogance; the little image by inheritance, and in unconscious imitation. The two so very much alike, and yet so monstrously contrasted.

On one of these occasions, when they had both been perfectly quiet for a long time, and Mr. Dombey only knew that the child was awake by occasionally glancing at his eye, where the bright fire was sparkling like a jewel, little Paul broke silence thus—

'Papa! what 's money?'

The abrupt question had such immediate reference to the subject of Mr. Dombey's thoughts, that Mr. Dombey was quite disconcerted.

'What is money, Paul?' he answered. 'Money?'

'Yes,' said the child, laying his hands upon the elbows of his little chair, and turning the old face up towards Mr. Dombey's; 'what is money?'

Mr. Dombey was in a difficulty. He would have liked to give him some explanation involving the terms circulating-medium, currency, depreciation of currency, paper, bullion, rates of exchange, value of precious metals in the market, and so forth; but looking down at the little chair, and seeing what a long way down it was, he answered: 'Gold, and silver, and copper. Guineas, shillings, half-pence. You know what they are?'

'Oh yes, I know what they are,' said Paul. 'I don't mean that, papa. I mean what 's money after all.'

Heaven and earth! how old his face was as he turned it up again towards his father's!

'What is money after all?' said Mr. Dombey, backing his chair a little, that he might the better gaze in sheer amazement at the presumptuous atom that propounded such an inquiry.

'I mean, papa, what can it do?' returned Paul, folding his arms (they were hardly long enough to fold), and looking at the fire, and up at him, and at the fire, and up at him again.

Mr. Dombey drew his chair back to its former place, and patted him on the head. 'You 'll know better by and by, my man,' he said. 'Money, Paul, can do anything.' He took hold of the little hand, and beat it softly against one of his own, as he said so.

But Paul got his hand free as soon as he could; and rubbing it gently to and fro on the elbow of his chair, as if his wit were in the palm, and he were sharpening it—and looking at the fire again, as though the fire had been his adviser and prompter—repeated, after a short pause—

'Anything, papa?'

'Yes. Anything—almost,' said Mr. Dombey.

'Anything means everything, don't it, papa?' asked his son: not observing, or possibly not understanding, the qualification.

'It includes it: yes,' said Mr. Dombey.

'Why didn't money save me my mamma?' returned the child. 'It isn't cruel, is it?'

'Cruel!' said Mr. Dombey, settling his neckcloth, and seeming to resent the idea. 'No. A good thing can't be cruel.'

'If it 's a good thing, and can do anything,' said the little fellow, thoughtfully, as he looked back at the fire, 'I wonder why it didn't save me my mamma.'

He didn't ask the question of his father this time. Perhaps he had seen, with a child's quickness, that it had already made his father uncomfortable. But he repeated the thought aloud, as if it were quite an old one to him, and had troubled him very much; and sat with his chin resting on his hand, still cogitating and looking for an explanation in the fire.

Mr. Dombey having recovered from his surprise, not to say his alarm (for it was the very first occasion on which the child had ever broached the subject of his mother to him, though he had had him sitting by his side, in this same manner, evening after evening), expounded to him how that money, though a very potent spirit, never to be disparaged on any account whatever, could not keep people alive whose time was come to die; and how that we must all die, unfortunately, even in the City, though we were never so rich. But how that money caused us to be honoured, feared, respected, courted, and admired, and made us powerful and glorious in the eyes of all men; and how that it could, very often, even keep off death, for a long time together. How, for example, it had secured to his mamma the services of Mr. Pilkins, by which he, Paul, had often profited himself; likewise of the great Doctor Parker Peps, whom he had never known. And how it could do all, that could be done. This, with more to the same purpose, Mr. Dombey instilled into the mind of his son, who listened attentively, and seemed to understand the greater part of what was said to him.

'It can't make me strong and quite well, either, papa; can it?' asked Paul, after a short silence; rubbing his tiny hands.

'Why, you *are* strong and quite well,' returned Mr. Dombey. 'Are you not?'

Oh! the age of the face that was turned up again, with an expression, half of melancholy, half of slyness, on it!

'You are as strong and well as such little people usually are? Eh?' said Mr. Dombey.

'Florence is older than I am, but I 'm not as strong and well as Florence, I know,' returned the child; 'but I believe that when Florence was as little as me, she could play a great deal longer at a time without tiring herself. I am so tired sometimes,' said little Paul, warming his hands, and looking in between the bars of the grate, as if some ghostly puppet-show were performing there, 'and my bones ache so (Wickam says it 's my bones), that I don't know what to do.'

'Aye! But that 's at night,' said Mr. Dombey, drawing his own chair closer to his son's, and laying his hand gently on his back; 'little people should be tired at night, for then they sleep well.'

'Oh, it 's not at night, papa,' returned the child, 'it 's in the day; and I lie down in Florence's lap, and she sings to me. At night I dream about such cu-ri-ous things!'

And he went on, warming his hands again, and thinking about them, like an old man or a young goblin.

Mr. Dombey was so astonished, and so uncomfortable, and so perfectly at a loss how to pursue the conversation, that he could only sit looking at his son by the light of the fire, with his hand resting on his back, as if it were detained there by some magnetic attraction. Once he advanced his other hand, and turned the contemplative face towards his own for a moment. But it sought the fire again as soon as he released it; and remained, addressed towards the flickering blaze, until the nurse appeared, to summon him to bed.

'I want Florence to come for me,' said Paul.

'Won't you come with your poor Nurse Wickam, Master Paul?' inquired that attendant, with great pathos.

'No, I won't,' replied Paul, composing himself in his arm-chair again, like the master of the house.

Invoking a blessing upon his innocence, Mrs. Wickam withdrew, and presently Florence appeared in her stead. The child immediately started up with sudden readiness and animation, and raised towards his father in bidding him good-night, a countenance so much brighter, so much younger, and so much more child-like altogether, that Mr. Dombey, while he felt greatly reassured by the change, was quite amazed at it.

After they had left the room together, he thought he heard a soft voice singing; and remembering that Paul had said his sister sung to him, he had the curiosity to open the door and listen, and look after them. She was toiling up the great, wide, vacant staircase, with him in her arms; his head was lying on her shoulder, one of his arms thrown negligently round her neck. So they went, toiling up; she singing all the way, and Paul sometimes crooning out a feeble accompaniment. Mr. Dombey looked after them until they reached the top of the staircase—not without halting to rest by the way—and passed out of his sight; and then he still stood gazing upwards, until the dull rays of the moon, glimmering in a melancholy manner through the dim skylight, sent him back to his own room.

Mrs. Chick and Miss Tox were convoked in council at dinner next day; and when the cloth was removed, Mr. Dombey opened the proceedings by requiring to be informed, without any gloss or reservation, whether there was anything the matter with Paul, and what Mr. Pilkins said about him.

'For the child is hardly,' said Mr. Dombey, 'as stout as I could wish.'

'With your usual happy discrimination, my dear Paul,' returned Mrs. Chick, 'you have hit the point at once. Our darling is *not* altogether as stout as we could wish. The fact is, that his mind is too much for him. His soul is a great deal too large for his frame.

I am sure the way in which that dear child talks!' said Mrs. Chick, shaking her head; 'no one would believe. His expressions, Lucretia, only yesterday upon the subject of funerals!—'

'I am afraid,' said Mr. Dombey, interrupting her testily, 'that some of those persons upstairs suggest improper subjects to the child. He was speaking to me last night about his—about his bones,' said Mr. Dombey, laying an irritated stress upon the word. 'What on earth has anybody to do with the—with the—bones of my son? He is not a living skeleton, I suppose.'

'Very far from it,' said Mrs. Chick, with unspeakable expression.

'I hope so,' returned her brother. 'Funerals again! who talks to the child of funerals? We are not undertakers, or mutes, or grave-diggers, I believe.'

'Very far from it,' interposed Mrs. Chick, with the same profound expression as before.

'Then who puts such things into his head?' said Mr. Dombey. 'Really I was quite dismayed and shocked last night. Who puts such things into his head, Louisa?'

'My dear Paul,' said Mrs. Chick, after a moment's silence, 'it is of no use inquiring. I do not think, I will tell you candidly, that Wickam is a person of very cheerful spirit, or what one would call a—'

'A daughter of Momus,' Miss Tox softly suggested.

'Exactly so,' said Mrs. Chick; 'but she is exceedingly attentive and useful, and not at all presumptuous; indeed I never saw a more biddable woman. If the dear child,' pursued Mrs. Chick, in a tone of one who was summing up what had been previously quite agreed upon, instead of saying it all for the first time, 'is a little weakened by that last attack, and is not in quite such vigorous health as we could wish; and if he has some temporary weakness in his system, and does occasionally seem about to lose, for the moment, the use of his—'

Mrs. Chick was afraid to say limbs, after Mr. Dombey's recent objection to bones, and therefore waited for a suggestion from Miss Tox, who, true to her office, hazarded 'members.'

'Members!' repeated Mr. Dombey.

'I think the medical gentleman mentioned legs this morning, my dear Louisa, did he not,' said Miss Tox.

'Why, of course he did, my love,' retorted Mrs. Chick, mildly reproachful. 'How can you ask me? You heard him. I say, if our dear Paul should lose, for the moment, the use of his legs, these are casualties common to many children at his time of life, and not to be prevented by any care or caution. The sooner you understand that, Paul, and admit that, the better.'

'Surely you must know, Louisa,' observed Mr. Dombey, 'that I don't question your natural devotion to, and natural regard for, the future head of my house. Mr. Pilkins saw Paul this morning, I believe?' said Mr. Dombey.

'Yes, he did,' returned his sister. 'Miss Tox and myself were present, Miss Tox and myself are always present. We make a point of it. Mr. Pilkins has seen him for some days past, and a very clever man I believe him to be. He says it is nothing to speak of; which I can confirm, if that is any consolation; but he recommended, to-day, sea-air. Very wisely, Paul, I feel convinced.'

'Sea-air,' repeated Mr. Dombey, looking at his sister.

'There is nothing to be made uneasy by, in that,' said Mrs. Chick. 'My George and Frederick were both ordered sea-air, when they were about his age; and I have been ordered it myself a great many times. I quite agree with you, Paul, that perhaps topics may be incautiously mentioned upstairs before him, which it would be as well for his little mind not to expatiate upon; but I really don't see how that is to be helped in the case of a child of his quickness. If he were a common child, there would be nothing in it. I must say I think, with Miss Tox, that a short absence from this house, the air of Brighton, and the bodily and mental training of so judicious a person as Mrs. Pipchin for instance—'

'Who is Mrs. Pipchin, Louisa?' asked Mr. Dombey; aghast at this familiar introduction of a name he had never heard before.

'Mrs. Pipchin, my dear Paul,' returned his sister, 'is an elderly lady—Miss Tox knows her whole history—who has for some time devoted all the energies of her mind, with the greatest success, to the study and treatment of infancy, and who has been extremely well connected. Her husband broke his heart in—how did you say her husband broke his heart, my dear? I forget the precise circumstances.'

'In pumping water out of the Peruvian mines,' replied Miss Tox.

'Not being a pumper himself, of course,' said Mrs. Chick, glancing at her brother; and it really did seem necessary to offer the explanation, for Miss Tox had spoken of him as if he had died at the handle; 'but having invested money in the speculation, which failed. I believe that Mrs. Pipchin's management of children is quite astonishing. I have heard it commended in private circles ever since I was—dear me—how high!' Mrs. Chick's eye wandered about the bookcase near the bust of Mr. Pitt, which was about ten feet from the ground.

'Perhaps I should say of Mrs. Pipchin, my dear sir,' observed Miss Tox, with an ingenuous blush, 'having been so pointedly referred to, that the encomium which has been passed upon her by your sweet sister is well merited. Many ladies and gentlemen, now grown up to be interesting members of society, have been indebted to her care. The humble individual who addresses you was once under her charge. I believe juvenile nobility itself is no stranger to her establishment.'

'Do I understand that this respectable matron keeps an establishment, Miss Tox?' inquired Mr. Dombey, condescendingly.

'Why, I really don't know,' rejoined that lady, 'whether I am justified in calling it so. It is not a preparatory school by any means. Should I express my meaning,' said Miss Tox, with peculiar sweetness, 'if I designated it an infantine boarding-house of a very select description?'

'On an exceedingly limited and particular scale,' suggested Mrs. Chick, with a glance at her brother.

'Oh! Exclusion itself!' said Miss Tox.

There was something in this. Mrs. Pipchin's husband having broken his heart of the Peruvian mines was good. It had a rich sound. Besides, Mr. Dombey was in a state almost amounting to consternation at the idea of Paul remaining where he was one hour after his removal had been recommended by the medical practitioner. It was a stoppage and delay upon the road the child must traverse, slowly at the best, before the goal was reached. Their recommendation of Mrs. Pipchin had great weight with him; for he knew that they were jealous of any interference with their charge, and he never for a moment took it into account that they might be solicitous to divide a responsibility, of which he had, as shown just now, his own established views. Broke his heart of the Peruvian mines, mused Mr. Dombey. Well, a very respectable way of doing it.

'Supposing we should decide, on to-morrow's inquiries, to send Paul down to Brighton to this lady, who would go with him?' inquired Mr. Dombey, after some reflection.

'I don't think you could send the child anywhere at present without Florence, my dear Paul,' returned his sister, hesitating. 'It's quite an infatuation with him. He's very young, you know, and has his fancies.'

Mr. Dombey turned his head away, and going slowly to the book-case, and unlocking it, brought back a book to read.

'Anybody else, Louisa?' he said, without looking up, and turning over the leaves.

'Wickam, of course. Wickam would be quite sufficient, I should say,' returned his sister. 'Paul being in such hands as Mrs. Pipchin's, you could hardly send anybody who would be a further check upon her. You would go down yourself once a week at least, of course.'

'Of course,' said Mr. Dombey; and sat looking at one page for an hour afterwards, without reading one word.

This celebrated Mrs. Pipchin was a marvellous ill-favoured, ill-conditioned old lady, of a stooping figure, with a mottled face, like bad marble, a hook nose, and a hard grey eye, that looked as if it might have been hammered at on an anvil without sustaining any injury. Forty years at least had elapsed since the Peruvian mines had been the death of Mr. Pipchin; but his relict still wore black bombazeen, of such a lustreless, deep, dead, sombre shade, that gas itself couldn't light her up after dark, and her presence was a quencher to any number of candles. She was generally spoken of as 'a great manager' of children; and the secret of her management was, to give them everything that they didn't like, and nothing that they did—which was found to sweeten their dispositions very much. She was such a bitter old lady, that one was tempted to believe there had been some mistake in the application of the Peruvian machinery, and that all her waters of gladness and milk of human kindness, had been pumped out dry, instead of the mines.

The Castle of this ogress and child-queller was in a steep by-street at Brighton; where the soil was more than usually chalky, flinty, and sterile, and the houses were more than usually brittle and thin; where the small front-gardens had the unaccountable property of producing nothing but marigolds, whatever was sown in them; and where snails were constantly discovered holding on to the street doors, and other public places they were not expected to ornament, with the tenacity of cupping-glasses. In the winter time the air couldn't be got out of the Castle, and in the summer time it couldn't be got in. There was such a continual reverberation of wind in it, that it sounded like a great shell, which the inhabitants were obliged to hold to their ears night and day, whether they liked it or no. It was not, naturally, a fresh-smelling house; and in the window of the front-parlour, which was never opened, Mrs. Pipchin kept a collection of plants in pots, which imparted an earthly flavour of their own to the establishment. However choice examples of their kind, too, these plants were of a kind peculiarly adapted to the embowerment of Mrs. Pipchin. There were half a dozen specimens of the cactus, writhing round bits of lath, like hairy serpents; another specimen shooting out broad claws, like a green lobster; several creeping vegetables, possessed of sticky and adhesive leaves; and one uncomfortable flower-pot hanging to the ceiling, which appeared to have boiled over, and tickling people underneath with its long green ends, reminded them of spiders—in which Mrs. Pipchin's dwelling was uncommonly prolific, though perhaps it challenged competition still more proudly, in the season, in point of earwigs.

Mrs. Pipchin's scale of charges being high, however, to all who could afford to pay, and Mrs. Pipchin very seldom sweetening the equable acidity of her nature in favour of anybody, she was held to be an old lady of remarkable firmness, who was quite scientific in her knowledge of the childish character. On this reputation, and on the broken heart of Mr. Pipchin, she had contrived, taking one year with another, to eke out a tolerable sufficient living since her husband's demise. Within three days after Mrs. Chick's first allusion to her, this excellent old lady had the satisfaction of anticipating a handsome addition to her current receipts, from the pocket of Mr. Dombey; and of receiving Florence and her little brother Paul, as inmates of the Castle.

Mrs. Chick and Miss Tox, who had brought them down on the previous night (which they all passed at an hotel), had just driven away from the door, on their journey home again; and Mrs. Pipchin, with her back to the fire, stood, reviewing the new comers, like an old soldier. Mrs. Pipchin's middle-aged niece, her good-natured and devoted slave, but possessing a gaunt and iron-bound aspect, and much afflicted with boils on her nose, was divesting Master Bitherstone of the clean collar he had worn on parade. Miss Pankey, the only other little boarder at present, had that moment been walked off to the Castle Dungeon (an empty apartment at the back, devoted to correctional purposes), for having sniffed thrice, in the presence of visitors.

'Well, sir,' said Mrs. Pipchin to Paul, 'how do you think you shall like me?'

'I don't think I shall like you at all,' replied Paul. 'I want to go away. This isn't my house.'

'No. It 's mine,' retorted Mrs. Pipchin.

'It 's a very nasty one,' said Paul.

'There 's a worse place in it than this though,' said Mrs. Pipchin, 'where we shut up our bad boys.'

'Has *he* ever been in it?' asked Paul: pointing out Master Bitherstone.

Mrs. Pipchin nodded assent; and Paul had enough to do, for the rest of that day, in surveying Master Bitherstone from head to foot, and watching all the workings of his countenance, with the interest attaching to a boy of mysterious and terrible experiences.

At one o'clock there was a dinner, chiefly of the farinaceous and vegetable kind, when Miss Pankey (a mild little blue-eyed morsel of a child, who was shampoo'd every morning, and seemed in danger of being rubbed away, altogether) was led in from captivity by the ogress herself, and instructed that nobody who sniffed before visitors ever went to heaven. When this great truth had been thoroughly impressed upon her, she was regaled with rice; and subsequently repeated the form of grace established in the Castle, in which there was a special clause, thanking Mrs. Pipchin for a good dinner. Mrs. Pipchin's niece, Berinthia, took cold pork. Mrs. Pipchin, whose constitution required warm nourishment, made a special repast of mutton-chops, which were brought in hot and hot, between two plates, and smelt very nice.

As it rained after dinner, and they couldn't go out walking on the beach, and Mrs. Pipchin's constitution required rest after chops, they went away with

Berry (otherwise Berinthia) to the Dungeon; an empty room looking out upon a chalk wall and a water-butt, and made ghastly by a ragged fireplace without any stove in it. Enlivened by company, however, this was the best place after all; for Berry played with them there, and seemed to enjoy a game at romps as much as they did; until Mrs. Pipchin knocking angrily at the wall, like the Cock Lane Ghost revived, they left off, and Berry told them stories in a whisper until twilight.

For tea there was plenty of milk and water, and bread and butter, with a little black tea-pot for Mrs. Pipchin and Berry, and buttered toast unlimited for Mrs. Pipchin, which was brought in, hot and hot, like the chops. Though Mrs. Pipchin got very greasy, outside, over this dish, it didn't seem to lubricate her internally, at all; for she was as fierce as ever and the hard grey eye knew no softening.

After tea, Berry brought out a little work-box, with the Royal Pavilion on the lid, and fell to working busily; while Mrs. Pipchin, having put on her spectacles and opened a great volume bound in green baize, began to nod. And whenever Mrs. Pipchin caught herself falling forward into the fire, and woke up, she filliped Master Bitherstone on the nose for nodding too.

At last it was the children's bedtime, and after prayers they went to bed. As little Miss Pankey was afraid of sleeping alone in the dark, Mrs. Pipchin always made a point of driving her upstairs herself, like a sheep; and it was cheerful to hear Miss Pankey moaning long afterwards, in the least eligible chamber, and Mrs. Pipchin now and then going in to shake her. At about half-past nine o'clock the odour of a warm sweet-bread (Mrs. Pipchin's constitution wouldn't go to sleep without sweet-bread) diversified the prevailing fragrance of the house, which Mrs. Wickam said was 'a smell of building'; and slumber fell upon the Castle shortly after.

The breakfast next morning was like the tea overnight, except that Mrs. Pipchin took her roll instead of toast, and seemed a little more irate when it was over. Master Bitherstone read aloud to the rest a pedigree from Genesis (judiciously selected by Mrs. Pipchin), getting over the names with the ease and clearness of a person tumbling up the treadmill. That done, Miss Pankey was borne away to be shampoo'd; and Master Bitherstone to have something else done to him with salt water, from which he always returned very blue and dejected. Paul and Florence went out in the meantime on the beach with Wickam—who was constantly in tears—and at about noon Mrs. Pipchin presided over some Early Readings. It being a part of Mrs. Pipchin's system not to encourage a child's mind to develop and expand itself like a young flower, but to open it by force like an oyster, the moral of these lessons was usually of a violent and stunning character: the hero—a naughty boy—seldom, in the mildest catastrophe, being finished off by anything less than a lion, or a bear.

Such was life at Mrs. Pipchin's. On Saturday Mr. Dombey came down; and Florence and Paul would go to his hotel, and have tea. They passed the whole of Sunday with him, and generally rode out before dinner; and on these occasions Mr. Dombey seemed to grow, like Falstaff's assailants, and instead of being one man in buckram, to become a dozen. Sunday evening was the most melancholy evening in the week; for Mrs. Pipchin always made a point of being particularly cross on Sunday nights. Miss Pankey was generally brought back from an aunt's at Rottingdean, in deep distress; and Master Bitherstone, whose relatives were all in India, and who was required to sit, between the services, in an erect position with his head against the parlour wall neither moving hand nor foot, suffered so acutely in his young spirits that he once asked Florence, on a Sunday night, if she could give him any idea of the way back to Bengal.

But it was generally said that Mrs. Pipchin was a woman of system with children; and no doubt she was. Certainly the wild ones went home tame enough, after sojourning for a few months beneath her hospitable roof. It was generally said, too, that it was highly creditable of Mrs. Pipchin to have devoted herself to this way of life, and to have made such a sacrifice of her feelings, and such a resolute stand against her troubles, when Mr. Pipchin broke his heart in the Peruvian mines.

At this exemplary old lady, Paul would sit staring in his little arm-chair by the fire, for any length of time. He never seemed to know what weariness was, when he was looking fixedly at Mrs. Pipchin. He was not fond of her; he was not afraid of her; but in those old old moods of his, she seemed to have a grotesque attraction for him. There he would sit, looking at her, and warming his hands, and looking at her, until he sometimes quite confounded Mrs. Pipchin, ogress as she was. Once she asked him, when they were alone, what he was thinking about.

'You,' said Paul, without the least reserve.

'And what are you thinking about me?' asked Mrs. Pipchin.

'I 'm thinking how old you must be,' said Paul.

'You mustn't say such things as that, young gentleman,' returned the dame. 'That 'll never do.'

'Why not?' asked Paul.

'Because it 's not polite,' said Mrs. Pipchin, snappishly.

'Not polite?' said Paul.

'No.'

'It 's not polite,' said Paul, innocently, 'to eat all the mutton-chops and toast, Wickam says.'

'Wickam,' retorted Mrs. Pipchin, colouring, 'is a wicked, impudent, bold-faced hussy.'

'What 's that?' inquired Paul.

'Never you mind, sir,' retorted Mrs. Pipchin. 'Remember the story of the little boy that was gored to death by a mad bull for asking questions.'

'If the bull was mad,' said Paul, 'how did *he* know that the boy had asked questions? Nobody can go and whisper secrets to a mad bull. I don't believe that story.'

'You don't believe it, sir?' repeated Mrs. Pipchin, amazed.

'No,' said Paul.

'Not if it should happen to have been a tame bull, you little infidel?' said Mrs. Pipchin.

As Paul had not considered the subject in that light, and had founded his conclusions on the alleged lunacy of the bull, he allowed himself to be put down for the present. But he sat turning it over in his mind, with such an obvious intention of fixing Mrs. Pipchin presently, that even that hardy old lady deemed it prudent to retreat until he should have forgotten the subject.

From that time, Mrs. Pipchin appeared to have something of the same odd kind of attraction towards Paul, as Paul had towards her. She would make him move his chair to her side of the fire, instead of sitting opposite; and there he would remain in a nook between Mrs. Pipchin and the fender, with all the light of his little face absorbed into the black bombazeen drapery, studying every line and wrinkle of her countenance, and peering at the hard grey eye, until Mrs. Pipchin was sometimes fain to shut it on pretence of dozing. Mrs. Pipchin had an old black cat, who generally lay coiled upon the centre foot of the fender, purring egotistically, and winking at the fire until the contracted pupils of his eyes were like two notes of admiration. The good old lady might have been—not to record it disrespectfully—a witch, and Paul and the cat her two familiars, as they all sat by the fire together. It would have been quite in keeping with the appearance of the party if they had all sprung up the chimney in a high wind one night, and never been heard of any more.

This, however, never came to pass. The cat, and Paul, and Mrs. Pipchin, were constantly to be found in their usual places after dark; and Paul, eschewing the companionship of Master Bitherstone, went on studying Mrs. Pipchin, and the cat, and the fire, night after night, as if they were a book of necromancy, in three volumes.

Mrs. Wickham put her own construction on Paul's eccentricities: and being confirmed in her low spirits by a perplexed view of chimneys from the room where she was accustomed to sit, and by the noise of the wind, and by the general dulness (gashliness was Mrs. Wickam's strong expression) of her present life, deduced the most dismal reflections from the foregoing premises. It was a part of Mrs. Pipchin's policy to prevent her own 'young hussy'—that was Mrs. Pipchin's generic name for female servant—from communicating with Mrs. Wickam: to which end she devoted much of her time to concealing herself behind doors, and springing out on that devoted maiden, whenever she made an approach towards Mrs. Wickam's apartment. But Berry was free to hold what converse she could in that quarter consistently with the discharge of the multifarious duties at which she toiled incessantly from morning to night; and to Berry Mrs. Wickam unburdened her mind.

'What a pretty fellow he is when he 's asleep!' said Berry, stopping to look at Paul in bed, one night when she took up Mrs. Wickam's supper.

'Ah!' sighed Mrs. Wickam. 'He need be.'

'Why, he 's not ugly when he 's awake,' observed Berry.

'No, ma'am. Oh no. No more was my uncle's Betsey Jane,' said Mrs. Wickam.

Berry looked as if she would like to trace the connection of ideas between Paul Dombey and Mrs. Wickam's uncle's Betsey Jane.

'My uncle's wife,' Mrs. Wickam went on to say, 'died just like his mamma. My uncle's child took on just as Master Paul do. My uncle's child made people's blood run cold, sometimes, she did!'

'How?' asked Berry.

'I wouldn't have sat up all night alone with Betsey Jane!' said Mrs. Wickam, 'not if you'd have put Wickam into business next morning for himself. I couldn't have done it, Miss Berry.'

Miss Berry naturally asked why not? But Mrs. Wickam, agreeably to the usage of some ladies in her condition, pursued her own branch of the subject without any compunction.

'Betsey Jane,' said Mrs. Wickam, 'was as sweet a child as I could wish to see. I couldn't wish to see a sweeter. Everything that a child could have in the way of illnesses, Betsey Jane had come through. The cramps was as common to her,' said Mrs. Wickam, 'as biles is to yourself, Miss Berry.' Miss Berry involuntarily wrinkled her nose.

'But Betsey Jane,' said Mrs. Wickam, lowering her

voice, and looking round the room, and towards Paul in bed, 'had been minded, in her cradle, by her departed mother. I couldn't say how, nor I couldn't say when, nor I couldn't say whether the dear child knew it or not, but Betsey Jane had been watched by her mother, Miss Berry! You may say nonsense! I an't offended, miss. I hope you may be able to think in your own conscience that it *is* nonsense; you 'll find your spirits all the better for it in this—you 'll excuse my being so free—in this burying-ground of a place; which is wearing of me down. Master Paul 's a little restless in his sleep. Pat his back, if you please.'

'Of course you think,' said Berry, gently doing what she was asked, 'that *he* has been nursed by his mother, too?'

'Betsey Jane,' returned Mrs. Wickam in her most solemn tones, 'was put upon as that child has been put upon, and changed as that child has changed. I have seen her sit, often and often, think, think, thinking, like him. I have seen her look, often and often, old, old, old, like him. I have heard her, many a time, talk just like him. I consider that child and Betsey Jane on the same footing entirely, Miss Berry.'

'Is your uncle's child alive?' asked Berry.

'Yes, miss, she is alive,' returned Mrs. Wickam with an air of triumph, for it was evident Miss Berry expected the reverse; 'and is married to a silver-chaser. Oh yes, miss, SHE is alive,' said Mrs. Wickam, laying strong stress on her nominative case.

It being clear that somebody was dead, Mrs. Pipchin's niece inquired who it was.

'I wouldn't wish to make you uneasy,' returned Mrs. Wickam, pursuing her supper. 'Don't ask me.'

This was the surest way of being asked again. Miss Berry repeated her question, therefore; and after some resistance, and reluctance, Mrs. Wickam laid down her knife, and again glancing round the room and at Paul in bed, replied—

'She took fancies to people; whimsical fancies, some of them; others, affections that one might expect to see—only stronger than common. They all died.'

This was so very unexpected and awful to Mrs. Pipchin's niece, that she sat upright on the hard edge of the bedstead, breathing short, and surveying her informant with looks of undisguised alarm.

Mrs. Wickam shook her left forefinger stealthily towards the bed where Florence lay; then turned it upside down, and made several emphatic points at the floor; immediately below, which was the parlour in which Mrs. Pipchin habitually consumed the toast.

'Remember my words, Miss Berry,' said Mrs. Wickam, 'and be thankful that Master Paul is not too fond of you. I am, that he 's not too fond of me, I assure you; though there isn't much to live for—you 'll excuse my being so free—in this gaol of a house!'

Miss Berry's emotion might have led to her patting Paul too hard on the back, or might have produced a cessation of that soothing monotony, but he turned in his bed just now, and, presently awaking, sat up in it with his hair hot and wet from the effects of some childish dream, and asked for Florence.

She was out of her own bed at the first sound of his voice; and bending over his pillow immediately, sang him to sleep again. Mrs. Wickam shaking her head, and letting fall several tears, pointed out the little group to Berry, and turned her eyes up to the ceiling.

'Good night, miss!' said Wickam, softly. 'Good night! Your aunt is an old lady, Miss Berry, and it 's what you must have looked for, often.'

This consolatory farewell, Mrs. Wickam accompanied with a look of heartfelt anguish; and being left alone with the two children again, and becoming conscious that the wind was blowing mournfully, she indulged in melancholy—that cheapest and most accessible of luxuries—until she was overpowered by slumber.

Although the niece of Mrs. Pipchin did not expect to find that exemplary dragon prostrate on the hearth-rug when she went downstairs, she was relieved to find her unusually fractious and severe, and with every present appearance of intending to live a long time to be a comfort to all who knew her. Nor had she any symptoms of declining, in the course of the ensuing week, when the constitutional viands still continued to disappear in regular succession, notwithstanding that Paul studied her as attentively as ever, and occupied his usual seat between the black skirts and the fender, with unwavering constancy.

But as Paul himself was no stronger at the expiration of that time than he had been on his first arrival, though he looked much healthier in the face, a little carriage was got for him, in which he could lie at his ease, with an alphabet and other elementary works of reference, and be wheeled down to the sea-side. Consistent in his odd tastes, the child set aside a ruddy-faced lad who was proposed as the drawer of this carriage, and selected, instead, his grandfather—a weazen, old, crab-faced man, in a suit of battered oil-skin, who had got tough and stringy from long pickling in salt water, and who smelt like a weedy sea-beach when the tide is out.

With this notable attendant to pull him along, and Florence always walking by his side, and the despondent Wickam bringing up the rear, he went down to the margin of the ocean every day; and there he would sit or lie in his carriage for hours together: never so distressed as by the company of children—Florence alone excepted, always.

'Go away, if you please,' he would say to any child who came to bear him company. 'Thank you, but I don't want you.'

Some small voice, near his ear, would ask him how he was, perhaps.

'I am very well, I thank you,' he would answer. 'But you had better go and play, if you please.'

Then he would turn his head, and watch the child away, and say to Florence, 'We don't want any others, do we? Kiss me, Floy.'

He had even a dislike, at such times, to the company of Wickham, and was well pleased when she strolled away, as she generally did, to pick up shells and acquaintances. His favourite spot was quite a lonely one, far away from most loungers; and with Florence sitting by his side at work, or reading to him, or talking to him, and the wind blowing on his face, and the water coming up among the wheels of his bed, he wanted nothing more.

'Floy,' he said one day, 'where 's India, where that boy's friends live?'

'Oh, it 's a long, long distance off,' said Florence, raising her eyes from her work.

'Weeks off?' asked Paul.

'Yes, dear. Many weeks' journey, night and day.'

'If you were in India, Floy,' said Paul, after being silent for a minute, 'I should—what is that mamma did? I forget.'

'Loved me!' answered Florence.

'No, no. Don't I love you now, Floy? What is it?—Died. If you were in India, I should die, Floy.'

She hurriedly put her work aside, and laid her head down on his pillow, caressing him. And so would she, she said, if he were there. He would be better soon.

'Oh! I am a great deal better now!' he answered. 'I don't mean that. I mean that I should die of being so sorry and so lonely, Floy!'

Another time, in the same place, he fell asleep, and slept quietly for a long time. Awaking suddenly, he listened, started up, and sat listening.

Florence asked him what he thought he heard.

'I want to know what it says,' he answered, looking steadily in her face. 'The sea, Floy, what is it that it keeps on saying?'

She told him that it was only the noise of the rolling waves.

'Yes, yes,' he said. 'But I know that they are always saying something. Always the same thing. What place is over there?' He rose up, looking eagerly at the horizon.

She told him that there was another country opposite, but he said he didn't mean that: he meant farther away—farther away!

Very often afterwards, in the midst of their talk, he would break off, to try to understand what it was that the waves were always saying; and would rise up in his couch to look towards that invisible region, far away.

## CHAPTER IX

### IN WHICH THE WOODEN MIDSHIPMAN GETS INTO TROUBLE

THAT spice of romance and love of the marvellous, of which there was a pretty strong infusion in the nature of young Walter Gay, and which the guardianship of his uncle, old Solomon Gills, had not very much weakened by the waters of stern practical experience, was the occasion of his attaching an uncommon and delightful interest to the adventure of Florence with Good Mrs. Brown. He pampered and cherished it in his memory, especially that part of it with which he had been associated: until it became the spoiled child of his fancy, and took its own way, and did what it liked with it.

The recollection of those incidents, and his own share in them, may have been made the more captivating, perhaps, by the weekly dreamings of old Sol and Captain Cuttle on Sundays. Hardly a Sunday passed, without mysterious references being made by one or other of those worthy chums to Richard Whittington; and the latter gentleman had even gone so far as to purchase a ballad of considerable antiquity, that had long fluttered among many others, chiefly expressive of maritime sentiments, on a dead wall in the Commercial Road: which poetical performance set forth the courtship and nuptials of a promising young coal-whipper with a certain 'lovely Peg,' the accomplished daughter of the master and part-owner of a Newcastle collier. In this stirring legend, Captain Cuttle descried a profound metaphysical bearing on the case of Walter and Florence; and it excited him so much, that on very festive occasions, as birthdays and a few other non-Dominical holidays, he would roar through the whole song in the little back-parlour; making an amazing shake on the word Pe—e—eg, with which every verse concluded, in compliment to the heroine of the piece.

But a frank, free-spirited, open-hearted boy, is not much given to analysing the nature of his own feelings, however strong their hold upon him: and Walter would have found it difficult to decide this point. He had a great affection for the wharf where he had encountered Florence, and for the streets (albeit not enchanting in themselves) by which they had come home. The shoes that had so often tumbled off by the way, he preserved in his own room; and, sitting in the little back-parlour of an evening, he had drawn a whole gallery of fancy portraits of Good Mrs. Brown. It may be that he became a little smarter in his dress after that memorable occasion; and he certainly liked in his leisure time to walk towards that quarter of the town where Mr. Dombey's house was situated, on the vague chance of passing little Florence in the street. But the sentiment of all this was as boyish and innocent as could be. Florence was very pretty, and it is pleasant to admire a pretty face. Florence was defenceless and weak, and it was a proud thought that he had been able to render her any protection and assistance. Florence was the most grateful little creature in the world, and it was delightful to see her bright gratitude beaming in her face. Florence was neglected and coldly looked upon, and his breast was full of youthful interest for the slighted child in her dull, stately home.

Thus it came about that, perhaps some half a dozen times in the course of the year, Walter pulled off his hat to Florence in the street, and Florence would stop to shake hands. Mrs. Wickam (who, with a characteristic alteration of his name invariably spoke of him as 'Young Graves') was so well used to this, knowing the story of their acquaintance, that she took no heed of it at all. Miss Nipper, on the other hand, rather looked out for these occasions: her sensitive young heart being secretly propitiated by Walter's good looks, and inclining to the belief that its sentiments were responded to.

In this way, Walter, so far from forgetting or losing sight of his acquaintance with Florence, only remembered it better and better. As to its adventurous beginning, and all those little circumstances which gave it a distinctive character and relish, he took them into account, more as a pleasant story very agreeable to his imagination, and not to be dismissed from it, than as a part of any matter of fact with which *he* was concerned. They set off Florence very much, to his fancy; but not himself. Sometimes he thought (and then he walked very fast) what a grand thing it would have been for him to have been going to sea on the day after that first meeting, and to have gone, and to have done wonders there, and to have stopped away a long time, and to have come back an admiral of all the colours of the dolphin, or at least a post-captain with epaulettes of insupportable brightness, and have married Florence (then a beautiful young woman) in spite of Mr. Dombey's teeth, cravat, and watch-chain, and borne her away to the blue shores of somewhere or other, triumphantly. But these flights of fancy seldom burnished the brass plate of Dombey and Son's offices into a tablet of golden hope, or shed a brilliant lustre on their dirty skylights; and when the captain and uncle Sol talked about Richard Whittington and masters' daughters, Walter felt that he understood his true position at Dombey and Son's much better than they did.

So it was that he went on doing what he had to do from day to day, in a cheerful, painstaking, merry spirit; and saw through the sanguine complexion of uncle Sol and Captain Cuttle; and yet entertained a thousand indistinct and visionary fancies of his own, to which theirs were workaday probabilities. Such was his condition at the Pipchin period, when he looked a little older than of yore, but not much; and was the same light-footed, light-hearted, light-headed lad, as when he charged into the parlour at the head of uncle Sol and the imaginary boarders, and lighted him to bring up *the* Madeira.

'Uncle Sol,' said Walter, 'I don't think you 're well. You haven't eaten any breakfast. I shall bring a doctor to you, if you go on like this.'

'He can't give me what I want, my boy,' said uncle Sol. 'At least he is in good practice if he can—and then he wouldn't.'

'What is it, uncle? Customers?'

'Aye,' returned Solomon, with a sigh. 'Customers would do.'

'Confound it, uncle!' said Walter, putting down his breakfast-cup with a clatter, and striking his hand on the table: 'when I see the people going up and down the street in shoals all day, and passing and repassing the shop every minute, by scores, I feel half tempted to rush out, collar somebody, bring him in, and *make* him buy fifty pounds' worth of instruments for ready money. What are you looking in at the door for?' continued Walter, apostrophising an old gentleman with a powdered head (inaudibly to him of course), who was staring at a ship's telescope with all his might and main. '*That 's* no use. I could do that. Come in and buy it!'

The old gentleman, however, having satiated his curiosity, walked calmly away.

'There he goes!' said Walter. 'That 's the way with 'em all. But, uncle—I say, uncle Sol'—for the old man was meditating, and had not responded to his first appeal. 'Don't be cast down. Don't be out of spirits, uncle. When orders *do* come, they 'll come in such a crowd, you won't be able to execute 'em.'

'I shall be past executing 'em, whenever they come, my boy,' returned Solomon Gills. 'They 'll never come to this shop again, till I am out of it.'

'I say, uncle! You mustn't really, you know!' urged Walter. 'Don't!'

Old Sol endeavoured to assume a cheery look, and smiled across the little table at him as pleasantly as he could.

'There 's nothing more than usual the matter; is there, uncle?' said Walter, leaning his elbows on the tea-tray, and bending over, to speak the more confidentially and kindly. 'Be open with me, uncle, if there is, and tell me all about it.'

'No, no, no,' returned old Sol. 'More than usual? No, no. What should there be the matter more than usual?'

Walter answered with an incredulous shake of his head. 'That 's what I want to know,' he said, 'and you ask *me*! I 'll tell you what, uncle, when I see you like this, I am quite sorry that I live with you.'

Old Sol opened his eyes involuntarily.

'Yes. Though nobody ever was happier than I am and always have been with you, I am quite sorry that I live with you, when I see you with anything on your mind.'

'I am a little dull at such times, I know,' observed Solomon, meekly rubbing his hands.

'What I mean, uncle Sol,' pursued Walter, bending over a little more to pat him on the shoulder, 'is, that then I feel you ought to have, sitting here and pouring out the tea instead of me, a nice little dumpling of a wife, you know,—a comfortable, capital, cosey old lady, who was just a match for you, and knew how to manage you, and keep you in good heart. Here am I, as loving a nephew as ever was (I am sure I ought to be!), but I am only a nephew, and I can't be such a companion to you when you 're low and out of sorts as she would have made herself, years ago, though I 'm sure I 'd give any money if I could cneer you up. And so I say, when I see you with anything on your mind, that I feel quite sorry you haven't got somebody better about you than a blundering young rough-and-tough boy like me, who has got the will to console you, uncle, but hasn't got the way—hasn't got the way,' repeated Walter, reaching over further yet, to shake his uncle by the hand.

'Wally, my dear boy,' said Solomon, 'if the cosey little old lady had taken her place in this parlour five-and forty years ago, I never could have been fonder of her than I am of you.'

'*I* know that, uncle Sol,' returned Walter. 'Lord bless you, I know that. But you wouldn't have had the whole weight of any uncomfortable secrets if she had been with you, because she would have known how to relieve you of 'em, and I don't.'

'Yes, yes, you do,' returned the instrument-maker.

'Well then, what 's the matter, uncle Sol?' said Walter, coaxingly. 'Come! What 's the matter?'

Solomon Gills persisted that there was nothing the matter; and maintained it so resolutely, that his nephew had no resource but to make a very indifferent imitation of believing him.

'All I can say is, uncle Sol, that if there is—'

'But there isn't,' said Solomon.

'Very well,' said Walter. 'Then I 've no more to say; and that 's lucky, for my time 's up for going to business. I shall look in by and by when I 'm out, to see how you get on, uncle. And mind, uncle! I 'll never believe you again, and never tell you anything more about Mr. Carker the junior, if I find out that you have been deceiving me!'

Solomon Gills laughingly defied him to find out anything of the kind; and Walter, revolving in his thoughts all sorts of impracticable ways of making fortunes and placing the wooden midshipman in a position of independence, betook himself to the offices of Dombey and Son with a heavier countenance than he usually carried there.

There lived in those days, round the corner—in Bishopsgate Street Without—one Brogley, sworn broker and appraiser, who kept a shop where every description of second-hand furniture was exhibited in the most uncomfortable aspect, and under circumstances and in combinations the most completely foreign to its purpose. Dozens of chairs hooked on to washing-stands, which with difficulty poised themselves on the shoulders of sideboards, which in their turn stood upon the wrong side of dining-tables, gymnastic with their legs upward on the tops of other dining-tables, were among its most reasonable arrangements. A banquet array of dish-covers, wine-glasses, and decanters was generally to be seen, spread forth upon the bosom of a four-post bedstead, for the entertainment of such genial company as half a dozen pokers, and a hall lamp. A set of window curtains with no windows belonging to them, would be seen gracefully draping a barricade of chests of drawers, loaded with little jars from chemists' shops; while a homeless hearthrug severed from its natural companion the fireside, braved the shrewd east wind in its adversity, and trembled in melancholy accord with the shrill complainings of a cabinet piano, wasting away, a string a day, and faintly resounding to the noises of the street in its jangling and distracted brain. Of motionless clocks that never stirred a finger, and seemed as incapable of being successfully wound up, as the pecuniary affairs of their former owners, there was always great choice in Mr. Brogley's shop; and various looking-glasses, accidentally placed at compound interest of reflection and refraction, presented to the eye an eternal perspective of bankruptcy and ruin.

Mr. Brogley himself was a moist-eyed, pink-complexioned, crisp-haired man, of a bulky figure and an easy temper—for that class of Caius Marius who sits upon the ruins of other people's Carthages, can keep up his spirits well enough. He had looked in at Solomon's shop sometimes to ask a question about articles in Solomon's way of business; and Walter knew him sufficiently to give him good day when they met in the street, but as that was the extent of the broker's acquaintance with Solomon Gills also, Walter was not a little surprised when he came back in the course of the forenoon, agreeably to his promise, to find Mr. Brogley sitting in the back-parlour with his hands in his pockets, and his hat hanging up behind the door.

'Well, uncle Sol!' said Walter. The old man was sitting ruefully on the opposite side of the table, with his spectacles over his eyes, for a wonder, instead of on his forehead. 'How are you now?'

Solomon shook his head, and waved one hand towards the broker, as introducing him.

'Is there anything the matter?' asked Walter, with a catching in his breath.

'No, no. There 's nothing the matter,' said Mr. Brogley. 'Don't let it put you out of the way.'

Walter looked from the broker to his uncle in mute amazement.

'The fact is,' said Mr. Brogley, 'there 's a little payment on a bond debt—three hundred and seventy odd, overdue: and I 'm in possession.'

'In possession!' cried Walter, looking round at the shop.

'Ah!' said Mr. Brogley, in confidential assent, and

nodding his head as if he would urge the advisability of their all being comfortable together. 'It 's an execution. That 's what it is. Don't let it put you out of the way. I come myself, because of keeping it quiet and sociable. You know me. It 's quite private.'

'Uncle Sol!' faltered Walter.

'Wally, my boy,' returned his uncle. 'It 's the first time. Such a calamity never happened to me before. I 'm an old man to begin.' Pushing up his spectacles again (for they were useless any longer to conceal his emotion), he covered his face with his hand, and sobbed aloud, and his tears fell down upon his coffee-coloured waistcoat.

'Uncle Sol! Pray! oh don't!' exclaimed Walter, who really felt a thrill of terror in seeing the old man weep. 'For God's sake don't do that. Mr. Brogley, what shall I do?'

'*I* should recommend you looking up a friend or so,' said Mr. Brogley, 'and talking it over.'

'To be sure!' cried Walter, catching at anything. 'Certainly! Thankee. Captain Cuttle 's the man, uncle. Wait till I run to Captain Cuttle. Keep your eye upon my uncle, will you, Mr. Brogley, and make him as comfortable as you can while I am gone? Don't despair, uncle Sol. Try and keep a good heart, there 's a dear fellow!'

Saying this with great fervour, and disregarding the old man's broken remonstrances, Walter dashed out of the shop again as hard as he could go; and, having hurried round to the office to excuse himself on the plea of his uncle's sudden illness, set off, full speed, for Captain Cuttle's residence.

Everything seemed altered as he ran along the streets. There were the usual entanglement and noise of carts, drays, omnibuses, waggons, and foot passengers, but the misfortune that had fallen on the wooden midshipman made it strange and new. Houses and shops were different from what they used to be, and bore Mr. Brogley's warrant on their fronts in large characters. The broker seemed to have got hold of the very churches; for their spires rose into the sky with an unwonted air. Even the sky itself was changed, and had an execution in it plainly.

Captain Cuttle lived on the brink of a little canal near the India Docks, where there was a swivel bridge which opened now and then to let some wandering monster of a ship come roaming up the street like a stranded leviathan. The gradual change from land to water, on the approach to Captain Cuttle's lodgings, was curious. It began with the erection of flagstaffs, as appurtenances to public-houses; then came slopsellers' shops, with Guernsey shirts, sou'wester hats, and canvas pantaloons, at once the tightest and the loosest of their order, hanging up outside. These were succeeded by anchor and chain-cable forges, where sledge-hammers were dinging upon iron all day long. Then came rows of houses, with little vane-surmounted masts uprearing themselves from among the scarlet beans. Then ditches. Then pollard willows. Then more ditches. Then unaccountable patches of dirty water, hardly to be descried, for the ships that covered them. Then the air was perfumed with chips; and all other trades were swallowed up in mast, oar, and block making, and boat building. Then the ground grew marshy and unsettled. Then there was nothing to be smelt but rum and sugar. Then Captain Cuttle's lodgings—at once a first floor and a top story, in Brig Place—were close before you.

The captain was one of those timber-looking men, suits of oak as well as hearts, whom it is almost impossible for the liveliest imagination to separate from any part of their dress, however insignificant. Accordingly, when Walter knocked at the door, and the captain instantly poked his head out of one of his little front-windows, and hailed him, with the hard glazed hat already on it, and the shirt-collar like a sail, and the wide suit of blue, all standing as usual, Walter was as fully persuaded that he was always in that state, as if the captain had been a bird and those had been his feathers.

'Wal'r, my lad!' said Captain Cuttle. 'Stand by and knock again. Hard! It 's washing-day.'

Walter, in his impatience, gave a prodigious thump with the knocker.

'Hard it is!' said Captain Cuttle, and immediately drew in his head, as if he expected a squall.

Nor was he mistaken: for a widow lady, with her sleeves rolled up to her shoulders, and her arms frothy with soap-suds and smoking with hot water, replied to the summons with startling rapidity. Before she looked at Walter, she looked at the knocker, and then, measuring him with her eyes from head to foot, said she wondered he had left any of it.

'Captain Cuttle 's at home, I know,' said Walter, with a conciliatory smile.

'Is he?' replied the widow lady. 'In-deed!'

'He has just been speaking to me,' said Walter, in breathless explanation.

'Has he?' replied the widow lady. 'Then p'raps you 'll give him Mrs. MacStinger's respects, and say that the next time he lowers himself and his lodgings by talking out of winder she 'll thank him to come down and open the door too.' Mrs. MacStinger spoke loud, and listened for any observations that might be offered from the first floor.

'I 'll mention it,' said Walter, 'if you 'll have the goodness to let me in, ma'am.'

For he was repelled by a wooden fortification extending across the doorway, and put there to prevent the little MacStingers in their moments of recreation from tumbling down the steps.

'A boy that can knock my door down,' said Mrs. MacStinger, contemptuously, 'can get over that, I should hope!' But Walter, taking this as a permission to enter, and getting over it, Mrs. MacStinger immediately demanded whether an Englishwoman's house was her castle or not; and whether she was to be broke in upon by 'raff.' On these subjects her thirst for information was still very importunate, when Walter, having made his way up the little staircase through an artificial fog occasioned by the washing, which covered the banisters with a clammy perspiration, entered Captain Cuttle's room, and found that gentleman in ambush behind the door.

'Never owed her a penny, Wal'r,' said Captain Cuttle, in a low voice, and with visible marks of trepidation on his countenance. 'Done her a world of good turns, and the children too. Vixen at times, though. Whew!'

'*I* should go away, Captain Cuttle,' said Walter.

'Dursn't do it, Wal'r,' returned the captain. 'She'd find me out, wherever I went. Sit down. How's Gills?'

The captain was dining (in his hat) off cold loin of mutton, porter, and some smoking hot potatoes, which he had cooked himself, and took out of a little saucepan before the fire as he wanted them. He unscrewed his hook at dinner-time, and screwed a knife into its wooden socket instead, with which he had already begun to peel one of these potatoes for Walter. His rooms were very small, and strongly impregnated with tobacco-smoke, but snug enough;

everything being stowed away, as if there were an earthquake regularly every half-hour.

'How 's Gills?' inquired the captain.

Walter, who had by this time recovered his breath, and lost his spirits—or such temporary spirits as his rapid journey had given him—looked at his questioner for a moment, said 'Oh, Captain Cuttle!' and burst into tears.

No words can describe the captain's consternation at this sight. Mrs. MacStinger faded into nothing before it. He dropped the potato and the fork—and would have dropped the knife too if he could—and sat gazing at the boy, as if he expected to hear next moment that a gulf had opened in the City, which had swallowed up his old friend, coffee-coloured suit, buttons, chronometer, spectacles, and all.

But when Walter told him what was really the matter, Captain Cuttle, after a moment's reflection, started up into full activity. He emptied out of a little tin canister on the top shelf of the cupboard, his whole stock of ready-money (amounting to thirteen pounds and half a crown), which he transferred to one of the pockets of his square blue coat; further enriched that repository with the contents of his plate chest, consisting of two withered atomies of teaspoons, and an obsolete pair of knock-knee'd sugar-tongs; pulled up his immense double-cased silver watch from the depths in which it reposed, to assure himself that that valuable was sound and whole; reattached the hook to his right wrist; and seizing the stick covered over with knobs, bade Walter come along.

Remembering, however, in the midst of his virtuous excitement, that Mrs. MacStinger might be lying in wait below, Captain Cuttle hesitated at last, not without glancing at the window, as if he had some thoughts of escaping by that unusual means of egress, rather than encounter his terrible enemy. He decided, however, in favour of stratagem.

'Wal'r,' said the captain, with a timid wink, 'go afore, my lad. Sing out, "good-bye, Captain Cuttle," when you 're in the passage, and shut the door. Then wait at the corner of the street till you see me.'

These directions were not issued without a previous knowledge of the enemy's tactics, for when Walter got downstairs, Mrs. MacStinger glided out of the little back-kitchen, like an avenging spirit. But not gliding out upon the captain, as she had expected, she merely made a further allusion to the knocker, and glided in again.

Some five minutes elapsed before Captain Cuttle could summon courage to attempt his escape; for Walter waited so long at the street-corner, looking back at the house, before there were any symptoms of the hard glazed hat. At length the captain burst out of the door with the suddenness of an explosion, and coming towards him at a great pace, and never once looking over his shoulder, pretended, as soon as they were well out of the street, to whistle a tune.

'Uncle much hove down, Wal'r?' inquired the captain, as they were walking along.

'I am afraid so. If you had seen him this morning, you would never have forgotten it.'

'Walk fast, Wal'r, my lad,' returned the captain, mending his pace; 'and walk the same all the days of your life. Overhaul the catechism for that advice, and keep it!'

The captain was too busy with his own thoughts of Solomon Gills, mingled perhaps with some reflections on his late escape from Mrs. MacStinger, to offer any further quotations on the way for Walter's moral improvement. They interchanged no other word until they arrived at old Sol's door, where the unfortunate wooden midshipman, with his instrument at his eye, seemed to be surveying the whole horizon in search of some friend to help him out of his difficulty.

'Gills!' said the captain, hurrying into the back-parlour, and taking him by the hand quite tenderly. 'Lay your head well to the wind, and we 'll fight through it. All you 've got to do,' said the captain, with the solemnity of a man who was delivering himself of one of the most precious practical tenets ever discovered by human wisdom, 'is to lay your head well to the wind, and we 'll fight through it!'

Old Sol returned the pressure of his hand, and thanked him.

Captain Cuttle, then, with a gravity suitable to the nature of the occasion, put down upon the table the two teaspoons and the sugar-tongs, the silver watch, and the ready money; and asked Mr. Brogley, the broker, what the damage was.

'Come! What do you make of it?' said Captain Cuttle.

'Why, Lord help you!' returned the broker; 'you don't suppose that property 's of any use, do you?'

'Why not?' inquired the captain.

'Why? The amount 's three hundred and seventy, odd,' replied the broker.

'Never mind,' returned the captain, though he was evidently dismayed by the figures; 'all 's fish that comes to your net, I suppose?'

'Certainly,' said Mr. Brogley. 'But sprats an't whales, you know.'

The philosophy of this observation seemed to strike the captain. He ruminated for a minute; eyeing the broker, meanwhile, as a deep genius; and then called the instrument-maker aside.

'Gills,' said Captain Cuttle, 'what 's the bearings of this business? Who 's the creditor?'

'Hush!' returned the old man. 'Come away. Don't speak before Wally. It 's a matter of security for Wally's father—an old bond. I 've paid a good deal of it, Ned, but the times are so bad with me that I can't do more just now. I 've foreseen it, but I couldn't help it. Not a word before Wally, for all the world.'

'You 've got *some* money, haven't you?' whispered the captain.

'Yes, yes—oh yes—I 've got some,' returned old Sol, first putting his hands into his empty pockets, and then squeezing his Welsh wig between them, as if he thought he might wring some gold out of it; 'but I—the little I have got, isn't convertible, Ned; it can't be got at. I have been trying to do something with it for Wally, and I 'm old-fashioned, and behind the time. It 's here and there, and—and, in short, it 's as good as nowhere,' said the old man, looking in bewilderment about him.

He had so much the air of a half-witted person who had been hiding his money in a variety of places, and had forgotten where, that the captain followed his eyes, not without a faint hope that he might remember some few hundred pounds concealed up the chimney, or down in the cellar. But Solomon Gills knew better than that.

'I 'm behind the time altogether, my dear Ned,' said Sol, in resigned despair, 'a long way. It 's no use my lagging on so far behind it. The stock had better be sold—it 's worth more than this debt—and I had better go and die somewhere, on the balance. I haven't any energy left. I don't understand things. This had better be the end of it. Let 'em sell the stock and take *him* down,' said the old man, pointing feebly to the wooden midshipman, 'and let us both be broken up together.'

'And what d' ye mean to do with Wal'r?' said the captain. 'There, there! Sit ye down, Gills, sit ye down, and let me think o' this. If I warn't a man on a small annuity, that was large enough till to-day, I hadn't need to think of it. But you only lay your head well to the wind,' said the captain, again administering that unanswerable piece of consolation, 'and you 're all right!'

Old Sol thanked him from his heart, and went and laid it against the back-parlour fireplace instead.

Captain Cuttle walked up and down the shop for some time, cogitating profoundly, and bringing his bushy black eyebrows to bear so heavily on his nose, like clouds setting on a mountain, that Walter was afraid to offer any interruption to the current of his reflections. Mr. Brogley, who was averse to being any constraint upon the party, and who had an ingenious cast of mind, went, softly whistling, among the stock; rattling weather glasses, shaking compasses as if they were physic, catching up keys with loadstones, looking through telescopes, endeavouring to make himself acquainted with the use of the globes, setting parallel rulers astride on to his nose, and amusing himself with other philosophical transactions.

'Wal'r?' said the captain at last. 'I 've got it.'

'Have you, Captain Cuttle?' cried Walter, with great animation.

'Come this way, my lad,' said the captain. 'The stock 's one security. I 'm another. Your governor 's the man to advance the money.'

'Mr. Dombey!' faltered Walter.

The captain nodded gravely. 'Look at him,' he said. 'Look at Gills. If they was to sell off these things now, he 'd die of it. You know he would.

We mustn't leave a stone unturned—and there 's a stone for you.'

'A stone!—Mr. Dombey!' faltered Walter.

'You run round to the office, first of all, and see if he 's there,' said Captain Cuttle, clapping him on the back. 'Quick!'

Walter felt he must not dispute the command—a glance at his uncle would have determined him if he had felt otherwise—and disappeared to execute it. He soon returned, out of breath, to say that Mr. Dombey was not there. It was Saturday, and he had gone to Brighton.

'I tell you what, Wal'r!' said the captain, who seemed to have prepared himself for this contingency in his absence. 'We 'll go to Brighton. I 'll back you, my boy. I 'll back you, Wal'r. We 'll go to Brighton by the afternoon's coach.'

If the application must be made to Mr. Dombey at all, which was awful to think of, Walter felt that he would rather prefer it alone and unassisted, than backed by the personal influence of Captain Cuttle, to which he hardly thought Mr. Dombey would attach much weight. But as the captain appeared to be of quite another opinion, and was bent upon it, and as his friendship was too zealous and serious to be trifled with by one so much younger than himself, he forbore to hint the least objection. Cuttle, therefore, taking a hurried leave of Solomon Gills, and returning the ready money, the teaspoons, the sugar-tongs, and the silver watch, to his pocket—with a view, as Walter thought, with horror, to making a gorgeous impression on Mr. Dombey—bore him off to the coach-office, without a minute's delay, and repeatedly assured him on the road, that he would stick by him to the last.

# CHAPTER X

## CONTAINING THE SEQUEL OF THE MIDSHIPMAN'S DISASTER

Major Bagstock, after long and frequent observation of Paul, across Princess's Place, through his double-barrelled opera-glass; and after receiving many minute reports, daily, weekly, and monthly, on that subject, from the native who kept himself in constant communication with Miss Tox's maid for that purpose; came to the conclusion that Dombey, sir, was a man to be known, and that J. B. was the boy to make his acquaintance.

Miss Tox, however, maintaining her reserved behaviour, and frigidly declining to understand the major whenever he called (which he often did) on any little fishing excursion connected with this project, the major, in spite of his constitutional toughness and slyness, was fain to leave the accomplishment of his desire in some measure to chance, 'which,' as he was used to observe with chuckles at his club, 'has been fifty to one in favour of Joey B., sir, ever since his elder brother died of Yellow Jack in the West Indies.'

It was some time coming to his aid in the present instance, but it befriended him at last. When the dark servant, with full particulars, reported Miss Tox absent on Brighton service, the major was suddenly touched with affectionate reminiscences of his friend Bill Bitherstone of Bengal, who had written to ask him, if he ever went that way, to bestow a call upon his only son. But when the same dark servant reported Paul at Mrs. Pipchin's, and the major, referring to the letter favoured by Master Bitherstone on his arrival in England—to which he had never had the least idea of paying any attention—saw the opening that presented itself, he was made so rabid by the gout, with which he happened to be then laid up, that he threw a footstool at the dark servant in return for his intelligence, and swore he would be the death of the rascal before he had done with him: which the dark servant was more than half disposed to believe.

At length the major being released from his fit, went one Saturday growling down to Brighton, with the native behind him; apostrophising Miss Tox all the way, and gloating over the prospect of carrying by storm the distinguished friend to whom she attached so much mystery, and for whom she had deserted him.

'Would you, ma'am, would you!' said the major, straining with vindictiveness, and swelling every already swollen vein in his head. 'Would you give Joey B. the go-by, ma'am? Not yet, ma'am, not yet! Damme, not yet, sir. Joe is awake, ma'am. Bagstock is alive, sir. J. B. knows a move or two, ma'am. Josh has his weather-eye open, sir. You'll find him tough, ma'am. Tough, sir, tough is Joseph. Tough, and de-vilish sly!'

And very tough indeed Master Bitherstone found him, when he took that young gentleman out for a walk. But the major, with his complexion like a Stilton cheese, and his eyes like a prawn's, went roving about, perfectly indifferent to Master Bitherstone's amusement, and dragging Master Bitherstone along, while he looked about him high and low, for Mr. Dombey and his children.

In good time the major, previously instructed by Mrs. Pipchin, spied out Paul and Florence, and bore down upon them; there being a stately gentleman (Mr. Dombey, doubtless) in their company. Charging with Master Bitherstone into the very heart of the little squadron, it fell out, of course, that Master Bitherstone spoke to his fellow-sufferers. Upon that the major stopped to notice and admire them; remembered with amazement that he had seen and spoken to them at his friend Miss Tox's in Princess's Place; opined that Paul was a devilish fine fellow, and his own little friend; inquired if he remembered Joey B. the major; and finally, with a sudden recollection of the conventionalities of life, turned and apologised to Mr. Dombey.

'But my little friend here, sir,' said the major, 'makes a boy of me again. An old soldier, sir—Major Bagstock, at your service—is not ashamed to confess it.' Here the major lifted his hat. 'Damme, sir,' cried the major with sudden warmth, 'I envy you.' Then he recollected himself, and added, 'Excuse my freedom.'

Mr. Dombey begged he wouldn't mention it.

'An old campaigner, sir,' said the major, 'a smoke-dried, sun-burnt, used-up, invalided old dog of a major, sir, was not afraid of being condemned for his whim by a man like Mr. Dombey. I have the honour of addressing Mr. Dombey, I believe?'

'I am the present unworthy representative of that name, major,' returned Mr. Dombey.

'By G—, sir,' said the major, 'it 's a great name. It 's a name, sir,' said the major firmly, as if he defied Mr. Dombey to contradict him, and would feel it his painful duty to bully him if he did, 'that is known and honoured in the British possessions abroad. It is a name, sir, that a man is proud to recognise. There is nothing adulatory in Joseph Bagstock, sir. His Royal Highness the Duke of York observed on more than one occasion, "there is no adulation in Joey. He is a plain old soldier is Joe. He is tough to a fault is Joseph": but it 's a great name, sir. By the Lord, it 's a great name!' said the major, solemnly.

'You are good enough to rate it higher than it deserves, perhaps, major,' returned Mr. Dombey.

'No, sir,' said the major. 'My little friend here, sir, will certify for Joseph Bagstock that he is a thorough-going, downright, plain-spoken old trump, sir, and nothing more. That boy, sir,' said the major in a lower tone, 'will live in history. That boy, sir, is not a common production. Take care of him, Mr. Dombey.

Mr. Dombey seemed to intimate that he would endeavour to do so.

'Here is a boy here, sir,' pursued the major, confidentially, and giving him a thrust with his cane. 'Son of Bitherstone of Bengal. Bill Bitherstone formerly of ours. That boy's father and myself, sir, were sworn friends. Wherever you went, sir, you heard of nothing but Bill Bitherstone and Joe Bagstock. Am I blind to that boy's defects? By no means. He 's a fool, sir.'

Mr. Dombey glanced at the libelled Master Bitherstone, of whom he knew at least as much as the major did, and said, in quite a complacent manner, 'Really?'

'That is what he is, sir,' said the major. 'He 's a fool. Joe Bagstock never minces matters. The son of my old friend Bill Bitherstone, of Bengal, is a born fool, sir.' Here the major laughed till he was almost black. 'My little friend is destined for a public school, I presume, Mr. Dombey?' said the major when he had recovered.

'I am not quite decided,' returned Mr. Dombey. 'I think not. He is delicate.'

'If he 's delicate, sir,' said the major, 'you are right. None but the tough fellows could live through it, sir, at Sandhurst. We put each other to the torture there, sir. We roasted the new fellows at a slow fire, and hung 'em out of a three pair of stairs window, with their heads downwards. Joseph Bagstock, sir, was held out of the window by the heels of his boots, for thirteen minutes by the college clock.'

The major might have appealed to his countenance in corroboration of this story. It certainly looked as if he had hung out a little too long.

'But it made us what we were, sir,' said the major, settling his shirt-frill. 'We were iron, sir, and it forged us. Are you remaining here, Mr. Dombey?'

'I generally come down once a week, major,' returned that gentleman. 'I stay at the Bedford.'

'I shall have the honour of calling at the Bedford, sir, if you'll permit me,' said the major. 'Joey B., sir, is not in general a calling man, but Mr. Dombey's is not a common name. I am much indebted to my little friend, sir, for the honour of this introduction.'

Mr. Dombey made a very gracious reply; and Major Bagstock, having patted Paul on the head, and said of Florence that her eyes would play the devil with the youngsters before long—'and the oldsters, too, sir, if you come to that,' added the major, chuckling very much—stirred up Master Bitherstone with his walking-stick, and departed with that young gentleman, at a kind of half-trot; rolling his head and coughing with great dignity, as he staggered away, with his legs very wide asunder.

In fulfilment of his promise, the major afterwards called on Mr. Dombey; and Mr. Dombey, having referred to the army list, afterwards called on the major. Then the major called at Mr. Dombey's house in town; and came down again, in the same coach as Mr. Dombey. In short, Mr. Dombey and the major got on uncommonly well together, and uncommonly fast: and Mr. Dombey observed of the major, to his sister, that besides being quite a military man he was really something more, as he had a very admirable idea of the importance of things unconnected with his own profession.

At length Mr. Dombey, bringing down Miss Tox and Mrs. Chick to see the children, and finding the major again at Brighton, invited him to dinner at the Bedford, and complimented Miss Tox highly, beforehand, on her neighbour and acquaintance. Notwithstanding the palpitation of the heart which these allusions occasioned her, they were anything but disagreeable to Miss Tox, as they enabled her to be extremely interesting, and to manifest an occasional incoherence and distraction which she was not at all unwilling to display. The major gave her abundant opportunities of exhibiting this emotion: being profuse in his complaints, at dinner, of her desertion of him and Princess's Place: and as he appeared to derive great enjoyment from making them, they all got on very well.

None the worse on account of the major taking charge of the whole conversation, and showing as great an appetite in that respect as in regard of the various dainties on the table, among which he may be almost said to have wallowed: greatly to the aggravation of his inflammatory tendencies. Mr. Dombey's habitual silence and reserve yielding readily to this usurpation, the major felt that he was coming out and shining: and in the flow of spirits thus engendered, rang such an infinite number of new changes on his own name that he quite astonished himself. In a word, they were all very well pleased. The major was considered to possess an inexhaustible fund of conversation; and when he took a late farewell, after a long rubber, Mr. Dombey again complimented the blushing Miss Tox on her neighbour and acquaintance.

But all the way home to his own hotel, the major incessantly said to himself, and of himself, 'Sly, sir—sly, sir—de-vil-ish sly!' And when he got there, sat down in a chair, and fell into a silent fit of laughter, with which he was sometimes seized, and which was always particularly awful. It held him so long on this occasion that the dark servant, who stood watching him at a distance, but dared not for his life approach, twice or thrice gave him over for lost. His whole form, but especially his face and head, dilated beyond all former experience; and presented to the dark man's view, nothing but a heavy mass of indigo. At length he burst into a violent paroxysm of coughing, and when that was a little better burst into such ejaculations as the following—

'Would you, ma'am, would you? Mrs. Dombey, eh, ma'am? I think not, ma'am. Not while Joe B. can put a spoke in your wheel, ma'am. J. B. 's even with you now, ma'am. He isn't altogether bowled out, yet, sir, isn't Bagstock. She 's deep, sir, deep, but Josh is deeper. Wide awake is old Joe—broad awake and staring, sir!' There was no doubt of this last assertion being true and to a very fearful extent; as it continued to be during the greater part of that night, which the major chiefly passed in similar exclamations, diversified with fits of coughing and choking that startled the whole house.

It was on the day after this occasion (being Sunday) when, as Mr. Dombey, Mrs. Chick, and Miss Tox were sitting at breakfast, still eulogising the major, Florence came running in; her face suffused with a bright colour, and her eyes sparkling joyfully: and cried—

'Papa! Papa! Here 's Walter! and he won't come in.'

'Who?' cried Mr. Dombey. 'What does she mean? What is this?'

'Walter, papa!' said Florence timidly; sensible of having approached the presence with too much familiarity. 'Who found me when I wast lost.'

'Does she mean young Gay, Louisa?' inquired Mr. Dombey, knitting his brows. 'Really, this child's manners have become very boisterous. She cannot mean young Gay, I think. See what it is, will you.'

Mrs. Chick hurried into the passage, and returned with the information that it was young Gay, accompanied by a very strange-looking person; and that young Gay said he would not take the liberty of coming in, hearing Mr. Dombey was at breakfast, but would wait until Mr. Dombey should signify that he might approach.

'Tell the boy to come in now,' said Mr. Dombey. 'Now, Gay, what is the matter? Who sent you down here? Was there nobody else to come?'

'I beg your pardon, sir,' returned Walter. 'I have not been sent. I have been so bold as to come on my own account, which I hope you 'll pardon when I mention the cause.'

But Mr. Dombey, without attending to what he said, was looking impatiently on either side of him (as if he were a pillar in his way) at some object behind.

'What 's that?' said Mr. Dombey. 'Who is that? I think you have made some mistake in the door, sir.'

'Oh, I 'm very sorry to intrude with any one, sir,' cried Walter hastily: 'but this is—this is Captain Cuttle, sir.'

'Wal'r, my lad,' observed the captain in a deep voice: 'stand by!'

At the same time the captain, coming a little further in, brought out his wide suit of blue, his conspicuous shirt-collar, and his knobby nose in full relief, and stood bowing to Mr. Dombey, and waving his hook politely to the ladies, with the hard glazed hat in his one hand, and a red equator round his head which it had newly imprinted there.

Mr. Dombey regarded this phenomenon with amazement and indignation, and seemed by his looks to appeal to Mrs. Chick and Miss Tox against it. Little Paul, who had come in after Florence, backed towards Miss Tox as the captain waved his hook, and stood on the defensive.

'Now, Gay,' said Mr. Dombey. 'What have you got to say to me?'

Again the captain observed, as a general opening of the conversation that could not fail to propitiate all parties, 'Wal'r, stand by!'

'I am afraid, sir,' began Walter, trembling, and looking down at the ground, 'that I take a very great liberty in coming—indeed, I am sure I do. I should hardly have had the courage to ask to see you, sir, even after coming down, I am afraid, if I had not overtaken Miss Dombey, and—'

'Well!' said Mr. Dombey, following his eyes as he glanced at the attentive Florence, and frowning unconsciously as she encouraged him with a smile. 'Go on, if you please.'

'Aye, aye,' observed the captain, considering it incumbent on him, as a point of good breeding, to support Mr. Dombey. 'Well said! Go on, Wal'r.'

Captain Cuttle ought to have been withered by the look which Mr. Dombey bestowed upon him in acknowledgment of his patronage. But quite innocent of this, he closed one eye in reply, and gave Mr. Dombey to understand by certain significant motions of his hook, that Walter was a little bashful at first, and might be expected to come out shortly.

'It is entirely a private and personal matter, that has brought me here, sir,' continued Walter, faltering, 'and Captain Cuttle—'

'Here!' interposed the captain, as an assurance that he was at hand, and might be relied upon.

'Who is a very old friend of my poor uncle's, and a most excellent man, sir,' pursued Walter, raising his eyes with a look of entreaty in the captain's behalf, 'was so good as to offer to come with me, which I could hardly refuse.'

'No, no, no,' observed the captain complacently. 'Of course not. No call for refusing. Go on, Wal'r.'

'And therefore, sir,' said Walter, venturing to meet Mr. Dombey's eye, and proceeding with better courage in the very desperation of the case, now that there was no avoiding it, 'therefore I have come, with him, sir, to say that my poor old uncle is in very great affliction and distress. That, through the gradual loss of his business, and not being able to make a payment, the apprehension of which has weighed very heavily upon his mind, months and months, as indeed I know, sir, he has an execution in his house, and is in danger of losing all he has, and breaking his heart. And that if you would, in your kindness, and in your old knowledge of him as a respectable man, do anything to help him out of his difficulty, sir, we never could thank you enough for it.'

Walter's eyes filled with tears as he spoke; and so did those of Florence. Her father saw them glistening, though he appeared to look at Walter only.

'It is a very large sum, sir,' said Walter. 'More than three hundred pounds. My uncle is quite beaten down by his misfortune, it lies so heavy on him; and is quite unable to do anything for his own relief. He doesn't even know yet, that I have come to speak to you. You would wish me to say, sir,' added Walter, after a moment's hesitation, 'exactly what it is I want. I really don't know, sir. There is my uncle's stock, on which I believe I may say, confidently, there are no other demands, and there is Captain Cuttle, who would wish to be security too. I—I hardly like to mention,' said Walter, 'such earnings as mine; but if you would allow them—accumulate—payment—advance—uncle—frugal, honourable, old man.' Walter trailed off, through these broken sentences, into silence; and stood, with downcast head, before his employer.

Considering this a favourable moment for the display of the valuables, Captain Cuttle advanced to the table; and clearing a space among the breakfast-cups at Mr. Dombey's elbow, produced the silver watch, the ready money, the teaspoons, and the sugar-tongs; and piling them up into a heap that they might look as precious as possible, delivered himself of these words—

'Half a loaf 's better than no bread, and the same remark holds good with crumbs. There 's a few. Annuity of one hundred pound prannum, also ready to be made over. If there is a man chock-full of science in the world, it 's old Sol Gills. If there is a lad of promise—one flowing,' added the captain, in one of his happy quotations, 'with milk and honey—it 's his nevy!'

The captain then withdrew to his former place, where he stood arranging his scattered locks with the air of a man who had given the finishing touch to a difficult performance.

When Walter ceased to speak, Mr. Dombey's eyes were attracted to little Paul, who, seeing his sister hanging down her head and silently weeping in her commiseration for the distress she had heard described, went over to her, and tried to comfort her: looking at Walter and his father as he did so, with a very expressive face. After the momentary distraction of Captain Cuttle's address, which he regarded with lofty indifference, Mr. Dombey again turned his eyes upon his son, and sat steadily regarding the child, for some moments, in silence.

'What was this debt contracted for?' asked Mr. Dombey at length. 'Who is the creditor?'

'He don't know,' replied the captain, putting his hand on Walter's shoulder. 'I do. It came of helping a man that 's dead now, and that 's cost my friend Gills many a hundred pound already. More particulars in private, if agreeable.'

'People who have enough to do to hold their own way,' said Mr. Dombey, unobservant of the captain's mysterious sign behind Walter, and still looking at his son, 'had better be content with their own obligations and difficulties, and not increase them by engaging for other men. It is an act of dishonesty and presumption, too,' said Mr. Dombey, sternly; 'great presumption; for the wealthy could do no more. Paul, come here!'

The child obeyed: and Mr. Dombey took him on his knee.

'If you had money now—' said Mr. Dombey. 'Look at me!'

Paul, whose eyes had wandered to his sister, and to Walter, looked his father in the face.

'If you had money now,' said Mr. Dombey; 'as much money as young Gay has talked about; what would you do?'

'Give it to his old uncle,' returned Paul.

'Lend it to his old uncle, eh?' retorted Mr. Dombey. 'Well! When you are old enough, you know, you will share my money, and we shall use it together.'

'Dombey and Son,' interrupted Paul, who had been tutored early in the phrase.

'Dombey and Son,' repeated his father. 'Would you like to begin to be Dombey and Son, now, and lend this money to young Gay's uncle?'

'Oh! if you please, papa!' said Paul: 'and so would Florence.'

'Girls,' said Mr. Dombey, 'have nothing to do with Dombey and Son. Would *you* like it?'

'Yes, papa, yes!'

'Then you shall do it,' returned his father. 'And you see, Paul,' he added, dropping his voice, 'how powerful money is, and how anxious people are to get it. Young Gay comes all this way to beg for money, and you, who are so grand and great, having got it, are going to let him have it, as a great favour and obligation.'

Paul turned up the old face for a moment, in which there was a sharp understanding of the reference conveyed in these words: but it was a young and childish face immediately afterwards, when he slipped down from his father's knee, and ran to tell Florence not to cry any more, for he was going to let young Gay have the money.

Mr. Dombey then turned to a side-table, and wrote a note and sealed it. During the interval, Paul and Florence whispered to Walter, and Captain Cuttle beamed on the three, with such aspiring and ineffably presumptuous thoughts as Mr. Dombey never could have believed in. The note being finished, Mr. Dombey turned round to his former place, and held it out to Walter.

'Give that,' he said, 'the first thing to-morrow morning, to Mr. Carker. He will immediately take care that one of my people releases your uncle from his present position, by paying the amount at issue; and that such arrangements are made for its repayment as may be consistent with your uncle's circumstances. You will consider that this is done for you by Master Paul.'

Walter, in the emotion of holding in his hand the means of releasing his good uncle from his trouble, would have endeavoured to express something of his gratitude and joy. But Mr. Dombey stopped him short.

'You will consider that it is done,' he repeated, 'by Master Paul. I have explained that to him, and he understands it. I wish no more to be said.'

As he motioned towards the door, Walter could only bow his head and retire. Miss Tox, seeing that the captain appeared about to do the same, interposed.

'My dear sir,' she said, addressing Mr. Dombey, at whose munificence both she and Mrs. Chick were shedding tears copiously; 'I think you have overlooked something. Pardon me, Mr. Dombey, I think in the nobility of your character, and its exalted scope, you have omitted a matter of detail.'

'Indeed, Miss Tox!' said Mr. Dombey.

'The gentleman with the—instrument,' pursued Miss Tox, glancing at Captain Cuttle, 'has left upon the table, at your elbow—'

'Good Heavens!' said Mr. Dombey, sweeping the captain's property from him, as if it were so much crumb indeed. 'Take these things away. I am obliged to you, Miss Tox; it is like your usual discretion. Have the goodness to take these things away, sir!'

Captain Cuttle felt he had no alternative but to comply. But he was so much struck by the magnanimity of Mr. Dombey, in refusing treasures lying heaped up to his hand, that when he had deposited the teaspoons and sugar-tongs in one pocket, and the ready money in another, and had lowered the great watch down slowly into its proper vault, he could not refrain from seizing that gentleman's right hand in his own solitary left, and while he held it open with his powerful fingers, bringing the hook down upon its palm in a transport of admiration. At this touch of warm feeling and cold iron, Mr. Dombey shivered all over.

Captain Cuttle then kissed his hook to the ladies several times, with great elegance and gallantry; and having taken a particular leave of Paul and Florence, accompanied Walter out of the room. Florence was running after them in the earnestness of her heart, to send some message to old Sol, when Mr. Dombey called her back, and bade her stay where she was.

'Will you *never* be a Dombey, my dear child!' said Mrs. Chick, with pathetic reproachfulness.

'Dear aunt,' said Florence. 'Don't be angry with me. I am so thankful to papa!'

She would have run and thrown her arms about his neck if she had dared; but as she did not dare, she glanced with thankful eyes towards him, as he sat musing; sometimes bestowing an uneasy glance on her, but, for the most part, watching Paul, who walked about the room with the newblown dignity of having let young Gay have the money.

And young Gay—Walter—what of him?

He was overjoyed to purge the old man's hearth from bailiffs and brokers, and to hurry back to his uncle with the good tidings. He was overjoyed to have it all arranged and settled next day before noon; and to sit down at evening in the little back-parlour with old Sol and Captain Cuttle; and to see the instrument-maker already reviving, and hopeful for the future, and feeling that the wooden midshipman was his own again. But without the least impeachment of his gratitude to Mr. Dombey, it must be confessed that Walter was humbled and cast down. It is when our budding hopes are nipped beyond recovery by some rough wind, that we are the most disposed to picture to ourselves what flowers they might have borne, if they had flourished; and now, when Walter felt himself cut off from that great Dombey height, by the depth of a new and terrible tumble, and felt that all his old wild fancies had been scattered to the winds in the fall, he began to suspect that they might have led him on to harmless visions of aspiring to Florence in the remote distance of time.

The captain viewed the subject in quite a different light. He appeared to entertain a belief that the interview at which he had assisted was so very satisfactory and encouraging, as to be only a step or two removed from a regular betrothal of Florence to Walter; and that the late transaction had immensely forwarded, if not thoroughly established, the Whittingtonian hopes. Stimulated by this conviction, and by the improvement in the spirits of his old friend, and by his own consequent gaiety, he even attempted, in favouring them with the ballad of 'Lovely Peg' for the third time in one evening, to make an extemporaneous substitution of the name 'Florence'; but finding this difficult, on account of the word Peg invariably rhyming to leg (in which personal beauty the original was described as having excelled all competitors), he hit upon the happy thought of changing it to Fle—e—eg which he accordingly did, with an archness almost supernatural, and a voice quite vociferous, notwithstanding that the time was close at hand when he must seek the abode of the dreadful Mrs. MacStinger.

## CHAPTER XI

### PAUL'S INTRODUCTION TO A NEW SCENE

Mrs. Pipchin's constitution was made of such hard metal, in spite of its liability to the fleshly weaknesses of standing in need of repose after chops, and of requiring to be coaxed to sleep by the soporific agency of sweet-breads, that it utterly set at naught the predictions of Mrs. Wickam, and showed no symptoms of decline. Yet, as Paul's rapt interest in the old lady continued unabated, Mrs. Wickam would not budge an inch from the position she had taken up. Fortifying and entrenching herself on the strong ground of her uncle's Betsey Jane, she advised Miss Berry, as a friend, to prepare herself for the worst; and forewarned her that her aunt might, at any time, be expected to go off suddenly, like a powder-mill.

Poor Berry took it all in good part, and drudged and slaved away as usual; perfectly convinced that Mrs. Pipchin was one of the most meritorious persons in the world, and making every day innumerable sacrifices of herself upon the altar of that noble old woman. But all these immolations of Berry were somehow carried to the credit of Mrs. Pipchin by Mrs. Pipchin's friends and admirers; and were made to harmonise with, and carry out, that melancholy fact of the deceased Mr. Pipchin having broken his heart in the Peruvian mines.

For example, there was an honest grocer and general dealer in the retail line of business, between whom and Mrs. Pipchin there was a small memorandum book, with a greasy red cover, perpetually in question, and concerning which divers secret councils and conferences were continually being held between the parties to the register, on the mat in the passage, and with closed doors in the parlour. Nor were there wanting dark hints from Master Bitherstone (whose temper had been made revengeful by the solar heats of India acting on his blood), of balances unsettled, and of a failure, on one occasion within his memory, in the supply of moist sugar at tea-time. This grocer being a bachelor, and not a man who looked upon the surface for beauty, had once made honourable offers for the hand of Berry, which Mrs. Pipchin had, with contumely and scorn, rejected. Everybody said how laudable this was in Mrs. Pipchin, relict of a man who had died of the Peruvian mines; and what a staunch, high, independent spirit the old lady had. But nobody said anything about poor Berry, who cried for six weeks (being soundly rated by her good aunt all the time), and lapsed into a state of hopeless spinsterhood.

'Berry's very fond of you, ain't she?' Paul once asked Mrs. Pipchin when they were sitting by the fire with the cat.

'Yes,' said Mrs. Pipchin.

'Why?' asked Paul.

'Why!' returned the disconcerted old lady. 'How can you ask such things, sir! Why are you fond of your sister Florence?'

'Because she's very good,' said Paul. 'There's nobody like Florence.'

'Well!' retorted Mrs. Pipchin, shortly, 'and there's nobody like me, I suppose.'

'Ain't there really though?' asked Paul, leaning forward in his chair, and looking at her very hard.

'No,' said the old lady.

'I am glad of that,' observed Paul, rubbing his hands thoughtfully. 'That 's a very good thing.'

Mrs. Pipchin didn't dare to ask him why, lest she should receive some perfectly annihilating answer. But as a compensation to her wounded feelings, she harassed Master Bitherstone to that extent until bed-time, that he began that very night to make arrangements for an overland return to India, by secreting from his supper a quarter of a round of bread and a fragment of moist Dutch cheese, as the beginning of a stock of provision to support him on the voyage.

Mrs. Pipchin had kept watch and ward over little Paul and his sister for nearly twelve months. They had been home twice, but only for a few days; and had been constant in their weekly visits to Mr, Dombey at the hotel. By little and little Paul had grown stronger, and had become able to dispense with his carriage; though he still looked thin and delicate; and still remained the same old, quiet, dreamy child that he had been when first consigned to Mrs. Pipchin's care. One Saturday afternoon, at dusk, great consternation was occasioned in the Castle by the unlooked-for announcement of Mr. Dombey as a visitor to Mrs. Pipchin. The population of the parlour was immediately swept upstairs as on the wings of a whirlwind, and after much slamming of bedroom doors, and trampling overhead, and some knocking about of Master Bitherstone by Mrs. Pipchin, as a relief to the perturbation of her spirits, the black bombazeen garments of the worthy old lady darkened the audience-chamber where Mr. Dombey was contemplating the vacant arm-chair of his son and heir.

'Mrs. Pipchin,' said Mr. Dombey, 'how do you do?'

'Thank you, sir,' said Mrs. Pipchin, 'I am pretty well, considering.'

Mrs. Pipchin always used that form of words. It meant, considering her virtues, sacrifices, and so forth.

'I can't expect, sir, to be very well,' said Mrs. Pipchin, taking a chair, and fetching her breath; 'but such health as I have, I am grateful for.'

Mr. Dombey inclined his head with the satisfied air of a patron, who felt that this was the sort of thing for which he paid so much a quarter. After a moment's silence, he went on to say—

'Mrs. Pipchin, I have taken the liberty of calling, to consult you in reference to my son. I have had it in my mind to do so for some time past; but have deferred it from time to time, in order that his health might be thoroughly re-established. You have no misgivings on that subject, Mrs. Pipchin?'

'Brighton has proved very beneficial, sir,' returned Mrs. Pipchin. 'Very beneficial, indeed.'

'I purpose,' said Mr. Dombey, 'his remaining at Brighton.'

Mrs. Pipchin rubbed her hands, and bent her grey eyes on the fire.

'But,' pursued Mr. Dombey, stretching out his forefinger, 'but possibly that he should now make a change, and lead a different kind of life here. In short, Mrs. Pipchin, that is the object of my visit. My son is getting on, Mrs. Pipchin. Really he is getting on.'

There was something melancholy in the triumphant air with which Mr. Dombey said this. It showed how long Paul's childish life had been to him, and how his hopes were set upon a later stage of his existence. Pity may appear a strange word to connect with any one so haughty and so cold, and yet he seemed a worthy subject for it at that moment.

'Six years old!' said Mr. Dombey, settling his neckcloth—perhaps to hide an irrepressible smile that rather seemed to strike upon the surface of his face and glance away, as finding no resting-place, than to play there for an instant. 'Dear me, six will be changed to sixteen, before we have time to look about us.'

'Ten years,' croaked the unsympathetic Pipchin, with a frosty glistening of her hard grey eye, and a dreary shaking of her bent head, 'is a long time.'

'It depends on circumstances,' returned Mr. Dombey; 'at all events, Mrs. Pipchin, my son is six years old, and there is no doubt, I fear, that in his studies he is behind many children of his age—of his youth,' said Mr. Dombey, quickly answering what he mistrusted was a shrewd twinkle of the frosty eye, 'his youth is a more appropriate expression. Now, Mrs. Pipchin, instead of being behind his peers, my son ought to be before them; far before them. There is an eminence ready for him to mount upon. There is nothing of chance or doubt in the course before my son. His way in life was clear and prepared, and marked out before he existed. The education of such a young gentleman must not be delayed. It must not be left imperfect. It must be very steadily and seriously undertaken, Mrs. Pipchin.'

'Well, sir,' said Mrs. Pipchin, 'I can say nothing to the contrary.'

'I was quite sure, Mrs. Pipchin,' returned Mr. Dombey, approvingly, 'that a person of your good sense could not, and would not.'

'There is a great deal of nonsense—and worse—talked about young people not being pressed too hard at first, and being tempted on, and all the rest of it, sir,' said Mrs. Pipchin, impatiently rubbing her hooked nose. 'It never was thought of in my time, and it has no business to be thought of now. My opinion is "keep 'em at it."'

'My good madam,' returned Mr. Dombey, 'you have not acquired your reputation undeservedly; and I beg you to believe, Mrs. Pipchin, that I am more than satisfied with your excellent system of management, and shall have the greatest pleasure in commending it whenever my poor commendation'—Mr. Dombey's loftiness when he affected to disparage his own importance, passed all bounds—'can be of any service. I have been thinking of Dr. Blimber's, Mrs. Pipchin.'

'My neighbour, sir?' said Mrs. Pipchin. 'I believe the Doctor's is an excellent establishment. I 've heard that it 's very strictly conducted, and there is nothing but learning going on from morning to night.'

'And it 's very expensive,' added Mr. Dombey.

'And it 's very expensive, sir,' returned Mrs. Pipchin, catching at the fact, as if in omitting that, she had omitted one of its leading merits.

'I have had some communication with the Doctor, Mrs. Pipchin,' said Mr. Dombey, hitching his chair anxiously a little nearer to the fire, 'and he does not consider Paul at all too young for the purpose. He mentioned several instances of boys in Greek at about the same age. If I have any little uneasiness in my own mind, Mrs. Pipchin, on the subject of this change, it is not on that head. My son not having known a mother has gradually concentrated much—too much—of his childish affection on his sister. Whether their separation—' Mr. Dombey said no more, but sat silent.

'Hoity-toity!' exclaimed Mrs. Pipchin, shaking out

her black bombazeen skirts, and plucking up all the ogress within her. 'If she don't like it, Mr. Dombey, she must be taught to lump it.' The good lady apologised immediately afterwards for using so common a figure of speech, but said (and truly) that that was the way *she* reasoned with 'em.

Mr. Dombey waited until Mrs. Pipchin had done bridling and shaking her head, and frowning down a legion of Bitherstones and Pankeys; and then said quietly, but correctively, 'He, my good madam, he.'

Mrs. Pipchin's system would have applied very much the same mode of cure to any uneasiness on the part of Paul, too; but as the hard grey eye was sharp enough to see that the recipe, however Mr. Dombey might admit its efficacy in the case of the daughter, was not a sovereign remedy for the son, she argued the point; and contended that change, and new society, and the different form of life he would lead at Dr. Blimber's, and the studies he would have to master, would very soon prove sufficient alienations. As this chimed in with Mr. Dombey's own hope and belief, it gave that gentleman a still higher opinion of Mrs. Pipchin's understanding: and as Mrs. Pipchin, at the same time, bewailed the loss of her dear little friend (which was not an overwhelming shock to her, as she had long expected it, and had not looked, in the beginning, for his remaining with her longer than three months), he formed an equally good opinion of Mrs. Pipchin's disinterestedness. It was plain that he had given the subject anxious consideration, for he had formed a plan, which he announced to the ogress, of sending Paul to the Doctor's as a weekly boarder for the first half-year, during which time Florence would remain at the Castle, that she might receive her brother there, on Saturdays. This would wean him by degrees, Mr. Dombey said; prob-

DR. BLIMBER'S YOUNG GENTLEMEN ENJOYING THEMSELVES.

ably with a recollection of his not having been weaned by degrees on a former occasion.

Mr. Dombey finished the interview by expressing his hope that Mrs. Pipchin would still remain in office as general superintendent and overseer of his son, pending his studies at Brighton; and having kissed Paul, and shaken hands with Florence, and beheld Master Bitherstone in his collar of state, and made Miss Pankey cry by patting her on the head (in which region she was uncommonly tender, on account of a habit Mrs. Pipchin had of sounding it with her knuckles, like a cask), he withdrew to his hotel and dinner: resolved that Paul, now that he was getting so old and well, should begin a vigorous course of education forthwith, to qualify him for the position in which he was to shine; and that Doctor Blimber should take him in hand immediately.

Whenever a young gentleman was taken in hand by Doctor Blimber, he might consider himself sure of a pretty tight squeeze. The Doctor only undertook the charge of ten young gentlemen, but he had, always ready, a supply of learning for a hundred, on the lowest estimate; and it was at once the business and delight of his life to gorge the unhappy ten with it.

In fact, Doctor Blimber's establishment was a great hot-house, in which there was a forcing apparatus incessantly at work. All the boys blew before their time. Mental green-peas were produced at Christmas, and intellectual asparagus all the year round. Mathematical gooseberries (very sour ones too) were common at untimely seasons, and from mere sprouts of bushes, under Doctor Blimber's cultivation. Every description of Greek and Latin vegetable was got off the driest twigs of boys, under the frostiest circumstances. Nature was of no consequence at all.

No matter what a young gentleman was intended to bear, Doctor Blimber made him bear to pattern, somehow or other.

This was all very pleasant and ingenious, but the system of forcing was attended with its usual disadvantages. There was not the right taste about the premature productions, and they didn't keep well. Moreover, one young gentleman, with a swollen nose and an excessively large head (the oldest of the ten who had 'gone through' everything), suddenly left off blowing one day, and remained in the establishment a mere stalk. And people did say that the Doctor had rather overdone it with young Toots, and that when he began to have whiskers he left off having brains.

There young Toots was, at any rate; possessed of the gruffest of voices and the shrillest of minds; sticking ornamental pins into his shirt, and keeping a ring in his waistcoat pocket to put on his little finger by stealth, when the pupils went out walking; constantly falling in love by sight with nurserymaids, who had no idea of his existence; and looking at the gas-lighted world over the little iron bars in the left-hand corner window of the front three pairs of stairs, after bed-time, like a greatly overgrown cherub who had sat up aloft much too long.

The Doctor was a portly gentleman in a suit of black, with strings at his knees, and stockings below them. He had a bald head, highly polished; a deep voice; and a chin so very double, that it was a wonder how he ever managed to shave into the creases. He had likewise a pair of little eyes that were always half shut up, and a mouth that was always half expanded into a grin, as if he had, that moment, posed a boy, and were waiting to convict him from his own lips. Insomuch that when the Doctor put his right hand into the breast of his coat; and with his other hand behind him, and a scarcely perceptible wag of his head, made the commonest observation to a nervous stranger, it was like a sentiment from the sphynx, and settled his business.

The Doctor's was a mighty fine house, fronting the sea. Not a joyful style of house within, but quite the contrary. Sad-coloured curtains, whose proportions were spare and lean, hid themselves despondently behind the windows. The tables and chairs were put away in rows, like figures in a sum: fires were so rarely lighted in the rooms of ceremony, that they felt like wells, and a visitor represented the bucket; the dining-room seemed the last place in the world where any eating or drinking was likely to occur; there was no sound through all the house but the ticking of a great clock in the hall, which made itself audible in the very garrets: and sometimes a dull crying of young gentlemen at their lessons, like the murmurings of an assemblage of melancholy pigeons.

Miss Blimber, too, although a slim and graceful maid, did no soft violence to the gravity of the house. There was no light nonsense about Miss Blimber. She kept her hair short and crisp, and wore spectacles. She was dry and sandy with working in the graves of deceased languages. None of your live languages for Miss Blimber. They must be dead—stone dead —and then Miss Blimber dug them up like a ghoul.

Mrs. Blimber, her mamma, was not learned herself, but she pretended to be, and that did quite as well. She said at evening parties, that if she could have known Cicero, she thought she could have died contented. It was the steady joy of her life to see the Doctor's young gentlemen go out walking, unlike all other young gentlemen, in the largest possible shirt-collars, and the stiffest possible cravats. It was so classical, she said.

As to Mr. Feeder, B.A., Dr. Blimber's assistant, he was a kind of human barrel-organ, with a little list of tunes at which he was continually working, over and over again, without any variation. He might have been fitted up with a change of barrels, perhaps, in early life, if his destiny had been favourable; but it had not been; and he had only one, with which, in a monotonous round, it was his occupation to bewilder the young ideas of Dr. Blimber's young gentlemen. The young gentlemen were prematurely full of carking anxieties. They knew no rest from the pursuit of stony-hearted verbs, savage noun-substantives, inflexible syntactic passages, and ghosts of exercises that appeared to them in their dreams. Under the forcing system, a young gentleman usually took leave of his spirits in three weeks. He had all the cares of the world on his head in three months. He conceived bitter sentiments against his parents or guardians in four; he was an old misanthrope, in five; envied Curtius that blessed refuge in the earth, in six; and at the end of the first twelvemonth had arrived at the conclusion, from which he never afterwards departed, that all the fancies of the poets, and lessons of the sages, were a mere collection of words and grammar, and had no other meaning in the world.

'But he went on blow, blow, blowing, in the Doctor's hothouse, all the time; and the Doctor's glory and reputation were great, when he took his wintry growth home to his relations and friends.

Upon the Doctor's door-steps one day, Paul stood with a fluttering heart, and with his small right hand in his father's. His other hand was locked in that of Florence. How tight the tiny pressure of that one; and how loose and cold the other!

Mrs. Pipchin hovered behind the victim, with her sable plumage and her hooked beak, like a bird of ill-omen. She was out of breath—for Mr. Dombey, full of great thoughts, had walked fast—and she croaked hoarsely as she waited for the opening of the door.

'Now, Paul,' said Mr. Dombey, exultingly. 'This is the way indeed to be Dombey and Son, and have money. You are almost a man already.'

'Almost,' returned the child.

Even his childish agitation could not master the sly and quaint yet touching look, with which he accompanied the reply.

It brought a vague expression of dissatisfaction into Mr. Dombey's face; but the door being opened, it was quickly gone.

'Doctor Blimber is at home I believe?' said Mr. Dombey.

The man said yes; and as they passed in, looked at Paul as if he were a little mouse, and the house were a trap. He was a weak-eyed young man, with the first faint streaks or early dawn of a grin on his countenance. It was mere imbecility; but Mrs. Pipchin took it into her head that it was impudence, and made a snap at him directly.

'How dare you laugh behind the gentleman's back?' said Mrs. Pipchin. 'And what do you take me for?'

'I ain't a laughing at nobody, and I 'm sure I don't take you for nothing, ma'am,' returned the young man, in consternation.

'A pack of idle dogs!' said Mrs. Pipchin, 'only fit to be turnspits. Go and tell your master that Mr. Dombey 's here, or it 'll be worse for you!'

The weak-eyed young man went, very meekly, to discharge himself of this commission; and soon came back to invite them to the Doctor's study.

'You 're laughing again, sir,' said Mrs. Pipchin, when it came to her turn, bringing up the rear, to pass him in the hall.

'I *ain't*,' returned the young man, grievously oppressed. 'I never see such a thing as this!'

'What is the matter, Mrs. Pipchin?' said Mr. Dombey, looking round. 'Softly! Pray!'

Mrs. Pipchin, in her deference, merely muttered at the young man as she passed on, and said, 'Oh! he was a precious fellow'—leaving the young man, who was all meekness and incapacity, affected even to tears by the incident. But Mrs. Pipchin had a way of falling foul of all meek people; and her friends said who could wonder at it, after the Peruvian mines!

The Doctor was sitting in his portentous study, with a globe at each knee, books all round him, Homer over the door, and Minerva on the mantelshelf. 'And how do you, sir?' he said to Mr. Dombey; 'and how is my little friend?' Grave as an organ was the Doctor's speech; and when he ceased, the great clock in the hall seemed (to Paul at least) to take him up, and to go on saying, 'how, is, my, lit, tle, friend? how, is, my, lit, tle, friend?' over and over and over again.

The little friend being something too small to be seen at all from where the Doctor sat, over the books on the table, the Doctor made several futile attempts to get a view of him round the legs; which Mr. Dombey perceiving, relieved the Doctor from his embarrassment by taking Paul up in his arms, and sitting him on another little table, over against the Doctor, in the middle of the room.

'Ha!' said the Doctor, leaning back in his chair with his hand in his breast. 'Now I see my little friend. How do you do, my little friend?'

The clock in the hall wouldn't subscribe to this alteration in the form of words, but continued to repeat 'how, is, my, lit, tle, friend? how, is, my, lit, tle, friend?'

'Very well, I thank you, sir,' returned Paul, answering the clock quite as much as the Doctor.

'Ha!' said Doctor Blimber. 'Shall we make a man of him?'

'Do you hear, Paul?' added Mr. Dombey; Paul being silent.

'Shall we make a man of him?' repeated the Doctor.

'I had rather be a child,' replied Paul.

'Indeed!' said the Doctor. 'Why?'

The child sat on the table looking at him, with a curious expression of suppressed emotion in his face, and beating one hand proudly on his knee as if he had the rising tears beneath it, and crushed them. But his other hand strayed a little way the while, a little farther—farther from him yet—until it lighted on the neck of Florence. 'This is why,' it seemed to say, and then the steady look was broken up and gone; the working lip was loosened; and the tears came streaming forth.

'Mrs. Pipchin,' said his father, in a querulous manner, 'I am really very sorry to see this.'

'Come away from him, do, Miss Dombey,' quoth the matron.

'Never mind,' said the Doctor, blandly nodding his head, to keep Mrs. Pipchin back, 'Ne-ver mind; we shall substitute new cares and new impressions, Mr. Dombey, very shortly. You would still wish my little friend to acquire—'

'Everything, if you please, Doctor,' returned Mr. Dombey, firmly.

'Yes,' said the Doctor, who, with his half-shut eyes, and his usual smile, seemed to survey Paul with the sort of interest that might attach to some choice little animal he was going to stuff. 'Yes, exactly. Ha! We shall impart a great variety of information to our little friend, and bring him quickly forward, I dare say. I dare say. Quite a virgin soil, I believe you said, Mr. Dombey?'

'Except some ordinary preparation at home, and from this lady,' replied Mr. Dombey, introducing Mrs. Pipchin, who instantly communicated a rigidity to her whole muscular system, and snorted defiance beforehand, in case the Doctor should disparage her; 'except so far, Paul has, as yet, applied himself to no studies at all.'

Doctor Blimber inclined his head, in gentle tolerance of such insignificant poaching as Mrs. Pipchin's, and said he was glad to hear it. It was much more satisfactory, he observed, rubbing his hands, to begin at the foundation. And again he leered at Paul, as if he would have liked to tackle him with the Greek alphabet on the spot.

'That circumstance, indeed, Doctor Blimber,' pursued Mr. Dombey, glancing at his little son, 'and the interview I have already had the pleasure of holding with you, renders any further explanation, and consequently, any further intrusion on your valuable time, so unnecessary that—'

'Now, Miss Dombey!' said the acid Pipchin.

'Permit me,' said the Doctor, 'one moment. Allow me to present Mrs. Blimber and my daughter, who will be associated with the domestic life of our young pilgrim to Parnassus. Mrs. Blimber,' for the lady, who had perhaps been in waiting, opportunely entered, followed by her daughter, that fair sexton in spectacles, 'Mr. Dombey. My daughter Cornelia, Mr. Dombey. Mr. Dombey, my love,' pursued the Doctor, turning to his wife, 'is so confiding as to—do you see our little friend?'

Mrs. Blimber, in an excess of politeness, of which Mr. Dombey was the object, apparently did not, for she was backing against the little friend, and very much endangering his position on the table. But, on this hint, she turned to admire his classical and intellectual lineaments, and turning again to Mr. Dombey, said, with a sigh, that she envied his dear son.

'Like a bee, sir,' said Mrs. Blimber, with uplifted eyes, 'about to plunge into a garden of the choicest flowers, and sip the sweets for the first time. Virgil, Horace, Ovid, Terence, Plautus, Cicero. What a world of honey have we here. It may appear remarkable, Mr. Dombey, in one who is a wife—the wife of such a husband—'

'Hush, hush,' said Doctor Blimber. 'Fie for shame.'

'Mr. Dombey will forgive the partiality of a wife,' said Mrs. Blimber, with an engaging smile.

Mr. Dombey answered 'Not at all': applying those words, it is to be presumed, to the partiality, and not to the forgiveness.

'—And it may seem remarkable in one who is a mother also,' resumed Mrs. Blimber.

'And such a mother,' observed Mr. Dombey, bowing with some confused idea of being complimentary to Cornelia.

'But really,' pursued Mrs. Blimber, 'I think if I could have known Cicero, and been his friend, and talked with him in his retirement at Tusculum (beautiful Tusculum!), I could have died contented.'

A learned enthusiasm is so very contagious, that Mr.

Dombey half believed this was exactly his case; and even Mrs. Pipchin, who was not, as we have seen, of an accommodating disposition generally, gave utterance to a little sound between a groan and a sigh, as if she would have said that nobody but Cicero could have proved a lasting consolation under that failure of the Peruvian mines, but that he indeed would have been a very Davy-lamp of refuge.

Cornelia looked at Mr. Dombey through her spectacles, as if she would have liked to crack a few quotations with him from the authority in question. But this design, if she entertained it, was frustrated by a knock at the room-door.

'Who is that?' said the Doctor. 'Oh! Come in, Toots; come in. Mr. Dombey, sir.' Toots bowed. 'Quite a coincidence!' said Dr. Blimber. 'Here we have the beginning and the end. Alpha and Omega. Our head boy, Mr. Dombey.'

The Doctor might have called him their head and shoulders boy, for he was at least that much taller than any of the rest. He blushed very much at finding himself among strangers, and chuckled aloud.

'An addition to our little portico, Toots,' said the Doctor. 'Mr. Dombey's son.'

Young Toots blushed again: and finding, from a solemn silence which prevailed, that he was expected to say something, said to Paul, 'How are you?' in a voice so deep, and a manner so sheepish, that if a lamb had roared it couldn't have been more surprising.

'Ask Mr. Feeder, if you please, Toots,' said the Doctor, 'to prepare a few introductory volumes for Mr. Dombey's son, and to allot him a convenient seat for study. My dear, I believe Mr. Dombey has not seen the dormitories.'

'If Mr. Dombey will walk upstairs,' said Mrs. Blimber, 'I shall be more than proud to show him the dominions of the drowsy god.'

With that, Mrs. Blimber, who was a lady of great suavity, and a wiry figure, and who wore a cap composed of sky-blue materials, proceeded upstairs with Mr. Dombey and Cornelia; Mrs. Pipchin following, and looking out sharp for her enemy the footman.

While they were gone, Paul sat upon the table, holding Florence by the hand, and glancing timidly from the Doctor round and round the room, while the Doctor, leaning back in his chair, with his hand in his breast, as usual, held a book from him at arm's-length, and read. There was something very awful in this manner of reading. It was such a determined, unimpassioned, inflexible, cold-blooded way of going to work. It left the Doctor's countenance exposed to view; and when the Doctor smiled auspiciously at his author, or knit his brows, or shook his head and made wry faces at him, as much as to say, 'Don't tell me, sir; I know better,' it was terrific.

Toots, too, had no business to be outside the door, ostentatiously examining the wheels in his watch, and counting his half-crowns. But that didn't last long; for Doctor Blimber, happening to change the position of his tight plump legs, as if he were going to get up, Toots swiftly vanished, and appeared no more.

Mr. Dombey and his conductress were soon heard coming downstairs again, talking all the way; and presently they re-entered the Doctor's study.

'I hope, Mr. Dombey,' said the Doctor, laying down his book, 'that the arrangements meet your approval.'

'They are excellent, sir,' said Mr. Dombey.

'Very fair, indeed,' said Mrs. Pipchin, in a low voice; never disposed to give too much encouragement.

'Mrs. Pipchin,' said Mr. Dombey, wheeling round, 'will, with your permission, Doctor and Mrs. Blimber, visit Paul now and then.'

'Whenever Mrs. Pipchin pleases,' observed the Doctor.

'Always happy to see her,' said Mrs. Blimber.

'I think,' said Mr. Dombey, 'I have given all the trouble I need, and may take my leave. Paul, my child,' he went close to him, as he sat upon the table. 'Good-bye.'

'Good-bye, papa.'

The limp and careless little hand that Mr. Dombey took in his, was singularly out of keeping with the wistful face. But he had no part in its sorrowful expression. It was not addressed to him. No, no. To Florence—all to Florence.

If Mr. Dombey in his insolence of wealth, had ever made an enemy, hard to appease and cruelly vindictive in his hate, even such an enemy might have received the pang that wrung his proud heart then, as compensation for his injury.

He bent down over his boy, and kissed him. If his sight were dimmed as he did so, by something that for a moment blurred the little face, and made it indistinct to him, his mental vision may have been, for that short time, the clearer perhaps.

'I shall see you soon, Paul. You are free on Saturdays and Sundays, you know.'

'Yes, papa,' returned Paul: looking at his sister. 'On Saturdays and Sundays.'

'And you 'll try and learn a great deal here, and be a clever man,' said Mr. Dombey; 'won't you?'

'I 'll try,' returned the child wearily.

'And you 'll soon be grown up now!' said Mr. Dombey.

'Oh! very soon!' replied the child. Once more the old, old look, passed rapidly across his features like a strange light. It fell on Mrs. Pipchin, and extinguished itself in her black dress. That excellent ogress stepped forward to take leave and to bear off Florence, which she had long been thirsting to do. The move on her part roused Mr. Dombey, whose eyes were fixed on Paul. After patting him on the head, and pressing his small hand again, he took leave of Doctor Blimber, Mrs. Blimber, and Miss Blimber, with his usual polite frigidity, and walked out of the study.

Despite his entreaty that they would not think of stirring, Doctor Blimber, Mrs. Blimber, and Miss Blimber all pressed forward to attend him to the hall; and thus Mrs. Pipchin got into a state of entanglement with Miss Blimber and the Doctor, and was crowded out of the study before she could clutch Florence. To which happy accident Paul stood afterwards indebted for the dear remembrance, that Florence ran back to throw her arms round his neck, and that hers was the last face in the doorway: turned towards him with a smile of encouragement, the brighter for the tears through which it beamed.

It made his childish bosom heave and swell when it was gone; and sent the globes, the books, blind Homer and Minerva, swimming round the room. But they stopped, all of a sudden; and then he heard the loud clock in the hall still gravely inquiring 'how, is, my, lit, tle, friend? how, is, my, lit, tle, friend?' as it had done before.

He sat, with folded hands, upon his pedestal, silently listening. But he might have answered 'weary, weary! very lonely, very sad!' And there, with an aching void in his young heart, and all outside so cold, and bare, and strange, Paul sat as if he had taken life unfurnished, and the upholsterer were never coming.

## CHAPTER XII

### PAUL'S EDUCATION

After the lapse of some minutes, which appeared an immense time to little Paul Dombey on the table, Doctor Blimber came back. The Doctor's walk was stately, and calculated to impress the juvenile mind with solemn feelings. It was a sort of march; but when the Doctor put out his right foot, he gravely turned upon his axis, with a semicircular sweep towards the left; and when he put out his left foot, he turned in the same manner towards the right. So that he seemed, at every stride he took, to look about him as though he were saying, 'Can anybody have the goodness to indicate any subject, in any direction, on which I am uninformed? I rather think not.'

Mrs. Blimber and Miss Blimber came back in the Doctor's company; and the Doctor, lifting his new pupil off the table, delivered him over to Miss Blimber.

'Cornelia,' said the Doctor, 'Dombey will be your charge at first. Bring him on, Cornelia, bring him on.'

Miss Blimber received her young ward from the Doctor's hands; and Paul, feeling that the spectacles were surveying him, cast down his eyes.

'How old are you, Dombey?' said Miss Blimber.

'Six,' answered Paul, wondering, as he stole a glance at the young lady, why her hair didn't grow long like Florence's, and why she was like a boy.

'How much do you know of your Latin Grammar, Dombey?' said Miss Blimber.

'None of it,' answered Paul. Feeling that the answer was a shock to Miss Blimber's sensibility, he looked up at the three faces that were looking down at him, and said—

'I haven't been well. I have been a weak child. I couldn't learn a Latin Grammar when I was out, every day, with old Glubb. I wish you 'd tell old Glubb to come and see me, if you please.'

'What a dreadful low name!' said Mrs. Blimber. 'Unclassical to a degree! Who is the monster, child?'

'What monster?' inquired Paul.

'Glubb,' said Mrs. Blimber, with a great disrelish.

'He 's no more a monster than you are,' returned Paul.

'What!' cried the Doctor, in a terrible voice. 'Aye, aye, aye? Aha! What 's that?'

Paul was dreadfully frightened; but still he made a stand for the absent Glubb, though he did it trembling.

'He 's a very nice old man, ma'am,' he said. 'He used to draw my couch. He knows all about the deep sea, and the fish that are in it, and the great monsters that come and lie on rocks in the sun, and dive into the water again when they 're startled, blowing and splashing so, that they can be heard for miles. There are some creatures,' said Paul, warming with his subject, 'I don't know how many yards long, and I forget their names, but Florence knows, that pretend to be in distress; and when a man goes near them, out of compassion, they open their great jaws, and attack him. But all he has got to do,' said Paul, boldly tendering this information to the very Doctor himself, 'is to keep on turning as he runs away, and then, as they turn slowly, because they are so long, and can't bend, he 's sure to beat them. And though old Glubb don't know why the sea should make me think of my mamma that 's dead, or what it is that it is always saying—always saying! he knows a great deal about it. And I wish,' the child concluded, with a sudden falling of his countenance, and failing in his animation, as he looked like one forlorn, upon the three strange faces, 'that you 'd let old Glubb come here to see me, for I know him very well; and he knows me.'

'Ha!' said the Doctor, shaking his head: 'this is bad, but study will do much.'

Mrs. Blimber opined, with something like a shiver, that he was an unaccountable child; and, allowing for the difference of visage, looked at him pretty much as Mrs. Pipchin had been used to do.

'Take him round the house, Cornelia,' said the Doctor, 'and familiarise him with his new sphere. Go with that young lady, Dombey.'

Dombey obeyed; giving his hand to the abstruse Cornelia, and looking at her sideways, with timid curiosity, as they went away together. For her spectacles, by reason of the glistening of the glasses, made her so mysterious, that he didn't know where she was looking, and was not indeed quite sure that she had any eyes at all behind them.

Cornelia took him first to the school-room, which was situated at the back of the hall, and was approached through two baize doors, which deadened and muffled the young gentlemen's voices. Here, there were eight young gentlemen in various stages of mental prostration, all very hard at work, and very grave indeed. Toots, as an old hand, had a desk to himself in one corner: and a magnificent man, of immense age, he looked, in Paul's young eyes, behind it.

Mr. Feeder, B.A., who sat at another little desk, had his Virgil stop on, and was slowly grinding that tune to four young gentlemen. Of the remaining four, two, who grasped their foreheads convulsively, were engaged in solving mathematical problems; one with his face like a dirty window, from much crying, was endeavouring to flounder through a hopeless number of lines before dinner; and one sat looking at his task in stony stupefaction and despair—which it seemed had been his condition ever since breakfast-time.

The appearance of a new boy did not create the sensation that might have been expected. Mr. Feeder, B.A. (who was in the habit of shaving his head for coolness, and had nothing but little bristles on it), gave him a bony hand, and told him he was glad to see him—which Paul would have been very glad to have told *him,* if he could have done so with the least sincerity. Then Paul, instructed by Cornelia, shook hands with the four young gentlemen at Mr. Feeder's desk; then with the two young gentlemen at work on the problems, who were very feverish; then with the young gentleman at work against time, who was very inky; and lastly with the young gentleman in a state of stupefaction, who was flabby and quite cold.

Paul having been already introduced to Toots, that pupil merely chuckled and breathed hard, as his custom was, and pursued the occupation in which he was engaged. It was not a severe one; for on account of his having 'gone through' so much (in more senses than one), and also of his having, as before hinted, left off blowing in his prime, Toots now had licence to pursue his own course of study: which was chiefly to write long letters to himself from persons of distinction, addressed 'P. Toots, Esquire, Brighton, Sussex,' and to preserve them in his desk with great care.

These ceremonies passed, Cornelia led Paul upstairs to the top of the house; which was rather a slow journey, on account of Paul being obliged to land both feet on every stair, before he mounted another. But they reached their journey's end at last; and there, in a front-room, looking over the wild sea, Cornelia showed him a nice little bed with white hangings, close to the window, on which there was already beautifully written on a card in round text—down-strokes very thick, and up-strokes very fine—DOMBEY; while two other little bedsteads in the same room were announced, through like means, as respectively appertaining unto BRIGGS and TOZER.

Just as they got downstairs again into the hall, Paul saw the weak-eyed young man who had given that mortal offence to Mrs. Pipchin, suddenly seize a very large drumstick, and fly at a gong that was hanging up, as if he had gone mad, or wanted vengeance. Instead of receiving warning, however, or being instantly taken into custody, the young man left off unchecked, after having made a dreadful noise. Then Cornelia Blimber said to Dombey that dinner would be ready in a quarter of an hour, and perhaps he had better go into the school-room among his 'friends.'

So Dombey, deferentially passing the great clock which was still as anxious as ever to know how he found himself, opened the school-room door a very little way, and strayed in like a lost boy: shutting it after him with some difficulty. His friends were all dispersed about the room except the stony friend, who remained immovable. Mr. Feeder was stretching himself in his grey gown, as if, regardless of expense, he were resolved to pull the sleeves off.

'Heigh ho hum!' cried Mr. Feeder, shaking himself like a cart-horse, 'oh dear me, dear me! Ya-a-a-ah!'

Paul was quite alarmed by Mr. Feeder's yawning; it was done on such a great scale, and he was so terribly in earnest. All the boys too (Toots excepted) seemed knocked up, and were getting ready for dinner—some newly tying their neckcloths, which were very stiff indeed; and others washing their hands or brushing their hair, in an adjoining antechamber—as if they didn't think they should enjoy it at all.

Young Toots, who was ready beforehand, and had therefore nothing to do, and had leisure to bestow upon Paul, said, with heavy good-nature—

'Sit down, Dombey.'

'Thank you, sir,' said Paul.

His endeavouring to hoist himself on to a very high window-seat, and his slipping down again, appeared to prepare Toots's mind for the reception of a discovery.

'You 're a very small chap,' said Mr. Toots.

'Yes, sir, I 'm small,' returned Paul. 'Thank you, sir.'

For Toots had lifted him into the seat, and done it kindly too.

'Who 's your tailor?' inquired Toots, after looking at him for some moments.

'It 's a woman that has made my clothes as yet,' said Paul. 'My sister's dressmaker.'

'My tailor 's Burgess and Co.,' said Toots. 'Fash-'nable. But very dear.'

Paul had wit enough to shake his head, as if he would have said it was easy to see *that;* and indeed he thought so.

'Your father 's regularly rich, ain't he?' inquired Mr. Toots.

'Yes, sir,' said Paul. 'He 's Dombey and Son.'

'And which?' demanded Toots.

'And Son, sir,' replied Paul.

Mr. Toots made one or two attempts, in a low voice, to fix the firm in his mind; but not quite succeeding, said he would get Paul to mention the name again to-morrow morning, as it was rather important. And indeed he purposed nothing less than writing himself a private and confidential letter from Dombey and Son immediately.

By this time the other pupils (always excepting the stony boy) gathered round. They were polite, but pale; and spoke low; and they were so depressed in their spirits, that in comparison with the general tone of that company, Master Bitherstone was a perfect Miller, or Complete Jest Book. And yet he had a sense of injury upon him, too, had Bitherstone.

'You sleep in my room, don't you?' asked a solemn young gentleman, whose shirt-collar curled up the lobes of his ears.

'Master Briggs?' inquired Paul.

'Tozer,' said the young gentleman.

Paul answered yes; and Tozer pointing out the stony pupil, said that was Briggs. Paul had already felt certain that it must be either Briggs or Tozer, though he didn't know why.

'Is yours a strong constitution?' inquired Tozer.

Paul said he thought not. Tozer replied that *he* thought not also judging from Paul's looks, and that it was a pity, for it need be. He then asked Paul if he were going to begin with Cornelia; and on Paul saying 'yes,' all the young gentlemen (Briggs excepted) gave a low groan.

It was drowned in the tintinnabulation of the gong, which sounding again with great fury, there was a general move towards the dining-room; still excepting Briggs the stony boy, who remained where he was, and as he was; and on its way to whom Paul presently encountered a round of bread, genteelly served on a plate and napkin, and with a silver fork lying crosswise on the top of it.

Doctor Blimber was already in his place in the

dining-room, at the top of the table, with Miss Blimber and Mrs. Blimber on either side of him. Mr. Feeder in a black coat was at the bottom. Paul's chair was next to Miss Blimber; but it being found, when he sat in it, that his eyebrows were not much above the level of the table-cloth, some books were brought in from the doctor's study, on which he was elevated, and on which he always sat from that time—carrying them in and out himself on after occasions, like a little elephant and castle.

Grace having been said by the Doctor, dinner began. There was some nice soup; also roast meat, boiled meat, vegetables, pie, and cheese. Every young gentleman had a massive silver fork, and a napkin; and all the arrangements were stately and handsome. In particular, there was a butler in a blue coat and bright buttons, who gave quite a winey flavour to the table beer; he poured it out so superbly.

Nobody spoke, unless spoken to, except Doctor Blimber, Mrs. Blimber, and Miss Blimber, who conversed occasionally. Whenever a young gentleman was not actually engaged with his knife and fork or spoon, his eye, with an irresistible attraction, sought the eye of Doctor Blimber, Mrs. Blimber, or Miss Blimber, and modestly rested there. Toots appeared to be the only exception to this rule. He sat next Mr. Feeder on Paul's side of the table, and frequently looked behind and before the intervening boys to catch a glimpse of Paul.

Only once during dinner was there any conversation that included the young gentlemen. It happened at the epoch of the cheese, when the Doctor, having taken a glass of port wine, and hemmed twice or thrice, said—

'It is remarkable, Mr. Feeder, that the Romans—'

At the mention of this terrible people, their implacable enemies, every young gentleman fastened his gaze upon the Doctor, with an assumption of the deepest interest. One of the number who happened to be drinking, and who caught the Doctor's eye glaring at him through the side of his tumbler, left off so hastily that he was convulsed for some moments, and in the sequel ruined Doctor Blimber's point.

'It is remarkable, Mr. Feeder,' said the Doctor, beginning again slowly, 'that the Romans, in those gorgeous and profuse entertainments of which we read in the days of the emperors, when luxury had attained a height unknown before or since, and when whole provinces were ravaged to supply the splendid means of one imperial banquet—'

Here the offender, who had been swelling and straining, and waiting in vain for a full stop, broke out violently.

'Johnson,' said Mr. Feeder, in a low reproachful voice, 'take some water.'

The Doctor, looking very stern, made a pause until the water was brought, and then resumed—

'And when, Mr. Feeder—'

But Mr. Feeder, who saw that Johnson must break out again, and who knew that the Doctor would never come to a period before the young gentlemen until he had finished all he meant to say, couldn't keep his eye off Johnson; and thus was caught in the fact of not looking at the Doctor, who consequently stopped.

'I beg your pardon, sir,' said Mr. Feeder, reddening. 'I beg your pardon, Doctor Blimber.'

'And when,' said the Doctor, raising his voice, 'when, sir, as we read, and have no reason to doubt—incredible as it may appear to the vulgar of our time—the brother of Vitellius prepared for him a feast, in which were served, of fish, two thousand dishes—'

'Take some water, Johnson—dishes, sir,' said Mr. Feeder.

'Of various sorts of fowl, five thousand dishes.'

'Or try a crust of bread,' said Mr. Feeder.

'And one dish,' pursued Doctor Blimber, raising his voice still higher as he looked all round the table, 'called, from its enormous dimensions, the Shield of Minerva, and made among other costly ingredients, of the brains of pheasants—'

'Ow, ow, ow!' (from Johnson).

'Woodcocks—'

'Ow, ow, ow!'

'The sounds of the fish called scari—'

'You 'll burst some vessel in your head,' said Mr. Feeder. 'You had better let it come.'

'And the spawn of the lamprey, brought from the Carpathian Sea,' pursued the Doctor, in his severest voice; 'when we read of costly entertainments such as these, and still remember, that we have a Titus—'

'What would be your mother's feelings if you died of apoplexy!' said Mr. Feeder.

'A Domitian—'

'And you 're blue, you know,' said Mr. Feeder.

'A Nero, a Tiberius, a Caligula, a Heliogabalus, and many more,' pursued the Doctor; 'it is, Mr. Feeder—if you are doing me the honour to attend—remarkable: VERY remarkable, sir—'

But Johnson, unable to suppress it any longer, burst at that moment into such an overwhelming fit of coughing, that although both his immediate neighbours thumped him on the back, and Mr. Feeder himself held a glass of water to his lips, and the butler walked him up and down several times between his own chair and the sideboard, like a sentry, it was full five minutes before he was moderately composed, and then there was a profound silence.

'Gentlemen,' said Doctor Blimber, 'rise for grace! Cornelia, lift Dombey down'—nothing of whom but his scalp was accordingly seen above the table-cloth. 'Johnson will repeat to me to-morrow morning before breakfast, without book, and from the Greek Testament, the first chapter of the Epistle of Saint Paul to the Ephesians. We will resume our studies, Mr. Feeder, in half an hour.'

The young gentlemen bowed and withdrew. Mr. Feeder did likewise. During the half-hour, the young gentlemen, broken into pairs, loitered arm-in-arm up and down a small piece of ground behind the house, or endeavoured to kindle a spark of animation in the breast of Briggs. But nothing happened so vulgar as play. Punctually at the appointed time, the gong sounded, and the studies, under the joint auspices of Doctor Blimber and Mr. Feeder, were resumed.

As the Olympic game of lounging up and down had been cut shorter than usual that day, on Johnson's account, they all went out for a walk before tea. Even Briggs (though he hadn't begun yet) partook of this dissipation; in the enjoyment of which he looked over the cliff two or three times darkly. Doctor Blimber accompanied them; and Paul had the honour of being taken in tow by the doctor himself: a distinguished state of things, in which he looked very little and feeble.

Tea was served in a style no less polite than the dinner; and after tea, the young gentlemen rising and bowing as before, withdrew to fetch up the unfinished tasks of that day, or to get up the already looming tasks of to-morrow. In the meantime Mr. Feeder withdrew to his own room; and Paul sat in a corner wondering whether Florence was thinking of him, and what they were all about at Mrs. Pipchin's.

Mr. Toots, who had been detained by an important letter from the Duke of Wellington, found Paul out after a time; and having looked at him for a long while, as before, inquired if he was fond of waistcoats.

Paul said 'Yes, sir.'

'So am I,' said Toots.

No word more spake Toots that night; but he stood looking at Paul as if he liked him; and as there was company in that, and Paul was not inclined to talk, it answered his purpose better than conversation.

At eight o'clock or so, the gong sounded again for prayers in the dining-room, where the butler afterwards presided over a side-table, on which bread and cheese and beer were spread for such young gentlemen as desired to partake of those refreshments. The ceremonies concluded by the Doctor's saying, 'Gentlemen, we will resume our studies at seven to-morrow'; and then, for the first time, Paul saw Cornelia Blimber's eye, and saw that it was upon him. When the Doctor had said these words, 'Gentlemen, we will resume our studies at seven to-morrow,' the pupils bowed again, and went to bed.

In the confidence of their own room upstairs, Briggs said his head ached ready to split, and that he should wish himself dead if it wasn't for his mother, and a blackbird he had at home. Tozer didn't say much, but he sighed a good deal, and told Paul to look out, for his turn would come to-morrow. After uttering those prophetic words, he undressed himself moodily, and got into bed. Briggs was in his bed too, and Paul in his bed too, before the weak-eyed young man appeared to take away the candle, when he wished them good night and pleasant dreams. But his benevolent wishes were in vain, as far as Briggs and Tozer were concerned; for Paul, who lay awake for a long while, and often woke afterwards, found that Briggs was ridden by his lesson as a nightmare: and that Tozer, whose mind was affected in his sleep by similar causes, in a minor degree, talked unknown tongues, or scraps of Greek and Latin—it was all one to Paul—which, in the silence of night, had an inexpressibly wicked and guilty effect.

Paul had sunk into a sweet sleep, and dreamed that he was walking hand in hand with Florence through beautiful gardens, when they came to a large sunflower which suddenly expanded itself into a gong, and began to sound. Opening his eyes, he found that it was a dark, windy morning, with a drizzling rain: and that the real gong was giving dreadful note of preparation, down in the hall.

So he got up directly, and found Briggs with hardly any eyes, for nightmare and grief had made his face puffy, putting his boots on: while Tozer stood shivering and rubbing his shoulders in a very bad humour. Poor Paul couldn't dress himself easily, not being used to it, and asked them if they would have the goodness to tie some strings for him; but as Briggs merely said 'Bother!' and Tozer, 'Oh, yes!' he went down when he was otherwise ready, to the next story, where he saw a pretty young woman in leather gloves, cleaning a stove. The young woman seemed surprised at his appearance, and asked him where his mother was. When Paul told her she was dead, she took her gloves off, and did what he wanted; and furthermore rubbed his hands to warm them; and gave him a kiss; and told him whenever he wanted anything of that sort—meaning in the dressing way—to ask for 'Melia; which Paul, thanking her very much, said he certainly would. He then proceeded softly on his journey downstairs, towards the room in which the young gentlemen resumed their studies, when, passing by a door that stood ajar, a voice from within cried, 'Is that Dombey?' On Paul replying, 'Yes, ma'am': for he knew the voice to be Miss Blimber's: Miss Blimber said, 'Come in, Dombey.' And in he went.

Miss Blimber presented exactly the appearance she had presented yesterday, except that she wore a shawl. Her little light curls were as crisp as ever, and she had already her spectacles on, which made Paul wonder whether she went to bed in them. She had a cool little sitting-room of her own up there, with some books in it, and no fire. But Miss Blimber was never cold, and never sleepy.

'Now, Dombey,' said Miss Blimber, 'I am going out for a constitutional.'

Paul wondered what that was, and why she didn't send the footman out to get it in such unfavourable weather. But he made no observation on the subject: his attention being devoted to a little pile of new books on which Miss Blimber appeared to have been recently engaged.

'These are yours, Dombey,' said Miss Blimber.

'All of 'em, ma'am?' said Paul.

'Yes,' returned Miss Blimber; 'and Mr. Feeder will look you out some more very soon, if you are as studious as I expect you will be, Dombey.'

'Thank you, ma'am,' said Paul.

'I am going out for a constitutional,' resumed Miss Blimber; 'and while I am gone, that is to say in the interval between this and breakfast, Dombey, I wish you to read over what I have marked in these books, and to tell me if you quite understand what you have got to learn. Don't lose time, Dombey, for you have none to spare, but take them downstairs, and begin directly.'

'Yes, ma'am,' answered Paul.

There were so many of them, that although Paul put one hand under the bottom book and his other hand and his chin on the top book, and hugged them all closely, the middle book slipped out before he reached the door, and then they all tumbled down on the floor. Miss Blimber said, 'Oh, Dombey, Dombey, this is really very careless!' and piled them up afresh for him; and this time, by dint of balancing them with great nicety, Paul got out of the room, and down a few stairs before two of them escaped again. But he held the rest so tight, that he only left one more on the first floor, and one in the passage; and when he had got the main body down into the schoolroom, he set off upstairs again to collect the stragglers. Having at last amassed the whole library, and climbed into his place, he fell to work, encouraged by a remark from Tozer to the effect that he 'was in for it now'; which was the only interruption he received till breakfast-time. At that meal, for which he had no appetite, everything was quite as solemn and genteel as at the others; and when it was finished, he followed Miss Blimber upstairs.

'Now, Dombey,' said Miss Blimber. 'How have you got on with those books?'

They comprised a little English, and a deal of Latin—names of things, declensions of articles and substantives, exercises thereon, and preliminary rules—a trifle of orthography, a glance at ancient history, a wink or two at modern ditto, a few tables, two or three weights and measures, and a little general information. When poor Paul had spelt out number two, he found he had no idea of number one; fragments whereof afterwards obtruded themselves into number three, which slided into number four, which grafted itself on to number two. So that whether twenty Romuluses made a Remus, or hic hæc hoc was troy weight, or a verb always agreed with an ancient Briton, or three times four was Taurus a bull, were open questions with him.

'Oh, Dombey, Dombey!' said Miss Blimber, 'this is very shocking.'

'If you please,' said Paul, 'I think if I might sometimes talk a little to old Glubb, I should be able to do better.'

'Nonsense, Dombey,' said Miss Blimber. 'I couldn't hear of it. This is not the place for Glubbs of any kind. You must take the books down, I suppose, Dombey, one by one, and perfect yourself in the day's instalment of subject A, before you turn at all to subject B. And now take away the top book, if you please, Dombey, and return when you are master of the theme.'

Miss Blimber expressed her opinions on the subject of Paul's uninstructed state with a gloomy delight, as if she had expected this result, and were glad to find that they must be in constant communication. Paul withdrew with the top task, as he was told, and laboured away at it, down below; sometimes remembering every word of it, and sometimes forgetting it all, and everything else besides: until at last he ventured upstairs again to repeat the lesson, when it was nearly all driven out of his head before he began, by Miss Blimber's shutting up the book, and saying, 'Go on, Dombey!' a proceeding so suggestive of the knowledge inside of her, that Paul looked upon the young lady with consternation, as a kind of learned Guy Faux, or artificial Bogle, stuffed full of scholastic straw.

He acquitted himself very well, nevertheless; and Miss Blimber, commending him as giving promise of getting on fast, immediately provided him with subject B; from which he passed to C, and even D before dinner. It was hard work, resuming his studies, soon after dinner; and he felt giddy and confused and drowsy and dull. But all the other young gentlemen had similar sensations, and were obliged to resume their studies too, if there were any comfort in that. It was a wonder that the great clock in the hall, instead of being constant to its first inquiry, never said, 'Gentlemen, we will now resume our studies,' for that phrase was often enough repeated in its neighbourhood. The studies went round like a mighty wheel, and the young gentlemen were always stretched upon it.

After tea there were exercises again, and preparations for next day by candle-light. And in due course there was bed; where, but for that resumption of the studies which took place in dreams, were rest and sweet forgetfulness.

Oh Saturdays! Oh happy Saturdays, when Florence always came at noon, and never would, in any weather, stay away, though Mrs. Pipchin snarled and growled, and worried her bitterly. Those Saturdays were Sabbaths for at least two little Christians among all the Jews, and did the holy Sabbath work of strengthening and knitting up a brother's and a sister's love.

Not even Sunday nights—the heavy Sunday nights, whose shadow darkened the first waking burst of light on Sunday mornings—could mar those precious Saturdays. Whether it was the great sea-shore, where they sat, and strolled together; or whether it was only Mrs. Pipchin's dull back-room, in which she sang to him so softly, with his drowsy head upon her arm; Paul never cared. It was Florence. That was all he thought of. So, on Sunday nights, when the Doctor's dark door stood agape to swallow him up for another week, the time was come for taking leave of Florence; no one else.

Mrs. Wickam had been drafted home to the house in town, and Miss Nipper, now a smart young woman, had come down. To many a single combat with Mrs. Pipchin, did Miss Nipper gallantly devote herself; and if ever Mrs. Pipchin in all her life had found her match, she had found it now. Miss Nipper threw away the scabbard the first morning she arose in Mrs. Pipchin's house. She asked and gave no quarter. She said it must be war, and war it was; and Mrs. Pipchin lived from that time in the midst of surprises, harassings, and defiances, and skirmishing attacks that came bouncing in upon her from the passage, even in unguarded moments of chops, and carried desolation to her very toast.

Miss Nipper had returned one Sunday night with Florence, from walking back with Paul to the Doctor's, when Florence took from her bosom a little piece of paper, on which she had pencilled down some words.

'See here, Susan,' she said: 'These are the names of the little books that Paul brings home to do those long exercises with, when he is so tired. I copied them last night while he was writing.'

'Don't show 'em to me, Miss Floy, if you please,' returned Nipper, 'I 'd as soon see Mrs. Pipchin.'

'I want you to buy them for me, Susan, if you will, to-morrow morning. I have money enough,' said Florence.

'Why, goodness gracious me, Miss Floy,' returned Miss Nipper, 'how can you talk like that, when you have books upon books already, and masterses and missesses a teaching of you everything continual, though my belief is that your pa, Miss Dombey, never would have learnt you nothing, never would have thought of it, unless you 'd asked him—when he couldn't well refuse; but giving consent when asked, and offering when unasked, miss, is quite two things; I may not have my objections to a young man's keeping company with me, and when he puts the question, may say "yes," but that 's not saying "would you be so kind as like me." '

'But you can buy me the books, Susan; and you will, when you know I want them.'

'Well, miss, and why do you want 'em?' replied Nipper; adding, in a lower voice, 'if it was to fling at Mrs. Pipchin's head, I 'd buy a cart-load.'

'I think I could perhaps give Paul some help, Susan, if I had these books,' said Florence, 'and make the coming week a little easier to him. At least I want to try. So buy them for me, dear, and I will never forget how kind it was of you to do it!'

It must have been a harder heart than Susan Nipper's that could have rejected the little purse Florence held out with these words, or the gentle look of entreaty with which she seconded her petition. Susan put the purse in her pocket without reply, and trotted out at once upon her errand.

The books were not easy to procure: and the answer at several shops was, either that they were just out of them, or that they never kept them, or that they had had a great many last month, or that they expected a great many next week. But Susan was not easily baffled in such an enterprise; and having entrapped a white-haired youth, in a black calico apron, from a library where she was known, to accompany her in her quest, she led him such a life in going up and down, that he exerted himself to the utmost, if it were only to get rid of her; and finally enabled her to return home in triumph.

With these treasures then, after her own daily lessons were over, Florence sat down at night to track Paul's footsteps through the thorny ways of learning; and being possessed of a naturally quick and sound capacity, and taught by that most wonderful of masters, love, it was not long before she gained upon Paul's heels, and caught and passed him.

Not a word of this was breathed to Mrs. Pipchin: but many a night when they were all in bed, and when Miss Nipper, with her hair in papers and herself asleep in some uncomfortable attitude, reposed unconscious by her side; and when the chinking ashes in the grate were cold and grey; and when the candles were burnt down and guttering out;—Florence tried so hard to be a substitute for one small Dombey, that her fortitude and perseverance might have almost won her a free right to bear the name herself.

And high was her reward, when one Saturday evening, as little Paul was sitting down as usual to 'resume his studies,' she sat down by his side, and showed him all that was so rough, made smooth, and all that was so dark, made clear and plain, before him. It was nothing but a startled look in Paul's wan face—a flush—a smile—and then a close embrace—but God knows how her heart leaped up at this rich payment for her trouble.

'Oh, Floy!' cried her brother, 'how I love you! How I love you, Floy!'

'And I you, dear!'

'Oh! I am sure of that, Floy.'

He said no more about it, but all that evening sat close by her, very quiet; and in the night he called out from his little room within hers, three or four times, that he loved her.

Regularly, after that. Florence was prepared to

sit down with Paul on Saturday night, and patiently assist him through so much as they could anticipate together, of his next week's work. The cheering thought that he was labouring on where Florence had just toiled before him, would, of itself, have been a stimulant to Paul in the perpetual resumption of his studies; but coupled with the actual lightening of his load, consequent on this assistance, it saved him, possibly, from sinking underneath the burden which the fair Cornelia Blimber piled upon his back.

It was not that Miss Blimber meant to be too hard upon him, or that Doctor Blimber meant to bear too heavily on the young gentlemen in general. Cornelia merely held the faith in which she had been bred; and the Doctor, in some partial confusion of his ideas, regarded the young gentlemen as if they were all Doctors, and were born grown up. Comforted by the applause of the young gentlemen's nearest relations, and urged on by their blind vanity and ill-considered haste, it would have been strange if Doctor Blimber had discovered his mistake, or trimmed his swelling sails to any other tack.

Thus in the case of Paul. When Doctor Blimber said he made great progress, and was naturally clever, Mr. Dombey was more bent than ever on his being forced and crammed. In the case of Briggs, when Doctor Blimber reported that he did not make great progress yet, and was not naturally clever, Briggs senior was inexorable in the same purpose. In short, however high and false the temperature at which the Doctor kept his hothouse, the owners of the plants were always ready to lend a helping hand at the bellows, and to stir the fire.

Such spirits as he had in the outset, Paul soon lost of course. But he retained all that was strange, and old, and thoughtful in his character: and under circumstances so favourable to the development of those tendencies, became even more strange, and old, and thoughtful, than before.

The only difference was, that he kept his character to himself. He grew more thoughtful and reserved, every day; and had no such curiosity in any living member of the Doctor's household, as he had had in Mrs. Pipchin. He loved to be alone; and in those short intervals when he was not occupied with his books, liked nothing so well as wandering about the house by himself, or sitting on the stairs, listening to the great clock in the hall. He was intimate with all the paperhanging in the house; saw things that no one else saw in the patterns; found out miniature tigers and lions running up the bed-room walls, and squinting faces leering in the squares and diamonds of the floor-cloth.

The solitary child lived on, surrounded by this arabesque work of his musing fancy, and no one understood him. Mrs. Blimber thought him 'odd,' and sometimes the servants said among themselves that little Dombey 'moped'; but that was all.

Unless young Toots had some idea on the subject, to the expression of which he was wholly unequal. Ideas, like ghosts (according to the common notion of ghosts), must be spoken to a little before they will explain themselves; and Toots had long left off asking any questions of his own mind. Some mist there may have been, issuing from that leaden casket, his cranium, which, if it could have taken shape and form, would have become a genie; but it could not; and it only so far followed the example of the smoke in the Arabian story, as to roll out in a thick cloud, and there hang and hover. But it left a little figure visible upon a lonely shore, and Toots was always staring at it.

'How are you?' he would say to Paul, fifty times a day.

'Quite well, sir, thank you,' Paul would answer.

'Shake hands,' would be Toots's next advance.

Which Paul, of course, would immediately do. Mr. Toots generally said again, after a long interval of staring and hard breathing, 'How are you?' To which Paul again replied, 'Quite well, sir, thank you.'

One evening Mr. Toots was sitting at his desk, oppressed by correspondence, when a great purpose seemed to flash upon him. He laid down his pen, and went off to seek Paul, whom he found at last, after a long search, looking through the window of his little bedroom.

'I say!' cried Toots, speaking the moment he entered the room, lest he should forget it; 'what do you think about?'

'Oh! I think about a great many things,' replied Paul.

'Do you, though?' said Toots, appearing to consider that fact in itself surprising.

'If you had to die,' said Paul, looking up into his face—

Mr. Toots started, and seemed much disturbed.

'—Don't you think you would rather die on a moonlight night when the sky was quite clear, and the wind blowing, as it did last night?'

Mr. Toots said, looking doubtfully at Paul, and shaking his head, that he didn't know about that.

'Not blowing, at least,' said Paul, 'but sounding in the air like the sea sounds in the shells. It was a beautiful night. When I had listened to the water for a long time, I got up and looked out. There was a boat over there, in the full light of the moon; a boat with a sail.'

The child looked at him so steadfastly, and spoke

so earnestly, that Mr. Toots, feeling himself called upon to say something about this boat, said, 'Smugglers.' But with an impartial remembrance of there being two sides to every question, he added, 'or Preventive.'

'A boat with a sail,' repeated Paul, 'in the full light of the moon. The sail like an arm, all silver. It went away into the distance, and what do you think it seemed to do as it moved with the waves?'

'Pitch,' said Mr. Toots.

'It seemed to beckon,' said the child, 'to beckon me to come!—There she is! There she is!'

Toots was almost beside himself with dismay at this sudden exclamation, after what had gone before, and cried, 'Who?'

'My sister Florence!' cried Paul, 'looking up here, and waving her hand. She sees me—she sees me! Good night, dear, good night, good night.'

His quick transition to a state of unbounded pleasure, as he stood at his window, kissing and clapping his hands: and the way in which the light retreated from his features as she passed out of his view, and left a patient melancholy on the little face: were too remarkable wholly to escape even Toots's notice. Their interview being interrupted at this moment by a visit from Mrs. Pipchin, who usually brought her black skirts to bear upon Paul just before dusk, once or twice a week, Toots had no opportunity of improving the occasion; but it left so marked an impression on his mind that he twice returned, after having exchanged the usual salutations, to ask Mrs. Pipchin how she did. This the irascible old lady conceived to be a deeply-devised and long-meditated insult, originating in the diabolical invention of the weak-eyed young man downstairs, against whom she accordingly lodged a formal complaint with Doctor Blimber that very night; who mentioned to the young man that if he ever did it again, he should be obliged to part with him.

The evenings being longer now, Paul stole up to his window every evening to look out for Florence. She always passed and repassed at a certain time, until she saw him; and their mutual recognition was a gleam of sunshine in Paul's daily life. Often after dark, one other figure walked alone before the Doctor's house. He rarely joined them on the Saturday now. He could not bear it. He would rather come unrecognised, and look up at the windows where his son was qualifying for a man; and wait, and watch, and plan, and hope.

Oh! could he but have seen, or seen as others did, the slight spare boy above, watching the waves and clouds at twilight, with his earnest eyes, and breasting the window of his solitary cage when birds flew by, as if he would have emulated them, and soared away!

## CHAPTER XIII

### SHIPPING INTELLIGENCE AND OFFICE BUSINESS

Mr. Dombey's offices were in a court where there was an old-established stall of choice fruit at the corner: where perambulating merchants, of both sexes, offered for sale at any time between the hours of ten and five, slippers, pocket-books, sponges, dogs' collars, and Windsor soap, and sometimes a pointer or an oil-painting.

The pointer always came that way, with a view to the Stock Exchange, where a sporting taste (originating generally in bets of new hats) is much in vogue. The other commodities were addressed to the general public; but they were never offered by the vendors to Mr. Dombey. When he appeared, the dealers in those wares fell off respectfully. The principal slipper and dogs' collar man—who considered himself a public character, and whose portrait was screwed on to an artist's door in Cheapside—threw up his forefinger to the brim of his hat as Mr. Dombey went by. The ticket-porter, if he were not absent on a job, always ran officiously before to open Mr. Dombey's office-door as wide as possible, and hold it open, with his hat off, while he entered.

The clerks within were not a whit behindhand in their demonstrations of respect. A solemn hush prevailed, as Mr. Dombey passed through the outer office. The wit of the counting-house became in a moment as mute, as the row of leather fire-buckets hanging up behind him. Such vapid and flat daylight as filtered through the ground-glass windows and skylights, leaving a black sediment upon the panes, showed the books and papers, and the figures bending over them, enveloped in a studious gloom, and as much abstracted in appearance, from the world without, as if they were assembled at the bottom of the sea; while a mouldy little strong room in the obscure perspective, where a shady lamp was always burning, might have represented the cavern of some ocean-monster, looking on with a red eye at these mysteries of the deep.

When Perch the messenger, whose place was on a little bracket, like a time-piece, saw Mr. Dombey come in—or rather when he felt that he was coming, for he had usually an instinctive sense of his approach—he hurried into Mr. Dombey's room, stirred the fire, quarried fresh coals from the bowels of the coal-box, hung the newspaper to air upon the fender, put the chair ready, and the screen in its place, and was round upon his heel on the instant of Mr. Dombey's entrance, to take his great-coat and hat, and hang them up. Then Perch took the newspaper, and gave it a turn or two in his hands before the fire, and laid it, deferentially, at Mr. Dombey's elbow. And so little objection had Perch to doing deferential in the last degree, that if he might have laid himself at Mr. Dombey's feet, or might have called him by some such title as used to be bestowed upon the Caliph Haroun Alraschid, he would have been all the better pleased.

As this honour would have been an innovation and an experiment, Perch was fain to content himself by expressing as well as he could, in his manner, You are the Light of my Eyes. You are the Breath of my Soul. You are the Commander of the Faithful Perch! With this imperfect happiness to cheer him, he would shut the door softly, walk away on tiptoe, and leave his great chief to be stared at, through a dome-shaped window in the leads, by ugly chimney pots and backs of houses, and especially by the bold window of a hair-cutting saloon on a first floor, where a waxen effigy, bald as a Mussulman in the morning, and covered after eleven o'clock in the day, with luxuriant hair and whiskers in the latest Christian fashion, showed him the wrong side of its head for ever.

Between Mr. Dombey and the common world, as it was accessible through the medium of the outer office—to which Mr. Dombey's presence in his own room may be said to have struck like damp, or cold air—there were two degrees of descent. Mr. Carker in his own office was the first step; Mr. Morfin, in *his* own office, was the second. Each of these gentlemen occupied a little chamber like a bath-room, opening from the passage outside Mr. Dombey's door. Mr. Carker, as Grand Vizier, inhabited the room that was nearest to the Sultan. Mr. Morfin, as an officer of inferior state, inhabited the room that was nearest to the clerks.

The gentleman last mentioned was a cheerful-looking, hazel-eyed elderly bachelor: gravely attired, as to his upper man, in black; and as to his legs, in pepper and salt colour. His dark hair was just touched here and there with specks of grey, as though the tread of Time had splashed it; and his whiskers were already white. He had a mighty respect for Mr. Dombey, and rendered him due homage; but as he was of a genial temper himself, and never wholly at his ease in that stately presence, he was disquieted by no jealousy of the many conferences enjoyed by Mr. Carker, and felt a secret satisfaction in having duties to discharge, which rarely exposed him to be singled out for such distinction. He was a great musical amateur in his way—after business; and had a paternal affection for his violoncello, which was once in every week transported from Islington, his place of abode, to a certain club-room hard by the Bank, where quartettes of the most tormenting and excruciating nature were executed every Wednesday evening by a private party.

Mr. Carker was a gentleman thirty-eight or forty years old, of a florid complexion, and with two unbroken rows of glistening teeth, whose regularity and whiteness were quite distressing. It was impossible to escape the observation of them, for he showed them whenever he spoke; and bore so wide a smile upon his countenance (a smile, however, very rarely, indeed, extending beyond his mouth), that there was something in it like the snarl of a cat. He affected a stiff white cravat, after the example of his principal, and was always closely buttoned up and tightly dressed. His manner towards Mr. Dombey was deeply conceived and perfectly expressed. He was familiar with him, in the very extremity of his sense of the distance between them. 'Mr. Dombey, to a man in your position from a man in mine, there is no show of subservience compatible with the transaction of business between us, that I should think sufficient. I frankly tell you, sir, I give it up altogether. I feel that I could not satisfy my own mind; and Heaven knows, Mr. Dombey, you can afford to dispense with the endeavour.' If he had carried these words about with him, printed on a placard, and had constantly offered it to Mr. Dombey's perusal on the breast of his coat, he could not have been more explicit than he was.

This was Carker the manager. Mr. Carker the junior, Walter's friend, was his brother; two or three years older than he, but widely removed in station. The younger brother's post was on the top of the official ladder; the elder brother's at the bottom. The elder brother never gained a stave, or raised his foot to mount one. Young men passed above his head, and rose and rose; but he was always at the bottom. He was quite resigned to occupy that low condition: never complained of it: and certainly never hoped to escape from it.

'How do you do this morning?' said Mr. Carker the manager, entering Mr. Dombey's room soon after his arrival one day: with a bundle of papers in his hand.

'How do you do, Carker?' said Mr. Dombey, rising from his chair, and standing with his back to the fire. 'Have you anything there for me?'

'I don't know that I need trouble you,' returned Carker, turning over the papers in his hand. 'You have a committee to-day at three, you know.'

'And one at three, three-quarters,' added Mr. Dombey.

'Catch you forgetting anything!' exclaimed Carker, still turning over his papers. 'If Mr. Paul inherits your memory, he 'll be a troublesome customer in the house. One of you is enough.'

'You have an accurate memory of your own,' said Mr. Dombey.

'Oh! *I!*' returned the manager. 'It 's the only capital of a man like *me*.'

Mr. Dombey did not look less pompous or at all displeased, as he stood leaning against the chimney-piece, surveying his (of course unconscious) clerk, from head to foot. The stiffness and nicety of Mr. Carker's dress, and a certain arrogance of manner, either natural to him or imitated from a pattern not far off, gave great additional effect to his humility. He seemed a man who would contend against the power that vanquished him, if he could, but who was utterly borne down by the greatness and superiority of Mr. Dombey.

'Is Morfin here?' asked Mr. Dombey, after a short pause, during which Mr. Carker had been fluttering his papers, and muttering little abstracts of their contents to himself.

'Morfin 's here,' he answered, looking up with his widest and most sudden smile; 'humming musical recollections—of his last night's quartette party, I suppose—through the walls between us, and driving me half mad. I wish he 'd make a bonfire of his violoncello, and burn his music-books in it.'

'You respect nobody, Carker, I think,' said Mr. Dombey.

'No?' inquired Carker, with another wide and most feline show of his teeth. 'Well! Not many people,

I believe. I wouldn't answer perhaps,' he murmured, as if he were only thinking it, 'for more than one.'

A dangerous quality, if real; and not a less dangerous one, if feigned. But Mr. Dombey hardly seemed to think so, as he still stood with his back to the fire, drawn up to his full height, and looking at his head-clerk with a dignified composure, in which there seemed to lurk a stronger latent sense of power than usual.

'Talking of Morfin,' resumed Mr. Carker, taking out one paper from the rest, 'he reports a junior dead in the agency at Barbados, and proposes to reserve a passage in the Son and Heir—she 'll sail in a month or so—for the successor. You don't care who goes, I suppose? We have nobody of that sort here.'

Mr. Dombey shook his head with supreme indifference.

'It 's no very precious appointment,' observed Mr. Carker, taking up a pen, with which to endorse a memorandum on the back of the paper. 'I hope he may bestow it on some orphan nephew of a musical friend. It may perhaps stop *his* fiddle-playing, if he has a gift that way. Who 's that? Come in!'

'I beg your pardon, Mr. Carker. I didn't know you were here, sir,' answered Walter, appearing with some letters in his hand, unopened, and newly arrived. 'Mr. Carker the junior, sir—'

At the mention of this name, Mr. Carker the manager was, or affected to be, touched to the quick with shame and humiliation. He cast his eyes full on Mr. Dombey with an altered and apologetic look, abased them on the ground, and remained for a moment without speaking.

'I thought, sir,' he said suddenly and angrily, turning on Walter, 'that you had been before requested not to drag Mr. Carker the junior into your conversation.'

'I beg your pardon,' returned Walter. 'I was only going to say that Mr. Carker the junior had told me he believed you were gone out, or I should not have knocked at the door when you were engaged with Mr. Dombey. These are letters for Mr. Dombey, sir.'

'Very well, sir,' returned Mr. Carker the manager, plucking them sharply from his hand. 'Go about your business.'

But in taking them with so little ceremony, Mr. Carker dropped one on the floor, and did not see what he had done; neither did Mr. Dombey observe the letter lying near his feet. Walter hesitated for a moment, thinking that one or other of them would notice it; but finding that neither did, he stopped, came back, picked it up, and laid it himself on Mr. Dombey's desk. The letters were post-letters; and it happened that the one in question was Mrs. Pipchin's regular report, directed as usual—for Mrs. Pipchin was but an indifferent penwoman—by Florence. Mr. Dombey, having his attention silently called to this letter by Walter, started, and looked fiercely at him, as if he believed that he had purposely selected it from all the rest.

'You can leave the room, sir!' said Mr. Dombey, haughtily.

He crushed the letter in his hand; and having watched Walter out at the door, put it in his pocket without breaking the seal.

'You want somebody to send to the West Indies, you were saying,' observed Mr. Dombey, hurriedly.

'Yes,' replied Carker.

'Send young Gay.'

'Good, very good indeed. Nothing easier,' said Mr. Carker, without any show of surprise, and taking up the pen to re-endorse the letter, as coolly as he had done before. '"Send young Gay."'

'Call him back,' said Mr. Dombey.

Mr. Carker was quick to do so, and Walter was quick to return.

'Gay,' said Mr. Dombey, turning a little to look at him over his shoulder. 'Here is a—'

'An opening,' said Mr. Carker, with his mouth stretched to the utmost.

'In the West Indies. At Barbados. I am going to send you,' said Mr. Dombey, scorning to embellish the bare truth, 'to fill a junior situation in the counting-house at Barbados. Let your uncle know from me, that I have chosen you to go to the West Indies.'

Walter's breath was so completely taken away by his astonishment, that he could hardly find enough for the repetition of the words, 'West Indies.'

'Somebody must go,' said Mr. Dombey, 'and you are young and healthy, and your uncle's circumstances are not good. Tell your uncle that you are appointed. You will not go yet. There will be an interval of a month—or two perhaps.'

'Shall I remain there, sir?' inquired Walter.

'Will you remain there, sir!' repeated Mr. Dombey, turning a little more round towards him. 'What do you mean? What does he mean, Carker?'

'Live there, sir,' faltered Walter.

'Certainly,' returned Mr. Dombey.

Walter bowed.

'That 's all,' said Mr. Dombey, resuming his letters, 'You will explain to him in good time about the usual outfit and so forth, Carker, of course. He needn't wait, Carker.'

'You needn't wait, Gay,' observed Mr. Carker: bare to the gums.

'Unless,' said Mr. Dombey, stopping in his reading without looking off the letter, and seeming to listen. 'Unless he has anything to say.'

'No, sir,' returned Walter agitated and confused, and almost stunned, as an infinite variety of pictures presented themselves to his mind; among which Captain Cuttle, in his glazed hat, transfixed with astonishment at Mrs. MacStinger's, and his uncle bemoaning his loss in the little back-parlour, held prominent places. 'I hardly know—I—I am much obliged, sir.'

'He needn't wait, Carker,' said Mr. Dombey.

And as Mr. Carker again echoed the words, and also collected his papers as if he were going away too, Walter felt that his lingering any longer would be an unpardonable intrusion—especially as he had nothing to say—and therefore walked out quite confounded.

Going along the passage, with the mingled consciousness and helplessness of a dream, he heard Mr. Dombey's door shut again, as Mr. Carker came out: and immediately afterwards that gentleman called to him.

'Bring your friend Mr. Carker the junior to my room, sir, if you please.'

Walter went to the outer office and apprised Mr. Carker the junior of his errand, who accordingly came out from behind a partition where he sat alone in one corner, and returned with him to the room of Mr. Carker the manager.

That gentleman was standing with his back to the fire, and his hands under his coat-tails, looking over his white cravat, as unpromisingly as Mr. Dombey himself could have looked. He received them without any change in his attitude or softening of his harsh and black expression: merely signing to Walter to close the door.

'John Carker,' said the manager, when this was done, turning suddenly upon his brother, with his two rows of teeth bristling as if he would have bitten him, 'what is the league between you and this young man, in virtue of which I am haunted and hunted by the mention of your name? Is it not enough for you, John Carker, that I am your near relation, and can't detach myself from that—'

'Say disgrace, James,' interposed the other in a low voice, finding that he stammered for a word. 'You mean it, and have reason, say disgrace.'

'From that disgrace,' assented his brother, with keen emphasis, 'but is the fact to be blurted out and trumpeted, and proclaimed continually in the presence of the very House? In moments of confidence too? Do you think your name is calculated to harmonise in this place with trust and confidence, John Carker?'

'No,' returned the other. 'No, James. God knows I have no such thought.'

'What is your thought, then?' said his brother, 'and why do you thrust yourself in my way? Haven't you injured me enough already?'

'I have never injured you, James, wilfully.'

'You are my brother,' said the manager. 'That 's injury enough.'

'I wish I could undo it, James.'

'I wish you could and would.'

During this conversation Walter had looked from one brother to the other, with pain and amazement. He who was the senior in years, and junior in the house, stood, with his eyes cast upon the ground, and his head bowed, humbly listening to the reproaches of the other. Though these were rendered very bitter by the tone and look with which they were accompanied, and by the presence of Walter, whom they so much surprised and shocked, he entered no other protest against them than by slightly raising his right hand in a deprecatory manner, as if he would have said, 'Spare me!' So, had they been blows, and he a brave man, under strong constraint, and weakened by bodily suffering, he might have stood before the executioner.

Generous and quick in all his emotions, and regarding himself as the innocent occasion of these taunts, Walter now struck in, with all the earnestness he felt.

'Mr. Carker,' he said, addressing himself to the manager. 'Indeed, indeed, this is my fault solely. In a kind of heedlessness, for which I cannot blame myself enough, I have, I have no doubt, mentioned Mr. Carker the junior much oftener than was necessary; and have allowed his name sometimes to slip through my lips, when it was against your express wish. But it has been my own mistake, sir. We have never exchanged one word upon the subject—very few, indeed, on any subject. And it has not been,' added Walter, after a moment's pause, 'all heedlessness on my part, sir; for I have felt an interest in Mr. Carker ever since I have been here, and have hardly been able to help speaking of him sometimes, when I have thought of him so much!'

Walter said this from his soul, and with the very breath of honour. For he looked upon the bowed head, and the downcast eyes, and upraised hand, and thought, 'I have felt it; and why should I not avow it in behalf of this unfriended, broken man!'

'In truth, you have avoided me, Mr. Carker,' said Walter, with the tears rising to his eyes; so true was his compassion. 'I know it, to my disappointment and regret. When I first came here, and ever since, I am sure, I have tried to be as much your friend, as one of my age could presume to be; but it has been of no use.'

'And observe,' said the manager, taking him up quickly, 'it will be of still less use, Gay, if you persist in forcing Mr. John Carker's name on people's attention. That is not the way to befriend Mr. John Carker. Ask him if he thinks it is.'

'It is no service to me,' said the brother. 'It only leads to such a conversation as the present, which I need not say I could have well spared. No one can be a better friend to me': he spoke here very distinctly, as if he would impress it upon Walter: 'than in forgetting me, and leaving me to go my way, unquestioned and unnoticed.'

'Your memory not being retentive, Gay, of what you are told by others,' said Mr. Carker the manager, warming himself with great and increased satisfaction, 'I thought it well that you should be told this from the best authority,' nodding towards his brother. 'You are not likely to forget it now, I hope. That 's all, Gay. You can go.'

Walter passed out at the door, and was about to close it after him, when hearing the voice of the brothers again, and also the mention of his own name, he stood irresolutely, with his hand upon the lock, and the door ajar, uncertain whether to return or go away. In this position he could not help overhearing what followed.

'Think of me more leniently, if you can, James,' said John Carker, 'when I tell you I have had—how could I help having, with my history, written here'—striking himself upon the breast—'my whole heart awakened by my observation of that boy, Walter Gay.

I saw in him when he first came here, almost my other self.'

'Your other self!' repeated the manager, disdainfully.

'Not as I am, but as I was when I first came here too; as sanguine, giddy, youthful, inexperienced; flushed with the same restless and adventurous fancies; and full of the same qualities, fraught with the same capacity of leading on to good or evil.'

'I hope not,' said his brother, with some hidden and sarcastic meaning in his tone.

'You strike me sharply; and your hand is steady, and your thrust is very deep,' returned the other, speaking (or so Walter thought) as if some cruel weapon actually stabbed him as he spoke. 'I imagined all this when he was a boy. I believed it. It was a truth to me. I saw him lightly walking on the edge of an unseen gulf where so many others walk with equal gaiety, and from which—'

'The old excuse,' interrupted his brother, as he stirred the fire. 'So many. Go on. Say, so many fall.'

'From which ONE traveller fell,' returned the other, 'who set forward, on his way, a boy like him, and missed his footing more and more, and slipped a little and a little lower, and went on stumbling still, until he fell headlong and found himself below a shattered man. Think what I suffered, when I watched that boy.'

'You have only yourself to thank for it,' returned the brother.

'Only myself,' he assented with a sigh. 'I don't seek to divide the blame or shame.'

'You *have* divided the shame,' James Carker muttered through his teeth. And through so many and such close teeth, he could mutter well.

'Ah, James,' returned his brother, speaking for the first time in an accent of reproach, and seeming, by the sound of his voice, to have covered his face with his hands, 'I have been, since then, a useful foil to you. You have trodden on me freely in your climbing up. Don't spurn me with your heel!'

A silence ensued. After a time, Mr. Carker the manager was heard rustling among his papers, as if he had resolved to bring the interview to a conclusion. At the same time his brother withdrew nearer to the door.

'That 's all,' he said. 'I watched him with such trembling and such fear, as was some little punishment to me, until he passed the place where I first fell; and then, though I had been his father, I believe I never could have thanked God more devoutly. I didn't dare to warn him, and advise him; but if I had seen direct cause, I would have shown him my example. I was afraid to be seen speaking with him, lest it should be thought I did him harm, and tempted him to evil, and corrupted him, or lest I really should. There may be such contagion in me; I don't know. Piece out my history, in connection with young Walter Gay, and what he has made me feel; and think of me more leniently, James, if you can.'

With these words he came out to where Walter was standing. He turned a little paler when he saw him there, and paler yet when Walter caught him by the hand, and said in a whisper—

'Mr. Carker, pray let me thank you! Let me say how much I feel for you! How sorry I am, to have been the unhappy cause of all this! How I almost look upon you now as my protector and guardian! How very, very much I feel obliged to you and pity you!' said Walter, squeezing both his hands, and hardly knowing, in his agitation, what he did or said.

Mr. Morfin's room being close at hand and empty, and the door wide open, they moved thither by one accord: the passage being seldom free from some one passing to or fro. When they were there, and Walter saw in Mr. Carker's face some traces of the emotion within, he almost felt as if he had never seen the face before; it was so greatly changed.

'Walter,' he said, laying his hand on his shoulder. 'I am far removed from you, and may I ever be. Do you know what I am?'

'What you are!' appeared to hang on Walter's lips, as he regarded him attentively.

'It was begun,' said Carker, 'before my twenty-first birthday—led up to, long before, but not begun till near that time. I had robbed them when I came of age. I robbed them afterwards. Before my twenty-second birthday, it was all found out; and then, Walter, from all men's society, I died.'

Again his lasts few words hung trembling upon Walter's lips, but he could neither utter them, nor any of his own.

'The House was very good to me. May Heaven reward the old man for his forbearance! This one, too, his son, who was then newly in the firm, where I had held great trust! I was called into that room which is now his—I have never entered it since—and came out, what you know me. For many years, I sat in my present seat, alone as now, but then a known and recognised example to the rest. They were all merciful to me, and I lived. Time has altered that part of my poor expiation; and I think, except the three heads of the House, there is no one here who knows my story rightly. Before the little boy grows up, and has it told to him, my corner may be vacant. I would rather that it might be so! This is the only change to me since that day, when I left all youth, and hope, and good men's company, behind me in that room. God bless you, Walter! Keep you, and all dear to you, in honesty, or strike them dead!'

Some recollection of his trembling from head to foot, as if with excessive cold, and of his bursting into tears, was all that Walter could add to this, when he tried to recall exactly what had passed between them.

When Walter saw him next, he was bending over his desk in his old silent, drooping, humbled way. Then, observing him at his work, and feeling how resolved he evidently was that no further intercourse should arise between them, and thinking again and again on all he had seen and heard that morning in so short a time, in connection with the history of both the Carkers, Walter could hardly believe that he was under orders for the West Indies, and would soon be lost to Uncle Sol, and Captain Cuttle, and to glimpses few and far between of Florence Dombey—no, he meant Paul—and to all he loved, and liked, and looked for, in his daily life.

But it was true, and the news had already penetrated to the outer office: for while he sat with a heavy heart, pondering on these things, and resting his head upon his arm, Perch the messenger, descending from his mahogany bracket, and jogging his elbow, begged his pardon, but wished to say in his ear, Did he think he could arrange to send home to England a jar of preserved ginger, cheap, for Mrs. Perch's own eating, in the course of her recovery from her next confinement?

# CHAPTER XIV

## PAUL GROWS MORE AND MORE OLD-FASHIONED, AND GOES HOME FOR THE HOLIDAYS

When the midsummer vacation approached, no indecent manifestations of joy were exhibited by the leaden-eyed young gentlemen assembled at Doctor Blimber's. Any such violent expression as 'breaking up,' would have been quite inapplicable to that polite establishment. The young gentlemen oozed away, semi-annually, to their own homes; but they never broke up. They would have scorned the action.

Tozer, who was constantly galled and tormented by a starched white cambric neckerchief, which he wore at the express desire of Mrs. Tozer, his parent, who, designing him for the Church, was of opinion that he couldn't be in that forward state of preparation too soon—Tozer said, indeed, that choosing between two evils, he thought he would rather stay where he was, than go home. However inconsistent this declaration might appear with that passage in Tozer's essay on the subject, wherein he had observed 'that the thoughts of home and all its recollections, awakened in his mind the most pleasing emotions of anticipation and delight,' and had also likened himself to a Roman general, flushed with a recent victory over the Iceni, or laden with Carthaginian spoil, advancing within a few hours' march of the Capitol, presupposed, for the purposes of the simile, to be the dwelling-place of Mrs. Tozer, still it was very sincerely made. For it seemed that Tozer had a dreadful uncle, who not only volunteered examinations of him, in the holidays, on abstruse points, but twisted innocent events and things, and wrenched them to the same fell purpose. So that if this uncle took him to the play, or, on a similar pretence of kindness, carried him to see a giant, or a dwarf, or a conjuror, or anything, Tozer knew he had read up some classical allusion to the subject beforehand, and was thrown into a state of mortal apprehension: not foreseeing where he might break out, or what authority he might not quote against him.

As to Briggs, *his* father made no show of artifice about it. He never would leave him alone. So numerous and severe were the mental trials of that unfortunate youth in vacation time, that the friends of the family (then resident near Bayswater, London) seldom approached the ornamental piece of water in Kensington Gardens, without a vague expectation of seeing Master Briggs's hat floating on the surface, and an unfinished exercise lying on the bank. Briggs, therefore, was not at all sanguine on the subject of holidays; and these two sharers of little Paul's bedroom were so fair a sample of the young gentlemen in general, that the most elastic among them contemplated the arrival of those festive periods with genteel resignation.

It was far otherwise with little Paul. The end of these first holidays was to witness his separation from Florence, but who ever looked forward to the end of holidays whose beginning was not yet come! Not Paul, assuredly. As the happy time drew near, the lions and tigers climbing up the bedroom walls, became quite tame and frolicsome. The grim sly faces in the squares and diamonds of the floorcloth, relaxed and peeped out at him with less wicked eyes. The grave old clock had more of personal interest in the tone of its formal inquiry; and the restless sea went rolling on all night, to the sounding of a melancholy strain—yet it was pleasant too—that rose and fell with the waves, and rocked him, as it were, to sleep.

Mr. Feeder, B.A., seemed to think that he, too, would enjoy the holidays very much. Mr. Toots projected a life of holidays from that time forth; for, as he regularly informed Paul every day, it was his 'last half' at Doctor Blimber's, and he was going to begin to come into his property directly.

It was perfectly understood between Paul and Mr. Toots, that they were intimate friends, notwithstanding their distance in point of years and station. As the vacation approached, and Mr. Toots breathed harder and stared oftener in Paul's society, than he had done before, Paul knew that he meant he was sorry they were going to lose sight of each other, and felt very much obliged to him for his patronage and good opinion.

It was even understood by Doctor Blimber, Mrs. Blimber, and Miss Blimber, as well as by the young gentlemen in general, that Toots had somehow constituted himself protector and guardian of Dombey, and the circumstance became so notorious, even to Mrs. Pipchin, that the good old creature cherished feelings of bitterness and jealousy against Toots; and, in the sanctuary of her own home, repeatedly denounced him as a 'chuckleheaded noodle.' Whereas the innocent Toots had no more idea of awakening Mrs. Pipchin's wrath, than he had of any other definite possibility or proposition. On the contrary, he was disposed to consider her rather a remarkable character, with many points of interest about her. For this reason he smiled on her with so much urbanity, and asked her how she did, so often, in the course of her visits to little Paul, that at last she one night told him plainly, she wasn't used to it, whatever he might think; and she could not, and she would not bear it, either from himself or any other puppy then existing:

at which unexpected acknowledgment of his civilities, Mr. Toots was so alarmed that he secreted himself in a retired spot until she had gone. Nor did he ever again face the doughty Mrs. Pipchin, under Doctor Blimber's roof.

They were within two or three weeks of the holidays, when, one day, Cornelia Blimber called Paul into her room, and said, 'Dombey, I am going to send home your analysis.'

'Thank you, ma'am,' returned Paul.

'You know what I mean, do you, Dombey?' inquired Miss Blimber, looking hard at him through the spectacles.

'No, ma'am,' said Paul.

'Dombey, Dombey,' said Miss Blimber, 'I begin to be afraid you are a sad boy. When you don't know the meaning of an expression, why don't you seek for information!'

'Mrs. Pipchin told me I wasn't to ask questions,' returned Paul.

'I must beg you not to mention Mrs. Pipchin to me, on any account, Dombey,' returned Miss Blimber. 'I couldn't think of allowing it. The course of study here, is very far removed from anything of that sort. A repetition of such allusions would make it necessary for me to request to hear, without a mistake, before breakfast-time to-morrow morning, from *Verbum personale* down to *simillima cygno*.'

'I didn't mean, ma'am—' began little Paul.

'I must trouble you not to tell me that you didn't mean, if you please, Dombey,' said Miss Blimber, who preserved an awful politeness in her admonitions. 'That is a line of argument, I couldn't dream of permitting.'

Paul felt it safest to say nothing at all, so he only looked at Miss Blimber's spectacles. Miss Blimber having shaken her head at him gravely, referred to a paper lying before her.

'"Analysis of the character of P. Dombey." If my recollection serves me,' said Miss Blimber breaking off, 'the word analysis as opposed to synthesis, is thus defined by Walker. "The resolution of an object, whether of the senses or of the intellect, into its first elements." As opposed to synthesis, you observe. *Now* you know what analysis is, Dombey.'

Dombey didn't seem to be absolutely blinded by the light let in upon his intellect, but he made Miss Blimber a little bow.

'"Analysis,"' resumed Miss Blimber, casting her eye over the paper, '"of the character of P. Dombey." I find that the natural capacity of Dombey is extremely good; and that his general disposition to study may be stated in an equal ratio. Thus, taking eight as our standard and highest number, I find these qualities in Dombey stated each at six three-fourths!'

Miss Blimber paused to see how Paul received this news. Being undecided whether six three-fourths, meant six pounds fifteen, or sixpence three farthings, or six foot three, or three quarters past six, or six somethings that he hadn't learnt yet, with three unknown something elses over, Paul rubbed his hands and looked straight at Miss Blimber. It happened to answer as well as anything else he could have done; and Cornelia proceeded.

'"Violence two. Selfishness two. Inclination to low company, as evinced in the case of a person named Glubb, originally seven, but since reduced. Gentlemanly demeanour four, and improving with advancing years." Now what I particularly wish to call your attention to, Dombey, is the general observation at the close of this analysis.'

Paul set himself to follow it with great care.

'"It may be generally observed of Dombey,"' said Miss Blimber, reading in a loud voice, and at every second word directing her spectacles towards the little figure before her: '"that his abilities and inclinations are good, and that he has made as much progress as under the circumstances could have been expected. But it is to be lamented of this young gentleman that he is singular (what is usually termed old-fashioned) in his character and conduct, and that, without presenting anything in either which distinctly calls for reprobation, he is often very unlike other young gentlemen of his age and social position." Now, Dombey,' said Miss Blimber, laying down the paper, 'do you understand that?'

'I think I do, ma'am,' said Paul.

'This analysis, you see, Dombey,' Miss Blimber continued, 'is going to be sent home to your respected parent. It will naturally be very painful to him to find that you are singular in your character and conduct. It is naturally painful to us; for we can't like you, you know, Dombey, as well as we could wish.'

She touched the child upon a tender point. He had secretly become more and more solicitous from day to day as the time of his departure drew more near, that all the house should like him. For some hidden reason, very imperfectly understood by himself—if understood at all—he felt a gradually increasing impulse of affection towards almost everything and everybody in the place. He could not bear to think that they would be quite indifferent to him when he was gone. He wanted them to remember him kindly; and he had made it his business even to conciliate a great hoarse shaggy dog, chained up at the back of the house, who had previously been the terror of his life; that even he might miss him when he was no longer there.

Little thinking that in this, he only showed again the difference between himself and his compeers, poor tiny Paul set it forth to Miss Blimber as well as he could, and begged her, in despite of the official analysis, to have the goodness to try and like him. To Mrs. Blimber, who had joined them, he preferred the same petition: and when that lady could not forbear, even in his presence, from giving utterance to her often-repeated opinion, that he was an odd child, Paul told her that he was sure she was quite right; that he thought it must be his bones, but he didn't know; and that he hoped she would overlook it, for he was fond of them all.

'Not so fond,' said Paul, with a mixture of timidity and perfect frankness, which was one of the most peculiar and most engaging qualities of the child, 'not so fond as I am of Florence, of course; that could never be. You couldn't expect that, could you, ma'am?'

'Oh! the old-fashioned little soul!' cried Mrs. Blimber, in a whisper.

'But I like everybody here very much,' pursued Paul, 'and I should grieve to go away, and think that any one was glad that I was gone, or didn't care.'

Mrs. Blimber was now quite sure that Paul was the oddest child in the world; and when she told the Doctor what had passed, the Doctor did not controvert his wife's opinion. But he said, as he had said before, when Paul first came, that study would do much; and he also said, as he had said on that occasion, 'Bring him on, Cornelia! Bring him on!'

Cornelia had always brought him on as vigorously as she could; and Paul had had a hard life of it.

But over and above the getting through his tasks, he had long had another purpose always present to him, and to which he still held fast. It was, to be a gentle, useful, quiet little fellow, always striving to secure the love and attachment of the rest; and though he was yet often to be seen at his old post on the stairs, or watching the waves and clouds from his solitary window, he was oftener found, too, among the other boys, modestly rendering them some little voluntary service. Thus it came to pass, that even among those rigid and absorbed young anchorites, who mortified themselves beneath the roof of Doctor Blimber, Paul was an object of general interest; a fragile little plaything that they all liked, and that no one would have thought of treating roughly. But he could not change his nature, or rewrite the analysis; and so they all agreed that Dombey was old-fashioned.

There were some immunities, however, attaching to the character enjoyed by no one else. They could have better spared a newer-fashioned child, and that alone was much. When the others only bowed to Doctor Blimber and family on retiring for the night, Paul would stretch out his morsel of a hand, and boldly shake the Doctor's; also Mrs. Blimber's; also Cornelia's. If anybody was to be begged off from impending punishment, Paul was always the delegate. The weak-eyed young man himself had once consulted him, in reference to a little breakage of glass and china. And it was darkly rumoured that the butler, regarding him with favour such as that stern man had never shown before to mortal boy, had sometimes mingled porter with his table-beer to make him strong.

Over and above these extensive privileges, Paul had free right of entry to Mr. Feeder's room, from which apartment he had twice led Mr. Toots into the open air in a state of faintness, consequent on an unsuccessful attempt to smoke a very blunt cigar: one of a bundle which that young gentleman had covertly purchased on the shingle from a most desperate smuggler, who had acknowledged, in confidence, that two hundred pounds was the price set upon his head, dead or alive, by the Custom House. It was a snug room, Mr. Feeder's, with his bed in another little room inside of it; and a flute, which Mr. Feeder couldn't play yet, but was going to make a point of learning, he said, hanging up over the fireplace. There were some books in it, too, and a fishing-rod; for Mr. Feeder said he should certainly make a point of learning to fish when he could fine time. Mr. Feeder had amassed, with similar intentions, a beautiful little curly second-hand key-bugle, a chess-board and men, a Spanish Grammar, a set of sketching materials, and a pair of boxing-gloves. The art of self-defence Mr. Feeder said he should undoubtedly make a point of learning, as he considered it the duty of every man to do; for it might lead to the protection of a female in distress.

But Mr. Feeder's great possession was a large green jar of snuff, which Mr. Toots had brought down as a present, at the close of the last vacation; and for which he had paid a high price, as having been the genuine property of the Prince Regent. Neither Mr. Toots nor Mr. Feeder could partake of this or any other snuff, even in the most stinted and moderate degree, without being seized with convulsions of sneezing. Nevertheless it was their great delight to moisten a boxful with cold tea, stir it up on a piece of parchment with a paper-knife, and devote themselves to its consumption then and there. In the course of which cramming of their noses, they endured surprising torments with the constancy of martyrs: and, drinking table-beer at intervals, felt all the glories of dissipation.

To little Paul sitting silent in their company, and by the side of his chief patron, Mr. Toots, there was a dread charm in these reckless occasions: and when Mr. Feeder spoke of the dark mysteries of London, and told Mr. Toots that he was going to observe it himself closely in all its ramifications in the approaching holidays, and for that purpose had made arrangements to board with two old maiden ladies at Peckham, Paul regarded him as if he were the hero of some book of travels or wild adventure, and was almost afraid of such a slashing person.

Going into this room one evening, when the holidays were very near, Paul found Mr. Feeder filling up the blanks in some printed letters, while some others, already filled up and strewn before him, were being folded and sealed by Mr. Toots. Mr. Feeder said, 'Aha, Dombey, there you are, are you?'—for they were always kind to him, and glad to see him—and then said, tossing one of the letters towards him, 'And *there* you are, too, Dombey. That 's yours.'

'Mine, sir?' said Paul.

'Your invitation,' returned Mr. Feeder.

Paul, looking at it, found, in copper-plate print, with the exception of his own name and date, which were in Mr. Feeder's penmanship, that Doctor and Mrs. Blimber requested the pleasure of Mr. P. Dombey's company at an early party on Wednesday evening the seventeenth instant; and that the hour was half-past seven o'clock; and that the object was quadrilles. Mr. Toots also showed him, by holding up a companion sheet of paper, that Doctor and Mrs. Blimber requested the pleasure of Mr. Toots's company at an early party on Wednesday evening the seventeenth instant, when the hour was half-past seven o'clock, and when the object was quadrilles. He also found, on glancing at the table where Mr. Feeder sat, that the pleasure of Mr. Briggs's company, and of Mr. Tozer's company, and of every young gentleman's company, was requested by Doctor and Mrs. Blimber on the same genteel occasion.

Mr. Feeder then told him, to his great joy, that his sister was invited, and that it was a half-yearly event, and that, as the holidays began that day, he could go away with his sister after the party, if he liked, which Paul interrupted him to say he *would* like, very much. Mr. Feeder then gave him to understand that he would be expected to inform Doctor and Mrs. Blimber, in superfine small-hand, that Mr. P. Dombey would be happy to have the honour of waiting on them, in accordance with their polite invitation. Lastly, Mr. Feeder said, he had better not refer to the festive occasion, in the hearing of Doctor and Mrs. Blimber; as these preliminaries, and the whole of the arrangements, were conducted on principles of classicality and high breeding; and that Doctor and Mrs. Blimber on the one hand, and the young gentlemen on the other, were supposed, in their scholastic capacities, not to have the least idea of what was in the wind.

Paul thanked Mr. Feeder for these hints, and pocketing his invitation, sat down on a stool by the side of Mr. Toots as usual. But Paul's head, which had long been ailing more or less, and was sometimes very heavy and painful, felt so uneasy that night, that he was obliged to support it on his hand. And yet it dropped so, that by little and little it sunk on Mr. Toots's knee, and rested there, as if it had no care to be ever lifted up again.

That was no reason why he should be deaf; but

he must have been, he thought, for, by and by, he heard Mr. Feeder calling in his ear, and gently shaking him to rouse his attention. And when he raised his head, quite scared, and looked about him, he found that Doctor Blimber had come into the room; and that the window was open, and that his forehead was wet with sprinkled water; though how all this had been done without his knowledge, was very curious indeed.

'Ah! Come, come! That 's well! How is my little friend now?' said Doctor Blimber, encouragingly.

'Oh, quite well, thank you, sir,' said Paul.

But there seemed to be something the matter with the floor, for he couldn't stand upon it steadily; and with the walls too, for they were inclined to turn round and round, and could only be stopped by being looked at very hard indeed. Mr. Toots's head had the appearance of being at once bigger and farther off than was quite natural: and when he took Paul in his arms, to carry him upstairs, Paul observed with astonishment that the door was in quite a different place from that in which he had expected to find it, and almost thought, at first, that Mr. Toots was going to walk straight up the chimney.

It was very kind of Mr. Toots to carry him to the top of the house so tenderly; and Paul told him that it was. But Mr. Toots said he would do a great deal more than that, if he could; and indeed he did more as it was: for he helped Paul to undress, and helped him to bed, in the kindest manner possible, and then sat down by the bedside and chuckled very much; while Mr. Feeder, B.A., leaning over the bottom of the bedstead, set all the little bristles on his head bolt upright with his bony hands, and then made believe to spar at Paul with great science, on account of his being all right again, which was so uncommonly facetious, and kind too in Mr. Feeder, that Paul, not being able to make up his mind whether it was best to laugh or cry at him, did both at once.

How Mr. Toots melted away, and Mr. Feeder changed into Mrs. Pipchin, Paul never thought of asking; neither was he at all curious to know; but when he saw Mrs. Pipchin standing at the bottom of the bed, instead of Mr. Feeder, he cried out, 'Mrs. Pipchin, don't tell Florence!'

'Don't tell Florence what, my little Paul?' said Mrs. Pipchin, coming round to the bedside, and sitting down in the chair.

'About me,' said Paul.

'No, no,' said Mrs. Pipchin.

'What do you think I mean to do when I grow up, Mrs. Pipchin?' inquired Paul, turning his face towards her on his pillow, and resting his chin wistfully on his folded hands.

Mrs. Pipchin couldn't guess.

'I mean,' said Paul, 'to put my money all together in one bank, never try to get any more, go away into the country with my darling Florence, have a beautiful garden, fields, and woods, and live there with her all my life!'

'Indeed!' cried Mrs. Pipchin.

'Yes,' said Paul. 'That 's what I mean to do, when I—' He stopped, and pondered for a moment.

Mrs. Pipchin's grey eye scanned his thoughtful face.

'If I grow up,' said Paul. Then he went on immediately to tell Mrs. Pipchin all about the party, about Florence's invitation, about the pride he would have in the admiration that would be felt for her by all the boys, about their being so kind to him and fond of him, about his being so fond of them, and about his being so glad of it. Then he told Mrs. Pipchin about the analysis, and about his being certainly old-fashioned, and took Mrs. Pipchin's opinion on that point, and whether she knew why it was, and what it meant. Mrs. Pipchin denied the fact altogether, as the shortest way of getting out of the difficulty; but Paul was far from satisfied with that reply, and looked so searchingly at Mrs. Pipchin for a truer answer, that she was obliged to get up and look out of the window to avoid his eyes.

There was a certain calm apothecary, who attended at the establishment when any of the young gentlemen were ill, and somehow *he* got into the room and appeared at the bedside, with Mrs. Blimber. How they came there, or how long they had been there, Paul didn't know; but when he saw them, he sat up in bed and answered all the apothecary's questions at full length, and whispered to him that Florence was not to know anything about it, if he pleased, and that he had set his mind upon her coming to the party. He was very chatty with the apothecary, and they parted excellent friends. Lying down again with his eyes shut, he heard the apothecary say, out of the room and quite a long way off—or he dreamed it—that there was a want of vital power (what was that, Paul wondered!) and great constitutional weakness. That as the little fellow had set his heart on parting with his schoolmates on the seventeenth, it would be better to indulge the fancy if he grew no worse. That he was glad to hear from Mrs. Pipchin, that the little fellow would go to his friends in London on the eighteenth. That he would write to Mr. Dombey, when he should have gained a better knowledge of the case, and before that day. That there was no immediate cause for—what? Paul lost that word

And that the little fellow had a fine mind, but was an old-fashioned boy.

What old fashion could that be, Paul wondered with a palpitating heart, that was so visibly expressed in him; so plainly seen by so many people?

He could neither make it out, nor trouble himself long with the effort. Mrs. Pipchin was again beside him, if she had ever been away (he thought she had gone out with the Doctor, but it was all a dream perhaps), and presently a bottle and glass got into her hands magically, and she poured out the contents for him. After that, he had some real good jelly, which Mrs. Blimber brought to him herself; and then he was so well, that Mrs. Pipchin went home, at his urgent solicitation, and Briggs and Tozer came to bed. Poor Briggs grumbled terribly about his own analysis, which could hardly have discomposed him more if it had been a chemical process; but he was very good to Paul, and so was Tozer, and so were all the rest, for they every one looked in before going to bed, and said, 'How are you now, Dombey?' 'Cheer up, little Dombey!' and so forth. After Briggs had got into bed, he lay awake for a long time, still bemoaning his analysis, and saying he knew it was all wrong, and they couldn't have analysed a murderer worse, and how would Doctor Blimber like it if his pocket-money depended on it? It was very easy, Briggs said, to make a galley-slave of a boy all the half-year, and then score him up idle; and to crib two dinners a week out of his board, and then score him up greedy; but that wasn't going to be submitted to, he believed, was it? Oh! Ah!

Before the weak-eyed young man performed on the gong next morning, he came upstairs to Paul and told him he was to lie still, which Paul very gladly did.

Mrs. Pipchin reappeared a little before the apothecary, and a little after the good young woman whom Paul had seen cleaning the stove on that first morning (how long ago it seemed now!) had brought him his breakfast. There was another consultation a long way off, or else Paul dreamed it again; and then the apothecary, coming back with Doctor and Mrs. Blimber, said—

'Yes, I think, Doctor Blimber, we may release this young gentleman from his books just now; the vacation being so very near at hand.'

'By all means,' said Doctor Blimber. 'My love, you will inform Cornelia, if you please.'

'Assuredly,' said Mrs. Blimber.

The apothecary bending down, looked closely into Paul's eyes, and felt his head, and his pulse, and his heart, with so much interest and care, that Paul said 'Thank you, sir.'

'Our little friend,' observed Doctor Blimber, 'has never complained.'

'Oh no!' replied the apothecary. 'He was not likely to complain.'

'You find him greatly better?' said Doctor Blimber.

'Oh! he is greatly better, sir,' returned the apothecary.

Paul had begun to speculate, in his own odd way, on the subject that might occupy the apothecary's mind just at that moment; so musingly had he answered the two questions of Doctor Blimber. But the apothecary happening to meet his little patient's eyes, as the latter set off on that mental expedition, and coming instantly out of his abstraction with a cheerful smile, Paul smiled in return and abandoned it.

He lay in bed all that day, dozing and dreaming,

and looking at Mr. Toots: but got up on the next, and went downstairs. Lo and behold, there was something the matter with the great clock; and a workman on a pair of steps had taken its face off, and was poking instruments into the works by the light of a candle! This was a great event for Paul, who sat down on the bottom stair, and watched the operation attentively: now and then glancing at the clock-face, leaning all askew, against the wall hard by, and feeling a little confused by a suspicion that it was ogling him.

The workman on the steps was very civil; and as he said, when he observed Paul, 'How do you do, sir?' Paul got into conversation with him, and told him he hadn't been quite well lately. The ice being thus broken, Paul asked him a multitude of questions about chimes and clocks: as, whether people watched up in the lonely church steeples by night to make them strike, and how the bells were rung when people died, and whether those were different bells from wedding bells, or only sounded dismal in the fancies of the living. Finding that his new acquaintance was not very well informed on the subject of the Curfew Bell of ancient days, Paul gave him an account of that institution; and also asked him, as a practical man, what he thought about King Alfred's idea of measuring time by the burning of candles; to which the workman replied, that he thought it would be the ruin of the clock trade if it was to come up again. In fine, Paul looked on, until the clock had quite recovered its familiar aspect, and resumed its sedate inquiry: when the workman, putting away his tools in a long basket, bade him good day, and went away. Though not before he had whispered something, on the door-mat, to the footman, in which there was the phrase 'old-fashioned'—for Paul heard it.

What could that old fashion be, that seemed to make the people sorry? What could it be?

Having nothing to learn now, he thought of this frequently; though not so often as he might have done, if he had had fewer things to think of. But he had a great many; and was always thinking, all day long.

First, there was Florence coming to the party. Florence would see that the boys were fond of him; and that would make her happy. This was his great theme. Let Florence once be sure that they were gentle and good to him, and that he had become a little favourite among them, and then she would always think of the time he had passed there, without being very sorry. Florence might be all the happier too for that, perhaps, when he came back.

When he came back! Fifty times a day, his noiseless little feet went up the stairs to his own room, as he collected every book and scrap, and trifle that belonged to him, and put them all together there, down to the minutest thing, for taking home! There was no shade of coming back on little Paul; no preparation for it, or other reference to it, grew out of anything he thought or did, except this slight one in connection with his sister. On the contrary, he had to think of everything familiar to him, in his contemplative moods and in his wanderings about the house, as being to be parted with; and hence the many things he had to think of, all day long.

He had to peep into those rooms upstairs, and think how solitary they would be when he was gone, and wonder through how many silent days, weeks, months, and years, they would continue just as grave and undisturbed. He had to think—would any other child (old-fashioned, like himself) stray there at any time, to whom the same grotesque distortions of pattern and furniture would manifest themselves; and would anybody tell that boy of little Dombey, who had been there once.

He had to think of a portrait on the stairs, which always looked earnestly after him as he went away, eyeing it over his shoulder: and which, when he passed it in the company of any one, still seemed to gaze at him, and not at his companion. He had much to think of, in association with a print that hung up in another place, where, in the centre of a wondering group, one figure that he knew, a figure with a light about its head—benignant, mild, and merciful—stood pointing upward.

At his own bedroom window, there were crowds of thoughts that mixed with these, and came on, one upon another, like the rolling waves. Where those wild birds lived, that were always hovering out at sea in troubled weather; where the clouds rose and first began; whence the wind issued on its rushing flight, and where it stopped; whether the spot where he and Florence had so often sat, and watched, and talked about these things, could ever be exactly as it used to be without them; whether it could ever be the same to Florence, if he were in some distant place, and she were sitting there alone.

He had to think, too, of Mr. Toots, and Mr. Feeder, B.A.; of all the boys; and of Doctor Blimber, Mrs. Blimber, and Miss Blimber; of home, and of his aunt and Miss Tox; of his father, Dombey and Son, Walter with the poor old uncle who had got the money he wanted, and that gruff-voiced captain with the iron hand. Besides all this, he had a number of little visits to pay, in the course of the day; to the schoolroom, to Doctor Blimber's study, to Mrs. Blimber's private apartment, to Miss Blimber's, and to the dog. For he was free of the whole house now, to range it as he chose; and, in his desire to part with everybody on affectionate terms, he attended, in his way, to them all. Sometimes he found places in books for Briggs, who was always losing them; sometimes he looked up words in dictionaries for other young gentlemen who were in extremity; sometimes he held skeins of silk for Mrs. Blimber to wind; sometimes he put Cornelia's desk to rights; sometimes he would even creep into the Doctor's study, and, sitting on the carpet near his learned feet, turn the globes softly, and go round the world, or take a flight among the far-off stars.

In those days immediately before the holidays, in short, when the other young gentlemen were labouring for dear life through a general resumption of the studies of the whole half-year, Paul was such a privileged pupil as had never been seen in that house before. He could hardly believe it himself; but his liberty lasted from hour to hour, and from day to day; and little Dombey was caressed by every one. Doctor Blimber was so particular about him, that he requested Johnson to retire from the dinner-table one day, for having thoughtlessly spoken to him as 'poor little Dombey'; which Paul thought rather hard and severe, though he had flushed at the moment, and wondered why Johnson should pity him. It was the more questionable justice, Paul thought, in the Doctor, from his having certainly overheard that great authority give his assent on the previous evening, to the proposition (stated by Mrs. Blimber) that poor dear little Dombey was more old-fashioned than ever. And now it was that Paul began to think it must surely be old-fashioned to be very thin, and light, and easily tired, and soon disposed to lie down anywhere and rest; for he couldn't help feeling that these were more and more his habits every day.

At last the party-day arrived; and Doctor Blimber

said at breakfast, 'Gentlemen, we will resume our studies on the twenty-fifth of next month.' Mr. Toots immediately threw off his allegiance, and put on his ring: and mentioning the Doctor in casual conversation shortly afterwards, spoke of him as 'Blimber'! This act of freedom inspired the older pupils with admiration and envy; but the younger spirits were appalled, and seemed to marvel that no beam fell down and crushed him.

Not the least allusion was made to the ceremonies of the evening, either at breakfast or at dinner; but there was a bustle in the house all day, and in the course of his perambulations, Paul made acquaintance with various strange benches and candlesticks, and met a harp in a green great-coat standing on the landing outside the drawing-room door. There was something queer, too, about Mrs. Blimber's head at dinner-time, as if she had screwed her hair up too tight; and though Miss Blimber showed a graceful bunch of plaited hair on each temple, she seemed to have her own little curls in paper underneath, and in a play-bill too: for Paul read 'Theatre Royal' over one of her sparkling spectacles, and 'Brighton' over the other.

There was a grand array of white waistcoats and cravats in the young gentlemen's bedrooms as evening approached; and such a smell of singed hair, that Doctor Blimber sent up the footman with his compliments, and wished to know if the house was on fire. But it was only the hairdresser curling the young gentlemen, and over-heating his tongs in the ardour of business.

When Paul was dressed—which was very soon done, for he felt unwell and drowsy, and was not able to stand about it very long—he went down into the drawing-room; where he found Doctor Blimber pacing up and down the room full dressed, but with a dignified and unconcerned demeanour, as if he thought it barely possible that one or two people might drop in by and by. Shortly afterwards, Mrs. Blimber appeared looking lovely, Paul thought; and attired in such a number of skirts that it was quite an excursion to walk round her. Miss Blimber came down soon after her mamma; a little squeezed in appearance, but very charming.

Mr. Toots and Mr. Feeder were the next arrivals. Each of these gentlemen brought his hat in his hand, as if he lived somewhere else; and when they were announced by the butler, Doctor Blimber said, 'Aye, aye, aye! God bless my soul!' and seemed extremely glad to see them. Mr. Toots was one blaze of jewellery and buttons: and he felt the circumstance so strongly, that when he had shaken hands with the Doctor, and had bowed to Mrs. Blimber and Miss Blimber, he took Paul aside, and said 'What do you think of this, Dombey!'

But notwithstanding this modest confidence in himself, Mr. Toots appeared to be involved in a good deal of uncertainty whether, on the whole, it was judicious to button the bottom button of his waistcoat, and whether, on a calm revision of all the circumstances, it was best to wear his wristbands turned up or turned down. Observing that Mr. Feeder's were turned up, Mr. Toots turned his up; but the wristbands of the next arrival being turned down, Mr. Toots turned his down. The differences in point of waistcoat buttoning, not only at the bottom, but at the top too, became so numerous and complicated as the arrivals thickened, that Mr. Toots was continually fingering that article of dress, as if he were performing on some instrument; and appeared to find the incessant execution it demanded, quite bewildering.

All the young gentlemen, tightly cravatted, curled, and pumped, and with their best hats in their hands, having been at different times announced and introduced, Mr. Baps, the dancing-master, came, accompanied by Mrs. Baps, to whom Mrs. Blimber was extremely kind and condescending. Mr. Baps was a very grave gentleman, with a slow and measured manner of speaking; and before he had stood under the lamp five minutes, he began to talk to Toots (who had been silently comparing pumps with him) about what you were to do with your raw materials when they came into your ports in return for your drain of gold. Mr. Toots, to whom the question seemed perplexing, suggested 'Cook 'em.' But Mr. Baps did not appear to think that would do.

Paul now slipped away from the cushioned corner of a sofa, which had been his post of observation, and went downstairs into the tea-room to be ready for Florence, whom he had not seen for nearly a fortnight, as he had remained at Doctor Blimber's on the previous Saturday and Sunday, lest he should take cold. Presently she came: looking so beautiful in her simple ball-dress, with her fresh flowers in her hand, that when she knelt down on the ground to take Paul round the neck and kiss him (for there was no one there, but his friend and another young woman waiting to serve out the tea), he could hardly make up his mind to let her go again, or to take away her bright and loving eyes from his face.

'But what is the matter, Floy?' asked Paul, almost sure that he saw a tear there.

'Nothing, darling; nothing,' returned Florence.

Paul touched her cheek gently with his finger—and it *was* a tear! 'Why, Floy!' said he.

'We 'll go home together, and I 'll nurse you, love,' said Florence.

'Nurse me!' echoed Paul.

Paul couldn't understand what that had to do with it, nor why the two young women looked on so seriously, nor why Florence turned away her face for a moment, and then turned it back, lighted up again with smiles.

'Floy,' said Paul, holding a ringlet of her dark hair in his hand. 'Tell me, dear. Do *you* think I have grown old-fashioned?'

His sister laughed, and fondled him, and told him 'No.'

'Because I know they say so,' returned Paul, 'and I want to know what they mean, Floy.'

But a loud double-knock coming at the door, and Florence hurrying to the table, there was no more said between them. Paul wondered again when he saw his friend whisper to Florence, as if she were comforting her; but a new arrival put that out of his head speedily.

It was Sir Barnet Skettles, Lady Skettles, and Master Skettles. Master Skettles was to be a new boy after the vacation, and Fame had been busy, in Mr. Feeder's room, with his father, who was in the House of Commons, and of whom Mr. Feeder had said that when he *did* catch the Speaker's eye (which he had been expected to do for three or four years), it was anticipated that he would rather touch up the Radicals.

'And what room is this now, for instance?' said Lady Skettles to Paul's friend, 'Melia.

'Doctor Blimber's study, ma'am,' was the reply.

Lady Skettles took a panoramic survey of it through her glass, and said to Sir Barnet Skettles, with a nod of approval, 'Very good.' Sir Barnet assented, but Master Skettles looked suspicious and doubtful.

'And this little creature, now,' said Lady Skettles, turning to Paul. 'Is he one of the—'

'Young gentlemen, ma'am; yes, ma'am,' said Paul's friend.

'And what is your name, my pale child?' said Lady Skettles.

'Dombey,' answered Paul.

Sir Barnet Skettles immediately interposed, and said that he had had the honour of meeting Paul's father at a public dinner, and that he hoped he was very well. Then Paul heard him say to Lady Skettles, 'City—very rich—most respectable—Doctor mentioned it.' And then he said to Paul, 'Will you tell your good papa that Sir Barnet Skettles rejoiced to hear that he was very well, and sent him his best compliments?'

'Yes, sir,' answered Paul.

'That is my brave boy,' said Sir Barnet Skettles. 'Barnet,' to Master Skettles, who was revenging himself for the studies to come, on the plum-cake, 'this is a young gentleman you ought to know. This is a young gentleman you *may* know, Barnet,' said Sir Barnet Skettles, with an emphasis on the permission.

'What eyes! What hair! What a lovely face!' exclaimed Lady Skettles softly, as she looked at Florence through her glass.

'My sister,' said Paul, presenting her.

The satisfaction of the Skettleses was now complete. And as Lady Skettles had conceived, at first sight, a liking for Paul, they all went upstairs together: Sir Barnet Skettles taking care of Florence, and young Barnet following.

Young Barnet did not remain long in the background after they had reached the drawing-room, for Doctor Blimber had him out in no time, dancing with Florence. He did not appear to Paul to be particularly happy, or particularly anything but sulky, or to care much what he was about; but as Paul heard Lady Skettles say to Mrs. Blimber, while she beat time with her fan, that her dear boy was evidently smitten to death by that angel of a child, Miss Dombey, it would seem that Skettles junior was in a state of bliss, without showing it.

Little Paul thought it a singular coincidence that nobody had occupied his place among the pillows; and that when he came into the room again, they should all make way for him to go back to it, remembering it was his. Nobody stood before him either, when they observed that he liked to see Florence dancing, but they left the space in front quite clear, so that he might follow her with his eyes. They were so kind, too, even the strangers, of whom there were soon a great many, that they came and spoke to him every now and then, and asked him how he was, and if his head ached, and whether he was tired. He was very much obliged to them for all their kindness and attention, and reclining propped up in his corner, with Mrs. Blimber and Lady Skettles on the same sofa, and Florence coming and sitting by his side as soon as every dance was ended, he looked on very happily indeed.

Florence would have sat by him all night, and would not have danced at all of her own accord, but Paul made her, by telling her how much it pleased him. And he told her the truth, too; for his small heart swelled, and his face glowed, when he saw how much they all admired her, and how she was the beautiful little rosebud of the room.

From his nest among the pillows, Paul could see and hear almost everything that passed, as if the whole were being done for his amusement. Among other little incidents that he observed, he observed Mr.

Baps the dancing-master get into conversation with Sir Barnet Skettles, and very soon ask him, as he had asked Mr. Toots, what you were to do with your raw materials, when they came into your ports in return for your drain of gold—which was such a mystery to Paul that he was quite desirous to know what ought to be done with them. Sir Barnet Skettles had much to say upon the question, and said it; but it did not appear to solve the question, for Mr. Baps retorted, Yes, but supposing Russia stepped in with her tallows; which struck Sir Barnet almost dumb, for he could only shake his head after that, and say, why then you must fall back upon your cottons, he supposed.

Sir Barnet Skettles looked after Mr. Baps when he went to cheer up Mrs. Baps (who, being quite deserted, was pretending to look over the music-book of the gentleman who played the harp), as if he thought him a remarkable kind of man; and shortly afterwards he said so in those words to Doctor Blimber, and inquired if he might take the liberty of asking who he was, and whether he had ever been in the Board of Trade. Doctor Blimber answered no, he believed not; and that in fact he was a Professor of—

'Of something connected with statistics, I 'll swear?' observed Sir Barnet Skettles.

'Why no, Sir Barnet,' replied Doctor Blimber, rubbing his chin. 'No, not exactly.'

'Figures of some sort, I would venture a bet,' said Sir Barnet Skettles.

'Why yes,' said Dr. Blimber, 'yes, but not of that sort. Mr. Baps is a very worthy sort of man, Sir Barnet, and—in fact he 's our professor of dancing.'

Paul was amazed to see that this piece of information quite altered Sir Barnet Skettles' opinion of Mr. Baps, and that Sir Barnet flew into a perfect rage, and glowered at Mr. Baps over on the other side of the room. He even went so far as to D Mr. Baps to Lady Skettles, in telling her what had happened, and to say that it was like his most con-summate and con-foun-ded impudence.

There was another thing that Paul observed. Mr. Feeder, after imbibing several custard-cups of negus, began to enjoy himself. The dancing in general was ceremonious, and the music rather solemn—a little like church music in fact—but after the custard-cups Mr. Feeder told Mr. Toots that he was going to throw a little spirit into the thing. After that, Mr. Feeder not only began to dance as if he meant dancing and nothing else, but secretly to stimulate the music to perform wild tunes. Further, he became particular in his attentions to the ladies; and dancing with Miss Blimber, whispered to her—whispered to her!—though not so softly but that Paul heard him say this remarkable poetry,

> 'Had I a heart for falsehood framed,
> I ne'er could injure You!'

This, Paul heard him repeat to four young ladies in succession. Well might Mr. Feeder say to Mr. Toots, that he was afraid he should be worse for it to-morrow!

Mrs. Blimber was a little alarmed by this—comparatively speaking—profligate behaviour; and especially by the alteration in the character of the music, which, beginning to comprehend low melodies that were popular in the streets, might not unnaturally be supposed to give offence to Lady Skettles. But Lady Skettles was so very kind as to beg Mrs. Blimber not to mention it; and to receive her explanation that Mr. Feeder's spirits sometimes betrayed him into excesses on these occasions, with the greatest courtesy and politeness; observing, that he seemed a very nice sort of person for his situation, and that she particularly liked the unassuming style of his hair—which (as already hinted) was about a quarter of an inch long.

Once, when there was a pause in the dancing, Lady Skettles told Paul that he seemed very fond of music. Paul replied, that he was; and if she was too, she ought to hear his sister Florence, sing. Lady Skettles presently discovered that she was dying with anxiety to have that gratification; and though Florence was at first very much frightened at being asked to sing before so many people, and begged earnestly to be excused, yet, on Paul calling her to him, and saying, 'Do, Floy! Please! For me, my dear!' she went straight to the piano, and began. When they all drew a little away, that Paul might see her; and when he saw her sitting there alone, so young, and good, and beautiful, and kind to him; and heard her thrilling voice, so natural and sweet, and such a golden link between him and all his life's love and happiness, rising out of the silence; he turned his face away, and hid his tears. Not, as he told them when they spoke to him, not that the music was too plaintive or too sorrowful, but it was so dear to him.

They all loved Florence! How could they help it? Paul had known beforehand that they must and would; and sitting in his cushioned corner, with calmly folded hands, and one leg loosely doubled under him, few would have thought what triumph and delight expanded his childish bosom while he watched her, or what a sweet tranquillity he felt. Lavish encomiums on 'Dombey's sister' reached his ears from all the boys; admiration of the self-possessed and modest little beauty was on every lip: reports of her intelligence and accomplishments floated past him, constantly; and, as if borne in upon the air of the summer night, there was a half-intelligible sentiment diffused around, referring to Florence and himself, and breathing sympathy for both, that soothed and touched him.

He did not know why. For all that the child observed, and felt, and thought, that night—the present and the absent; what was then and what had been—were blended like the colours in the rainbow, or in the plumage of rich birds when the sun is shining on them, or in the softening sky when the same sun is setting. The many things he had had to think of lately, passed before him in the music; not as claiming his attention over again, or as likely evermore to occupy it, but as peacefully disposed of and gone. A solitary window, gazed through years ago, looked out upon an ocean, miles and miles away; upon its waters, fancies, busy with him only yesterday, were hushed and lulled to rest like broken waves. The same mysterious murmur he had wondered at, when lying on his couch upon the beach, he thought he still heard sounding through his sister's song, and through the hum of voices, and the tread of feet, and having some part in the faces flitting by, and even in the heavy gentleness of Mr. Toots, who frequently came up to shake him by the hand. Through the universal kindness he still thought he heard it, speaking to him; and even his old-fashioned reputation seemed to be allied to it, he knew not how. Thus little Paul sat musing, listening, looking on, and dreaming; and was very happy.

Until the time arrived for taking leave: and then, indeed, there was a sensation in the party. Sir Barnet Skettles brought up Skettles Junior to shake hands with him, and asked him if he would remember to tell his good papa, with his best compliments, that he, Sir Barnet Skettles, had said he hoped the two young gentlemen would become intimately acquainted. Lady Skettles kissed him, and parted his hair upon his brow, and held him in her arms; and even Mrs. Baps—poor Mrs. Baps! Paul was glad of that—came over from beside the music-book of the gentleman who played the harp, and took leave of him quite as heartily as anybody in the room.

'Good-bye, Doctor Blimber,' said Paul, stretching out his hand.

'Good-bye, my little friend,' returned the doctor.

'I 'm very much obliged to you, sir,' said Paul, looking innocently up into his awful face. 'Ask them to take care of Diogenes, if you please.'

Diogenes was the dog: who had never in his life received a friend into his confidence, before Paul. The doctor promised that every attention should be paid to Diogenes in Paul's absence, and Paul having again thanked him, and shaken hands with him, bade adieu to Mrs. Blimber and Cornelia with such heartfelt earnestness that Mrs. Blimber forgot from that moment to mention Cicero to Lady Skettles, though she had fully intended it all the evening. Cornelia, taking both Paul's hands in hers, said, 'Dombey, Dombey, you have always been my favourite pupil. God bless you!' And it showed, Paul thought, how easily one might do injustice to a person; for Miss Blimber meant it—though she *was* a Forcer.

A buzz then went round among the young gentlemen, of 'Dombey 's going!' 'Little Dombey 's going!' and there was a general move after Paul and Florence down the staircase and into the hall, in which the whole Blimber family were included. Such a circumstance, Mr. Feeder said aloud, as had never happened in the case of any former young gentleman within his experience; but it would be difficult to say if this were sober fact or custard-cups. The servants with the butler at their head, had all an interest in seeing little Dombey go; and even the weak-eyed young man, taking out his books and trunks to the coach that was to carry him and Florence to Mrs. Pipchin's for the night, melted visibly.

Not even the influence of the softer passion on the young gentlemen—and they all, to a boy, doted on Florence—could restrain them from taking quite a noisy leave of Paul; waving hats after him, pressing downstairs to shake hands with him, crying individually 'Dombey, don't forget me!' and indulging in many such ebullitions of feeling, uncommon among those young Chesterfields. Paul whispered Florence, as she wrapped him up before the door was opened. Did she hear them? Would she ever forget it? Was she glad to know it? And a lively delight was in his eyes as he spoke to her.

Once, for a last look, he turned and gazed upon the faces thus addressed to him, surprised to see how shining and how bright, and numerous they were, and how they were all piled and heaped up, as faces are at crowded theatres. They swam before him as he looked, like faces in an agitated glass; and next moment he was in the dark coach outside, holding close to Florence. From that time, whenever he thought of Doctor Blimber's, it came back as he had seen it in this last view; and it never seemed to be a real place again, but always a dream, full of eyes.

This was not quite the last of Doctor Blimber's, however. There was something else. There was Mr. Toots. Who, unexpectedly letting down one of the coach-windows, and looking in, said, with a most egregious chuckle, 'Is Dombey there?' and immediately put it up again, without waiting for an answer. Nor was this quite the last of Mr. Toots, even; for before the coachman could drive off, he as suddenly let down the other window, and looking in with a precisely similar chuckle, said in a precisely similar tone of voice, 'Is Dombey there?' and disappeared precisely as before.

How Florence laughed! Paul often remembered it, and laughed himself whenever he did so.

But there was much, soon afterwards—next day, and after that—which Paul could only recollect confusedly. As, why they stayed at Mrs. Pipchin's days and nights, instead of going home; why he lay in bed, with Florence sitting by his side; whether that had been his father in the room, or only a tall shadow on the wall; whether he had heard his doctor say, of some one, that if they had removed him before the occasion on which he had built up fancies, strong in proportion to his own weakness, it was very possible he might have pined away.

He could not even remember whether he had often said to Florence, 'Oh Floy, take me home, and never leave me!' but he thought he had. He fancied sometimes he had heard himself repeating, 'Take me home, Floy! take me home!'

But he could remember, when he got home, and was carried up the well-remembered stairs, that there had been the rumbling of a coach for many hours together, while he lay upon the seat, with Florence still beside him, and old Mrs. Pipchin sitting opposite. He remembered his old bed too, when they laid him down in it: his aunt, Miss Tox, and Susan: but there was something else, and recent too, that still perplexed him.

'I want to speak to Florence, if you please,' he said, 'To Florence by herself, for a moment!'

She bent down over him, and the others stood away.

'Floy, my pet, wasn't that papa in the hall, when they brought me from the coach?'

'Yes, dear.'

'He didn't cry, and go into his room, Floy, did he, when he saw me coming in?'

Florence shook her head, and pressed her lips against his cheek.

'I'm very glad he didn't cry,' said little Paul. 'I thought he did. Don't tell them that I asked.'

## CHAPTER XV

### AMAZING ARTFULNESS OF CAPTAIN CUTTLE, AND A NEW PURSUIT FOR WALTER GAY

WALTER could not, for several days, decide what to do in the Barbados business; and even cherished some faint hope that Mr. Dombey might not have meant what he had said, or that he might change his mind, and tell him he was not to go. But as nothing occurred to give this idea (which was sufficiently improbable in itself) any touch of confirmation, and as time was slipping by, and he had none to lose, he felt that he must act, without hesitating any longer.

Walter's chief difficulty was, how to break the change in his affairs to uncle Sol, to whom he was sensible it would be a terrible blow. He had the greater difficulty in dashing uncle Sol's spirits with such an astounding piece of intelligence, because they had lately recovered very much, and the old man had become so cheerful, that the little back-parlour was itself again. Uncle Sol had paid the first appointed portion of the debt to Mr. Dombey, and was hopeful of working his way through the rest; and to cast him down afresh, when he had sprung up so manfully from his troubles, was a very distressing necessity.

Yet it would never do to run away from him. He

must know of it beforehand; and how to tell him was the point. As to the question of going or not going, Walter did not consider that he had any power of choice in the matter. Mr. Dombey had truly told him that he was young, and that his uncle's circumstances were not good; and Mr. Dombey had plainly expressed, in the glance with which he had accompanied that reminder, that if he declined to go he might stay at home if he chose, but not in his counting-house. His uncle and he lay under a great obligation to Mr. Dombey, which was of Walter's own soliciting. He might have begun in secret to despair of ever winning that gentleman's favour, and might have thought that he was now and then disposed to put a slight upon him, which was hardly just. But what would have been duty without that, was still duty with it—or Walter thought so—and duty must be done.

When Mr. Dombey had looked at him, and told him he was young, and that his uncle's circumstances were not good, there had been an expression of disdain in his face; a contemptuous and disparaging assumption that he would be quite content to live idly on a reduced old man, which stung the boy's generous soul. Determined to assure Mr. Dombey, in so far as it was possible to give him the assurance without expressing it in words, that indeed he mistook his nature, Walter had been anxious to show even more cheerfulness and activity after the West Indian interview than he had shown before: if that were possible, in one of his quick and zealous disposition. He was too young and inexperienced to think, that possibly this very quality in him was not agreeable to Mr. Dombey, and that it was no stepping-stone to his good opinion to be elastic and hopeful of pleasing under the shadow of his powerful displeasure, whether it were right or wrong. But it may have been—it may have been—that the great man thought himself defied in this new exposition of an honest spirit, and purposed to bring it down.

'Well! at last and at least, uncle Sol must be told,' thought Walter, with a sigh. And as Walter was apprehensive that his voice might perhaps quaver a little, and that his countenance might not be quite as hopeful as he could wish it to be, if he told the old man himself, and saw the first effects of his communication on his wrinkled face, he resolved to avail himself of the services of that powerful mediator, Captain Cuttle. Sunday coming round, he set off, therefore, after breakfast, once more to beat up Captain Cuttle's quarters.

It was not unpleasant to remember, on the way thither, that Mrs. MacStinger resorted to a great distance every Sunday morning, to attend the ministry of the Reverend Melchisedech Howler, who, having been one day discharged from the West India Docks on a false suspicion (got up expressly against him by the general enemy) of screwing gimlets into puncheons, and applying his lips to the orifice, had announced the destruction of the world for that day two years, at ten in the morning, and opened a front-parlour for the reception of ladies and gentlemen of the Ranting persuasion, upon whom, on the first occasion of their assemblage, the admonitions of the Reverend Melchisedech had produced so powerful an effect, that, in their rapturous performance of a sacred jig, which closed the service, the whole flock broke through into a kitchen below, and disabled a mangle belonging to one of the fold.

This the captain, in a moment of uncommon conviviality, had confided to Walter and his uncle, between the repetitions of Lovely Peg, on the night when Brogley the broker was paid out. The captain himself was punctual in his attendance at a church in his own neighbourhood, which hoisted the Union Jack every Sunday morning; and where he was good enough—the lawful beadle being infirm—to keep an eye upon the boys, over whom he exercised great power, in virtue of his mysterious hook. Knowing the regularity of the captain's habits, Walter made all the haste he could, that he might anticipate his going out; and he made such good speed, that he had the pleasure, on turning into Brig Place, to behold the broad blue coat and waistcoat hanging out of the captain's open window, to air in the sun.

It appeared incredible that the coat and waistcoat could be seen by mortal eyes without the captain: but he certainly was not in them, otherwise his legs—the houses in Brig Place not being lofty—would have obstructed the street door, which was perfectly clear. Quite wondering at this discovery, Walter gave a single knock.

'Stinger,' he distinctly heard the captain say, up in his room, as if that were no business of his. Therefore Walter gave two knocks.

'Cuttle,' he heard the captain say upon that; and immediately afterwards the captain, in his clean shirt and braces, with his neckerchief hanging loosely round his throat like a coil of rope, and his glazed hat on, appeared at the window, leaning out over the broad blue coat and waistcoat.

'Wal'r!' cried the captain, looking down upon him in amazement.

'Ay, ay, Captain Cuttle,' returned Walter, 'only me.'

'What 's the matter, my lad?' inquired the captain, with great concern. 'Gills an't been and sprung nothing again?'

'No, no,' said Walter. 'My uncle 's all right, Captain Cuttle.'

The captain expressed his gratification, and said he would come down below and open the door, which he did.

'Though you 're early, Wal'r,' said the captain, eyeing him still doubtfully, when they got upstairs.

'Why, the fact is, Captain Cuttle,' said Walter, sitting down, 'I was afraid you would have gone out, and I want to benefit by your friendly counsel.'

'So you shall,' said the captain; 'what 'll you take?'

'I want to take your opinion, Captain Cuttle,' returned Walter, smiling. 'That 's the only thing for me.'

'Come on then,' said the captain. 'With a will, my lad!'

Walter related to him what had happened; and the difficulty in which he felt respecting his uncle, and the relief it would be to him if Captain Cuttle, in his kindness, would help him to smooth it away; Captain Cuttle's infinite consternation and astonishment at the prospect unfolded to him gradually swallowing that gentleman up, until it left his face quite vacant, and the suit of blue, the glazed hat, and the hook, apparently without an owner.

'You see, Captain Cuttle,' pursued Walter, 'for myself, I am young, as Mr. Dombey said, and not to be considered. I am to fight my way through the world, I know; but there are two points I was thinking, as I came along, that I should be very particular about, in respect to my uncle. I don't mean to say that I deserve to be the pride and delight of his life—you believe me, I know—but I am. Now, don't you think I am?'

The captain seemed to make an endeavour to rise from the depths of his astonishment, and get back to his face; but the effort being ineffectual, the glazed hat merely nodded with a mute, unutterable meaning.

'If I live and have my health,' said Walter, 'and I am not afraid of that, still, when I leave England I can hardly hope to see my uncle again. He is old, Captain Cuttle; and besides, his life is a life of custom—'

'Steady, Wal'r! Of a want of custom?' said the Captain, suddenly reappearing.

'Too true,' returned Walter, shaking his head; 'but I meant a life of habit, Captain Cuttle—that sort of custom. And if (as you very truly said, I am sure) he would have died the sooner for the loss of the stock, and all those objects to which he has been accustomed for so many years, don't you think he might die a little sooner for the loss of—'

'Of his nevy,' interposed the captain. 'Right!'

'Well then,' said Walter, trying to speak gaily, 'we must do our best to make him believe that the separation is but a temporary one, after all; but as I know better, or dread that I know better, Captain Cuttle, and as I have so many reasons for regarding him with affection, and duty, and honour, I am afraid I should make but a very poor hand at that, if I tried to persuade him of it. That's my great reason for wishing you to break it out to him; and that's the first point.'

'Keep her off a point or so!' observed the captain, in a contemplative voice.

'What did you say, Captain Cuttle?' inquired Walter.

'Stand by!' returned the captain, thoughtfully.

Walter paused to ascertain if the captain had any particular information to add to this, but as he said no more, went on.

'Now, the second point, Captain Cuttle. I am sorry to say, I am not a favourite with Mr. Dombey. I have always tried to do my best, and I have always done it; but he does not like me. He can't help his likings and dislikings, perhaps, I say nothing of that. I only say that I am certain he does not like me. He does not send me to this post as a good one; he disdains to represent it as being better than it is; and I doubt very much if it will ever lead me to advancement in the House—whether it does not, on the contrary, dispose of me for ever, and put me out of the way. Now, we must say nothing of this to my uncle, Captain Cuttle, but must make it out to be as favourable and promising as we can; and when I tell you what it really is, I only do so, that in case any means should ever arise of lending me a hand, so far off, I may have one friend at home who knows my real situation.'

'Wal'r, my boy,' replied the captain, 'in the Proverbs of Solomon you will find the following words, "May we never want a friend in need, nor a bottle to give him!" When found, make a note of.'

Here the captain stretched out his hand to Walter, with an air of downright good faith that spoke volumes; at the same time repeating (for he felt proud of the accuracy and pointed application of his quotation), 'When found, make a note of.'

'Captain Cuttle,' said Walter, taking the immense fist extended to him by the captain in both his hands, which it completely filled, 'next to my uncle Sol, I love you. There is no one on earth in whom I can more safely trust, I am sure. As to the mere going away, Captain Cuttle, I don't care for that; why should I care for that! If I were free to seek my own fortune—if I were free to go as a common sailor—if I were free to venture on my own account to the farthest end of the world—I would gladly go! I would have gladly gone, years ago, and taken my chance of what might come of it. But it was against my uncle's wishes, and against the plans he had formed for me; and there was an end of that. But what I feel, Captain Cuttle, is that we have been a little mistaken all along, and that, so far as my improvement in my prospects is concerned, I am no better off now than I was when I first entered Dombey's House—perhaps a little worse, for the House may have been kindly inclined towards me then, and it certainly is not now.'

'Turn again, Whittington,' muttered the disconsolate captain, after looking at Walter for some time.

'Aye!' replied Walter, laughing, 'and turn a great many times, too, Captain Cuttle, I 'm afraid, before such fortune as his ever turns up again. Not that I complain,' he added, in his lively, animated, energetic way. 'I have nothing to complain of. I am provided for. I can live. When I leave my uncle, I leave him to you; and I can leave him to no one better, Captain Cuttle. I haven't told you all this because I despair, not I; it 's to convince you that I can't pick and choose in Dombey's House, and that where I am sent, there I must go, and what I am offered, that I must take. It 's better for my uncle that I should be sent away; for Mr. Dombey is a valuable friend to him, as he proved himself, you know when, Captain Cuttle; and I am persuaded he won't be less valuable when he hasn't me there, every day, to awaken his dislike. So hurrah for the West Indies, Captain Cuttle! How does that tune go that the sailors sing?

'"For the Port of Barbados, boys!
Cheerily!

Leaving old England behind us, boys!
Cheerily!" '

Here the captain roared in chorus—

'Oh cheerily, cheerily!
'Oh cheer—i—ly!'

The last line reaching the quick ears of an ardent skipper not quite sober, who lodged opposite, and who instantly sprung out of bed, threw up his window, and joined in, across the street, at the top of his voice, produced a fine effect. When it was impossible to sustain the concluding note any longer, the skipper bellowed forth a terrific 'ahoy!' intended in part as a friendly greeting, and in part to show that he was not at all breathed. That done, he shut down his window, and went to bed again.

'And now, Captain Cuttle,' said Walter, handing him the blue coat and waistcoat, and bustling very much, 'if you 'll come and break the news to uncle Sol (which he ought to have known, days upon days ago, by rights), I 'll leave you at the door, you know, and walk about until the afternoon.'

The captain, however, scarcely appeared to relish the commission, or to be by any means confident of his powers of executing it. He had arranged the future life and adventures of Walter so very differently, and so entirely to his own satisfaction; he had felicitated himself so often on the sagacity and foresight displayed in that arrangement, and had found it so complete and perfect in all its parts; that to suffer it to go to pieces all at once, and even to assist in breaking it up, required a great effort of his resolution. The captain, too, found it difficult to unload his old ideas upon the subject, and to take a perfectly new cargo on board, with that rapidity which the circumstances required, or without jumbling and confounding the two. Consequently, instead of putting on his coat and waistcoat with anything like the impetuosity that could alone have kept pace with Walter's mood, he declined to invest himself with those garments at all at present; and informed Walter that on such a serious matter, he must be allowed to 'bite his nails a bit.'

'It 's an old habit of mine, Wal'r,' said the captain, 'any time these fifty year. When you see Ned Cuttle bite his nails, Wal'r, then you may know that Ned Cuttle 's aground.'

Thereupon the captain put his iron hook between his teeth, as if it were a hand; and with an air of wisdom and profundity that was the very concentration and sublimation of all philosophical reflection and grave inquiry, applied himself to the consideration of the subject in its various branches.

'There 's a friend of mine,' murmured the captain, in an absent manner, 'but he 's at present coasting round to Whitby, that would deliver such an opinion on this subject, or any other that cold be named, as would give Parliament six and beat 'em. Been knocked overboard, that man,' said the captain, 'twice, and none the worse for it. Was beat in his apprenticeship, for three weeks (off and on), about the head with a ringbolt. And yet a clearer-minded man don't walk.'

In spite of his respect for Captain Cuttle, Walter could not help inwardly rejoicing at the absence of this sage, and devoutly hoping that his limpid intellect might not be brought to bear on his difficulties until they were quite settled.

'If you was to take and show that man the buoy at the Nore,' said Captain Cuttle in the same tone, 'and ask him his opinion of it, Wal'r, he 'd give you an opinion that was no more like that buoy than your uncle's buttons are. There ain't a man that walks—certainly not on *two* legs—that can come near him. Not near him!'

'What 's his name, Captain Cuttle?' inquired Walter, determined to be interested in the captain's friend.

'His name 's Bunsby,' said the captain. 'But, Lord, it might be anything for the matter of that, with such a mind as his!'

The exact idea which the captain attached to this concluding piece of praise, he did not further elucidate; neither did Walter seek to draw it forth. For on his beginning to review, with the vivacity natural to himself and to his situation, the leading points in his own affairs, he soon discovered that the captain had relapsed into his former profound state of mind; and that while he eyed him steadfastly from beneath his bushy eyebrows, he evidently neither saw nor heard him, but remained immersed in cogitation.

In fact, Captain Cuttle was labouring with such great designs, that far from being aground, he soon got off into the deepest of water, and could find no bottom to his penetration. By degrees it became perfectly plain to the captain that there was some mistake here; that it was undoubtedly much more likely to be Walter's mistake than his; that if there were really any West India scheme afoot, it was a very different one from what Walter, who was young and rash, supposed; and could only be some new device for making his fortune with unusual celerity. 'Or if there should be any little hitch between 'em,' thought the captain, meaning between Walter and Mr. Dombey, 'it only wants a word in season from a friend of both parties, to set it right and smooth, and make all taut again.' Captain Cuttle's deduction from these considerations was, that as he already enjoyed the pleasure of knowing Mr. Dombey, from having spent a very agreeable half-hour in his company at Brighton (on the morning when they borrowed the money); and that, as a couple of men of the world, who understood each other, and were mutually disposed to make things comfortable, could easily arrange any little difficulty of this sort, and come at the real facts; the friendly thing for him to do would be, without saying anything about it to Walter at present, just to step up to Mr. Dombey's house—say to the servant 'Would ye be so good, my lad, as report Cap'en Cuttle here?' —meet Mr. Dombey in a confidential spirit—hook him by the button-hole—talk it over—make it all right—and come away triumphant!

As these reflections presented themselves to the captain's mind, and by slow degrees assumed this shape and form, his visage cleared like a doubtful morning when it gives place to a bright noon. His eyebrows, which had been in the highest degree portentous, smoothed their rugged bristling aspect, and became serene; his eyes, which had been nearly closed in the severity of his mental exercise, opened freely; a smile which had been at first but three specks—one at the right-hand corner of his mouth, and one at the corner of each eye—gradually overspread his whole face, and rippling up into his forehead, lifted the glazed hat: as if that too had been aground with Captain Cuttle, and were now, like him, happily afloat again.

Finally the captain left off biting his nails, and said, 'Now, Wal'r, my boy, you may help me on with them slops.' By which the captain meant his coat and waistcoat.

Walter little imagined why the captain was so particular in the arrangement of his cravat, as to twist the pendent ends into a sort of pigtail, and pass them through a massive gold ring with a picture of a tomb upon it, and a neat iron railing, and a tree, in memory of some deceased friend. Nor why the captain pulled up his shirt-collar to the utmost limits allowed by the Irish linen below, and by so doing decorated himself with a complete pair of blinkers; nor why he changed his shoes, and put on an unparalleled pair of ankle-jacks, which he only wore on extraordinary occasions. The captain being at length attired to his own complete satisfaction, and having glanced at himself from head to foot in a shaving-glass which he removed from a nail for that purpose, took up his knotted stick, and said he was ready.

The captain's walk was more complacent than usual when they got out into the street; but this Walter supposed to be the effect of the ankle-jacks, and took little heed of. Before they had gone very far they encountered a woman selling flowers; when the captain stopping short, as if struck by a happy idea, made a purchase of the largest bundle in her basket: a most glorious nosegay, fan-shaped, some two feet and a half round, and composed of all the jolliest-looking flowers that blow.

Armed with this little token which he designed for Mr. Dombey, Captain Cuttle walked on with Walter until they reached the instrument-maker's door, before which they both paused.

'You 're going in?' said Walter.

'Yes,' returned the captain, who felt that Walter must be got rid of before he proceeded any further, and that he had better time his projected visit somewhat later in the day.

'And you won't forget anything?'

'No,' returned the captain.

'I'll go upon my walk at once,' said Walter, 'and

then I shall be out of the way, Captain Cuttle.'

'Take a good long 'un, my lad!' replied the captain calling after him. Walter waved his hand in assent, and went his way.

His way was nowhere in particular; but he thought he would go out into the fields, where he could reflect upon the unknown life before him, and resting under some tree, ponder quietly. He knew no better fields than those near Hampstead, and no better means of getting at them than by passing Mr. Dombey's house.

It was as stately and as dark as ever, when he went by and glanced up at its frowning front. The blinds were all pulled down, but the upper windows stood wide open, and the pleasant air stirring those curtains and waving them to and fro, was the only sign of animation in the whole exterior. Walter walked softly as he passed, and was glad when he had left the house a door or two behind.

He looked back then; with the interest he had always felt for the place since the adventure of the lost child, years ago; and looked especially at those upper windows. While he was thus engaged, a chariot drove to the door, and a portly gentleman in black, with a heavy watch-chain, alighted, and went in. When he afterwards remembered this gentleman and his equipage together, Walter had no doubt he was a physician; and then he wondered who was ill; but the discovery did not occur to him until he had walked some distance, thinking listlessly of other things.

Though still, of what the house had suggested to him; for Walter pleased himself with thinking that perhaps the time might come, when the beautiful child who was his old friend and had always been so grateful to him and so glad to see him since, might interest her brother in his behalf and influence his fortunes for the better. He liked to imagine this

—more, at that moment, for the pleasure of imagining her continued remembrance of him, than for any worldly profit he might gain: but another and more sober fancy whispered to him that if he were alive then, he would be beyond the sea and forgotten; she married, rich, proud, happy. There was no more reason why she should remember him with any interest in such an altered state of things, than any plaything she ever had. No, not so much.

Yet Walter so idealised the pretty child whom he had found wandering in the rough streets, and so identified her with her innocent gratitude of that night and the simplicity and truth of its expression, that he blushed for himself as a libeller when he argued that she could ever grow proud. On the other hand, his meditations were of that fantastic order that it seemed hardly less libellous in him to imagine her grown a woman: to think of her as anything but the same artless, gentle, winning little creature, that she had been in the days of Good Mrs. Brown. In a word, Walter found out that to reason with himself about Florence at all, was to become very unreasonable indeed; and that he could do no better than preserve her image in his mind as something precious, unattainable, unchangeable, and indefinite—indefinite in all but its power of giving him pleasure, and restraining him like an angel's hand from anything unworthy.

It was a long stroll in the fields that Walter took that day, listening to the birds, and the Sunday bells, and the softened murmur of the town—breathing sweet scents; glancing sometimes at the dim horizon beyond which his voyage and his place of destination lay; then looking round on the green English grass and the home landscape. But he hardly once thought, even of going away, distinctly; and seemed to put off reflection idly, from hour to hour, and from minute to minute, while he yet went on reflecting all the time.

Walter had left the fields behind him, and was plodding homeward in the same abstracted mood, when he heard a shout from a man, and then a woman's voice calling to him loudly by name. Turning quickly in his surprise, he saw that a hackney-coach, going in the contrary direction, had stopped at no great distance; that the coachman was looking back from his box and making signals to him with his whip; and that a young woman inside was leaning out of the window, and beckoning with immense energy. Running up to this coach, he found that the young woman was Miss Nipper, and that Miss Nipper was in such a flutter as to be almost beside herself.

'Staggs's Gardens, Mr. Walter!' said Miss Nipper; 'if you please, oh do!'

'Eh?' cried Walter; 'what is the matter?'

'Oh, Mr. Walter, Staggs's Gardens, if you please!' said Susan.

'There!' cried the coachman, appealing to Walter, with a sort of exulting despair; 'that 's the way the young lady 's been a goin' on for up'ards of a mortal hour, and me continivally backing out of no thoroughfares, where she *would* drive up. I 've had a many fares in this coach, first and last, but never such a fare as her.'

'Do you want to go to Staggs's Gardens, Susan?' inquired Walter.

'Ah! *She* wants to go there! WHERE IS IT?' growled the coachman.

'I don't know where it is!' exclaimed Susan, wildly. 'Mr. Walter, I was there once myself, along with Miss Floy and our poor darling Master Paul, on the very day when you found Miss Floy in the City, for we lost her coming home, Mrs. Richards and me, and a mad bull, and Mrs. Richards's eldest, and though I went there afterwards, I can't remember where it is, I think it 's sunk into the ground. Oh, Mr. Walter, don't desert me, Staggs's Gardens, if you please! Miss Floy's darling—all our darlings—little, meek, meek Master Paul! Oh Mr. Walter!'

'Good God!' cried Walter. 'Is he very ill?'

'The pretty flower!' cried Susan, wringing her hands, 'has took the fancy that he 'd like to see his old nurse, and I've come to bring her to his bedside, Mrs. Staggs, of Polly Toodle's Gardens, some one pray!'

Greatly moved by what he heard, and catching Susan's earnestness immediately, Walter, now that he understood the nature of her errand, dashed into it with such ardour that the coachman had enough to do to follow closely as he ran before, inquiring here and there and everywhere, the way to Staggs's Gardens.

There was no such place as Staggs's Gardens. It had vanished from the earth. Where the old rotten summer-houses once had stood, palaces now reared their heads, and granite columns of gigantic girth opened a vista to the railway world beyond. The miserable waste ground, where the refuse-matter had been heaped of yore, was swallowed up and gone; and in its frowsy stead were tiers of warehouses, crammed with rich goods and costly merchandise. The old by-streets now swarmed with passengers and vehicles of every kind: the new streets that had stopped disheartened in the mud and waggon-ruts, formed towns within themselves, originating wholesome comforts and conveniences belonging to themselves, and never tried nor thought of until they sprung into existence. Bridges that had led to nothing, led to villas, gardens, churches, healthy public walks. The carcasses of houses, and beginnings of new thoroughfares, had started off upon the line at steam's own speed, and shot away into the country in a monster train.

As to the neighbourhood which had hesitated to acknowledge the railroad in its straggling days, that had grown wise and penitent, as any Christian might in such a case, and now boasted of its powerful and prosperous relation. There were railway patterns in its drapers' shops, and railway journals in the windows of its newsmen. There were railway hotels, coffee-houses, lodging-houses, boarding-houses; railway plans, maps, views, wrappers, bottles, sandwich-boxes, and time-tables; railway hackney-coach and cabstands; railway omnibuses, railway streets and buildings, railway hangers-on and parasites, and flatterers out of all calculation. There was even railway time observed in clocks, as if the sun itself had given in. Among the vanquished was the master chimney-sweeper, whilom incredulous at Staggs's Gardens, who now lived in a stuccoed house three stories high, and gave himself out, with golden flourishes upon a varnished board, as contractor for the cleansing of railway chimneys by machinery.

To and from the heart of this great change, all day and night, throbbing currents rushed and returned incessantly like its life's blood. Crowds of people and mountains of goods, departing and arriving scores upon scores of times in every four-and-twenty hours, produced a fermentation in the place that was always in action. The very houses seemed disposed to pack up and take trips. Wonderful Members of Parliament, who, little more than twenty years before, had made themselves merry with the wild railroad theories of engineers, and given them the liveliest rubs in cross-examination, went down into the north with their watches in their hands, and sent on messages before by the electric telegraph, to say that they were coming. Night and day the conquering engines rumbled at their distant work, or, advancing smoothly to their journey's end, and gliding like tame dragons into the allotted corners grooved out to the inch for their reception, stood bubbling and trembling there, making the walls quake, as if they were dilating with the secret knowledge of great powers yet unsuspected in them, and strong purposes not yet achieved.

But Staggs's Gardens had been cut up root and branch. Oh woe the day when 'not a rood of English ground'—laid out in Staggs's Gardens—is secure!

At last, after much fruitless inquiry, Walter, followed by the coach and Susan, found a man who had once resided in that vanished land, and who was no other than the master sweep before referred to, grown stout, and knocking a double-knock at his own door. He knowed Toodle, he said, well. Belonged to the railroad, didn't he?

'Yes, sir, yes!' cried Susan Nipper from the coach-window.

Where did he live now? hastily inquired Walter.

He lived in the Company's own Buildings, second turning to the right, down the yard, cross over, and take the second on the right again. It was number eleven; they couldn't mistake it; but if they did, they had only to ask for Toodle, Engine Fireman, and any one would show them which was his house. At this unexpected stroke of success, Susan Nipper dismounted from the coach with all speed, took Walter's arm and set off at a breathless pace on foot; leaving the coach there to await their return.

'Has the little boy been long ill, Susan?' inquired Walter, as they hurried on.

'Ailing for a deal of time, but no one knew how much,' said Susan; adding, with excessive sharpness, 'Oh, them Blimbers!'

'Blimbers?' echoed Walter.

'I couldn't forgive myself at such a time as this, Mr. Walter,' said Susan, 'and when there 's so much serious distress to think about, if I rested hard on any one, especially on them that little darling Paul speaks well of, but I *may* wish that the family was set to work in a stony soil to make new roads, and that Miss Blimber went in front, and had the pick-axe!'

Miss Nipper then took breath, and went on faster than before, as if this extraordinary aspiration had relieved her. Walter, who had by this time no breath of his own to spare, hurried along without asking any more questions; and they soon, in their impatience, burst in at a little door and came into a clean parlour full of children.

'Where 's Mrs. Richards?' exclaimed Susan Nipper, looking round. 'Oh Mrs. Richards, Mrs. Richards, come along with me, my dear creetur!'

'Why, if it an't Susan!' cried Polly, rising with her honest face and motherly figure from among the group, in great surprise.

'Yes, Mrs. Richards, it 's me,' said Susan, 'and I wish it wasn't, though I may not seem to flatter when I say so, but little Master Paul is very ill, and told his pa to-day that he would like to see the face of his old nurse, and him and Miss Floy hope you 'll come along with me—and Mr. Walter, Mrs. Richards—forgetting what is past, and do a kindness to the sweet dear that is withering away. Oh, Mrs. Richards, withering away!' Susan Nipper crying, Polly shed tears to see her, and to hear what she had said; and all the children gathered round (including numbers of new babies); and Mr. Toodle, who had just come home from Birmingham, and was eating his dinner out of a basin, laid down his knife and fork, and put on his wife's bonnet and shawl for her, which were hanging up behind the door; then tapped her on the back; and said, with more fatherly feeling than eloquence, 'Polly! cut away!'

So they got back to the coach, long before the coachman expected them; and Walter, putting Susan and Mrs. Richards inside, took his seat on the box himself that there might be no more mistakes, and deposited them safely in the hall of Mr. Dombey's house—where, by the bye, he saw a mighty nosegay lying, which reminded him of the one Captain Cuttle had purchased in his company that morning. He would have lingered to know more of the young invalid, or waited any length of time to see if he could render the least service; but, painfully sensible that such conduct would be looked upon by Mr. Dombey as presumptuous and forward, he turned slowly, sadly, anxiously away.

He had not gone five minutes' walk from the door, when a man came running after him, and begged him to return. Walter retraced his steps as quickly as he could, and entered the gloomy house with a sorrowful foreboding.

## CHAPTER XVI

### WHAT THE WAVES WERE ALWAYS SAYING

PAUL had never risen from his little bed. He lay there, listening to the noises in the street, quite tranquilly; not caring much how the time went, but watching it and watching everything about him with observing eyes.

When the sunbeams struck into his room through the rustling blinds, and quivered on the opposite wall like golden water, he knew that evening was coming on, and that the sky was red and beautiful. As the reflection died away, and a gloom went creeping up the wall, he watched it deepen, deepen, deepen, into night. Then he thought how the long streets were dotted with lamps, and how the peaceful stars were shining overhead. His fancy had a strange tendency to wander to the river, which he knew was flowing through the great city; and now he thought how black it was, and how deep it would look, reflecting the hosts of stars—and more than all, how steadily it rolled away to meet the sea.

As it grew later in the night, and footsteps in the street became so rare that he could hear them coming, count them as they paused, and lose them in the hollow distance, he would lie and watch the many-coloured ring about the candle, and wait patiently for day. His only trouble was, the swift and rapid river. He felt forced, sometimes, to try to stop it—to stem it with his childish hands—or choke its way with sand—and when he saw it coming on, resistless, he cried out! But a word from Florence, who was always at his side, restored him to himself; and leaning his poor head upon her breast, he told Floy of his dream, and smiled.

When day began to dawn again, he watched for the sun; and when its cheerful light began to sparkle in the room, he pictured to himself—pictured! he saw —the high church towers rising up into the morning sky, the town reviving, waking, starting into life once more, the river glistening as it rolled (but rolling fast as ever), and the country bright with dew. Familiar sounds and cries came by degrees into the street below; the servants in the house were roused and busy; faces looked in at the door, and voices asked his attendants softly how he was. Paul always answered for himself, 'I am better. I am a great deal better, thank you! Tell papa so!'

By little and little, he got tired of the bustle of the day, the noise of carriages and carts, and people passing and repassing; and would fall asleep, or be troubled with a restless and uneasy sense again—the child could hardly tell whether this were in his sleeping or his waking moments—of that rushing river. 'Why, will it never stop, Floy?' he would sometimes ask her. 'It is bearing me away, I think!'

But Floy could always soothe and reassure him; and it was his daily delight to make her lay her head down on his pillow, and take some rest.

'You are always watching me, Floy. Let me watch *you*, now!' They would prop him up with cushions in a corner of his bed, and there he would recline the while she lay beside him: bending forward oftentimes to kiss her, and whispering to those who were near that she was tired, and how she had sat up so many nights beside him.

Thus, the flush of the day, in its heat and light, would gradually decline; and again the golden water would be dancing on the wall.

He was visited by as many as three grave doctors —they used to assemble downstairs, and come up together—and the room was so quiet, and Paul was so observant of them (though he never asked of anybody what they said), that he even knew the difference in the sound of their watches. But his interest centred in Sir Parker Peps, who always took his seat on the side of the bed. For Paul had heard them say long ago, that that gentleman had been with his mamma when she clasped Florence in her arms, and died. And he could not forget it, now. He liked him for it. He was not afraid.

The people round him changed as unaccountably as on that first night at Doctor Blimber's—except Florence; Florence never changed—and what had been Sir Parker Peps was now his father, sitting with his head upon his hand. Old Mrs. Pipchin dozing in an easy chair, often changed to Miss Tox, or his aunt; and Paul was quite content to shut his eyes again, and see what happened next without emotion. But this figure with its head upon its hand returned so often and remained so long, and sat so still and solemn, never speaking, never being spoken to, and rarely lifting up its face, that Paul began to wonder languidly, if it were real; and in the night-time saw it sitting there, with fear.

'Floy!' he said. 'What *is* that?'

'Where, dearest?'

'There! at the bottom of the bed.'

'There 's nothing there, except papa!'

The figure lifted up its head, and rose, and coming to the bedside, said, 'My own boy! Don't you know me?'

Paul looked it in the face, and thought, was this his father? But the face so altered to his thinking, thrilled while he gazed, as if it were in pain; and before he could reach out both his hands to take it between them, and draw it towards him, the figure turned away quickly from the little bed, and went out at the door.

Paul looked at Florence with a fluttering heart, but he knew what she was going to say, and stopped her with his face against her lips. The next time he observed the figure sitting at the bottom of the bed, he called to it.

'Don't be so sorry for me, dear papa! Indeed I am quite happy!'

His father coming and bending down to him—which he did quickly, and without first pausing by the bedside—Paul held him round the neck, and repeated those words to him several times, and very earnestly; and Paul never saw him in his room again at any time, whether it were day or night, but he called out, 'Don't be so sorry for me! Indeed I am quite happy!' This was the beginning of his always saying in the morning that he was a great deal better, and that they were to tell his father so.

How many times the golden water danced upon the wall; how many nights the dark dark river rolled towards the sea in spite of him; Paul never counted, never sought to know. If their kindness or his sense of it, could have increased, they were more kind, and he more grateful every day; but whether they were many days or few, appeared of little moment now, to the gentle boy.

One night he had been thinking of his mother, and her picture in the drawing-room downstairs, and thought she must have loved sweet Florence better than his father did, to have held her in her arms when she felt that she was dying—for even he, her brother, who had such dear love for her, could have no greater wish than that. The train of thought suggested to him to inquire if he had ever seen his mother; for he could not remember whether they had told him, yes or no, the river running very fast, and confusing his mind.

'Floy, did I ever see mamma?'

'No, darling, why?'

'Did I ever see any kind face, like mamma's, looking at me when I was a baby, Floy?'

He asked, incredulously, as if he had some vision of a face before him.

'Oh yes, dear!'

'Whose, Floy?'

'Your old nurse's. Often.'

'And where is my old nurse?' said Paul. 'Is she dead too? Floy, are we *all* dead, except you?'

There was a hurry in the room, for an instant—longer, perhaps; but it seemed no more—then all was still again; and Florence, with her face quite colourless, but smiling, held his head upon her arm. Her arm trembled very much.

'Show me that old nurse, Floy, if you please!'

'She is not here, darling. She shall come to-morrow.'

'Thank you, Floy!'

Paul closed his eyes with those words, and fell asleep. When he awoke, the sun was high, and the broad day was clear and warm. He lay a little, looking at the windows, which were open, and the curtains rustling in the air, and waving to and fro: then he said, 'Floy, is it to-morrow? Is she come?'

Some one seemed to go in quest of her. Perhaps it was Susan. Paul thought he heard her telling him when he had closed his eyes again, that she would soon be back; but he did not open them to see. She kept her word—perhaps she had never been away—but the next thing that happened was a noise of footsteps on the stairs, and then Paul woke—woke mind and body—and sat upright in his bed. He saw them now about him. There was no grey mist before them, as there had been sometimes in the night. He knew them every one, and called them by their names.

'And who is this? Is this my old nurse?' said the child, regarding with a radiant smile, a figure coming in.

'Yes, yes. No other stranger would have shed those tears at sight of him, and called him her dear boy, her pretty boy, her own poor blighted child. No other woman would have stooped down by his bed, and taken up his wasted hand, and put it to her lips and breast, as one who had some right to fondle it. No other woman would have so forgotten everybody there but him and Floy, and been so full of tenderness and pity.

'Floy! this is a kind good face!' said Paul. 'I am glad to see it again. Don't go away, old nurse! Stay here.'

His senses were all quickened, and he heard a name he knew.

'Who was that, who said "Walter?"' he asked, looking round. 'Some one said "Walter." Is he here? I should like to see him very much.'

Nobody replied directly; but his father soon said to Susan, 'Call him back, then: let him come up!' After a short pause of expectation, during which he looked with smiling interest and wonder, on his nurse, and saw that she had not forgotten Floy, Walter was brought into the room. His open face and manner, and his cheerful eyes, had always made him a favourite with Paul; and when Paul saw him, he stretched out his hand, and said 'Good-bye!'

'Good-bye, my child!' cried Mrs. Pipchin, hurrying to his bed's head. 'Not good-bye?'

For an instant, Paul looked at her with the wistful face with which he had so often gazed upon her in his corner by the fire. 'Ah yes,' he said placidly, 'good-bye! Walter dear, good-bye!'—turning his head to where he stood, and putting out his hand again. 'Where is papa?'

He felt his father's breath upon his cheek, before the words had parted from his lips.

'Remember Walter, dear papa,' he whispered, looking in his face. 'Remember Walter. I was fond of Walter!' The feeble hand waved in the air, as if it cried 'good-bye!' to Walter once again.

'Now lay me down,' he said, 'and Floy, come close to me, and let me see you!'

Sister and brother wound their arms around each other, and the golden light came streaming in, and fell upon them, locked together.

'How fast the river runs, between its green banks and the rushes, Floy! But it 's very near the sea. I hear the waves! They always said so!'

Presently he told her that the motion of the boat upon the stream was lulling him to rest. How green the banks were now, how bright the flowers growing on them, and how tall the rushes! Now the boat was out at sea, but gliding smoothly on. And now there was a shore before him. Who stood on the bank!

He put his hands together, as he had been used to do at his prayers. He did not remove his arms to do it; but they saw him fold them so, behind her neck.

'Mamma is like you, Floy. I know her by the face! But tell them that the print upon the stairs at school is not divine enough. The light about the head is shining on me as I go!'

The golden ripple on the wall came back again, and nothing else stirred in the room. The old, old fashion! The fashion that came in with our first garments, and will last unchanged until our race has run its course, and the wide firmament is rolled up like a scroll. The old, old fashion—Death!

Oh thank God, all who see it, for that older fashion yet, of Immortality! And look upon us, angels of young children, with regards not quite estranged, when the swift river bears us to the ocean!

## CHAPTER XVII

### CAPTAIN CUTTLE DOES A LITTLE BUSINESS FOR THE YOUNG PEOPLE

Captain Cuttle, in the exercise of that surprising talent for deep-laid and unfathomable scheming, with which (as is not unusual in men of transparent simplicity) he sincerely believed himself to be endowed by nature, had gone to Mr. Dombey's house on the eventful Sunday, winking all the way as a vent for his superfluous sagacity, and had presented himself in the full lustre of the ankle-jacks before the eyes of Towlinson. Hearing from that individual, to his great concern, of the impending calamity, Captain Cuttle, in his delicacy, sheered off again confounded; merely handing in the nosegay as a small mark of his solicitude, and leaving his respectful compliments for the family in general, which he accompanied with an expression of his hope that they would lay their heads well to the wind under existing circumstances, and a friendly intimation that he would 'look up again' to-morrow.

The captain's compliments were never heard of

any more. The captain's nosegay, after lying in the hall all night, was swept into the dust-bin next morning; and the captain's sly arrangement, involved in one catastrophe with greater hopes and loftier designs, was crushed to pieces. So, when an avalanche bears down a mountain-forest, twigs and bushes suffer with the trees, and all perish together.

When Walter returned home on the Sunday evening from his long walk, and its memorable close, he was too much occupied at first by the tidings he had to give them, and by the emotions naturally awakened in his breast by the scene through which he had passed, to observe either that his uncle was evidently unacquainted with the intelligence the captain had undertaken to impart, or that the captain made signals with his hook, warning him to avoid the subject. Not that the captain's signals were calculated to have proved very comprehensible, however attentively observed; for, like those Chinese sages who are said in their conferences to write certain learned words in the air that are wholly impossible of pronunciation, the captain made such waves and flourishes as nobody without a previous knowledge of his mystery, would have been at all likely to understand.

Captain Cuttle, however, becoming cognisant of what had happened, relinquished these attempts, as he perceived the slender chance that now existed of his being able to obtain a little easy chat with Mr. Dombey before the period of Walter's departure. But in admitting to himself, with a disappointed and crestfallen countenance, that Sol Gills must be told, and that Walter must go—taking the case for the present as he found it, and not having it enlightened or improved beforehand by the knowing management of a friend—the captain still felt an unabated confidence that he, Ned Cuttle, was the man for Mr.

Dombey; and that, to set Walter's fortunes quite square, nothing was wanted but that they two should come together. For the captain never could forget how well he and Mr. Dombey had got on at Brighton; with what nicety each of them had put in a word when it was wanted; how exactly they had taken one another's measure; nor how Ned Cuttle had pointed out that resource in the first extremity, and had brought the interview to the desired termination. On all these grounds the captain soothed himself with thinking that though Ned Cuttle was forced by the pressure of events to 'stand by' almost useless for the present, Ned would fetch up with a wet sail in good time, and carry all before him.

Under the influence of this good-natured delusion, Captain Cuttle even went so far as to revolve in his own bosom, while he sat looking at Walter and listening with a tear on his shirt-collar to what he related, whether it might not be at once genteel and politic to give Mr. Dombey a verbal invitation, whenever they should meet, to come and cut his mutton in Brig Place on some day of his own naming, and enter on the question of his young friend's prospects over a social glass. But the uncertain temper of Mrs. MacStinger, and the possibility of her setting up her rest in the passage during such an entertainment, and there delivering some homily of an uncomplimentary nature, operated as a check on the captain's hospitable thoughts, and rendered him timid of giving them encouragement.

One fact was quite clear to the captain, as Walter, sitting thoughtfully over his untasted dinner, dwelt on all that had happened; namely, that however Walter's modesty might stand in the way of his perceiving it himself, he was, as one might say, a member of Mr. Dombey's family. He had been, in his own person, connected with the incident he so pathetically described; he had been by name remembered and commended in close association with it; and his fortunes must have a particular interest in his employer's eyes. If the captain had any lurking doubt whatever of his own conclusions, he had not the least doubt that they were good conclusions for the peace of mind of the instrument-maker. Therefore he availed himself of so favourable a moment for breaking the West Indian intelligence to his old friend, as a piece of extraordinary preferment; declaring that for his part he would freely give a hundred thousand pounds (if he had it) for Walter's gain in the long-run, and that he had no doubt such an investment would yield a handsome premium.

Solomon Gills was at first stunned by the communication, which fell upon the little back-parlour like a thunderbolt, and tore up the hearth savagely. But the captain flashed such golden prospects before his dim sight: hinted so mysteriously at Whittingtonian consequences: laid such emphasis on what Walter had just now told them: and appealed to it so confidently as a corroboration of his predictions, and a great advance towards the realisation of the romantic legend of Lovely Peg: that he bewildered the old man. Walter, for his part, feigned to be so full of hope and ardour, and so sure of coming home again soon, and backed up the captain with such expressive shakings of his head and rubbings of his hands, that Solomon, looking first at him and then at Captain Cuttle, began to think he ought to be transported with joy.

'But I'm behind the time, you understand,' he observed in apology, passing his hand nervously down the whole row of bright buttons on his coat, and then up again, as if they were beads and he were telling them twice over: 'and I would rather have my dear boy here. It 's an old-fashioned notion, I dare say. He was always fond of the sea. He 's—and he looked wistfully at Walter—'he 's glad, to go.'

'Uncle Sol!' cried Walter, quickly, 'if you say that, I *won't* go. No, Captain Cuttle, I won't. If my uncle thinks I could be glad to leave him, though I was going to be made Governor of all the Islands in the West Indies, that 's enough. I 'm a fixture.'

'Wal'r, my lad,' said the captain. 'Steady! Sol Gills, take an observation of your nevy.'

Following with his eyes the majestic action of the captain's hook, the old man looked at Walter.

'Here is a certain craft,' said the captain, with a magnificent sense of the allegory into which he was soaring, 'a going to put out on a certain voyage. What name is wrote upon that craft indelibly? Is it The Gay? or,' said the captain, raising his voice as much as to say, observe the point of this, 'is it The Gills?'

'Ned,' said the old man, drawing Walter to his side, and taking his arm tenderly through his, 'I know. I know. Of course I know that Wally considers me more than himself always. That 's in my mind. When I say he is glad to go, I mean I hope he is. Eh? look you, Ned, and you too, Wally, my dear, this is new and unexpected to me; and I 'm afraid my being behind the time, and poor, is at the bottom of it. Is it really good fortune for him, do you tell me, now?' said the old man, looking anxiously from one to the other. 'Really and truly? Is it? I can reconcile myself to almost anything that advances Wally, but I won't have Wally putting himself at any disadvantage for me, or keeping anything from me. You, Ned Cuttle!' said the old man, fastening on the captain, to the manifest confusion of that diplomatist; 'are you dealing plainly by your old

THE WOODEN MIDSHIPMAN ON THE LOOK OUT.

friend? Speak out, Ned Cuttle? Is there anything behind? Ought he to go? How do you know it first, and why?'

As it was a contest of affection and self-denial, Walter struck in with infinite effect, to the captain's relief; and between them they tolerably reconciled old Sol Gills, by continued talking, to the project; or rather so confused him, that nothing, not even the pain of separation, was distinctly clear to his mind.

He had not much time to balance the matter; for on the very next day, Walter received from Mr. Carker the manager, the necessary credentials for his passage and outfit, together with the information that the Son and Heir would sail in a fortnight, or within a day or two afterwards at latest. In the hurry of preparation: which Walter purposely enhanced as much as possible: the old man lost what little self-possession he ever had; and so the time of departure drew on rapidly.

The captain, who did not fail to make himself acquainted with all that passed, through inquiries of Walter from day to day, found the time still tending on towards his going away, without any occasion offering itself, or seeming likely to offer itself, for a better understanding of his position. It was after much consideration of this fact, and much pondering over such an unfortunate combination of circumstances, that a bright idea occurred to the captain. Suppose he made a call on Mr. Carker, and tried to find out from *him* how the land really lay!

Captain Cuttle liked this idea very much. It came upon him in a moment of inspiration, as he was smoking an early pipe in Brig Place after breakfast; and it was worthy of the tobacco. It would quiet his conscience, which was an honest one, and was made a little uneasy by what Walter had confided to him, and what Sol Gills had said; and it would be a deep, shrewd act of friendship. He would sound Mr. Carker carefully, and say much or little, just as he read that gentleman's character, and discovered that they got on well together or the reverse.

Accordingly without the fear of Walter before his eyes (who he knew was at home packing), Captain Cuttle again assumed his ankle-jacks and mourning brooch, and issued forth on this second expedition. He purchased no propitiatory nosegay on the present occasion, as he was going to a place of business; but he put a small sunflower in his button-hole to give himself an agreeable relish of the country; and with this, and the knobby stick, and the glazed hat, bore down upon the offices of Dombey and Son.

After taking a glass of warm rum-and-water at a tavern close by, to collect his thoughts, the captain made a rush down the court, lest its good effects should evaporate, and appeared suddenly to Mr. Perch.

'Matey,' said the captain, in persuasive accents. 'One of your Governors is named Carker.'

Mr. Perch admitted it; but gave him to understand, as in official duty bound, that all his governors were engaged, and never expected to be disengaged any more.

'Look 'ee here, mate,' said the captain in his ear; 'my name 's Cap'en Cuttle.'

The captain would have hooked Perch gently to him, but Mr. Perch eluded the attempt; not so much in design, as in starting at the sudden thought that such a weapon unexpectedly exhibited to Mrs. Perch might, in her then condition, be destructive to that lady's hopes.

'If you 'll be so good as just report Cap'en Cuttle

here, when you get a chance,' said the captain, 'I 'll wait.'

Saying which, the captain took his seat on Mr. Perch's bracket, and drawing out his handkerchief from the crown of the glazed hat, which he jammed between his knees (without injury to its shape, for nothing human could bend it), rubbed his head well all over, and appeared refreshed. He subsequently arranged his hair with his hook, and sat looking round the office, contemplating the clerks with a serene respect.

The captain's equanimity was so impenetrable, and he was altogether so mysterious a being, that Perch the messenger was daunted.

'What name was it you said?' asked Mr. Perch, bending down over him as he sat on the bracket.

'Cap'en,' in a deep hoarse whisper.

'Yes,' said Mr. Perch, keeping time with his head.

'Cuttle.'

'Oh!' said Mr. Perch, in the same tone, for he caught it, and couldn't help it; the captain, in his diplomacy, was so impressive. 'I 'll see if he 's disengaged now. I don't know. Perhaps he may be for a minute.'

'Aye, aye, my lad, I won't detain him longer than a minute,' said the captain, nodding with all the weighty importance that he felt within him. Perch, soon returning, said, 'Will Captain Cuttle walk this way?'

Mr. Carker the manager, standing on the hearth-rug before the empty fireplace, which was ornamented with a castellated sheet of brown paper, looked at the captain as he came in, with no very special encouragement.

'Mr. Carker?' said Captain Cuttle.

'I believe so,' said Mr. Carker, showing all his teeth.

The captain liked his answering with a smile; it looked pleasant. 'You see,' began the captain, rolling his eyes slowly round the little room, and taking in as much of it as his shirt collar permitted; 'I 'm a seafaring man myself, Mr. Carker, and Wal'r, as is on your books here, is a'most a son of mine.'

'Walter Gay?' said Mr. Carker, showing all his teeth again.

'Wal'r Gay it is,' replied the captain, 'right!' The captain's manner expressed a warm approval of Mr. Carker's quickness of perception. 'I 'm a intimate friend of his and his uncle's. Perhaps,' said the captain, 'you may have heard your head governor mention my name?—Captain Cuttle.'

'No!' said Mr. Carker, with a still wider demonstration than before.

'Well,' resumed the captain, 'I 've the pleasure of his acquaintance. I waited upon him down on the Sussex coast there, with my young friend Wal'r, when—in short, when there was a little accommodation wanted.' The captain nodded his head in a manner that was at once comfortable, easy, and expressive. 'You remember, I dare say?'

'I think,' said Mr. Carker, 'I had the honour of arranging the business.'

'To be sure!' returned the captain. 'Right again! you had. Now I 've took the liberty of coming here—'

'Won't you sit down?' said Mr. Carker, smiling.

'Thank 'ee,' returned the captain, availing himself of the offer. 'A man does get more way upon himself, perhaps, in his conversation, when he sits down. Won't you take a cheer yourself?'

'No thank you,' said the manager, standing, perhaps from the force of winter habit, with his back against the chimney-piece, and looking down upon the captain with an eye in every tooth and gum. 'You have taken the liberty, you were going to say—though it 's none—'

'Thank 'ee kindly, my lad,' returned the captain: 'of coming here, on account of my friend Wal'r. Sol Gills, his uncle, is a man of science, and in science he may be considered a clipper; but he ain't what I should altogether call a able seaman—not a man of practice. Wal'r is as trim a lad as ever stepped; but he 's a little down by the head in one respect, and that is modesty. Now what I should wish to put to you,' said the captain, lowering his voice, and speaking in a kind of confidential growl, 'in a friendly way, entirely between you and me, and for my own private reckoning, till your head governor has wore round a bit, and I can come alongside of him, is this.—Is everything right and comfortable here, and is Wal'r out'ard bound, with a pretty fair wind?'

'What do you think now, Captain Cuttle,' returned Carker, gathering up his skirts and settling himself in his position. '*You* are a practical man; what do you think?'

The acuteness and significance of the captain's eye as he cocked it in reply, no words short of those unutterable Chinese words before referred to could describe.

'Come!' said the captain, unspeakably encouraged, 'what do you say? Am I right or wrong?'

So much had the captain expressed in his eye, emboldened and incited by Mr. Carker's smiling urbanity, that he felt himself in as fair a condition to put the question, as if he had expressed his sentiments with the utmost elaboration.

'Right,' said Mr. Carker, 'I have no doubt.'

'Out'ard bound with fair weather, then, I say,' cried Captain Cuttle.

Mr. Carker smiled assent.

'Wind right astarn, and plenty of it,' pursued the captain.

Mr. Carker smiled assent again.

'Aye, aye!' said Captain Cuttle, greatly relieved and pleased. 'I know'd how she headed, well enough; I told Wal'r so. Thank 'ee, thank 'ee.'

'Gay has brilliant prospects,' observed Mr. Carker, stretching his mouth wider yet: 'all the world before him.'

'All the world and his wife too, as the saying is,' returned the delighted captain.

At the word 'wife' (which he had uttered without design), the captain stopped, cocked his eye again, and putting the glazed hat on the top of the knobby stick, gave it a twirl, and looked sideways at his always smiling friend.

'I'd bet a gill of old Jamaica,' said the captain, eyeing him attentively, 'that I know what you 're smiling at.'

Mr. Carker took his cue, and smiled the more.

'It goes no farther?' said the captain, making a poke at the door with the knobby stick to assure himself that it was shut.

'Not an inch,' said Mr. Carker.

'You 're a thinking of a capital F perhaps?' said the captain.

Mr. Carker didn't deny it.

'Anything about a L,' said the captain, 'or a O?'

Mr. Carker still smiled.

'Am I right again?' inquired the captain in a whisper, with the scarlet circle on his forehead swelling in his triumphant joy.

Mr. Carker, in reply, still smiling, and now nodding assent, Captain Cuttle rose and squeezed him by the hand, assuring him, warmly, that they were on the same tack, and that as for him (Cuttle) he had laid his course that way all along. 'He know'd her first,' said the captain, with all the secrecy and gravity that the subject demanded, 'in an uncommon manner —*you* remember his finding her in the street when she was a'most a babby—he has liked her ever since, and she him, as much as two such youngsters can. We 've always said, Sol Gills and me, that they was cut out for each other.'

A cat, or a monkey, or a hyena, or a death's head, could not have shown the captain more teeth at one time, than Mr. Carker showed him at this period of their interview.

'There 's a general in-draught that way,' observed the happy captain. 'Wind and water sets in that direction, you see. Look at his being present t' other day!'

'Most favourable to his hopes,' said Mr. Carker.

'Look at his being towed along in the wake of that day!' pursued the captain. 'Why, what can cut him adrift now?'

'Nothing,' replied Mr. Carker.

'You 're right again,' returned the captain, giving his hand another squeeze. 'Nothing it is. So! steady! There 's a son gone: pretty little creetur. Ain't there?'

'Yes, there 's a son gone,' said the acquiescent Carker.

'Pass the word, and there 's another ready for you,' quoth the captain. 'Nevy of a scientific uncle! Nevy of Sol Gills! Wal'r! Wal'r, as is already in your business! And'—said the captain, rising gradually to a quotation he was preparing for a final burst, 'who—comes from Sol Gills's daily, *to* your business, and your buzzums.'

The captain's complacency as he gently jogged Mr. Carker with his elbow, on concluding each of the foregoing short sentences, could be surpassed by nothing but the exultation with which he fell back and eyed him when he had finished this brilliant display of eloquence and sagacity; his great blue waistcoat heaving with the throes of such a masterpiece, and his nose in a state of violent inflammation from the same cause.

'Am I right?' said the captain.

'Captain Cuttle,' said Mr. Carker, bending down at the knees, for a moment, in an odd manner, as if he were falling together to hug the whole of himself at once, 'your views in reference to Walter Gay are thoroughly and accurately right. I understand that we speak together in confidence.'

'Honour!' interposed the captain. 'Not a word.'

'To him or any one?' pursued the manager.

Captain Cuttle frowned and shook his head.

'But merely for your own satisfaction and guidance—and guidance, of course,' repeated Mr. Carker, 'with a view to your future proceedings.'

'Thank 'ee kindly, I am sure,' said the captain, listening with great attention.

'I have no hesitation in saying, that 's the fact. You have hit the probabilities exactly.'

'And with regard to your head governor,' said the captain, 'why an interview had better come about nat'ral between us. There 's time enough.'

Mr. Carker, with his mouth from ear to ear, repeated, 'Time enough.' Not articulating the words, but bowing his head affably, and forming them with his tongue and lips.

'And as I know—it 's what I always said—that

Wal'r 's in a way to make his fortune,' said the captain.

'To make his fortune,' Mr. Carker repeated, in the same dumb manner.

'And as Wal'r's going on this little voyage is, as I may say, in his day's work, and a part of his general expectations here,' said the captain.

'Of his general expectations here,' assented Mr. Carker, dumbly as before.

'Why, so long as I know that,' pursued the captain, 'there 's no hurry, and my mind 's at ease.'

Mr. Carker still blandly assenting in the same voiceless manner, Captain Cuttle was strongly confirmed in his opinion that he was one of the most agreeable men he had ever met, and that even Mr. Dombey might improve himself on such a model. With great heartiness, therefore, the captain once again extended his enormous hand (not unlike an old block in colour), and gave him a grip that left upon his smoother flesh a proof impression of the chinks and crevices with which the captain's palm was liberally tatooed.

'Farewell!' said the captain. 'I an't a man of many words, but I take it very kind of you to be so friendly, and above-board. You'll excuse me if I 've been at all intruding, will you?' said the captain.

'Not at all,' returned the other.

'Thank 'ee. My berth an't very roomy,' said the captain, turning back again, 'but it 's tolerably snug; and if you was to find yourself near Brig Place, number nine, at any time—will you make a note of it?—and would come upstairs, without minding what was said by the person at the door, I should be proud to see you.'

With that hospitable invitation, the captain said 'Good day!' and walked out and shut the door; leaving Mr. Carker still reclining against the chimney-piece. In whose sly look and watchful manner; in whose false mouth, stretched but not laughing; in whose spotless cravat and very whiskers; even in whose silent passing of his soft hand over his white linen and his smooth face; there was something desperately cat-like.

The unconscious captain walked out in a state of self-glorification that imparted quite a new cut to the broad blue suit. 'Stand by, Ned!' said the captain to himself. 'You 've done a little business for the youngsters to-day, my lad!'

In his exultation, and in his familiarity, present and prospective, with the House, the captain, when he reached the outer office, could not refrain from rallying Mr. Perch a little, and asking him whether he thought everybody was still engaged. But not to be bitter on a man who had done his duty, the captain whispered in his ear, that if he felt disposed for a glass of rum-and-water, and would follow, he would be happy to bestow the same upon him.

Before leaving the premises, the captain, somewhat to the astonishment of the clerks, looked round from a central point of view, and took a general survey of the office as part and parcel of a project in which his young friend was nearly interested. The strong-room excited his especial admiration; but, that he might not appear too particular, he limited himself to an approving glance, and, with a graceful recognition of the clerks as a body, that was full of politeness and patronage, passed out into the court. Being promptly joined by Mr. Perch, he conveyed that gentleman to the tavern, and fulfilled his pledge—hastily, for Perch's time was precious.

'I 'll give you for a toast,' said the Captain, 'Wal'r!'

'Who?' submitted Mr. Perch.

'Wal'r!' repeated the captain, in a voice of thunder.

Mr. Perch, who seemed to remember having heard in infancy that there was once a poet of that name, made no objection; but he was much astonished at the captain's coming into the City to propose a poet; indeed, if he had proposed to put a poet's statue up—say Shakespeare's for example—in a civic thoroughfare, he could hardly have done a greater outrage to Mr. Perch's experience. On the whole, he was such a mysterious and incomprehensible character, that Mr. Perch decided not to mention him to Mrs. Perch at all, in case of giving rise to any disagreeable consequences.

Mysterious and incomprehensible, the captain, with that lively sense upon him of having done a little business for the youngsters, remained all day, even to his most intimate friends; and but that Walter attributed his winks and grins, and other such pantomimic reliefs of himself, to his satisfaction in the success of their innocent deception upon old Sol Gills, he would assuredly have betrayed himself before night. As it was, however, he kept his own secret; and went home late from the instrument-maker's house, wearing the glazed hat so much on one side, and carrying such a beaming expression in his eyes, that Mrs. MacStinger (who might have been brought up at Doctor Blimber's, she was such a Roman matron) fortified herself, at the first glimpse of him, behind the open street door, and refused to come out to the contemplation of her blessed infants, until he was securely lodged in his own room.

# CHAPTER XVIII

## FATHER AND DAUGHTER

THERE is a hush through Mr. Dombey's house. Servants gliding up and down stairs rustle but make no sound of footsteps. They talk together constantly, and sit long at meals, making much of their meat and drink, and enjoying themselves after a grim unholy fashion. Mrs. Wickam, with her eyes suffused with tears, relates melancholy anecdotes; and tells them how she always said at Mrs. Pipchin's that it would be so, and takes more table-ale than usual, and is very sorry but sociable. Cook's state of mind is similar. She promises a little fry for supper, and struggles about equally against her feelings and the onions. Towlinson begins to think there 's a fate in it, and wants to know if anybody can tell him of any good that ever came of living in a corner house. It seems to all of them as having happened a long time ago; though yet the child lies, calm and beautiful, upon his little bed.

After dark there come some visitors—noiseless visitors, with shoes of felt—who have been there before; and with them comes that bed of rest which is so strange a one for infant sleepers. All this time, the bereaved father has not been seen even by his attendant; for he sits in an inner corner of his own dark room when any one is there, and never seems to move at other times, except to pace it to and fro. But in the morning it is whispered among the household that he was heard to go upstairs in the dead night, and that he stayed there—in the room—until the sun was shining.

At the offices in the City, the ground-glass windows are made more dim by shutters; and while the lighted lamps upon the desks are half extinguished by the day that wanders in, the day is half extinguished by the lamps, and an unusual gloom prevails. There is not much business done. The clerks are indisposed to work; and they make assignations to eat chops in the afternoon, and go up the river. Perch, the messenger, stays long upon his errands; and finds himself in bars of public-houses, invited thither by friends, and holding forth on the uncertainty of human affairs. He goes home to Ball's Pond earlier in the evening than usual, and treats Mrs. Perch to a veal cutlet and Scotch ale. Mr. Carker the manager treats no one; neither is he treated; but alone in his own room he shows his teeth all day; and it would seem that there is something gone from Mr. Carker's path—some obstacle removed—which clears his way before him.

Now the rosy children living opposite to Mr. Dombey's house, peep from their nursery windows down into the street; for there are four black horses at his door, with feathers on their heads; and feathers tremble on the carriage that they draw; and these, and an array of men with scarves and staves, attract a crowd. The juggler who was going to twirl the basin, puts his loose coat on again over his fine dress; and his trudging wife, one-sided with her heavy baby in her arms, loiters to see the company come out. But closer to her dingy breast she presses her baby, when the burden that is so easily carried is borne forth; and the youngest of the rosy children at the high window opposite, needs no restraining hand to check her in her glee, when, pointing with her dimpled finger, she looks into her nurse's face, and asks, 'What 's that?'

And now, among the knot of servants dressed in mourning, and the weeping women, Mr. Dombey passes through the hall to the other carriage that is waiting to receive him. He is not 'brought down,' these observers think, by sorrow and distress of mind. His walk is as erect, his bearing is as stiff as ever it has been. He hides his face behind no handkerchief, and looks before him. But that his face is something sunk and rigid, and is pale, it bears the same expression as of old. He takes his place within the carriage, and three other gentlemen follow. Then the grand funeral moves slowly down the street. The feathers are yet nodding in the distance, when the juggler has the basin spinning on a cane, and has the same crowd to admire it. But the juggler's wife is less alert than usual with the money-box, for a child's burial has set her thinking that perhaps the baby underneath her shabby shawl may not grow up to be a man, and wear a sky-blue fillet round his head, and salmon-coloured worsted drawers, and tumble in the mud.

The feathers wind their gloomy way along the streets, and come within the sound of a church bell. In this same church, the pretty boy received all that will soon be left of him on earth—a name. All of him that is dead, they lay there, near the perishable substance of his mother. It is well. Their ashes lie where Florence in her walks—oh lonely, lonely walks!—may pass them any day.

The service over, and the clergyman withdrawn, Mr. Dombey looks round, demanding in a low voice, whether the person who has been requested to attend to receive instructions for the tablet, is there?

Some one comes forward, and says 'Yes.'

Mr. Dombey intimates where he would have it placed; and shows him, with his hand upon the wall, the shape and size; and how it is to follow the memorial to the mother. Then, with his pencil, he writes out the inscription, and gives it to him: adding, 'I wish to have it done at once.'

'It shall be done immediately, sir.'

'There is really nothing to inscribe but name and age, you see.'

The man bows, glancing at the paper, but appears to hesitate. Mr. Dombey not observing his hesitation, turns away, and leads towards the porch.

'I beg your pardon, sir'; a touch falls gently on his mourning cloak; 'but as you wish it done immediately, and it may be put in hand when I get back—'

'Well?'

'Will you be so good as read it over again? I think there 's a mistake.'

'Where?'

The statuary gives him back the paper, and points out, with his pocket rule, the words 'beloved and only child.'

'It should be "son," I think, sir?'

'You are right. Of course. Make the correction.'

The father, with a hastier step, pursues his way to the coach. When the other three, who follow closely, take their seats, his face is hidden for the first time—shaded by his cloak. Nor do they see it any more that day. He alights first, and passes immediately into his own room. The other mourners (who are only Mr. Chick, and two of the medical attendants) proceed upstairs to the drawing-room, to be received by Mrs. Chick and Miss Tox. And what the face is, in the shut-up chamber underneath: or what the thoughts are: what the heart is, what the contest or the suffering: no one knows.

The chief thing that they know below-stairs, in the kitchen, is that 'it seems like Sunday.' They can hardly persuade themselves but that there is something unbecoming, if not wicked, in the conduct of the people out of doors, who pursue their ordinary occupations, and wear their every-day attire. It is quite a novelty to have the blinds up, and the shutters open: and they make themselves dismally comfortable over bottles of wine, which are freely broached as on a festival. They are much inclined to moralise. Mr. Towlinson proposes with a sigh, 'Amendment to us all!' for which, as cook says with another sigh, 'There 's room enough, God knows.' In the evening, Mrs. Chick and Miss Tox take to needlework again. In the evening also, Mr. Towlinson goes out to take the air, accompanied by the housemaid, who has not yet tried her mourning bonnet. They are very tender to each other at dusky street-corners, and Towlinson has visions of leading an altered and blameless existence as a serious greengrocer in Oxford Market.

There is sounder sleep and deeper rest in Mr. Dombey's house to-night, than there has been for many nights. The morning sun awakens the old household, settled down once more in their old ways. The rosy children opposite run past with hoops. There is a splendid wedding in the church. The juggler's wife is active with the money-box in another quarter of the town. The mason sings and whistles as he chips out P-A-U-L in the marble slab before him.

And can it be that in a world so full and busy, the loss of one weak creature makes a void in any heart, so wide and deep that nothing but the width and depth of vast eternity can fill it up! Florence, in her innocent affliction, might have answered, 'Oh my brother, oh my dearly loved and loving brother! Only friend and companion of my slighted childhood! Could any less idea shed the light already dawning on your early grave, or give birth to the softened sorrow that is springing into life beneath this rain of tears!'

'My dear child,' said Mrs. Chick, who held it as a duty incumbent on her, to improve the occasion, 'when you are as old as I am—'

'Which will be the prime of life,' observed Miss Tox.

'You will then,' pursued Mrs. Chick, gently squeezing Miss Tox's hand in acknowledgment of her friendly remark, 'you will then know that all grief is unavailing, and that it is our duty to submit.'

'I will try, dear aunt. I do try,' answered Florence, sobbing.

'I am glad to hear it,' said Mrs. Chick, 'because, my love, as our dear Miss Tox—of whose sound sense and excellent judgment, there cannot possibly be two opinions—'

'My dear Louisa, I shall really be proud, soon,' said Miss Tox.

—'will tell you, and confirm by her experience,' pursued Mrs. Chick, 'we are called upon on all occasions to make an effort. It is required of us. If any—my dear,' turning to Miss Tox, 'I want a word. Mis—Mis—'

'Demeanour?' suggested Miss Tox.

'No, no, no,' said Mrs. Chick. 'How can you! Goodness me, it 's on the end of my tongue. Mis—'

'Placed affection?' suggested Miss Tox, timidly.

'Good gracious, Lucretia!' returned Mrs. Chick. 'How very monstrous! Misanthrope, is the word I want. The idea! Misplaced affection! I say, if any misanthrope were to put, in my presence, the question, "Why were we born?" I should reply, "Tc make an effort." '

'Very good indeed,' said Miss Tox, much impressed by the originality of the sentiment. '*Very* good.'

'Unhappily,' pursued Mrs. Chick, 'we have a warning under our own eyes. We have but too much reason to suppose, my dear child, that if an effort had been made in time, in this family, a train of the most trying and distressing circumstances might have been avoided. Nothing shall ever persuade me,' observed the good matron, with a resolute air, 'but that if that effort had been made by poor dear Fanny, the poor dear darling child would at least have had a stronger constitution.'

Mrs. Chick abandoned herself to her feelings for half a moment; but, as a practical illustration of her doctrine, brought herself up short, in the middle of a sob, and went on again.

'Therefore, Florence, pray let us see that you have some strength of mind, and do not selfishly aggravate the distress in which your poor papa is plunged.'

'Dear aunt,' said Florence, kneeling quickly down before her, that she might the better and more earnestly look into her face. 'Tell me more about papa. Pray tell me about him! Is he quite heart-broken?'

Miss Tox was of a tender nature, and there was something in this appeal that moved her very much. Whether she saw it in a succession, on the part of the neglected child, to the affectionate concern so often expressed by her dead brother—or a love that sought to twine itself about the heart that had loved him, and that could not bear to be shut out from sympathy with such a sorrow, in such sad community of love and grief—or whether she only recognised the earnest and devoted spirit which, although discarded and repulsed, was wrung with tenderness long unreturned, and in the waste and solitude of this bereavement cried to him to seek a comfort in it, and to give some, by some small response—whatever may have been her understanding of it, it moved Miss Tox. For the moment she forgot the majesty of Mrs. Chick, and, patting Florence hastily on the cheek, turned aside and suffered the tears to gush from her eyes, without waiting for a lead from that wise matron.

Mrs. Chick herself lost, for a moment, the presence of mind on which she so much prided herself; and remained mute, looking on the beautiful young face that had so long, so steadily, and patiently, been turned towards the little bed. But recovering her voice—which was synonymous with her presence of mind, indeed they were one and the same thing—she replied with dignity—

'Florence, my dear child, your poor papa is peculiar at times; and to question me about him, is to question me upon a subject which I really do not pretend to understand. I believe I have as much influence with your papa as anybody has. Still, all I can say is, that he has said very little to me; and that I have only seen him once or twice for a minute at a time, and indeed have hardly seen him then, for his room has been dark. I have said to your papa, "Paul!"—that is the exact expression I used—"Paul! why do you not take something stimulating?" Your papa's reply has always been, "Louisa, have the goodness to leave me. I want nothing. I am better by myself." If I was to be put upon my oath to-morrow, Lucretia, before a magistrate,' said Mrs. Chick, 'I have no doubt I could venture to swear to those identical words.'

Miss Tox expressed her admiration by saying, 'My Louisa is ever methodical!'

'In short, Florence,' resumed her aunt, 'literally nothing has passed between your poor papa and myself, until to-day; when I mentioned to your papa that

Sir Barnet and Lady Skettles had written exceedingly kind notes—our sweet boy! Lady Skettles loved him like a—where 's my pocket-handkerchief!'

Miss Tox produced one.

'Exceedingly kind notes, proposing that you should visit them for change of scene. Mentioning to your papa that I thought Miss Tox and myself might now go home (in which he quite agreed), I inquired if he had any objection to your accepting this invitation. He said, "No, Louisa, not the least!" '

Florence raised her tearful eyes.

'At the same time, if you would prefer staying here, Florence, to paying this visit at present, or to going home with me—'

'I should much prefer it, aunt,' was the faint rejoinder.

'Why then, child,' said Mrs. Chick, 'you can. It's a strange choice, I must say. But you always *were* strange. Anybody else at your time of life, and after what has passed—my dear Miss Tox, I have lost my pocket-handkerchief again—would be glad to leave here, one would suppose.'

'I should not like to feel,' said Florence, 'as if the house was avoided. I should not like to think that the—his—the rooms upstairs were quite empty and dreary, aunt. I would rather stay here, for the present. Oh my brother! oh my brother!'

It was a natural emotion, not to be suppressed; and it would make way even between the fingers of the hands with which she covered up her face. The overcharged and heavy-laden breast must sometimes have that vent, or the poor wounded solitary heart within it would have fluttered like a bird with broken wings, and sunk down in the dust.

'Well, child!' said Mrs. Chick, after a pause. 'I wouldn't on any account say anything unkind to you, and that I 'm sure you know. You will remain here, then, and do exactly as you like. No one will interfere with you, Florence, or wish to interfere with you, I 'm sure.'

Florence shook her head in sad assent.

'I had no sooner begun to advise your poor papa that he really ought to seek some distraction and restoration in a temporary change,' said Mrs. Chick, 'than he told me he had already formed the intention of going into the country for a short time. I'm sure I hope he 'll go very soon. He can't go too soon. But I suppose there are some arrangements connected with his private papers and so forth, consequent on the affliction that has tried us all so much—I can't think what 's become of mine: Lucretia, lend me yours, my dear—that may occupy him for one or two evenings in his own room. Your papa 's a Dombey, child, if ever there was one,' said Mrs. Chick, drying both her eyes at once with great care on opposite corners of Miss Tox's handkerchief. 'He 'll make an effort. There 's no fear of him.'

'Is there nothing, aunt,' asked Florence, trembling, 'I might do to—'

'Lord, my dear child,' interposed Mrs. Chick, hastily, 'what are you talking about? If your papa said to me—I have given you his exact words, "Louisa, I want nothing; I am better by myself"—what do you think he 'd say to you? You mustn't show yourself to him, child. Don't dream of such a thing.'

'Aunt,' said Florence, 'I will go and lie down on my bed.'

Mrs. Chick approved of this resolution, and dismissed her with a kiss. But Miss Tox, on a faint pretence of looking for the mislaid handkerchief, went upstairs after her; and tried in a few stolen minutes to comfort her, in spite of great discouragement from Susan Nipper. For Miss Nipper, in her burning zeal, disparaged Miss Tox as a crocodile; yet her sympathy seemed genuine, and had at least the vantage-ground of disinterestedness—there was little favour to be won by it.

And was there no one nearer and dearer than Susan, to uphold the striving heart in its anguish? Was there no other neck to clasp? no other face to turn to? no one else to say a soothing word to such deep sorrow? Was Florence so alone in the bleak world that nothing else remained to her? Nothing. Stricken motherless and brotherless at once—for in the loss of little Paul, that first and greatest loss fell heavily upon her—this was the only help she had. Oh, who can tell how much she needed help at first?

At first, when the house subsided into its accustomed course, and they had all gone away, except the servants, and her father shut up in his own rooms, Florence could do nothing but weep, and wander up and down, and sometimes, in a sudden pang of desolate remembrance, fly to her own chamber, wring her hands, lay her face down on her bed, and know no consolation: nothing but the bitterness and cruelty of grief. This commonly ensued upon the recognition of some spot or object very tenderly associated with him; and it made the miserable house, at first, a place of agony.

But it is not in the nature of pure love to burn so fiercely and unkindly long. The flame that in its grosser composition has the taint of earth, may prey upon the breast that gives it shelter; but the sacred fire from heaven is as gentle in the heart, as when it rested on the heads of the assembled twelve, and showed each man his brother, brightened and unhurt. The image conjured up, there soon returned the placid face, the softened voice, the loving looks, the quiet trustfulness and peace; and Florence, though she wept still, wept more tranquilly, and courted the remembrance.

It was not very long before the golden water, dancing on the wall, in the old place, at the old serene time, had her calm eye fixed upon it as it ebbed away. It was not very long before that room again knew her, often; sitting there alone, as patient and as mild as when she had watched beside the little bed. When any sharp sense of its being empty smote upon her, she could kneel beside it, and pray GOD—it was the pouring out of her full heart—to let one angel love her and remember her.

It was not very long before, in the midst of the dismal house so wide and dreary, her low voice in the twilight, slowly and stopping sometimes, touched the old air to which he had so often listened, with his drooping head upon her arm. And after that, and when it was quite dark, a little strain of music trembled in the room: so softly played and sung, that it was more like the mournful recollection of what she had done at his request on that last night, than the reality repeated. But it was repeated, often—very often, in the shadowy solitude; and broken murmurs of the strain still trembled on the keys, when the sweet voice was hushed in tears.

Thus she gained heart to look upon the work with which her fingers had been busy by his side on the sea-shore; and thus it was not very long before she took to it again—with something of a human love for it, as if it had been sentient and had known him; and, sitting in a window, near her mother's picture, in the unused room so long deserted, wore away the thoughtful hours.

Why did the dark eyes turn so often from this

work to where the rosy children lived? They were not immediately suggestive of her loss; for they were all girls: four little sisters. But they were motherless like her—and had a father.

It was easy to know when he had gone out and was expected home, for the elder child was always dressed and waiting for him at the drawing-room window, or in the balcony; and when he appeared, her expectant face lighted up with joy, while the others at the high window, and always on the watch too, clapped their hands, and drummed them on the sill, and called to him. The elder child would come down to the hall, and put her hand in his, and lead him up the stairs; and Florence would see her afterwards sitting by his side, or on his knee, or hanging coaxingly about his neck and talking to him: and though they were always gay together, he would often watch her face as if he thought her like her mother that was dead. Florence would sometimes look no more at this, and bursting into tears would hide behind the curtain as if she were frightened, or would hurry from the window. Yet she could not help returning; and her work would soon fall unheeded from her hands again.

It was the house that had been empty, years ago. It had remained so for a long time. At last, and while she had been away from home, this family had taken it; and it was repaired and newly painted; and there were birds and flowers about it; and it looked very different from its old self. But she never thought of the house. The children and their father were all in all.

When he had dined, she could see them, through the open windows, go down with their governess or nurse, and cluster round the table; and in the still summer weather, the sound of their childish voices and clear laughter would come ringing across the street, into the drooping air of the room in which she sat. Then they would climb and clamber upstairs with him, and romp about him on the sofa, or group themselves at his knee, a very nosegay of little faces, while he seemed to tell them some story. Or they would come running out into the balcony; and then Florence would hide herself quickly, lest it should check them in their joy, to see her in her black dress, sitting there alone.

The elder child remained with her father when the rest had gone away, and made his tea for him—happy little housekeeper she was then!—and sat conversing with him, sometimes at the window, sometimes in the room, until the candles came. He made her his companion, though she was some years younger than Florence; and she could be as staid and pleasantly demure with her little book or work-box, as a woman. When they had candles, Florence from her own dark room was not afraid to look again. But when the time came for the child to say 'Good night, papa,' and go to bed, Florence would sob and tremble as she raised her face to him, and could look no more.

Though still she would turn, again and again, before going to bed herself, from the simple air that had lulled him to rest so often, long ago, and from the other low soft broken strain of music, back to that house. But that she ever thought of it, or watched it, was a secret which she kept within her own young breast.

And did that breast of Florence—Florence, so ingenuous and true—so worthy of the love that he had borne her, and had whispered in his last faint words—whose guileless heart was mirrored in the beauty of her face, and breathed in every accent of her gentle voice—did that young breast hold any other secret? Yes. One more.

When no one in the house was stirring, and the

lights were all extinguished, she would softly leave her own room, and with noiseless feet descend the staircase, and approach her father's door. Against it, scarcely breathing, she would rest her face and head, and press her lips, in the yearning of her love. She crouched upon the cold stone floor outside it, every night, to listen even for his breath; and in her one absorbing wish to be allowed to show him some affection, to be a consolation to him, to win him over to the endurance of some tenderness from her, his solitary child, she would have knelt down at his feet, if she had dared, in humble supplication.

No one knew it. No one thought of it. The door was ever closed, and he shut up within. He went out once or twice, and it was said in the house that he was very soon going on his country journey; but he lived in those rooms, and lived alone, and never saw her, or inquired for her. Perhaps he did not even know that she was in the house.

One day, about a week after the funeral, Florence was sitting at her work, when Susan appeared, with a face half laughing and half crying, to announce a visitor.

'A visitor! To me, Susan!' said Florence, looking up in astonishment.

'Well, it *is* a wonder, ain't it now, Miss Floy,' said Susan; 'but I wish you had a many visitors, I do, indeed, for you 'd be all the better for it, and it 's my opinion that the sooner you and me goes even to them old Skettleses, miss, the better for both, I may not wish to live in crowds, Miss Floy, but still I 'm not a oyster.'

To do Miss Nipper justice, she spoke more for her young mistress than herself; and her face showed it.

'But the visitor, Susan,' said Florence.

Susan, with an hysterical explosion that was as

much a laugh as a sob, and as much a sob as a laugh, answered—

'Mr. Toots!'

The smile that appeared on Florence's face passed from it in a moment, and her eyes filled with tears. But at any rate it was a smile, and that gave great satisfaction to Miss Nipper.

'My own feelings exactly, Miss Floy,' said Susan, putting her apron to her eyes, and shaking her head. 'Immediately I see that innocent in the hall, Miss Floy, I burst out laughing first, and then I choked.'

Susan Nipper involuntarily proceeded to do the like again on the spot. In the meantime Mr. Toots, who had come upstairs after her, all unconscious of the effect he produced, announced himself with his knuckles on the door, and walked in very briskly.

'How d' ye do, Miss Dombey?' said Mr. Toots. 'I 'm very well, I thank you; how are you?'

Mr. Toots—than whom there were few better fellows in the world, though there may have been one or two brighter spirits—had laboriously invented this long burst of discourse with the view of relieving the feelings both of Florence and himself. But finding that he had run through his property, as it were, in an injudicious manner, by squandering the whole before taking a chair, or before Florence had uttered a word, or before he had well got in at the door, he deemed it advisable to begin again.

'How d' ye do, Miss Dombey?' said Mr. Toots. 'I 'm very well, I thank you; how are you?'

Florence gave him her hand, and said she was very well.

'I 'm very well indeed,' said Mr. Toots, taking a chair. 'Very well indeed, I am. I don't remember,' said Mr. Toots, after reflecting a little, 'that I was ever better, thank you.'

'It 's very kind of you to come,' said Florence, taking up her work. 'I am very glad to see you.'

Mr. Toots responded with a chuckle. Thinking that might be too lively, he corrected it with a sigh. Thinking that might be too melancholy, he corrected it with a chuckle. Not thoroughly pleasing himself with either mode of reply, he breathed hard.

'You were very kind to my dear brother,' said Florence, obeying her own natural impulse to relieve him by saying so. 'He often talked to me about you.'

'Oh, it 's of no consequence,' said Mr. Toots hastily. 'Warm, ain't it?'

'It is beautiful weather,' replied Florence.

'It agrees with *me*!' said Mr. Toots. 'I don't think I ever was so well as I find myself at present, I 'm obliged to you.'

After stating this curious and unexpected fact, Mr. Toots fell into a deep well of silence.

'You have left Doctor Blimber's, I think?' said Florence, trying to help him out.

'I should hope so,' returned Mr. Toots. And tumbled in again.

He remained at the bottom, apparently drowned, for at least ten minutes. At the expiration of that period, he suddenly floated, and said—

'Well! Good morning, Miss Dombey.'

'Are you going?' asked Florence, rising.

'I don't know, though. No, not just at present,' said Mr. Toots, sitting down again, most unexpectedly. 'The fact is— I say, Miss Dombey!'

'Don't be afraid to speak to me,' said Florence, with a quiet smile, 'I should be very glad if you would talk about my brother.'

'Would you, though?' retorted Mr. Toots, with sympathy in every fibre of his otherwise expressionless face. 'Poor Dombey! I 'm sure I never thought that Burgess and Co.—fashionable tailors (but very dear), that we used to talk about—would make this suit of clothes for such a purpose.' Mr. Toots was dressed in mourning. 'Poor Dombey! I say! Miss Dombey!' blubbered Toots.

'Yes,' said Florence.

'There 's a friend he took to very much at last. I thought you 'd like to have him, perhaps, as a sort of keepsake. You remember his remembering Diogenes?'

'Oh yes! oh yes!' cried Florence.

'Poor Dombey! So do I,' said Mr. Toots.

Mr. Toots, seeing Florence in tears, had great difficulty in getting beyond this point, and had nearly tumbled into the well again. But a chuckle saved him on the brink.

'I say,' he proceeded, 'Miss Dombey! I could have had him stolen for ten shillings, if they hadn't given him up: and I would: but they were glad to get rid of him, I think. If you 'd like to have him, he 's at the door. I brought him on purpose for you. He ain't a lady's dog, you know,' said Mr. Toots, 'but you won't mind that, will you?'

In fact Diogenes was at that moment, as they presently ascertained from looking down into the street, staring through the window of a hackney cabriolet, into which, for conveyance to that spot, he had been ensnared, on a false pretence of rats among the straw. Sooth to say, he was as unlike a lady's dog as dog might be; and in his gruff anxiety to get out, presented an appearance sufficiently unpromising, as he gave short yelps out of one side of his mouth, and overbalancing himself by the intensity of every one of those efforts, tumbled down into the straw, and then sprung panting up again, puttng out his tongue, as if he had come express to a dispensary to be examined for his health.

But though Diogenes was as ridiculous a dog as one would meet with on a summer's day; a blundering, ill-favoured, clumsy, bullet-headed dog, continually acting on a wrong idea that there was an enemy in the neighbourhood, whom it was meritorious to bark at; and though he was far from good-tempered, and certainly was not clever, and had hair all over his eyes, and a comic nose, and an inconsistent tail, and a gruff voice; he was dearer to Florence, in virtue of that parting remembrance of him, and that request that he might be taken care of, than the most valuable and beautiful of his kind. So dear, indeed, was this same ugly Diogenes, and so welcome to her, that she took the jewelled hand of Mr. Toots and kissed it in her gratitude. And when Diogenes, released, came tearing up the stairs and bouncing into the room (such a business as there was first, to get him out of the cabriolet!), dived under all the furniture, and wound a long iron chain, that dangled from his neck, round legs of chairs and tables, and then tugged at it until his eyes became unnaturally visible, in consequence of their nearly starting out of his head; and when he growled at Mr. Toots, who affected familiarity; and went pell-mell at Towlinson, morally convinced that he was the enemy whom he had barked at round the corner all his life and had never seen yet; Florence was as pleased with him as if he had been a miracle of discretion.

Mr. Toots was so overjoyed by the success of his present, and was so delighted to see Florence bending down over Diogenes, smoothing his coarse back with her little delicate hand—Diogenes graciously allowing it from the first moment of their acquaintance—that he felt it difficult to take leave, and would, no doubt, have been a much longer time in making up his mind to do so, if he had not been assisted by Diogenes himself, who suddenly took it into his head to bay Mr. Toots, and to make short runs at him with his mouth open. Not exactly seeing his way to the end of these demonstrations, and sensible that they placed the pantaloons constructed by the art of Burgess and Co. in jeopardy, Mr. Toots, with chuckles, lapsed out at the door: by which, after looking in again two or three times, without any object at all, and being on each occasion greeted with a fresh run from Diogenes, he finally took himself off and got away.

'Come, then, Di! Dear Di! Make friends with your new mistress. Let us love each other, Di!' said Florence, fondling his shaggy head. And Di, the rough and gruff, as if his hairy hide were pervious to the tear that dropped upon it, and his dog's heart melted as it fell, put his nose up to her face and swore fidelity.

Diogenes the man did not speak plainer to Alexander the Great than Diogenes the dog spoke to Florence. He subscribed to the offer of his little mistress cheerfully, and devoted himself to her service. A banquet was immediately provided for him in a corner; and when he had eaten and drunk his fill, he went to the window where Florence was sitting, looking on, rose up on his hind legs, with his awkward fore paws on her shoulders, licked her face and hands, nestled his great head against her heart, and wagged his tail till he was tired. Finally, Diogenes coiled himself up at her feet and went to sleep.

Although Miss Nipper was nervous in regard of dogs, and felt it necessary to come into the room with her skirts carefully collected about her, as if she were crossing a brook on stepping-stones; also to utter little screams and stand up on chairs when Diogenes stretched himself: she was in her own manner affected by the kindness of Mr. Toots, and could not see Florence so alive to the attachment and society of this rude friend of little Paul's, without some mental comments thereupon that brought the water to her eyes. Mr. Dombey, as a part of her reflections, may have been, in the association of ideas, connected with the dog; but, at any rate, after observing Diogenes and his mistress all the evening, and after exerting herself with much goodwill to provide Diogenes a bed in an antechamber outside his mistress's door, she said hurriedly to Florence, before leaving her for the night—

'Your pa 's a going off, Miss Floy, to-morrow morning.'

'To-morrow morning, Susan?'

'Yes, miss; that 's the orders. Early.'

'Do you know,' asked Florence, without looking at her, 'where papa is going, Susan?'

'Not exactly, miss. He 's going to meet that precious major first, and I must say if I was acquainted with any major myself (which Heavens forbid), it shouldn't be a blue one!'

'Hush, Susan!' urged Florence gently.

'Well, Miss Floy,' returned Miss Nipper, who was full of burning indignation, and minded her stops even less than usual. 'I can't help it, blue he is, and while I was a Christian, although humble, I would have natural-coloured friends, or none.'

It appeared from what she added and had gleaned downstairs, that Mrs. Chick had proposed the major for Mr. Dombey's companion, and that Mr. Dombey, after some hesitation, had invited him.

'Talk of *him* being a change, indeed!' observed Miss Nipper to herself with boundless contempt. 'If he 's a change give me a constancy.'

'Good night, Susan,' said Florence.

'Good night, my darling dear Miss Floy.'

Her tone of commiseration smote the chord so often roughly touched, but never listened to while she or any one looked on. Florence left alone, laid her head upon her hand, and pressing the other over her swelling heart, held free communication with her sorrows.

It was a wet night; and the melancholy rain fell pattering and dropping with a wearied sound. A sluggish wind was blowing, and went moaning round the house, as if it were in pain or grief. A shrill noise quivered through the trees. While she sat weeping, it grew late, and dreary midnight tolled out from the steeples.

Florence was little more than a child in years—not yet fourteen—and the loneliness and gloom of such an hour in the great house where Death had lately made its own tremendous devastation, might have set an older fancy brooding on vague terrors. But her innocent imagination was too full of one theme to admit them. Nothing wandered in her thoughts but love—a wandering love, indeed, and cast away—but turning always to her father.

There was nothing in the dropping of the rain, the moaning of the wind, the shuddering of the trees, the striking of the solemn clocks, that shook this one thought, or diminished its interest. Her recollections of the dear dead boy—and they were never absent—were itself; the same thing. And oh, to be shut out: to be so lost: never to have looked into her father's face or touched him since that hour!

She could not go to bed, poor child, and never had gone yet, since then, without making her nightly pilgrimage to his door. It would have been a strange sad sight, to see her now, stealing lightly down the stairs through the thick gloom, and stopping at it with a beating heart, and blinded eyes, and hair that fell down loosely and unthought of; and touching it outside with her wet cheek. But the night covered it, and no one knew.

The moment that she touched the door on this night, Florence found that it was open. For the first time it stood open, though by but a hair's-breadth: and there was a light within. The first impulse of the timid child—and she yielded to it—was to retire swiftly. Her next, to go back, and to enter; and this second impulse held her in irresolution on the staircase.

In its standing open, even by so much as that chink, there seemed to be hope. There was encouragement in seeing a ray of light from within, stealing through the dark stern doorway, and falling in a thread upon the marble floor. She turned back, hardly knowing what she did, but urged on by the love within her, and the trial they had undergone together, but not shared: and with her hands a little raised and trembling, glided in.

Her father sat at his old table in the middle room. He had been arranging some papers, and destroying others, and the latter lay in fragile ruins before him. The rain dripped heavily upon the glass panes in the outer room, where he had so often watched poor Paul, a baby; and the low complainings of the wind were heard without.

But not by him. He sat with his eyes fixed on the table, so immersed in thought, that a far heavier tread than the light foot of his child could make, might have failed to rouse him. His face was turned towards her. By the waning lamp and at that haggard hour, it looked worn and dejected; and in the utter loneliness surrounding him, there was an appeal to Florence that struck home.

'Papa! papa! Speak to me, dear papa!'

He started at her voice, and leaped up from his seat. She was close before him, with extended arms, but he fell back.

'What is the matter?' he said, sternly. 'Why do you come here? What has frightened you?'

If anything had frightened her, it was the face he turned upon her. The glowing love within the breast of his young daughter froze before it, and she stood and looked at him as if stricken into stone.

There was not one touch of tenderness or pity in it. There was not one gleam of interest, parental recognition, or relenting in it. There was a change in it, but not of that kind. The old indifference and cold constraint had given place to something: what, she never thought and did not dare to think, and yet she felt it in its force, and knew it well without a name: that as it looked upon her, seemed to cast a shadow on her head.

Did he see before him the successful rival of his son, in health and life? Did he look upon his own successful rival in that son's affection? Did a mad jealousy and withered pride, poison sweet remembrances that should have endeared and made her precious to him? Could it be possible that it was gall to him to look upon her in her beauty and her promise: thinking of his infant boy?

Florence had no such thoughts. But love is quick to know when it is spurned and hopeless: and hope died out of hers, as she stood looking in her father's face.

'I ask you, Florence, are you frightened? Is there anything the matter, that you come here?'

'I came, papa—'

'Against my wishes. Why?'

She saw he knew why: it was written broadly on his face: and dropped her head upon her hands with one prolonged low cry.

Let him remember it in that room, years to come. It has faded from the air, before he breaks the silence. It may pass as quickly from his brain, as he believes, but it is there. Let him remember it in that room, years to come!

He took her by the arm. His hand was cold, and loose, and scarcely closed upon her.

'You are tired, I dare say,' he said, taking up the light, and leading her towards the door, 'and want rest. We all want rest. Go, Florence. You have been dreaming.'

The dream she had had, was over then, God help her! and she felt that it could never more come back.

'I will remain here to light you up the stairs. The whole house is yours above there,' said her father, slowly. 'You are its mistress now. Good night!'

Still covering her face, she sobbed, and answered, 'Good night, dear papa,' and silently ascended. Once she looked back as if she would have returned to him, but for fear. It was a momentary thought, too hopeless to encourage; and her father stood there with the light—hard, unresponsive, motionless—until the fluttering dress of his fair child was lost in the darkness.

Let him remember it in that room, years to come. The rain that falls upon the roof: the wind that mourns outside the door: may have foreknowledge in their melancholy sound. Let him remember it in that room, years to come!

The last time he had watched her, from the same place, winding up those stairs, she had had her brother in her arms. It did not move his heart towards her now, it steeled it: but he went into his room, and locked his door, and sat down in his chair, and cried for his lost boy.

Diogenes was broad awake upon his post, and waiting for his little mistress.

'Oh Di! Oh dear Di! Love me for his sake!'

Diogenes already loved her for her own, and didn't care how much he showed it. So he made himself vastly ridiculous by performing a variety of uncouth bounces in the antechamber, and concluded, when poor Florence was at last asleep, and dreaming of the rosy children opposite, by scratching open her bedroom door: rolling up his bed into a pillow: lying down on the boards, at the full length of his tether, with his head towards her: and looking lazily at her, upside down, out of the tops of his eyes, until from winking and winking he fell asleep himself, and dreamed, with gruff barks, of his enemy.

## CHAPTER XIX

### WALTER GOES AWAY

THE wooden midshipman at the instrument-maker's door, like the hard-hearted little midshipman he was, remained supremely indifferent to Walter's going away, even when the very last day of his sojourn in the back-parlour was on the decline. With his quadrant at his round black knob of an eye, and his figure in its old attitude of indomitable alacrity, the midshipman displayed his elfin small-clothes to the best advantage, and, absorbed in scientific pursuits, had no sympathy with worldly concerns. He was so far the creature of circumstances, that a dry day covered him with dust, and a misty day peppered him with little bits of soot, and a wet day brightened up his tarnished uniform for the moment, and a very hot day blistered him; but otherwise he was a callous, obdurate, conceited midshipman, intent on his own discoveries, and caring as little for what went on about him, terrestrially, as Archimedes at the taking of Syracuse.

Such a midshipman he seemed to be, at least, in the then position of domestic affairs. Walter eyed him kindly many a time in passing in and out; and poor old Sol, when Walter was not there, would come and lean against the door-post, resting his weary wig as near the shoe-buckles of the guardian genius of his trade and shop as he could. But no fierce idol with a mouth from ear to ear, and a murderous visage made of parrot's feathers, was ever more indifferent to the appeals of its savage votaries, than was the midshipman to these marks of attachment.

Walter's heart felt heavy as he looked round his old bedroom, up among the parapets and chimney-pots, and thought that one more night already darkening would close his acquaintance with it, perhaps for ever. Dismantled of his little stock of books and pictures, it looked coldly and reproachfully on him for his desertion, and had already a foreshadowing upon it of its coming strangeness. 'A few hours more,' thought Walter, 'and no dream I ever had here when I was a school-boy will be so little mine as this old room. The dream may come back in my sleep, and I may return waking to this place, it may be: but the dream at least will serve no other master, and the room may have a score, and every one of them may change, neglect, misuse it.'

But his uncle was not to be left alone in the little back-parlour, where he was then sitting by himself:

for Captain Cuttle, considerate in his roughness, stayed away against his will, purposely that they should have some talk together unobserved: so Walter, newly returned home from his last day's bustle, descended briskly, to bear him company.

'Uncle,' he said gaily, laying his hand upon the old man's shoulder, 'what shall I send you home from Barbados?'

'Hope, my dear Wally. Hope that we shall meet again, on this side of the grave. Send me as much of that as you can.'

'So I will, uncle: I have enough and to spare, and I 'll not be chary of it! And as to lively turtles, and limes for Captain Cuttle's punch, and preserves for you on Sundays, and all that sort of thing, why I 'll send you ship-loads, uncle: when I 'm rich enough.'

Old Sol wiped his spectacles, and faintly smiled.

'That 's right, uncle!' cried Walter, merrily, and clapping him half a dozen times more upon the shoulder. 'You cheer up me! I 'll cheer up you! We 'll be as gay as larks to-morrow morning, uncle, and we 'll fly as high! As to my anticipations, they are singing out of sight now.'

'Wally, my dear boy,' returned the old man, 'I 'll do my best, I 'll do my best.'

'And *your* best, uncle,' said Walter, with his pleasant laugh, 'is the best best that I know. You 'll not forget what you 're to send *me,* uncle?'

'No, Wally, no,' replied the old man; 'everything I hear about Miss Dombey, now that she is left alone, poor lamb, I 'll write. I fear it won't be much though, Wally.'

'Why, I 'll tell you what, uncle,' said Walter, after a moment's hesitation, 'I have just been up there.'

'Ay, ay, ay?' murmured the old man, raising his eyebrows, and his spectacles with them.

'Not to see *her,*' said Walter, 'though I could have seen her, I dare say, if I had asked, Mr. Dombey being out of town: but to say a parting word to Susan. I thought I might venture to do that, you know, under the circumstances, and remembering when I saw Miss Dombey last.'

'Yes, my boy, yes,' replied his uncle, rousing himself from a temporary abstraction.

'So I saw her,' pursued Walter, 'Susan, I mean; and I told her I was off and away to-morrow. And I said, uncle, that you had always had an interest in Miss Dombey since that night when she was here, and always wished her well and happy, and always would be proud and glad to serve her in the least: I thought I might say that, you know, under the circumstances. Don't you think so?'

'Yes, my boy, yes,' replied his uncle, in the same tone as before.

'And I added,' pursued Walter, 'that if she—Susan, I mean—could ever let you know, either through herself, or Mrs. Richards, or anybody else who might be coming this way, that Miss Dombey *was* well and happy, you would take it very kindly, and would write so much to me, and I should take it very kindly too. There! Upon my word, uncle,' said Walter, 'I scarcely slept all last night through thinking of doing this; and could not make up my mind when I was out, whether to do it or not; and yet I am sure it is the true feeling of my heart, and I should have been quite miserable afterwards if I had not relieved it.'

His honest voice and manner corroborated what he said, and quite established its ingenuousness.

'So, if you ever see her, uncle,' said Walter, 'I mean Miss Dombey now—and perhaps you may, who knows!—tell her how much I felt for her; how much I used to think of her when I was here; how I spoke of her, with the tears in my eyes, uncle, on this last night before I went away. Tell her that I said I never could forget her gentle manner, or her beautiful face, or her sweet kind disposition that was better than all. And as I didn't take them from a woman's feet, or a young lady's: only a little innocent child's,' said Walter: 'tell her, if you don't mind, uncle, that I kept those shoes—she 'll remember how often they fell off, that night—and took them away with me as a remembrance!'

They were at that very moment going out at the door in one of Walter's trunks. A porter carrying off his baggage on a truck for shipment at the docks on board the Son and Heir, had got possession of them; and wheeled them away under the very eye of the insensible midshipman before their owner had well finished speaking.

But that ancient mariner might have been excused his insensibility to the treasure as it rolled away. For, under his eye, at the same moment, accurately within his range of observation, coming full into the sphere of his startled and intensely wide-awake lookout, were Florence and Susan Nipper: Florence looking up into his face half timidly, and receiving the whole shock of his wooden ogling!

More than this, they passed into the shop, and passed in at the parlour-door before they were observed by anybody but the midshipman. And Walter, having his back to the door, would have known nothing of their apparition even then, but for seeing his uncle spring out of his own chair, and nearly tumble over another.

'Why, uncle!' exclaimed Walter. 'What 's the matter?'

Old Solomon replied, 'Miss Dombey!'

'Is it possible!' cried Walter, looking round and starting up in his turn. 'Here!'

Why it was so possible and so actual, that, while the words were on his lips, Florence hurried past him; took uncle Sol's snuff-coloured lappels, one in each hand; kissed him on the cheek; and turning, gave her hand to Walter with a simple truth and earnestness that was her own, and no one else's in the world!

'Going away, Walter!' said Florence.

'Yes, Miss Dombey,' he replied, but not so hopefully as he endeavoured: 'I have a voyage before me.'

'And your uncle,' said Florence, looking back at Solomon. 'He is sorry you are going, I am sure. Ah! I see he is! Dear Walter, I am very sorry too.'

'Goodness knows,' exclaimed Miss Nipper, 'there 's a many we could spare instead, if numbers is a object, Mrs. Pipchin as a overseer would come cheap at her weight in gold, and if a knowledge of black slavery should be required, them Blimbers is the very people for the sitiwation.'

With that Miss Nipper untied her bonnet strings, and after looking vacantly for some moments into a little black tea-pot that was set forth with the usual homely service, on the table, shook her head and a tin canister, and began unasked to make the tea.

In the meantime Florence had turned again to the instrument-maker, who was as full of admiration as surprise. 'So grown!' said old Sol. 'So improved! And yet not altered! Just the same!'

'Indeed!' said Florence.

'Ye—yes,' returned old Sol, rubbing his hands slowly, and considering the matter half aloud, as something pensive in the bright eyes looking at him arrested his attention. 'Yes, that expression was in the younger face, too!'

'You remember me,' said Florence with a smile, 'and what a little creature I was then?'

'My dear young lady,' returned the instrument-maker, 'how could I forget you, often as I have thought of you and heard of you since! At the very moment, indeed, when you came in, Wally was talking about you to me, and leaving messages for you, and—'

'Was he?' said Florence. 'Thank you, Walter! Oh thank you, Walter! I was afraid you might be going away and hardly thinking of me'; and again she gave him her little hand so freely and so faithfully that Walter held it for some moments in his own, and could not bear to let it go.

Yet Walter did not hold it as he might have held it once, nor did its touch awaken those old day-dreams of his boyhood that had floated past him sometimes even lately, and confused him with their indistinct and broken shapes. The purity and innocence of her endearing manner, and its perfect trustfulness and the undisguised regard for him that lay so deeply seated in her constant eyes, and glowed upon her fair face through the smile that shaded—for alas! it was a smile too sad to brighten—it, were not of their romantic race. They brought back to his thoughts the early death-bed he had seen her tending, and the love the child had borne her; and on the wings of such remembrances she seemed to rise up, far above his idle fancies, into clearer and serener air.

'I—I am afraid I must call you Walter's Uncle, sir,' said Florence to the old man, 'if you'll let me.'

'My dear young lady,' cried old Sol. 'Let you! Good gracious!'

'We always knew you by that name, and talked of you,' said Florence, glancing round, and sighing gently. 'The nice old parlour! Just the same! How well I recollect it!'

Old Sol looked first at her, then at his nephew, and then rubbed his hands, and rubbed his spectacles, and said below his breath, 'Ah! time, time, time!'

There was a short silence; during which Susan Nipper skilfully impounded two extra cups and saucers from the cupboard, and awaited the drawing of the tea with a thoughtful air.

'I want to tell Walter's Uncle,' said Florence, laying her hand timidly upon the old man's as it rested on the table, to bespeak his attention, 'something that I am anxious about. He is going to be left alone, and if he will allow me—not to take Walter's place, for that I couldn't do, but to be his true friend and help him if I ever can while Walter is away, I shall be very much obliged to him indeed. Will you? May I, Walter's Uncle?'

The instrument-maker, without speaking, put her hand to his lips, and Susan Nipper, leaning back with her arms crossed, in the chair of presidency into which she had voted herself, bit one end of her bonnet strings, and heaved a gentle sigh as she looked up at the skylight.

'You will let me come to see you,' said Florence, 'when I can; and you will tell me everything about yourself and Walter; and you will have no secrets from Susan when she comes and I do not, but will confide in us, and trust us, and rely upon us. And you'll try to let us be a comfort to you? Will you, Walter's Uncle?'

The sweet face looking into his, the gently pleading eyes, the soft voice, and the light touch on his arm made the more winning by a child's respect and honour for his age, that gave to all an air of graceful doubt and modest hesitation—these, and her natural earnestness, so overcame the poor old instrument-maker that he only answered—

'Wally! say a word for me, my dear. I'm very grateful.'

'No, Walter,' returned Florence with her quiet smile. 'Say nothing for him, if you please. I understand him very well, and we must learn to talk together without you, dear Walter.'

The regretful tone in which she said these latter words, touched Walter more than all the rest.

'Miss Florence,' he replied, with an effort to recover the cheerful manner he had preserved while talking with his uncle, 'I know no more than my uncle, what to say in acknowledgment of such kindness, I am sure. But what could I say, after all, if I had the power of talking for an hour, except that it is like you?'

Susan Nipper began upon a new part of her bonnet string, and nodded at the skylight, in approval of the sentiment expressed.

'Oh! but Walter,' said Florence, 'there is something that I wish to say to you before you go away, and you must call me Florence, if you please, and not speak like a stranger.'

'Like a stranger!' returned Walter. 'No. I couldn't speak so. I am sure, at least, I couldn't feel like one.'

'Aye, but that is not enough, and is not what I mean. For, Walter,' added Florence, bursting into tears, 'he liked you very much, and said before he died that he was fond of you, and said, "Remember Walter!" and if you'll be a brother to me, Walter, now that he is gone and I have none on earth, I'll be your sister all my life, and think of you like one wherever we may be! This is what I wished to say, dear Walter, but I cannot say it as I would, because my heart is full.'

And in its fulness and its sweet simplicity, she held out both her hands to him. Walter taking them, stooped down and touched the tearful face that neither shrunk nor turned away, nor reddened as he did so, but looked up at him with confidence and truth. In that one moment, every shadow of doubt or agitation passed away from Walter's soul. It seemed to him that he responded to her innocent appeal, beside the dead child's bed: and, in the solemn presence he had seen there, pledged himself to cherish and protect her very image, in his banishment, with brotherly regard; to garner up her simple faith, inviolate; and hold himself degraded if he breathed upon it any thought that was not in her own breast when she gave it to him.

Susan Nipper, who had bitten both her bonnet strings at once, and imparted a great deal of private emotion to the skylight, during this transaction, now changed the subject by inquiring who took milk and who took sugar; and being enlightened on these points, poured out the tea. They all four gathered socially about the little table, and took tea under that young lady's active superintendence; and the presence of Florence in the back-parlour, brightened the Tartar frigate on the wall.

Half an hour ago Walter, for his life, would have hardly called her by her name. But he could do so now when she entreated him. He could think of her being there without a lurking misgiving that it would have been better if she had not come. He could calmly think how beautiful she was, how full of promise, what a home some happy man would find in such a heart one day. He could reflect upon his own place in that heart, with pride; and with a brave determination, if not to deserve it—he still thought that far above him—never to deserve it less.

Some fairy influence must surely have hovered round the hands of Susan Nipper when she made the tea, engendering the tranquil air that reigned in the back-parlour during its discussion. Some counter-influence must surely have hovered round the hands of uncle Sol's chronometer, and moved them faster than the Tartar frigate ever went before the wind. Be this as it may, the visitors had a coach in waiting at a quiet corner not far off; and the chronometer, on being incidentally referred to, gave such a positive opinion that it had been waiting a long time, that it was impossible to doubt the fact, especially when stated on such unimpeachable authority. If uncle Sol had been going to be hanged by his own time, he never would have allowed that the chronometer was too fast, by the least fraction of a second.

Florence at parting recapitulated to the old man all that she had said before, and bound him to their compact. Uncle Sol attended her lovingly to the legs of the wooden midshipman, and there resigned her to Walter, who was ready to escort her and Susan Nipper to the coach.

'Walter,' said Florence by the way, 'I have been afraid to ask before your uncle. Do you think you will be absent very long?'

'Indeed,' said Walter, 'I don't know. I fear so. Mr. Dombey signified as much, I thought, when he appointed me.'

'Is it a favour, Walter?' inquired Florence, after a moment's hesitation, and looking anxiously in his face.

'The appointment?' returned Walter.

'Yes.'

Walter would have given anything to have answered in the affirmative, but his face answered before his lips could, and Florence was too attentive to it not to understand its reply.

'I am afraid you have scarcely been a favourite with papa,' she said, timidly.

'There is no reason,' replied Walter, smiling, 'why I should be.'

'No reason, Walter!'

'There *was* no reason,' said Walter, understanding what she meant. 'There are many people employed in the house. Between Mr. Dombey and a young man like me, there's a wide space of separation. If I do my duty, I do what I ought, and do no more than all the rest.'

Had Florence any misgiving of which she was hardly conscious: any misgiving that had sprung into an indistinct and undefined existence since that recent night when she had gone down to her father's room: that Walter's accidental interest in her, and early knowledge of her, might have involved him in that powerful displeasure and dislike? Had Walter any such idea, or any sudden thought that it was in her mind at that moment? Neither of them hinted at it. Neither of them spoke at all, for some short time. Susan, walking on the other side of Walter, eyed them both sharply; and certainly Miss Nipper's thoughts travelled in that direction, and very confidently too.

'You may come back very soon,' said Florence, 'perhaps, Walter.'

'I *may* come back,' said Walter, 'an old man, and find you an old lady. But I hope for better things.'

'Papa,' said Florence, after a moment, 'will—will

recover from his grief, and—speak more freely to me one day, perhaps; and if he should, I will tell him how much I wish to see you back again, and ask him to recall you for my sake.'

There was a touching modulation in these words about her father, that Walter understood too well.

The coach being close at hand, he would have left her without speaking, for now he felt what parting was; but Florence held his hand when she was seated, and then he found there was a little packet in her own.

'Walter,' she said, looking full upon him with her affectionate eyes, 'like you, I hope for better things. I will pray for them, and believe that they will arrive. I made this little gift for Paul. Pray take it with my love, and do not look at it until you are gone away. And now, God bless you, Walter! never forget me. You are my brother, dear!'

He was glad that Susan Nipper came between them, or he might have left her with a sorrowful remembrance of him. He was glad too that she did not look out of the coach again, but waved the little hand to him instead, as long as he could see it.

In spite of her request, he could not help opening the packet that night when he went to bed. It was a little purse: and there was money in it.

Bright rose the sun next morning, from his absence in strange countries, and up rose Walter with it to receive the captain, who was already at the door: having turned out earlier than was necessary, in order to get under weigh while Mrs. MacStinger was yet slumbering. The captain pretended to be in tip-top spirits, and brought a very smoky tongue in one of the pockets of the broad blue coat for breakfast.

'And, Wal'r,' said the captain, when they took

their seats at table, 'if your uncle 's the man I think him, he 'll bring out the last bottle of *the* Madeira on the present occasion.'

'No, no, Ned,' returned the old man. 'No! That shall be opened when Walter comes home again.'

'Well said!' cried the captain. 'Hear him!'

'There it lies,' said Sol Gills, 'down in the little cellar, covered with dirt and cobwebs. There may be dirt and cobwebs over you and me perhaps, Ned, before it sees the light.'

'Hear him!' cried the captain. 'Good morality! Wal'r, my lad. Train up a fig-tree in the way it should go, and when you are old sit under the shade on it. Overhaul the—Well,' said the captain on second thoughts, 'I an't quite certain where that 's to be found, but when found, make a note of it. Sol Gills, heave ahead again!'

'But there, or somewhere, it shall lie, Ned, until Wally comes back to claim it,' said the old man. 'That 's all I meant to say.'

'And well said too,' returned the captain; 'and if we three don't crack that bottle in company, I 'll give you two leave to drink my allowance!'

Notwithstanding the captain's excessive joviality, he made but a poor hand at the smoky tongue, though he tried very hard, when anybody looked at him, to appear as if he were eating with a vast appetite. He was terribly afraid, likewise, of being left alone with either uncle or nephew; appearing to consider that his only chance of safety as to keeping up appearances, was in their being always three together. This terror on the part of the captain, reduced him to such ingenious evasions as running to the door, when Solomon went to put his coat on, under pretence of having seen an extraordinary hackney-coach pass: and darting out into the road when Walter went upstairs to take leave of the lodgers, on a feint of smelling fire in a neighbouring chimney. These artifices Captain Cuttle deemed inscrutable by any uninspired observer.

Walter was coming down from his parting expedition upstairs, and was crossing the shop to go back to the little parlour, when he saw a faded face he knew, looking in at the door, and darted towards it.

'Mr. Carker!' cried Walter, pressing the hand of John Carker the junior. 'Pray come in! This is kind of you, to be here so early to say good-bye to me. You knew how glad it would make me to shake hands with you, once, before going away. I cannot say how glad I am to have this opportunity. Pray come in.'

'It is not likely that we may ever meet again, Walter,' returned the other, gently resisting his invitation, 'and I am glad of this opportunity too. I may venture to speak to you, and to take you by the hand, on the eve of separation. I shall not have to resist your frank approaches, Walter, any more.'

There was a melancholy in his smile as he said it, that showed he had found some company and friendship for his thoughts even in that.

'Ah, Mr. Carker!' returned Walter. 'Why did you resist them? You could have done me nothing but good, I am very sure.'

He shook his head. 'If there were any good,' he said, 'I could do on this earth, I would do it, Walter, for you. The sight of you from day to day, has been at once happiness and remorse to me. But the pleasure has outweighed the pain. I know that, now, by knowing what I lose.'

'Come in, Mr. Carker, and make acquaintance with my good old uncle,' urged Walter. 'I have often talked to him about you, and he will be glad to tell you all he hears from me. I have not,' said Walter, noticing his hesitation, and speaking with embarrassment himself: 'I have not told him anything about our last conversation, Mr. Carker; not even him, believe me.'

The grey junior pressed his hand, and tears rose in his eyes.

'If I ever make acquaintance with him, Walter,' he returned, 'it will be that I may hear tidings of you. Rely on my not wronging your forbearance and consideration. It would be to wrong it, not to tell him all the truth, before I sought a word of confidence from him. But I have no friend or acquaintance except you: and even for your sake, am little likely to make any.'

'I wish,' said Walter, 'you had suffered me to be your friend indeed. I always wished it, Mr. Carker, as you know; but never half so much as now, when we are going to part.'

'It is enough,' replied the other, 'that you have been the friend of my own breast, and that when I have avoided you most, my heart inclined the most towards you, and was fullest of you. Walter, good-bye!'

'Good-bye, Mr. Carker. Heaven be with you, sir!' cried Walter, with emotion.

'If,' said the other, retaining his hand while he spoke; 'if when you come back, you miss me from my old corner, and should hear from any one where I am lying, come and look upon my grave. Think that I might have been as honest and as happy as you! And let *me* think, when I know my time is coming on, that some one like my former self may stand there, for a moment, and remember me with pity and forgiveness! Walter, good-bye!'

His figure crept like a shadow down the bright, sunlighted street, so cheerful yet so solemn in the early summer morning; and slowly passed away.

The relentless chronometer at last announced that Walter must turn his back upon the wooden midshipman: and away they went, himself, his uncle, and the captain, in a hackney-coach to a wharf, where they were to take steamboat for some Reach down the river, the name of which, as the captain gave it out, was a hopeless mystery to the ears of landsmen. Arrived at this Reach (whither the ship had repaired by last night's tide), they were boarded by various excited water-men, and among others by a dirty Cyclops of the captain's acquaintance, who, with his one eye, had made the captain out some mile and a half off, and had been exchanging unintelligible roars with him ever since. Becoming the lawful prize of this personage, who was frightfully hoarse and constitutionally in want of shaving, they were all three put aboard the Son and Heir. And the Son and Heir was in a pretty state of confusion, with sails lying all bedraggled on the wet decks, loose ropes tripping people up, men in red shirts running barefoot to and fro, casks blockading every foot of space, and, in the thickest of the fray, a black cook in a black caboose up to his eyes in vegetables and blinded with smoke.

The captain immediately drew Walter into a corner, and with a great effort, that made his face very red, pulled up the silver watch, which was so big, and so tight in his pocket, that it came out like a bung.

'Wal'r,' said the captain, handing it over, and shaking him heartily by the hand, 'a parting gift, my lad. Put it back half an hour every morning, and about another quarter towards the arternoon, and it 's a watch that 'll do you credit.'

'Captain Cuttle! I couldn't think of it!' cried Walter, detaining him, for he was running away. 'Pray take it back. I have one already.'

'Then, Wal'r,' said the captain, suddenly diving into one of his pockets and bringing up the two teaspoons and the sugar-tongs, with which he had armed himself to meet such an objection, 'take this here trifle of plate, instead.'

'No, no, I couldn't indeed!' cried Walter, 'a thousand thanks! Don't throw them away, Captain Cuttle!' for the captain was about to jerk them overboard. 'They 'll be of much more use to you than me. Give me your stick. I have often thought that I should like to have it. There! Good-bye, Captain Cuttle! Take care of my uncle! Uncle Sol, God bless you!'

They were over the side in the confusion, before Walter caught another glimpse of either; and when he ran up to the stern, and looked after them, he saw his uncle hanging down his head in the boat, and Captain Cuttle rapping him on the back with the great silver watch (it must have been very painful), and gesticulating hopefully with the teaspoons and sugar-tongs. Catching sight of Walter, Captain Cuttle dropped the property into the bottom of the boat with perfect unconcern, being evidently oblivious of its existence, and pulling off the glazed hat hailed him lustily. The glazed hat made quite a show in the sun with its glistening, and the captain continued to wave it until he could be seen no longer. Then the confusion on board, which had been rapidly increasing, reached its height; two or three other boats went away with a cheer; the sails shone bright and full above, as Walter watched them spread their surface to the favourable breeze; the water flew in sparkles from the prow; and off upon her voyage went the Son and Heir, as hopefully and trippingly as many another son and heir, gone down, had started on his way before her.

Day after day, Old Sol and Captain Cuttle kept her reckoning in the little back-parlour and worked out her course, with the chart spread before them on the round table. At night, when Old Sol climbed upstairs, so lonely, to the attic where it sometimes blew great guns, he looked up at the stars and listened to the wind, and kept a longer watch than would have fallen to his lot on board the ship. The last bottle of the old Madeira, which had had its cruising days, and known its dangers of the deep, lay silently beneath its dust and cobwebs, in the meanwhile, undisturbed.

## CHAPTER XX

### MR. DOMBEY GOES UPON A JOURNEY

'Mr. Dombey, sir,' said Major Bagstock, 'Joey B. is not in general a man of sentiment, for Joseph is tough. But Joe has his feelings, sir, and when they *are* awakened—damme, Mr. Dombey,' cried the major with sudden ferocity, 'this is weakness, and I won't submit to it!'

Major Bagstock delivered himself of these expressions on receiving Mr. Dombey as his guest at the head of his own staircase in Princess's Place. Mr. Dombey had come to breakfast with the major, previous to their setting forth on their trip; and the ill-starred native had already undergone a world of misery arising out of the muffins, while, in connection with the general question of boiled eggs, life was a burden to him.

'It is not for an old soldier of the Bagstock breed,' observed the major, relapsing into a mild state, 'to deliver himself up, a prey to his own emotions; but —damme, sir,' cried the major, in another spasm of ferocity, 'I condole with you!'

The major's purple visage deepened in its hue, and the major's lobster eyes stood out in bolder relief, as he shook Mr. Dombey by the hand, imparting to that peaceful action as defiant a character as if it had been the prelude to his immediately boxing Mr. Dombey for a thousand pounds a side and the championship of England. With a rotary motion of his head, and a wheeze very like the cough of a horse, the major then conducted his visitor to the sitting-room, and there welcomed him (having now composed his feelings) with the freedom and frankness of a travelling companion.

'Dombey,' said the major, 'I'm glad to see you. I'm proud to see you. There are not many men in Europe to whom J. Bagstock would say that—for Josh is blunt, sir: it's his nature—but Joey B. is proud to see you, Dombey.'

'Major,' returned Mr. Dombey, 'you are very obliging.'

'No, sir,' said the major, 'devil a bit! That's not my character. If that had been Joe's character, Joe might have been, by this time, Lieutenant-General Sir Joseph Bagstock, K.C.B., and might have received you in very different quarters. You don't know old Joe yet, I find. But this occasion, being special, is a source of pride to me. By the Lord, sir,' said the major resolutely, 'it's an honour to me!'

Mr. Dombey, in his estimation of himself and his money, felt that this was very true, and therefore did not dispute the point. But the instinctive recognition of such a truth by the major, and his plain avowal of it, were very agreeable. It was a confirmation to Mr. Dombey, if he had required any, of his not being mistaken in the major. It was an assurance to him that his power extended beyond his own immediate sphere; and that the major as an officer and a gentleman, had a no less becoming sense of it, than the beadle of the Royal Exchange.

And if it were ever consolatory to know this, or the like of this, it was consolatory then, when the impotence of his will, the instability of his hopes, the feebleness of wealth, had been so direfully impressed upon him. What could it do, his boy had asked him. Sometimes, thinking of the baby question, he could hardly forbear inquiring, himself, what *could* it do indeed: what had it done?

But these were lonely thoughts, bred late at night in the sullen despondency and gloom of his retirement, and pride easily found its reassurance in many testimonies to the truth, as unimpeachable and precious as the major's. Mr. Dombey, in his friendlessness, inclined to the major. It cannot be said that he warmed towards him, but he thawed a little. The major had had some part—and not too much—in the days by the seaside. He was a man of the world, and knew some great people. He talked much, and told stories; and Mr. Dombey was disposed to regard him as a choice spirit who shone in society, and who had not that poisonous ingredient of poverty with which choice spirits in general are too much adulterated. His station was undeniable. Altogether the major was a creditable companion, well accustomed to a life of leisure, and to such places as that they were about to visit, and having an air of gentlemanly ease about him that mixed well enough with his own

City character, and did not compete with it at all. If Mr. Dombey had any lingering idea that the major, as a man accustomed, in the way of his calling, to make light of the ruthless hand that had lately crushed his hopes, might unconsciously impart some useful philosophy to him, and scare away his weak regrets, he hid it from himself, and left it lying at the bottom of his pride, unexamined.

'Where is my scoundrel?' said the major, looking wrathfully round the room.

The native, who had no particular name, but answered to any vituperative epithet, presented himself instantly at the door and ventured to come no nearer.

'You villain!' said the choleric major, 'where 's the breakfast?'

The dark servant disappeared in search of it, and was quickly heard reascending the stairs in such a tremulous state, that the plates and dishes on the tray he carried, trembling sympathetically as he came, rattled again, all the way up.

'Dombey,' said the major, glancing at the native as he arranged the table, and encouraging him with an awful shake of his fist when he upset a spoon, 'here is a devilled grill, a savoury pie, a dish of kidneys, and so forth. Pray sit down. Old Joe can give you nothing but camp fare, you see.'

'Very excellent fare, major,' replied his guest; and not in mere politeness either; for the major always took the best possible care of himself, and indeed ate rather more of rich meats than was good for him, insomuch that his imperial complexion was mainly referred by the faculty to that circumstance.

'You have been looking over the way, sir,' observed the major. 'Have you seen our friend?'

'You mean Miss Tox,' retorted Mr. Dombey. 'No.'

'Charming woman, sir,' said the major, with a fat laugh rising in his short throat, and nearly suffocating him.

'Miss Tox is a very good sort of person, I believe,' replied Mr. Dombey.

The haughty coldness of the reply seemed to afford Major Bagstock infinite delight. He swelled and swelled, exceedingly: and even laid down his knife and fork for a moment, to rub his hands.

'Old Joe, sir,' said the major, 'was a bit of a favourite in that quarter once. But Joe has had his day. J. Bagstock is extinguished—outrivalled—floored, sir. I tell you what, Dombey.' The major paused in his eating, and looked mysteriously indignant. 'That 's a de-vilish ambitious woman, sir.'

Mr. Dombey said 'Indeed?' with frigid indifference: mingled perhaps with some contemptuous incredulity as to Miss Tox having the presumption to harbour such a superior quality.

'That woman, sir,' said the major, 'is, in her way, a Lucifer. Joey B. has had his day, sir, but he keeps his eyes. He sees, does Joe. His Royal Highness the late Duke of York observed of Joey, at a levee, that he saw.'

The major accompanied this with such a look, and, between eating, drinking, hot tea, devilled grill, muffins, and meaning, was altogether so swollen and inflamed about the head, that even Mr. Dombey showed some anxiety for him.

'That ridiculous old spectacle, sir,' pursued the major, 'aspires. She aspires sky-high, sir. Matrimonially, Dombey.'

'I am sorry for her,' said Mr. Dombey.

'Don't say that, Dombey,' returned the major in a warning voice.

'Why should I not, Major?' said Mr. Dombey.

The major gave no answer but the horse's cough, and went on eating vigorously.

'She has taken an interest in your household,' said the major, stopping short again, 'and has been a frequent visitor at your house for some time now."

'Yes,' replied Mr. Dombey, with great stateliness, 'Miss Tox was originally received there, at the time of Mrs. Dombey's death, as a friend of my sister's; and being a well-behaved person, and showing a liking for the poor infant, she was permitted—I may say encouraged—to repeat her visits with my sister, and gradually to occupy a kind of footing of familiarity in the family. I have,' said Mr. Dombey, in the tone of a man who was making a great and valuable concession, 'I have a respect for Miss Tox. She has been so obliging as to render many little services in my house; trifling and insignificant services perhaps, major, but not to be disparaged on that account: and I hope I have had the good fortune to be enabled to acknowledge them by such attention and notice as it has been in my power to bestow. I hold myself indebted to Miss Tox, major,' added Mr. Dombey, with a slight wave of his hand, 'for the pleasure of your acquaintance.'

'Dombey,' said the major, warmly: 'no! No, sir! Joseph Bagstock can never permit that assertion to pass uncontradicted. Your knowledge of old Joe, sir, such as he is, and old Joe's knowledge of you, sir, had its origin in a noble fellow, sir—in a great creature, sir. Dombey!' said the major, with a struggle which it was not very difficult to parade, his whole life being a struggle against all kinds of apoplectic symptoms, 'we knew each other through your boy.'

Mr. Dombey seemed touched, as it is not improbable the major designed he should be, by this allusion.

He looked down and sighed: and the major, rousing himself fiercely, again said, in reference to the state of mind into which he felt himself in danger of falling, that this was weakness, and nothing should induce him to submit to it.

'Our friend had a remote connection with that event,' said the major, 'and all the credit that belongs to her, J. B. is willing to give her, sir. Notwithstanding which, ma'am,' he added, raising his eyes from his plate, and casting them across Princess's Place, to where Miss Tox was at that moment visible at her window watering her flowers, 'you're a scheming jade, ma'am, and your ambition is a piece of monstrous impudence. If it only made yourself ridiculous, ma'am,' said the major, rolling his head at the unconscious Miss Tox, while his starting eyes appeared to make a leap towards her, 'you might do that to your heart's content, ma'am, without any objection, I assure you, on the part of Bagstock.' Here the major laughed frightfully up in the tips of his ears and in the veins of his head. 'But when, ma'am,' said the major, 'you compromise other people, and generous, unsuspicious people too, as a repayment for their condescension, you stir the blood of old Joe in his body.'

'Major,' said Mr. Dombey, reddening, 'I hope you do not hint at anything so absurd on the part of Miss Tox as—'

'Dombey,' returned the major, 'I hint at nothing. But Joey B. has lived in the world, sir: lived in the world with his eyes open, sir, and his ears cocked: and Joe tells you, Dombey, that there 's a de-vilish artful and ambitious woman over the way.'

Mr. Dombey involuntarily glanced over the way, and an angry glance he sent in that direction, too.

'That 's all on such a subject that shall pass the

lips of Joseph Bagstock,' said the major firmly. 'Joe is not a talebearer, but there are times when he must speak, when he *will* speak!—confound your arts, ma'am,' cried the major, again apostrophising his fair neighbour, with great ire, '—when the provocation is too strong to admit of his remaining silent.'

The emotion of this outbreak threw the major into a paroxysm of horse's coughs, which held him for a long time. On recovering he added—

'And now, Dombey, as you have invited Joe—old Joe, who has no other merit, sir, but that he is tough and hearty—to be your guest and guide at Leamington, command him in any way you please, and he is wholly yours. I don't know, sir,' said the major, wagging his double chin with a jocose air, 'what it is you people see in Joe to make you hold him in such great request, all of you; but this I know, sir, that if he wasn't pretty tough, and obstinate in his refusals, you 'd kill him among you with your invitations and so forth, in double-quick time.'

Mr. Dombey, in a few words, expressed his sense of the preference he received over those other distinguished members of society who were clamouring for the possession of Major Bagstock. But the major cut him short by giving him to understand that he followed his own inclinations, and that they had risen up in a body and said with one accord, 'J. B., Dombey is the man for you to choose as a friend.'

The major being by this time in a state of repletion, with essence of savoury pie oozing out at the corners of his eyes, and devilled grill and kidneys tightening his cravat: and the time moreover approaching for the departure of the railway train to Birmingham, by which they were to leave town: the native got him into his great-coat wth immense difficulty, and buttoned him up until his face looked staring and gasping, over the top of that garment, as if he were in a barrel. The native then handed him separately, and with a decent interval between each supply, his wash-leather gloves, his thick stick, and his hat; which latter article the major wore with a rakish air on one side of his head, by way of toning down his remarkable visage. The native had previously packed, in all possible and impossible parts of Mr. Dombey's chariot, which was in waiting, an unusual quantity of carpetbags and small portmanteaus, no less apoplectic in appearance than the major himself: and having filled his own pockets with Seltzer water, East India sherry, sandwiches, shawls, telescopes, maps, and newspapers, any or all of which light baggage the major might require at any instant of the journey, he announced that everything was ready. To complete the equipment of this unfortunate foreigner (currently believed to be a prince in his own country), when he took his seat in the rumble by the side of Mr. Towlinson, a pile of the major's cloaks and great-coats was hurled upon him by the landlord, who aimed at him from the pavement with those great missiles like a Titan, and so covered him up, that he proceeded, in a living tomb, to the railroad station.

But before the carriage moved away, and while the native was in the act of sepulture, Miss Tox appearing at her window, waved a lily-white handkerchief. Mr. Dombey received this parting salutation very coldly—very coldly even for him—and honouring her with the slightest possible inclination of his head, leaned back in the carriage with a very discontented look. His marked behaviour seemed to afford the major (who was all politeness in his recognition of Miss Tox) unbounded satisfaction; and he sat for a long time afterwards, leering, and choking, like an over-fed Mephistopheles.

During the bustle of preparation at the railway, Mr. Dombey and the major walked up and down the platform side by side; the former taciturn and gloomy, and the latter entertaining him, or entertaining himself, with a variety of anecdotes and reminiscences, in most of which Joe Bagstock was the principal performer. Neither of the two observed that in the course of these walks, they attracted the attention of a working man who was standing near the engine, and who touched his hat every time they passed; for Mr. Dombey habitually looked over the vulgar herd, not at them; and the major was looking, at the time, into the core of one of his stories. At length, however, this man stepped before them as they turned round, and pulling his hat off, and keeping it off, ducked his head to Mr. Dombey.

'Beg your pardon, sir,' said the man, 'but I hope your a doin' pretty well, sir.'

He was dressed in a canvas suit abundantly besmeared with coal-dust and oil, and had cinders in his whiskers, and a smell of half-slaked ashes all over him. He was not a bad-looking fellow, nor even what could be fairly called a dirty-looking fellow, in spite of this; and, in short, he was Mr. Toodle, professionally clothed.

'I shall have the honour of stokin' of you down, sir,' said Mr. Toodle. 'Beg your pardon, sir. I hope you find yourself a coming round!'

Mr. Dombey looked at him, in return for his tone of interest, as if a man like that would make his very eyesight dirty.

''Scuse the liberty, sir,' said Toodle, seeing he was not clearly remembered, 'but my wife Polly, as was called Richards in your family—'

A change in Mr. Dombey's face, which seemed to express recollection of him. and so it did, but it expressed in a much stronger degree an angry sense of humiliation, stopped Mr. Toodle short.

'Your wife wants money, I suppose,' said Mr. Dombey, putting his hand in his pocket, and speaking (but that he always did) haughtily.

'No thank 'ee, sir,' returned Toodle, 'I can't say she does. *I* don't.'

Mr. Dombey was stopped short now in his turn: and awkwardly: with his hand in his pocket.

'No, sir,' said Toodle, turning his oilskin cap round and round; 'we 're a doin' pretty well, sir; we haven't no cause to complain in the worldly way, sir. We 've had four more since then, sir, but we rubs on.'

Mr. Dombey would have rubbed on to his own carriage, though in so doing he had rubbed the stoker underneath the wheels; but his attention was arrested by something in connection with the cap still going slowly round and round in the man's hand.

'We lost one babby,' observed Toodle, 'there 's no denyin'.'

'Lately,' added Mr. Dombey, looking at the cap.

'No, sir, up'ard of three years ago, but all the rest is hearty. And in the matter o' readin', sir,' said Toodle, ducking again, as if to remind Mr. Dombey of what had passed between them on that subject long ago, 'them boys o' mine, they learned me, among 'em, arter all. They 've made a wery tolerable scholar of me, sir, them boys.'

'Come, major!' said Mr. Dombey.

'Beg your pardon, sir,' resumed Toodle, taking a step before them and deferentially stopping them again, still cap in hand; 'I wouldn't have troubled you with such a pint except as a way of gettin' in the name of my son Biler—christened Robin—him as you was so good as to make a Charitable Grinder on.'

'Well, man,' said Mr. Dombey in his severest manner. 'What about him?'

'Why, sir,' returned Toodle, shaking his head with a face of great anxiety and distress. I'm forced to say, sir, that he 's gone wrong.'

'He has gone wrong, has he?' said Mr. Dombey, with a hard kind of satisfaction.

'He has fell into bad company, you see, gentlemen,' pursued the father looking wistfully at both, and evidently taking the major into the conversation with the hope of having his sympathy. 'He has got into bad ways. God send he may come to again, genelmen, but he 's on the wrong track now! You could hardly be off hearing of it somehow, sir,' said Toodle, again addressing Mr. Dombey individually; 'and it 's better I should out and say my boy 's gone rather wrong. Polly 's dreadful down about it, genelmen,' said Toodle with the same dejected look, and another appeal to the major.

'A son of this man's whom I caused to be educated, major,' said Mr. Dombey, giving him his arm. 'The usual return!'

'Take advice from plain old Joe, and never educate that sort of people, sir,' returned the major. 'Damme, sir, it never does! It always fails!'

The simple father was beginning to submit that he hoped his son, the quondam Grinder, huffed and cuffed, and flogged and badged, and taught, as parrots are, by a brute jobbed into his place of schoolmaster with as much fitness for it as a hound, might not have been educated on quite a right plan in some undiscovered respect, when Mr. Dombey angrily repeating 'The usual return!' led the major away. And the major being heavy to hoist into Mr. Dombey's carriage, elevated in mid-air, and having to stop and swear that he would flay the native alive, and break every bone in his skin, and visit other physical torments upon him, every time he couldn't get his foot on the step, and fell back on that dark exile, had barely time before they started to repeat hoarsely that it would never do: that it always failed: and that if he were to educate 'his own vagabond,' he would certainly be hanged.

Mr. Dombey assented bitterly; but there was something more in his bitterness, and in his moody way of falling back in the carriage, and looking with knitted brows at the changing objects without, than the failure of that noble educational system administered by the Grinders' Company. He had seen upon the man's rough cap a piece of new crape, and he had assured himself, from his manner and his answers, that he wore it for his son.

So! from high to low, at home or abroad, from Florence in his great house to the coarse churl who was feeding the fire then smoking before them, every one set up some claim or other to a share in his dead boy, and was a bidder against him! Could he ever forget how that woman had wept over his pillow, and called him her own child? or how he, waking from his sleep, had asked for her, and had raised himself in his bed and brightened when she came in?

To think of this presumptuous raker among coals and ashes going on before there, with his sign of mourning! To think that he dared to enter, even by a common show like that, into the trial and disappointment of a proud gentleman's secret heart! To think that this lost child, who was to have divided with him his riches, and his projects, and his power, and allied with whom he was to have shut out all the world as with a double door of gold, should have let in such a herd to insult him with their knowledge of his defeated hopes, and their boasts of claiming community of feeling with himself, so far removed: if not of having crept into the place wherein he would have lorded it, alone!

He found no pleasure or relief in the journey. Tortured by these thoughts he carried monotony with him, through the rushing landscape, and hurried headlong, not through a rich and varied country, but a wilderness of blighted plans and gnawing jealousies. The very speed at which the train was whirled along mocked the swift course of the young life that had been borne away so steadily and so inexorably to its fore-doomed end. The power that forced itself upon its iron way—its own—defiant of all paths and roads, piercing through the heart of every obstacle, and dragging living creatures of all classes, ages, and degrees behind it, was a type of the triumphant monster, Death.

Away, with a shriek, and a roar, and a rattle, from the town, burrowing among the dwellings of men and making the streets hum, flashing out into the meadows for a moment, mining in through the damp earth, booming on in darkness and heavy air, bursting out again into the sunny day so bright and wide; away, with a shriek, and a roar, and a rattle, through the fields, through the woods, through the corn, through the hay, through the chalk, through the mould, through the clay, through the rock, among objects close at hand and almost in the grasp, ever flying from the traveller, and a deceitful distance ever moving slowly within him: like as in the track of the remorseless monster, Death!

Through the hollow, on the height, by the heath, by the orchard, by the park, by the garden, over the canal, across the river, where the sheep are feeding, where the mill is going, where the barge is floating, where the dead are lying, where the factory is smoking, where the stream is runnnig, where the village clusters, where the great cathedral rises, where the bleak moor lies, and the wild breeze smooths or ruffles it at its constant will; away, with a shriek, and a roar, and a rattle, and no trace to leave behind but dust and vapour: like as in the track of the remorseless monster, Death!

Breasting the wind and light, the shower and sunshine, away, and still away, it rolls and roars, fierce and rapid, smooth and certain, and great works and massive bridges crossing up above, fall like a beam of shadow an inch broad, upon the eye, and then are lost. Away, and still away, onward and onward ever: glimpses of cottage-homes, of houses, mansions, rich estates, of husbandry and handicraft, of people, of old roads and paths that look deserted, small, and insignificant as they are left behind: and so they do, and what else is there but such glimpses, in the track of the indomitable monster, Death!

Away, with a shriek, and a roar, and a rattle, plunging down into the earth again, and working on in such a storm of energy and perseverance, that amidst the darkness and whirlwind the motion seems reversed, and to tend furiously backward, until a ray of light upon the wet wall shows its surface flying past like a fierce stream. Away once more into the day, and through the day, with a shrill yell of exultation, roaring, rattling, tearing on, spurning everything with its dark breath, sometimes pausing for a minute where a crowd of faces are, that in a minute more are not: sometimes lapping water greedily, and before the spout at which it drinks has ceased to drip upon the ground, shrieking, roaring, rattling through the purple distance!

Louder and louder yet, it shrieks and cries as it comes tearing on resistless to the goal: and now its way, still like the way of Death, is strewn with ashes thickly. Everything around is blackened. There are dark pools of water, muddy lanes, and miserable habitations far below. There are jagged walls and falling houses close at hand, and through the battered roofs and broken windows, wretched rooms are seen, where want and fever hide themselves in many wretched shapes, while smoke and crowded gables, and distorted chimneys, and deformity of brick and mortar penning up deformity of mind and body, choke the murky distance. As Mr. Dombey looks out of his carriage window, it is never in his thoughts that the monster who has brought him there has let the light of day in on these things: not made or caused them. It was the journey's fitting end, and might have been the end of everything; it was so ruinous and dreary.

So, pursuing the one course of thought, he had the one relentless monster still before him. All things looked black, and cold, and deadly upon him, and he on them. He found a likeness to his misfortune everywhere. There was a remorseless triumph going on about him, and it galled and stung him in his pride and jealousy, whatever form it took: though most of all when it divided with him the love and memory of his lost boy.

There was a face—he had looked upon it, on the previous night, and it on him with eyes that read his soul, though they were dim with tears, and hidden soon behind two quivering hands—that often had attended him in fancy, on this ride. He had seen it, with the expression of last night, timidly pleading to him. It was not reproachful, but there was something of doubt, almost of hopeful incredulity in it, which, as he once more saw that fade away into a desolate certainty of his dislike, was like reproach. It was a trouble to him to think of this face of Florence.

Because he felt any new compunction towards it? No. Because the feeling it awakened in him—of which he had had some old fore-shadowing in older times—was full-formed now, and spoke out plainly, moving him too much, and threatening to grow too strong for his composure. Because the face was abroad, in the expression of defeat and persecution that seemed to encircle him like the air. Because it barbed the arrow of that cruel and remorseless enemy on which his thoughts so ran, and put into its grasp a double-handed sword. Because he knew full well, in his own breast, as he stood there, tingeing the scene of transition before him with the morbid colours of his own mind, and making it a ruin and a picture of decay, instead of hopeful change, and promise of better things, that life had quite as much to do with his complainings as death. One child was gone, and one child left. Why was the object of his hope removed instead of her?

The sweet, calm, gentle presence in his fancy, moved him to no reflection but that. She had been unwelcome to him from the first; she was an aggravation of his bitterness now. If his son had been his only child, and the same blow had fallen on him, it would have been heavy to bear; but infinitely lighter than now, when it might have fallen on her (whom he could have lost, or he believed it, without a pang), and had not. Her loving and innocent face rising before him, had no softening or winning influence. He rejected the angel, and took up with the tormenting spirit crouching in his bosom. Her patience, goodness, youth, devotion, love, were as so many atoms in the ashes upon which he set his heel. He saw her image in the blight and blackness all round him, not irradiating but deepening the gloom. More than once upon this journey, and now again as he stood pondering at this journey's end, tracing figures in the dust with his stick, the thought came into his mind, what was there he could interpose between himself and it?

The major, who had been blowing and panting all the way down, like another engine, and whose eye had often wandered from his newspaper to leer at the prospect, as if there were a procession of discomfited Miss Toxes pouring out in the smoke of the train, and flying away over the fields to hide themselves in any place of refuge, aroused his friend by informing him that the post-horses were harnessed and the carriage ready.

'Dombey,' said the major, rapping him on the arm with his cane, 'don't be thoughtful. It's a bad habit. Old Joe, sir, wouldn't be as tough as you see him, if he had ever encouraged it. You are too great a man, Dombey, to be thoughtful. In your position, sir, you're far above that kind of thing.'

The major, even in his friendly remonstrances, thus consulting the dignity and honour of Mr. Dombey, and showing a lively sense of their importance, Mr. Dombey felt more than ever disposed to defer to a gentleman possessing so much good sense and such a well-regulated mind; accordingly he made an effort to listen to the major's stories, as they trotted along the turnpike-road; and the major, finding both the pace and the road a great deal better adapted to his conversational powers than the mode of travelling they had just relinquished, came out for his entertainment.

In this flow of spirits and conversation, only interrupted by his usual plethoric symptoms, and by intervals of lunch, and from time to time by some violent assault upon the native, who wore a pair of earrings in his dark-brown ears, and on whom his European clothes sat with an outlandish impossibility of adjustment—being, of their own accord, and without any reference to the tailor's art, long where they ought to be short, short where they ought to be long, tight where they ought to be loose, and loose where they ought to be tight—and to which he imparted a new grace, whenever the major attacked him, by shrinking into them like a shrivelled nut, or a cold monkey—in this flow of spirits and conversation, the major continued all day: so that when evening came on, and found them trotting through the green and leafy road near Leamington, the major's voice, what with talking and eating and chuckling and choking, appeared to be in the box under the rumble, or in some neighbouring haystack. Nor did the major improve it at the Royal Hotel, where rooms and dinner had been ordered, and where he so oppressed his organs of speech by eating and drinking, that when he retired to bed he had no voice at all, except to cough with, and could only make himself intelligible to the dark servant by gasping at him.

He not only rose next morning, however, like a giant refreshed, but conducted himself, at breakfast, like a giant refreshing. At this meal they arranged their daily habits. The major was to take the responsibility of ordering everything to eat and drink; and they were to have a late breakfast together every morning, and a late dinner together every day. Mr. Dombey would prefer remaining in his own room, or walking in the country by himself, on that first day of their sojourn at Leamington; but next morning he would be happy to accompany the major to the Pump-room, and about the town. So they parted until dinner-time. Mr. Dombey retired to nurse his wholesome thoughts in his own way. The major, attended by the native carrying a camp-stool, a great-coat, and an umbrella, swaggered up and down through all the public places: looking into subscription books to find out who was there, looking up old ladies by whom he was much admired, reporting J. B. tougher than ever, and puffing his rich friend Dombey wherever he went. There never was a man who stood by a friend more staunchly than the major, when in puffing them, he puffed himself.

It was surprising how much new conversation the major had to let off at dinner-time, and what occasion he gave Mr. Dombey to admire his social qualities. At breakfast next morning, he knew the contents of the latest newspapers received; and mentioned several subjects in connection with them, on which his opinion had recently been sought by persons of such power and might, that they were only to be obscurely hinted at. Mr. Dombey, who had been so long shut up within himself, and who had rarely, at any time, overstepped the enchanted circle within which the operations of Dombey and Son were conducted, began to think this an improvement on his solitary life; and in place of excusing himself for another day, as he had thought of doing when alone, walked out with the major arm-in-arm.

## CHAPTER XXI

### NEW FACES

THE major, more blue-faced and staring—more overripe, as it were, than ever—and giving vent, every now and then, to one of the horse's coughs, not so much of necessity as in a spontaneous explosion of importance, walked arm-in-arm with Mr. Dombey, up the sunny side of the way, with his cheeks swelling over his tight stock, his legs majestically wide apart, and his great head wagging from side to side, as if he were remonstrating within himself for being such a captivating object. They had not walked many yards, before the major encountered somebody he knew, nor many yards farther before the major encountered somebody else he knew, but he merely shook his fingers at them as he passed, and led Mr. Dombey on: pointing out the localities as they went, and enlivening the walk with any current scandal suggested by them.

In this manner the major and Mr. Dombey were walking arm-in-arm, much to their own satisfaction, when they beheld advancing towards them, a wheeled chair, in which a lady was seated, indolently steering her carriage by a kind of rudder in front, while it was propelled by some unseen power in the rear. Although the lady was not young, she was very blooming in the face—quite rosy—and her dress and attitude were perfectly juvenile. Walking by the side of the chair, and carrying her gossamer parasol with a proud and weary air, as if so great an effort must be soon abandoned and the parasol dropped, sauntered a much younger lady, very handsome, very haughty, very wilful, who tossed her head and drooped her eyelids, as though, if there were anything in all the world worth looking into, save a mirror, it certainly was not the earth or sky.

'Why, what the devil have we here, sir!' cried the major, stopping as this little cavalcade drew near.

'My dearest Edith!' drawled the lady in the chair, 'Major Bagstock!'

The major no sooner heard the voice, than he relinquished Mr. Dombey's arm, darted forward, took the hand of the lady in the chair and pressed it to his lips. With no less gallantry, the major folded both his gloves upon his heart, and bowed low to the other lady. And, now, the chair having stopped, the motive power became visible in the shape of a flushed page pushing behind, who seemed to have in part outgrown and in part out-pushed his strength, for when he stood upright he was tall, and wan, and thin, and his plight appeared the more forlorn from his having injured the shape of his hat, by butting at the carriage with his head to urge it forward, as is sometimes done by elephants in Oriental countries.

'Joe Bagstock,' said the major to both ladies, 'is a proud and happy man for the rest of his life.'

'You false creature,' said the old lady in the chair, insipidly. 'Where do you come from? I can't bear you.'

'Then suffer old Joe to present a friend, ma'am,' said the major, promptly, 'as a reason for being tolerated. Mr. Dombey, Mrs. Skewton.' The lady in the chair was gracious. 'Mr. Dombey, Mrs. Granger.' The lady with the parasol was faintly conscious of Mr. Dombey's taking off his hat, and bowing low. 'I am delighted, sir,' said the major, 'to have this opportunity.'

The major seemed in earnest, for he looked at all the three, and leered in his ugliest manner.

'Mrs. Skewton, Dombey,' said the major, 'makes havoc in the heart of old Josh.'

Mr. Dombey signified that he didn't wonder at it.

'You perfidious goblin,' said the lady in the chair, 'have done! How long have you been here, bad man?'

'One day,' replied the major.

'And can you be a day, or even a minute,' returned the lady, slightly settling her false curls and false eyebrows with her fan, and showing her false teeth, set off by her false complexion, 'in the garden of what 's-its-name—'

'Eden, I suppose, mamma,' interrupted the younger lady, scornfully.

'My dear Edith,' said the other, 'I cannot help it. I never can remember those frightful names—without having your whole soul and being inspired by the sight of Nature; by the perfume,' said Mrs. Skewton, rustling a handkerchief that was faint and sickly with essences, 'of her artless breath, you creature!'

The discrepancy between Mrs. Skewton's fresh enthusiasm of words, and forlornly faded manner, was hardly less observable than that between her age, which was about seventy, and her dress, which would have been youthful for twenty-seven. Her attitude in the wheeled chair (which she never varied) was one in which she had been taken in a barouche, some fifty years before, by a then fashionable artist who had appended to his published sketch the name of Cleopatra: in consequence of a discovery made by the critics of the time, that it bore an exact resemblance to that princess as she reclined on board her galley. Mrs. Skewton was a beauty then, and bucks threw wine-glasses over their heads by dozens in her honour. The beauty and the barouche had both passed away, but she still preserved the attitude, and for this reason expressly, maintained the wheeled chair and the butting page: there being nothing whatever, except the attitude, to prevent her from walking.

'Mr. Dombey is devoted to Nature, I trust?' said Mrs. Skewton, settling her diamond brooch. And by the way, she chiefly lived upon the reputation of some diamonds, and her family connections.

'My friend Dombey, ma'am,' returned the major, 'may be devoted to her in secret, but a man who is paramount in the greatest city in the universe—'

'No one can be a stranger,' said Mrs. Skewton, 'to Mr. Dombey's immense influence.'

As Mr. Dombey acknowledged the compliment with a bend of his head, the younger lady glancing at him, met his eyes.

'You reside here, madam?' said Mr. Dombey, addressing her.

'No, we have been to a great many places. To Harrowgate and Scarborough, and into Devonshire. We have been visiting, and resting here and there. Mamma likes change.'

'Edith of course does not,' said Mrs. Skewton, with a ghastly archness.

'I have not found that there is any change in such places,' was the answer, delivered with supreme indifference.

'They libel me. There is only one change, Mr. Dombey,' observed Mrs. Skewton, with a mincing sigh, 'for which I really care, and that I fear I shall never be permitted to enjoy. People cannot spare one. But seclusion and contemplation are my what 's-his-name—'

'If you mean Paradise, mamma, you had better say so, to render yourself intelligible,' said the younger lady.

'My dearest Edith,' returned Mrs. Skewton, 'you know that I am wholly dependent upon you for those odious names. I assure you, Mr. Dombey, Nature intended me for an Arcadian. I am thrown away in society. Cows are my passion. What I have ever sighed for, has been to retreat to a Swiss farm, and live entirely surrounded by cows—and china.'

This curious association of objects, suggesting a remembrance of the celebrated bull who got by mistake into a crockery shop, was received with perfect gravity by Mr. Dombey, who intimated his opinion that Nature was, no doubt, a very respectable institution.

'What I want,' drawled Mrs. Skewton, pinching her shrivelled throat, 'is heart.' It was frightfully true in one sense, if not in that in which she used the phrase. 'What I want, is frankness, confidence, less conventionality, and freer play of soul. We are so dreadfully artificial.'

We were, indeed.

'In short,' said Mrs. Skewton, 'I want Nature everywhere. It would be so extremely charming.'

'Nature is inviting us away now, mamma, if you are ready,' said the younger lady, curling her handsome lip. At this hint, the wan page, who had been surveying the party over the top of the chair, vanished behind it, as if the ground had swallowed him up.

'Stop a moment, Withers!' said Mrs. Skewton, as the chair began to move; calling to the page with all the languid dignity with which she had called in days of yore to a coachman with a wig, cauliflower nosegay, and silk stockings. 'Where are you staying, abomination?'

The major was staying at the Royal Hotel, with his friend Dombey.

'You may come and see us any evening when you are good,' lisped Mrs. Skewton. 'If Mr. Dombey will honour us, we shall be happy. Withers, go on!'

The major again pressed to his blue lips the tips of the fingers that were disposed on the ledge of the wheeled chair with careful carelessness, after the Cleopatra model: and Mr. Dombey bowed. The elder lady honoured them both with a very gracious smile and a girlish wave of her hand; the younger lady with the very slightest inclination of her head that common courtesy allowed.

The last glimpse of the wrinkled face of the mother, with that patched colour on it which the sun made infinitely more haggard and dismal than any want of colour could have been, and of the proud beauty of the daughter with her graceful figure and erect deportment, engendered such an involuntary disposition on the part of both the major and Mr. Dombey to look after them, that they both turned at the same moment. The page, nearly as much aslant as his own shadow, was toiling after the chair, uphill, like a slow battering-ram; the top of Cleopatra's bonnet was fluttering in exactly the same corner to the inch as before; and the Beauty, loitering by herself a little in advance, expressed in all her elegant form, from head to foot, the same supreme disregard of everything and everybody.

'I tell you what, sir,' said the major, as they resumed their walk again. 'If Joe Bagstock were a younger man, there 's not a woman in the world whom he 'd prefer for Mrs. Bagstock to that woman. By George, sir!' said the major, 'she 's superb!'

'Do you mean the daughter?' inquired Mr. Dombey.

'Is Joey B. a turnip, Dombey,' said the major, 'that he should mean the mother!'

'You were complimentary to the mother,' returned Mr. Dombey.

'An ancient flame, sir,' chuckled Major Bagstock, 'Devilish ancient. I humour her.'

'She impresses me as being perfectly genteel,' said Mr. Dombey.

'Genteel, sir,' said the major, stopping short, and staring in his companion's face. 'The Honourable Mrs. Skewton, sir, is sister to the late Lord Feenix, and aunt to the present lord. The family are not wealthy—they 're poor, indeed—and she lives upon a small jointure; but if you come to blood, sir!' The major gave a flourish with his stick and walked on again, in despair of being able to say what you came to, if you came to that.

'You addressed the daughter, I observed,' said Mr. Dombey, after a short pause, 'as Mrs. Granger.'

'Edith Skewton, sir,' returned the major, stopping short again, and punching a mark in the ground with his cane, to represent her, 'married (at eighteen) Granger of Ours'; whom the major indicated by another punch. 'Granger, sir,' said the major, tapping the last ideal portrait, and rolling his head emphatically, 'was Colonel of Ours; a de-vilish handsome fellow, sir, of forty-one. He died, sir, in the second year of his marriage.' The major ran the representative of the deceased Granger through and through the body with his walking-stick, and went on again, carrying his stick over his shoulder.

'How long is this ago?' asked Mr. Dombey, making another halt.

'Edith Granger, sir,' replied the major, shutting one eye, putting his head on one side, passing his cane into his left hand, and smoothing his shirt-frill with his right, 'is, at this present time, not quite thirty. And, damme, sir,' said the major, shouldering his stick once more, and walking on again, 'she 's a peerless woman!'

'Was there any family?' asked Mr. Dombey presently.

'Yes, sir,' said the major. 'There was a boy.'

Mr. Dombey's eyes sought the ground, and a shade came over his face.

'Who was drowned, sir,' pursued the major. 'When a child of four or five years old.'

'Indeed?' said Mr. Dombey, raising his head.

'By the upsetting of a boat in which his nurse had

no business to have put him,' said the major. 'That's *his* history. Edith Granger is Edith Granger still; but if tough old Joey B., sir, were a little younger and a little richer, the name of that immortal paragon should be Bagstock.'

The major heaved his shoulders, and his cheeks, and laughed more like an over-fed Mephistopheles than ever, as he said the words.

'Provided the lady made no objection, I suppose?' said Mr. Dombey coldly.

'By Gad, sir,' said the major, 'the Bagstock breed are not accustomed to that sort of obstacle. Though it's true enough that Edith might have married twen-ty times, but for being proud, sir, proud.'

Mr. Dombey seemed, by his face, to think no worse of her for that.

'It's a great quality after all,' said the major. 'By the Lord, it's a high quality! Dombey! You are proud yourself, and your friend, Old Joe, respects you for it, sir.'

With this tribute to the character of his ally, which seemed to be wrung from him by the force of circumstances and the irresistible tendency of their conversation, the major closed the subject, and glided into a general exposition of the extent to which he had been beloved and gloated on by splendid women and brilliant creatures.

On the next day but one, Mr. Dombey and the major encountered the Honourable Mrs. Skewton and her daughter in the Pump-room; on the day after, they met them again very near the place where they had met them first. After meeting them thus, three or four times in all, it became a point of mere civility to old acquaintances that the major should go there one evening. Mr. Dombey had not originally intended to pay visits, but on the major announcing this intention, he said he would have the pleasure of accompanying him. So the major told the native to go round before dinner, and say, with his and Mr. Dombey's compliments, that they would have the honour of visiting the ladies that same evening, if the ladies were alone. In answer to which message, the native brought back a very small note with a very large quantity of scent about it, indited by the Honourable Mrs. Skewton to Major Bagstock, and briefly saying, 'You are a shocking bear, and I have a great mind not to forgive you, but if you are very good indeed,' which was underlined, 'you may come. Compliments (in which Edith unites) to Mr. Dombey.'

The Honourable Mrs. Skewton and her daughter, Mrs. Granger, resided while at Leamington, in lodgings that were fashionable enough and dear enough, but rather limited in point of space and conveniences; so that the Honourable Mrs. Skewton, being in bed, had her feet in the window and her head in the fireplace, while the Honourable Mrs. Skewton's maid was quartered in a closet within the drawing-room, so extremely small, that, to avoid developing the whole of its accommodations, she was obliged to writhe in and out of the door like a beautiful serpent. Withers, the wan page, slept out of the house immediately under the tiles at a neighbouring milk-shop; and the wheeled chair, which was the stone of that young Sisyphus, passed the night in a shed belonging to the same dairy, where new-laid eggs were produced by the poultry connected with the establishment, who roosted on a broken donkey-cart, persuaded, to all appearance, that it grew there, and was a species of tree.

Mr. Dombey and the major found Mrs. Skewton arranged, as Cleopatra, among the cushions of a sofa:

very airily dressed; and certainly not resembling Shakespeare's Cleopatra, whom age could not wither. On their way upstairs they had heard the sound of a harp, but it had ceased on their being announced, and Edith now stood beside it handsomer and haughtier than ever. It was a remarkable characteristic of this lady's beauty that it appeared to vaunt and assert itself without her aid, and against her will. She knew that she was beautiful: it was impossible that it could be otherwise: but she seemed with her own pride to defy her very self.

Whether she held cheap, attractions that could only call forth admiration that was worthless to her, or whether she designed to render them more precious to admirers by this usage of them, those to whom they *were* precious seldom paused to consider.

'I hope, Mrs. Granger,' said Mr. Dombey, advancing a step towards her, 'we are not the cause of your ceasing to play?'

'*You?* oh no!'

'Why do you not go on, then, my dearest Edith?' said Cleopatra.

'I left off as I began—of my own fancy.'

The exquisite indifference of her manner in saying this: an indifference quite removed from dulness or insensibility, for it was pointed with proud purpose: was well set off by the carelessness with which she drew her hand across the strings, and came from that part of the room.

'Do you know, Mr. Dombey,' said her languishing mother, playing with a hand-screen, 'that occasionally my dearest Edith and myself actually almost differ—'

'Not quite, sometimes, mamma?' said Edith.

'Oh never quite, my darling! Fie, fie, it would break my heart,' returned her mother, making a faint attempt to pat her with the screen, which Edith made no movement to meet, 'about these cold conventionalities of manner that are observed in little things? Why are we not more natural! Dear me! With all those yearnings, and gushings, and impulsive throbbings that we have implanted in our souls, and which are so very charming, why are we not more natural?'

Mr. Dombey said it was very true, very true.

'We could be more natural I suppose if we tried,' said Mrs. Skewton.

Mr. Dombey thought it possible.

'Devil a bit, ma'am,' said the major. 'We couldn't afford it. Unless the world was peopled with J. B.'s—tough and blunt, old Joes, ma'am, plain red herrings, with hard roes, sir—we couldn't afford it. It wouldn't do.'

'You naughty infidel,' said Mrs. Skewton, 'be mute.'

'Cleopatra commands,' returned the major, kissing his hand, 'and Antony Bagstock obeys.'

'The man has no sensitiveness,' said Mrs. Skewton, cruelly holding up the hand-screen so as to shut the major out. 'No sympathy. And what do we live for *but* sympathy! What else is so extremely charming! without that gleam of sunshine on our cold cold earth,' said Mrs. Skewton, arranging her lace tucker, and complacently observing the effect of her bare lean arm, looking upward from the wrist, 'how could we possibly bear it? In short, obdurate man!' glancing at the major round the screen, 'I would have my world all heart; and Faith is so excessively charming, that I won't allow you to disturb it, do you hear?'

The major replied that it was hard in Cleopatra to require the world to be all heart, and yet to appropriate to herself the hearts of all the world; which obliged Cleopatra to remind him that flattery was insupportable to her, and that if he had the boldness to address her in that strain any more, she would positively send him home.

Withers the wan, at this period, handing round the tea, Mr. Dombey again addressed himself to Edith.

'There is not much company here, it would seem?' said Mr. Dombey, in his own portentous gentlemanly way.

'I believe not. We see none.'

'Why really,' observed Mrs. Skewton from her couch, 'there are no people here just now with whom we care to associate.'

'They have not enough heart,' said Edith, with a smile. The very twilight of a smile: so singularly were its light and darkness blended.

'My dearest Edith rallies me, you see!' said her mother, shaking her head: which shook a little of itself sometimes, as if the palsy twinkled now and then in opposition to the diamonds. 'Wicked one!'

'You have been here before, if I am not mistaken?' said Mr. Dombey. Still to Edith.

'Oh, several times. I think we have been everywhere.'

'A beautiful country.'

'I suppose it is. Everybody says so.'

'Your cousin Feenix raves about it, Edith,' interposed her mother from her couch.

The daughter slightly turned her graceful head, and raising her eyebrows by a hair's-breadth, as if her cousin Feenix were of all the mortal world the least to be regarded, turned her eyes again towards Mr. Dombey.

'I hope, for the credit of my good taste, that I am tired of the neighbourhood,' she said.

'You have almost reason to be, madam,' he replied, glancing at a variety of landscape drawings, of which he had already recognised several as representing neighbouring points of view, and which were strewn abundantly about the room, 'if these beautiful productions are from your hand.'

She gave him no reply, but sat in a disdainful beauty, quite amazing.

'Have they that interest?' said Mr. Dombey. 'Are they yours?'

'Yes.'

'And you play, I already know.'

'Yes.'

'And sing?'

'Yes.'

She answered all these questions with a strange reluctance; and with that remarkable air of opposition to herself, already noticed as belonging to her beauty. Yet she was not embarrassed, but wholly self-possessed. Neither did she seem to wish to avoid the conversation, for she addressed her face, and—so far as she could—her manner also, to him; and continued to do so, when he was silent.

'You have many resources against weariness at least,' said Mr. Dombey.

'Whatever their efficiency may be,' she returned, 'you know them all now. I have no more.'

'May I hope to prove them all?' said Mr. Dombey, with solemn gallantry, laying down a drawing he had held, and motioning towards the harp.

'Oh certainly! If you desire it!'

She rose as she spoke, and crossing by her mother's couch, and directing a stately look towards her, which was instantaneous in its duration, but inclusive (if any one had seen it) of a multitude of expressions, among which that of the twilight smile, without the smile itself, overshadowed all the rest, went out of the room.

The major, who was quite forgiven by this time, had wheeled a little table up to Cleopatra, and was sitting down to play picquet with her. Mr. Dombey, not knowing the game, sat down to watch them for his edification until Edith should return.

'We are going to have some music, Mr. Dombey, I hope?' said Cleopatra.

'Mrs. Granger has been kind enough to promise so,' said Mr. Dombey.

'Ah! That 's very nice. Do you propose, major?'

'No, ma'am,' said the major. 'Couldn't do it.'

'You 're a barbarous being,' replied the lady, 'and my hand 's destroyed. You are fond of music, Mr. Dombey?'

'Eminently so,' was Mr. Dombey's answer.

'Yes. It 's very nice,' said Cleopatra, looking at her cards. 'So much heart in it—undeveloped recollections of a previous state of existence—and all that—which is so truly charming. Do you know,' simpered Cleopatra, reversing the knave of clubs, who had come into her game with his heels uppermost, 'that if anything could tempt me to put a period to my life, it would be curiosity to find out what it 's all about, and what it means; there are so many provoking mysteries, really, that are hidden from us. Major, you to play.'

The major played; and Mr. Dombey, looking on for his instruction, would soon have been in a state of dire confusion, but that he gave no attention to the game whatever, and sat wondering instead when Edith would come back.

She came at last, and sat down to her harp, and Mr. Dombey rose and stood beside her, listening. He had little taste for music, and no knowledge of the strains she played, but he saw her bending over it, and perhaps he heard among the sounding strings some distant music of his own, that tamed the monster of the iron road, and made it less inexorable.

Cleopatra had a sharp eye, verily, at picquet. It glistened like a bird's, and did not fix itself upon the game, but pierced the room from end to end, and gleamed on harp, performer, listener, everything.

When the haughty beauty had concluded, she arose, and receiving Mr. Dombey's thanks and compliments in exactly the same manner as before, went with scarcely any pause to the piano, and began there.

Edith Granger, any song but that! Edith Granger, you are very handsome, and your touch upon the keys is brilliant, and your voice is deep and rich; but not the air that his neglected daughter sang to his dead son!

Alas, he knows it not; and if he did, what air of hers would stir him, rigid man! Sleep, lonely Florence, sleep! Peace in thy dreams, although the night has turned dark, and the clouds are gathering, and threaten to discharge themselves in hail!

## CHAPTER XXII

### A TRIFLE OF MANAGEMENT BY MR. CARKER THE MANAGER

MR. CARKER the manager sat at his desk, smooth and soft as usual, reading those letters which were reserved for him to open, backing them occasionally with such memoranda and references as their business purport required, and parcelling them out into little heaps for distribution through the several departments of the House. The post had come in heavy that morning, and Mr. Carker the manager had a good deal to do.

The general action of a man so engaged—pausing to look over a bundle of papers in his hand, dealing them round in various portions, taking up another bundle and examining its contents with knitted brows and pursed-out lips—dealing, and sorting, and pondering by turns—would easily suggest some whimsical resemblance to a player at cards. The face of Mr. Carker the manager was in good keeping with such a fancy. It was the face of a man who studied his play, warily: who made himself master of all the strong and weak points of the game: who registered the cards in his mind as they fell about him, knew exactly what was on them, what they missed, and what they made: who was crafty to find out what the other players held, and who never betrayed his own hand.

The letters were in various languages, but Mr. Carker the manager read them all. If there had been anything in the offices of Dombey and Son that he could *not* read, there would have been a card wanting in the pack. He read almost at a glance, and made combinations of one letter with another and one business with another as he went on, adding new matter to the heaps—much as a man would know the cards at sight, and work out their combinations in his mind after they were turned. Something too deep for a partner, and much too deep for an adversary, Mr. Carker the manager sat in the rays of the sun that came down slanting on him through the skylight, playing his game alone.

And although it is not among the instincts wild or domestic of the cat tribe to play at cards, feline from sole to crown was Mr. Carker the manager, as he basked in the strip of summer-light and warmth that shone upon his table and the ground as if they were a crooked dial-plate, and himself the only figure on it. With hair and whiskers deficient in colour at all times, but feebler than common in the rich sunshine, and more like the coat of a sandy tortoiseshell cat; with long nails, nicely pared and sharpened; with a natural antipathy to any speck of dirt, which made him pause sometimes and watch the falling motes of dust, and rub them off his smooth white hand or glossy linen: Mr. Carker the manager, sly of manner, sharp of tooth, soft of foot, watchful of eye, oily of tongue, cruel of heart, nice of habit, sat with a dainty steadfastness and patience at his work, as if he were waiting at a mouse's hole.

At length the letters were disposed of, excepting one which he reserved for a particular audience. Having locked the more confidential correspondence in a drawer, Mr. Carker the manager rang his bell.

'Why do *you* answer it?' was his reception of his brother.

'The messenger is out, and I am the next,' was the submissive reply.

'You are the next?' muttered the manager. 'Yes! Creditable to me! There!'

Pointing to the heaps of opened letters, he turned disdainfully away, in his elbow-chair, and broke the seal of that one which he held in his hand.

'I am sorry to trouble you, James,' said the brother, gathering them up, 'but—'

'Oh! you have something to say. I knew that. Well?'

Mr. Carker the manager did not raise his eyes or turn them on his brother, but kept them on his letter, though without opening it.

'Well?' he repeated sharply.

'I am uneasy about Harriet.'

'Harriet who? what Harriet? I know nobody of that name.'

'She is not well, and has changed very much of late.'

'She changed very much, a great many years ago,' replied the manager; 'and that is all I have to say.'

'I think if you would hear me—'

'Why should I hear you, brother John?' returned the manager, laying a sarcastic emphasis on those two words, and throwing up his head, but not lifting his eyes. 'I tell you, Harriet Carker made her choice many years ago between her two brothers. She may repent it, but she must abide by it.'

'Don't mistake me. I do not say she *does* repent it. It would be black ingratitude in me to hint at such a thing,' returned the other. 'Though believe me, James, I am as sorry for her sacrifice as you.'

'As I?' exclaimed the manager. 'As I?'

'As sorry for her choice—for what you call her choice—as you are angry at it,' said the junior.

'Angry?' repeated the other, with a wide show of his teeth.

'Displeased. Whatever word you like best. You know my meaning. There is no offence in my intention.'

'There is offence in everything you do,' replied his brother, glancing at him with a sudden scowl, which in a moment gave place to a wider smile than the last. 'Carry those papers away, if you please. I am busy.'

His politeness was so much more cutting than his wrath, that the junior went to the door. But stopping at it, and looking round, he said—

'When Harriet tried in vain to plead for me with you, on your first just indignation, and my first disgrace; and when she left you, James, to follow my broken fortunes, and devote herself, in her mistaken affection, to a ruined brother, because without her he had no one, and was lost; she was young and pretty. I think if you could see her now—if you would go and see her—she would move your admiration and compassion.'

The manager inclined his head, and showed his

teeth, as who should say, in answer to some careless small-talk, 'Dear me! Is that the case?' but said never a word.

'We thought in those days: you and I both: that she would marry young, and lead a happy and light-hearted life,' pursued the other. 'Oh if you knew how cheerfully she cast those hopes away; how cheerfully she has gone forward on the path she took and never once looked back; you never could say again that her name was strange in your ears. Never!'

Again the manager inclined his head, and showed his teeth, and seemed to say, 'Remarkable indeed! You quite surprise me!' And again he uttered never a word.

'May I go on?' said John Carker, mildly.

'On your way?' replied his smiling brother. 'If you will have the goodness.'

John Carker, with a sigh, was passing slowly out at the door, when his brother's voice detained him for a moment on the threshold.

'If she has gone, and goes, her own way cheerfully,' he said, throwing the still unfolded letter on his desk, and putting his hands firmly in his pockets, 'you may tell her that I go as cheerfully on mine. If she has never once looked back, you may tell her that I have, sometimes, to recall her taking part with you, and that my resolution is no easier to wear away'; he smiled very sweetly here; 'than marble.'

'I tell her nothing of you. We never speak about you. Once a year, on your birthday, Harriet says always, "Let us remember James by name, and wish him happy," but we say no more.'

'Tell it then, if you please,' returned the other, 'to yourself. You can't repeat it too often, as a lesson to you to avoid the subject in speaking to me. I know no Harriet Carker. There is no such person.

*You* may have a sister; make much of her. I have none.'

Mr. Carker the manager took up the letter again, and waved it with a smile of mock courtesy towards the door. Unfolding it as his brother withdrew, and looking darkly after him as he left the room, he once more turned round in his elbow-chair, and applied himself to a diligent perusal of its contents.

It was in the writing of his great chief, Mr. Dombey, and dated from Leamington. Though he was a quick reader of all other letters, Mr. Carker read this slowly; weighing the words as he went, and bringing every tooth in his head to bear upon them. When he had read it through once, he turned it over again, and picked out these passages. 'I find myself benefited by the change, and am not yet inclined to name any time for my return.' 'I wish, Carker, you would arrange to come down once and see me here, and let me know how things are going on, in person.' 'I omitted to speak to you about young Gay. If not gone per Son and Heir, or if Son and Heir still lying in the Docks, appoint some other young man and keep him in the City for the present. I am not decided.' 'Now that 's unfortunate!' said Mr. Carker the manager, expanding his mouth, as if it were made of india-rubber: 'for he is far away.'

Still that passage which was in a postscript, attracted his attention and his teeth, once more.

'I think,' he said, 'my good friend Captain Cuttle mentioned something about being towed along in the wake of that day. What a pity he 's so far away.'

He refolded the letter, and was sitting trifling with it, standing it long-wise and broad-wise on his table, and turning it over and over on all sides—doing pretty much the same thing perhaps, by its contents—

when Mr. Perch the messenger knocked softly at the door, and coming in on tiptoe, bending his body at every step as if it were the delight of his life to bow, laid some papers on the table.

'Would you please to be engaged, sir?' asked Mr. Perch, rubbing his hands, and deferentially putting his head on one side, like a man who felt he had no business to hold it up in such a presence, and would keep it as much out of the way as possible.

'Who wants me?'

'Why, sir,' said Mr. Perch, in a soft voice, 'really nobody, sir, to speak of at present. Mr. Gills the ship's instrument-maker, sir, has looked in, about a little matter of payment, he says; but I mentioned to him, sir, that you was engaged several deep; several deep.'

Mr. Perch coughed once behind his hand, and waited for further orders.

'Anybody else?'

'Well, sir,' said Mr. Perch, 'I wouldn't of my own self take the liberty of mentioning, sir, that there was anybody else; but that same young lad that was here yesterday, sir, and last week, has been hanging about the place; and it looks, sir,' added Mr. Perch, stopping to shut the door, 'dreadful unbusiness-like to see him whistling to the sparrows down the court and making of 'em answer him.'

'You said he wanted something to do, didn't you, Perch?' asked Mr. Carker, leaning back in his chair and looking at that officer.

'Why, sir,' said Mr. Perch, coughing behind his hand again, 'his expression certainly were that he was in wants of a sitiwation, and that he considered something might be done for him about the Docks, being used to fishing with a rod and line: but—' Mr. Perch shook his head very dubiously indeed.

'What does he say when he comes?' asked Mr. Carker.

'Indeed, sir,' said Mr. Perch, coughing another cough behind his hand, which was always his resource as an expression of humility when nothing else occurred to him, 'his observation generally air that he would humbly wish to see one of the gentlemen, and that he wants to earn a living. But you see, sir,' added Perch, dropping his voice to a whisper, and turning, in the inviolable nature of his confidence, to give the door a thrust with his hand and knee, as if that would shut it any more when it was shut already, 'it 's hardly to be bore, sir, that a common lad like that should come a prowling here, and saying that his mother nursed our House's young gentleman, and that he hopes our House will give him a chance on that account. I am sure, sir,' observed Mr. Perch, 'that although Mrs. Perch was at that time nursing as thriving a little girl, sir, as we 've ever took the liberty of adding to our family, I wouldn't have made so free as drop a hint of her being capable of imparting nourishment, not if it was never so!'

Mr. Carker grinned at him like a shark, but in an absent, thoughtful manner.

'Whether,' submitted Mr. Perch, after a short silence, and another cough, 'it mightn't be best for me to tell him, that if he was seen here any more he would be given into custody; and to keep to it! With respect to bodily fear,' said Mr. Perch, 'I 'm so timid, myself, by nature, sir, and my nerves is so unstrung by Mrs. Perch's state, that I could take my affidavit easy.'

'Let me see this fellow, Perch,' said Mr. Carker. 'Bring him in!'

'Yes, sir. Begging your pardon, sir,' said Mr.

Perch, hesitating at the door, 'he 's rough, sir, in appearance.'

'Never mind. If he 's there, bring him in. I 'll see Mr. Gills directly. Ask him to wait.'

Mr. Perch bowed; and shutting the door, as precisely and carefully as if he were not coming back for a week, went on his quest among the sparrows in the court. While he was gone, Mr. Carker assumed his favourite attitude before the fireplace, and stood looking at the door; presenting, with his under-lip tucked into the smile that showed his whole row of upper teeth, a singularly crouching appearance.

The messenger was not long in returning, followed by a pair of heavy boots that came bumping along the passage like boxes. With the unceremonious words, 'Come along with you!'—a very unusual form of introduction from his lips—Mr. Perch then ushered into the presence a strong-built lad of fifteen, with a round red face, a round sleek head, round black eyes, round limbs, and round body, who, to carry out the general rotundity of his appearance, had a round hat in his hand, without a particle of brim to it.

Obedient to a nod from Mr. Carker, Perch had no sooner confronted the visitor with that gentleman than he withdrew. The moment they were face to face alone, Mr. Carker, without a word of preparation, took him by the throat, and shook him until his head seemed loose upon his shoulders.

The boy, who in the midst of his astonishment could not help staring wildly at the gentleman with so many white teeth who was choking him, and at the office walls, as though determined, if he *were* choked, that his last look should be at the mysteries for his intrusion into which he was paying such a severe penalty, at last contrived to utter—

'Come, sir! You let me alone, will you?'

'Let you alone!' said Mr. Carker. 'What! I have got you, have I?' There was no doubt of that, and tightly too. 'You dog,' said Mr. Carker, through his set jaws, 'I'll strangle you!'

Biler whimpered, would he though? oh no he wouldn't—and what was he doing of—and why didn't he strangle somebody of his own size and not *him*: but Biler was quelled by the extraordinary nature of his reception, and, as his head became stationary, and he looked the gentleman in the face, or rather in the teeth, and saw him snarling at him, he so far forgot his manhood as to cry.

'I haven't done nothing to you, sir,' said Biler, otherwise Rob, otherwise Grinder, and always Toodle.

'You young scoundrel!' replied Mr. Carker, slowly releasing him and moving back a step into his favourite position. 'What do you mean by daring to come here?'

'I didn't mean no harm, sir,' whimpered Rob, putting one hand to his throat, and the knuckles of the other to his eyes. 'I'll never come again, sir, I only wanted work.'

'Work, young Cain that you are!' repeated Mr. Carker, eyeing him narrowly. 'An't you the idlest vagabond in London?'

The impeachment, while it much affected Mr. Toodle junior, attached to his character so justly, that he could not say a word in denial. He stood looking at the gentleman, therefore, with a frightened, self-convicted, and remorseful air. As to his looking at him, it may be observed that he was fascinated by Mr. Carker, and never took his round eyes off him for an instant.

'An't you a thief?' said Mr. Carker, with his hands behind him in his pockets.

'No, sir,' pleaded Rob.

'You are!' said Mr. Carker.

'I an't indeed, sir,' whimpered Rob. 'I never did such a thing as thieve, sir, if you 'll believe me. I know I 've been going wrong, sir, ever since I took to bird-catching and walking-matching. I 'm sure a cove might think,' said Mr. Toodle junior, with a burst of penitence, 'that singing birds was innocent company, but nobody knows what harm is in them little creeturs and what they brings you down to.'

They seemed to have brought *him* down to a velveteen jacket and trousers very much the worse for wear, a particularly small red waistcoat like a gorget, an interval of blue check, and the hat before mentioned.

'I an't been home twenty times since them birds got their will of me,' said Rob, 'and that 's ten months. How can I go home when everybody 's miserable to see me! I wonder,' said Biler, blubbering outright, and smearing his eyes with his coat-cuff, 'that I haven't been and drownded myself over and over again.'

All of which, including his expression of surprise at not having achieved this last scarce performance, the boy said, just as if the teeth of Mr. Carker drew it out of him, and he had no power of concealing anything with that battery of attraction in full play.

'You 're a nice young gentleman!' said Mr. Carker, shaking his head at him. 'There 's hemp-seed sown for *you,* my fine fellow!'

'I 'm sure, sir,' returned the wretched Biler, blubbering again, and again having recourse to his coat-cuff: 'I shouldn't care, sometimes, if it was growed too. My misfortunes all began in wagging, sir; but what could I do, exceptin' wag?'

'Excepting what?' said Mr. Carker.

'Wag, sir. Wagging from school.'

'Do you mean pretending to go there, and not going?' said Mr. Carker.

'Yes, sir, that 's wagging, sir,' returned the quondam Grinder, much affected. 'I was chivied through the streets, sir, when I went there, and pounded when I got there. So I wagged and hid myself, and that began it.'

'And you mean to tell me,' said Mr. Carker, taking him by the throat again, holding him out at arm's-length, and surveying him in silence for some moments, 'that you want a place, do you?'

'I should be thankful to be tried, sir,' returned Toodle junior, faintly.

Mr. Carker the manager pushed him backward into a corner—the boy submitting quietly, hardly venturing to breathe, and never once removing his eyes from his face—and rang the bell.

'Tell Mr. Gills to come here.'

Mr. Perch was too deferential to express surprise or recognition of the figure in the corner: and uncle Sol appeared immediately.

'Mr. Gills!' said Carker, with a smile, 'sit down. How do you do? You continue to enjoy your health, I hope?'

'Thank you, sir,' returned uncle Sol, taking out his pocketbook, and handing over some notes as he spoke. 'Nothing ails me in body but old age. Twenty-five, sir.'

'You are as punctual and exact, Mr. Gills,' replied the smiling manager, taking a paper from one of his many drawers, and making an endorsement on it, while uncle Sol looked over him, 'as one of your own chronometers. Quite right.'

'The Son and Heir has not been spoken, I find by the list, sir,' said uncle Sol, with a slight addition to the usual tremor in his voice.

'The Son and Heir has not been spoken,' returned Carker. 'There seems to have been tempestuous weather, Mr. Gills, and she has probably been driven out of her course.'

'She is safe, I trust in Heaven!' said old Sol.

'She is safe, I trust in Heaven!' assented Mr. Carker in that voiceless manner of his: which made the observant young Toodle tremble again. 'Mr. Gills,' he added aloud, throwing himself back in his chair, 'you must miss your nephew very much?'

Uncle Sol, standing by him, shook his head and heaved a deep sigh.

'Mr. Gills,' said Carker, with his soft hand playing round his mouth, and looking up into the instrument-maker's face, 'it would be company to you to have a young fellow in your shop just now, and it would be obliging me if you would give one house-room for the present. No, to be sure,' he added quickly, in anticipation of what the old man was going to say, 'there 's not much business doing there, I know; but you can make him clean the place out, polish up the instruments; drudge, Mr. Gills. That 's the lad!'

Sol Gills pulled down his spectacles from his forehead to his eyes, and looked at Toodle junior standing upright in the corner: his head presenting the appearance (which it always did) of having been newly drawn out of a bucket of cold water; his small waistcoat rising and falling quickly in the play of his emotions; and his eyes intently fixed on Mr. Carker, without the least reference to his proposed master.

'Will you give him house-room, Mr. Gills?' said the manager.

Old Sol, without being quite enthusiastic on the subject, replied that he was glad of any opportunity, however slight, to oblige Mr. Carker, whose wish on such a point was a command: and that the wooden midshipman would consider himself happy to receive in his berth any visitor of Mr. Carker's selecting.

Mr. Carker bared himself to the tops and bottoms of his gums: making the watchful Toodle junior tremble more and more: and acknowledged the instrument-maker's politeness in his most affable manner.

'I'll dispose of him so, then, Mr. Gills,' he answered, rising, and shaking the old man by the hand, 'until I make up my mind what to do with him, and what he deserves. As I consider myself responsible for him, Mr. Gills,' here he smiled a wide smile at Rob, who shook before it: 'I shall be glad if you'll look sharply after him, and report his behaviour to me. I'll ask a question or two of his parents as I ride home this afternoon—respectable people—to confirm some particulars in his own account of himself; and that done, Mr. Gills, I'll send him round to you to-morrow morning. Good-bye!'

His smile at parting was so full of teeth, that it confused old Sol, and made him vaguely uncomfortable. He went home, thinking of raging seas, foundering ships, drowning men, an ancient bottle of Madeira never brought to light, and other dismal matter.

'Now, boy!' said Mr. Carker, putting his hand on young Toodle's shoulder, and bringing him out into the middle of the room. 'You have heard me?'

Rob said 'Yes, sir.'

'Perhaps you understand,' pursued his patron, 'that if you ever deceive or play tricks with me, you had better have drowned yourself, indeed, once for all, before you came here?'

There was nothing in any branch of mental acquisition that Rob seemed to understand better than that.

'If you have lied to me,' said Mr. Carker, 'in anything, never come in my way again. If not, you may let me find you waiting for me somewhere near your mother's house this afternoon. I shall leave this at five o'clock, and ride there on horseback. Now, give me the address.'

Rob repeated it slowly as Mr. Carker wrote it down. Rob even spelt it over a second time, letter by letter, as if he thought that the omission of a dot or scratch would lead to his destruction. Mr. Carker then handed him out of the room; and Rob, keeping his round eyes fixed upon his patron to the last, vanished for the time being.

Mr. Carker the manager did a great deal of business in the course of the day, and bestowed his teeth upon a great many people. In the office, in the court, in the street, and on 'Change, they glistened and bristled to a terrible extent. Five o'clock arriving, and with it Mr. Carker's bay horse, they got on horseback, and went gleaming up Cheapside.

As no one can easily ride fast, even if inclined to do so, through the press and throng of the City at that hour, and as Mr. Carker was not inclined, he went leisurely along, picking his way among the carts and carriages, avoiding whenever he could the wetter and more dirty places in the over-watered road, and taking infinite pains to keep himself and his steed clean. Glancing at the passers-by while he was thus ambling on his way, he suddenly encountered the round eyes of the sleek-headed Rob intently fixed upon his face as if they had never been taken off, while the boy himself, with a pocket-handkerchief twisted up like a speckled eel and girded round his waist, made a very conspicuous demonstration of being prepared to attend upon him, at whatever pace he might think proper to go.

This attention, however flattering, being one of an unusual kind, and attracting some notice from the other passengers, Mr. Carker took advantage of a clearer thoroughfare and a cleaner road, and broke into a trot. Rob immediately did the same. Mr. Carker presently tried a canter. Rob was still in attendance. Then a short gallop; it was all one to the boy. Whenever Mr. Carker turned his eyes to that side of the road, he still saw Toodle junior holding his course, apparently without distress, and working himself along by the elbows after the most approved manner of professional gentlemen who got over the ground for wagers.

Ridiculous as this attendance was, it was a sign of an influence established over the boy, and therefore Mr. Carker, affecting not to notice it, rode away into the neighbourhood of Mr. Toodle's house. On his slackening his pace here, Rob appeared before him to point out the turnings; and when he called to a man at a neighbouring gateway to hold his horse, pending his visit to the Buildings that had succeeded Staggs's Gardens, Rob dutifully held the stirrup, while the manager dismounted.

'Now, sir,' said Mr. Carker, taking him by the shoulder, 'come along!'

The prodigal son was evidently nervous of visiting the parental abode; but Mr. Carker pushing him on before, he had nothing for it but to open the right door, and suffer himself to be walked into the midst of his brothers and sisters, mustered in overwhelming force round the family tea-table. At sight of the prodigal in the grasp of a stranger, these tender relations united in a general howl, which smote upon the prodigal's breast so sharply when he saw his mother stand up among them, pale and trembling with the baby in her arms, that he lent his own voice to the chorus.

Nothing doubting now that the stranger, if not

Mr. Ketch in person, was one of that company, the whole of the young family wailed the louder, while its more infantine members, unable to control the transports of emotion appertaining to their time of life, threw themselves on their backs like young birds when terrified by a hawk, and kicked violently. At length, poor Polly making herself audible, said, with quivering lips, 'Oh Rob, my poor boy, what have you done at last!'

'Nothing, mother,' cried Rob, in a piteous voice, 'ask the gentleman!'

'Don't be alarmed,' said Mr. Carker, 'I want to do him good.'

At this announcement, Polly, who had not cried yet, began to do so. The elder Toodles, who appeared to have been meditating a rescue, unclenched their fists. The younger Toodles clustered round their mother's gown, and peeped from under their own chubby arms at their desperado brother and his unknown friend. Everybody blessed the gentleman with the beautiful teeth, who wanted to do good.

'This fellow,' said Mr. Carker to Polly, giving him a gentle shake, 'is your son, eh, ma'am?'

'Yes, sir,' sobbed Polly, with a curtsey; 'yes, sir.'

'A bad son, I am afraid?' said Mr. Carker.

'Never a bad son to me, sir,' returned Polly.

'To whom then?' demanded Mr. Carker.

'He has been a little wild, sir,' replied Polly, checking the baby, who was making convulsive efforts with his arms and legs to launch himself on Biler, through the ambient air, 'and has gone with wrong companions: but I hope he has seen the misery of that, sir, and will do well again.'

Mr. Carker looked at Polly, and the clean room, and the clean children, and the simple Toodle face, combined of father and mother, that was reflected and repeated everywhere about him—and seemed to have achieved the real purpose of his visit.

'Your husband, I take it, is not at home?' he said.

'No, sir,' replied Polly. 'He 's down the line at present.'

The prodigal Rob seemed very much relieved to hear it; though still in the absorption of all his faculties in his patron, he hardly took his eyes from Mr. Carker's face, unless for a moment at a time to steal a sorrowful glance at his mother.

'Then,' said Mr. Carker, 'I'll tell you how I have stumbled on this boy of yours, and who I am, and what I am going to do for him.'

This Mr. Carker did, in his own way; saying that he at first intended to have accumulated nameless terrors on his presumptuous head, for coming to the whereabout of Dombey and Son. That he had relented, in consideration of his youth, his professed contrition, and his friends. That he was afraid he took a rash step in doing anything for the boy, and one that might expose him to the censure of the prudent; but that he did it of himself and for himself, and risked the consequences single-handed; and that his mother's past connection with Mr. Dombey's family had nothing to do with it, and that Mr. Dombey had nothing to do with it, but that he, Mr. Carker, was the be-all, and the end-all of this business. Taking great credit to himself for his goodness, and receiving no less from all the family then present, Mr. Carker signified, indirectly but still pretty plainly, that Rob's implicit fidelity, attachment, and devotion, were for evermore his due, and the least homage he could receive. And with this great truth Rob himself was so impressed, that standing gazing on his patron with tears rolling down his cheeks, he nodded his shiny head until it seemed almost as loose as it had done under the same patron's hands that morning.

Polly, who had passed Heaven knows how many sleepless nights on account of this her dissipated first-born, and had not seen him for weeks and weeks, could have almost kneeled to Mr. Carker the manager, as to a good spirit—in spite of his teeth. But Mr. Carker rising to depart, she only thanked him with her mother's prayers and blessings; thanks so rich when paid out of the heart's mint, especially for any service Mr. Carker had rendered, that he might have given back a large amount of change, and yet been overpaid.

As that gentleman made his way among the crowding children to the door, Rob retreated on his mother, and took her and the baby in the same repentant hug.

'I'll try hard, dear mother, now. Upon my soul I will!' said Rob.

'Oh do, my dear boy! I am sure you will, for our sakes and your own!' cried Polly, kissing him. 'But you're coming back to speak to me, when you have seen the gentleman away?'

'I don't know, mother.' Rob hesitated, and looked down. 'Father—when's he coming home?'

'Not till two o'clock to-morrow morning.'

'I'll come back, mother dear!' cried Rob. And passing through the shrill cry of his brothers and sisters in reception of this promise, he followed Mr. Carker out.

'What!' said Mr. Carker, who had heard this. 'You have a bad father, have you?'

'No, sir!' returned Rob, amazed. 'There ain't a better nor a kinder father going, than mine is.'

'Why don't you want to see him then?' inquired his patron.

'There's such a difference between a father and a

mother, sir,' said Rob, after faltering for a moment. 'He couldn't hardly believe yet that I was going to do better—though I know he'd try to—but a mother—*she* always believes what's good, sir; at least I know my mother does, God bless her!'

Mr. Carker's mouth expanded, but he said no more until he was mounted on his horse, and had dismissed the man who held it, when, looking down from the saddle steadily into the attentive and watchful face of the boy, he said—

'You'll come to me to-morrow morning, and you shall be shown where that old gentleman lives; that old gentleman who was with me this morning; where you are going, as you heard me say.'

'Yes, sir,' returned Rob.

'I have a great interest in that old gentleman, and in serving him, you serve me, boy, do you understand? Well,' he added, interrupting him, for he saw his round face brighten when he was told that: 'I see you do. I want to know all about that old gentleman, and how he goes on from day to day—for I am anxious to be of service to him—and especially who comes there to see him. Do you understand?'

Rob nodded his steadfast face, and said 'Yes, sir,' again.

'I should like to know that he has friends who are attentive to him, and that they don't desert him—for he lives very much alone now, poor fellow; but that they are fond of him, and of his nephew who has gone abroad. There is a very young lady who may perhaps come to see him. I want particularly to know all about *her*.'

'I'll take care, sir,' said the boy.

'And take care,' returned his patron, bending forward to advance his grinning face closer to the boy's, and pat him on the shoulder with the handle of his whip; 'take care you talk about affairs of mine to nobody but me.'

'To nobody in the world, sir,' replied Rob, shaking his head.

'Neither there,' said Mr. Carker, pointing to the place they had just left, 'nor anywhere else. I 'll try how true and grateful you can be. I 'll prove you!' Making this, by his display of teeth and by the action of his head, as much a threat as a promise, he turned from Rob's eyes, which were nailed upon him as if he had won the boy by a charm, body and soul, and rode away. But again becoming conscious, after trotting a short distance, that his devoted henchman, girt as before, was yielding him the same attendance, to the great amusement of sundry spectators, he reined up, and ordered him off. To insure his obedience, he turned in the saddle and watched him as he retired. It was curious to see that even then Rob could not keep his eyes wholly averted from his patron's face, but, constantly turning and turning again to look after him, involved himself in a tempest of buffetings and jostlings from the other passengers in the street; of which, in the pursuit of the one paramount idea, he was perfectly heedless.

Mr. Carker the manager rode on at a foot-pace, with the easy air of one who had performed all the business of the day in a satisfactory manner, and got it comfortably off his mind. Complacent and affable as man could be, Mr. Carker picked his way along the streets and hummed a soft tune as he went. He seemed to purr, he was so glad.

And in some sort, Mr. Carker, in his fancy, basked upon a hearth too. Coiled up snugly at certain feet, he was ready for a spring, or for a tear, or for a scratch, or for a velvet touch, as the humour took him and occasion served. Was there any bird in a cage, that came in for a share of his regards?

'A very young lady!' thought Mr. Carker the manager, through his song. 'Ay! when I saw her last, she was a little child. With dark eyes and hair, I recollect, and a good face; a very good face! I dare say she 's pretty.'

More affable and pleasant yet, and humming his song until his many teeth vibrated to it, Mr. Carker picked his way along, and turned at last into the shady street where Mr. Dombey's house stood. He had been so busy, winding webs round good faces, and obscuring them with meshes, that he hardly thought of being at this point of his ride, until, glancing down the cold perspective of tall houses, he reined in his horse quickly within a few yards of the door. But to explain why Mr. Carker reined in his horse quickly, and what he looked at in no small surprise, a few digressive words are necessary.

Mr. Toots, emancipated from the Blimber thraldom and coming into the possession of a certain portion of his worldly wealth, 'which,' as he had been wont, during his last half-year's probation, to communicate to Mr. Feeder every evening as a new discovery, 'the executors couldn't keep him out of,' had applied himself, with great diligence, to the science of life. Fired with a noble emulation to pursue a brilliant and distinguished career, Mr. Toots had furnished a choice set of apartments; had established among them a sporting bower, embellished with the portraits of winning horses in which he took no particle of interest; and a divan, which made him poorly. In this delicious abode, Mr. Toots devoted himself to the cultivation of those gentle arts which refine and humanise existence, his chief instructor in which was an interesting character called the Game Chicken, who was always to be heard of at the bar of the Black Badger, wore a shaggy white great-coat in the warmest weather, and knocked Mr. Toots about the head three times a week, for the small consideration of ten and six per visit.

The Game Chicken, who was quite the Apollo of Mr. Toots's Pantheon, had introduced to him a marker who taught billiards, a Life Guard who taught fencing, a jobmaster who taught riding, a Cornish gentleman who was up to anything in the athletic line, and two or three other friends connected no less intimately with the fine arts. Under whose auspices Mr. Toots could hardly fail to improve apace, and under whose tuition he went to work.

But however it came about, it came to pass, even while these gentlemen had the gloss of novelty upon them, that Mr. Toots felt, he didn't know how, unsettled and uneasy. There were husks in his corn, that even Game Chickens couldn't peck up; gloomy giants in his leisure, that even Game Chickens couldn't knock down. Nothing seemed to do Mr. Toots so much good as incessantly leaving cards at Mr. Dombey's door. No tax-gatherer in the British dominions—that wide-spread territory on which the sun never sets, and where the tax-gatherer never goes to bed—was more regular and persevering in his calls than Mr. Toots.

Mr. Toots never went upstairs; and always performed the same ceremonies, richly dressed for the purpose, at the hall-door.

'Oh! Good morning!' would be Mr. Toots's first remark to the servant. 'For Mr. Dombey,' would be Mr. Toots's next remark, as he handed in a card. 'For Miss Dombey,' would be his next, as he handed in another.

Mr. Toots would then turn round as if to go away;

but the man knew him by this time, and knew he wouldn't.

'Oh, I beg your pardon,' Mr. Toots would say, as if a thought had suddenly descended on him. 'Is the young woman at home?'

The man would rather think she was, but wouldn't quite know. Then he would ring a bell that rang upstairs, and would look up the staircase, and would say, yes, she *was* at home, and was coming down. Then Miss Nipper would appear, and the man would retire.

'Oh! How de do?' Mr. Toots would say, with a chuckle and a blush.

Susan would thank him, and say she was very well.

'How 's Diogenes going on?' would be Mr. Toots's second interrogation.

Very well indeed. Miss Florence was fonder and fonder of him every day. Mr. Toots was sure to hail this with a burst of chuckles, like the opening of a bottle of some effervescent beverage.

'Miss Florence is quite well, sir,' Susan would add.

'Oh, it 's of no consequence, thank 'ee,' was the invariable reply of Mr. Toots; and when he had said so, he always went away very fast.

Now it is certain that Mr. Toots had a filmy something in his mind, which led him to conclude that if he could aspire successfully in the fulness of time, to the hand of Florence, he would be fortunate and blest. It is certain that Mr. Toots, by some remote and roundabout road, had got to that point, and that there he made a stand. His heart was wounded; he was touched; he was in love. He had made a desperate attempt, one night, and had sat up all night for the purpose, to write an acrostic on Florence, which affected him to tears in the conception. But he never proceeded in the execution further than the words 'For when I gaze,'—the flow of imagination in which he had previously written down the initial letters of the other seven lines, deserting him at that point.

Beyond devising that very artful and politic measure of leaving a card for Mr. Dombey daily, the brain of Mr. Toots had not worked much in reference to the subject that held his feelings prisoner. But deep consideration at length assured Mr. Toots that an important step to gain, was the conciliation of Miss Susan Nipper, preparatory to giving her some inkling of his state of mind.

A little light and playful gallantry towards this lady seemed the means to employ in that early chapter of the history, for winning her to his interests. Not being able quite to make up his mind about it, he consulted the Chicken—without taking that gentleman into his confidence; merely informing him that a friend in Yorkshire had written to him (Mr. Toots) for his opinion on such a question. The Chicken replying that his opinion always was, 'Go in and win,' and further, 'When your man 's before you and your work cut out, go in and do it,' Mr. Toots considered this a figurative way of supporting his own view of the case, and heroically resolved to kiss Miss Nipper next day.

Upon the next day, therefore, Mr. Toots, putting into requisition some of the greatest marvels that Burgess and Co. had ever turned out, went off to Mr. Dombey's upon this design. But his heart failed him so much as he approached the scene of action, that, although he arrived on the ground at three o'clock in the afternoon, it was six before he knocked at the door.

Everything happened as usual, down to the point where Susan said her young mistress was well, and

Mr. Toots said it was of no consequence. To her amazement, Mr. Toots, instead of going off, like a rocket, after that observation, lingered and chuckled.

'Perhaps you 'd like to walk upstairs, sir!' said Susan.

'Well, I think I will come in!' said Mr. Toots.

But instead of walking upstairs, the bold Toots made an awkward plunge at Susan when the door was shut, and embracing that fair creature, kissed her on the cheek.

'Go along with you!' cried Susan, 'or I 'll tear your eyes out.'

'Just another!' said Mr. Toots.

'Go along with you!' exclaimed Susan, giving him a push. 'Innocents like you, too! Who 'll begin next? Go along, sir!'

Susan was not in any serious strait, for she could hardly speak for laughing; but Diogenes, on the staircase, hearing a rustling against the wall, and a shuffling of feet, and seeing through the banisters that there was some contention going on, and foreign invasion in the house, formed a different opinion, dashed down to the rescue, and in the twinkling of an eye had Mr. Toots by the leg.

Susan screamed, laughed, opened the street-door, and ran downstairs; the bold Toots tumbled staggering out into the street, with Diogenes holding on to one leg of his pantaloons, as if Burgess and Co. were his cooks, and had provided that dainty morsel for his holiday entertainment; Diogenes shaken off, rolled over and over in the dust, got up again, whirled round the giddy Toots and snapped at him: and all this turmoil, Mr. Carker, reining up his horse and sitting a little at a distance, saw to his amazement, issue from the stately house of Mr. Dombey.

Mr. Carker remained watching the discomfited

Toots, when Diogenes was called in, and the door shut: and while that gentleman, taking refuge in a doorway near at hand, bound up the torn leg of his pantaloons with a costly silk handkerchief that had formed part of his expensive outfit for the adventure.

'I beg your pardon, sir,' said Mr. Carker, riding up, with his most propitiatory smile. 'I hope you are not hurt?'

'Oh no, thank you,' replied Mr. Toots, raising his flushed face, 'it 's of no consequence.' Mr. Toots would have signified, if he could, that he liked it very much.

'If the dog's teeth have entered the leg, sir—' began Carker, with a display of his own.

'No, thank you,' said Mr. Toots, 'it 's all quite right. It 's very comfortable, thank you.'

'I have the pleasure of knowing Mr. Dombey,' observed Carker.

'Have you though?' rejoined the blushing Toots.

'And you will allow me, perhaps, to apologise, in his absence,' said Mr. Carker, taking off his hat, 'for such a misadventure, and to wonder how it can possibly have happened.'

Mr. Toots is so much gratified by this politeness, and the lucky chance of making friends with a friend of Mr. Dombey, that he pulls out his card-case, which he never loses an opportunity of using, and hands his name and address to Mr. Carker: who responds to that courtesy by giving him his own, and with that they part.

As Mr. Carker picks his way so softly past the house, glancing up at the windows, and trying to make out the pensive face behind the curtain looking at the children opposite, the rough head of Diogenes came clambering up close by it, and the dog, regardless of all soothing, barks and growls, and makes at him from that height, as if he would spring down and tear him limb from limb.

Well spoken, Di, so near your mistress! Another, and another with your head up, your eyes flashing, and your vexed mouth worrying itself, for want of him. Another, as he picks his way along! You have a good scent, Di,—cats, boy, cats!

## CHAPTER XXIII

### FLORENCE SOLITARY, AND THE MIDSHIPMAN MYSTERIOUS

FLORENCE lived alone in the great dreary house, and day succeeded day and still she lived alone; and the blank walls looked down upon her with a vacant stare, as if they had a Gorgon-like mind to stare her youth and beauty into stone.

No magic dwelling-place in magic story, shut up in the heart of a thick wood, was ever more solitary and deserted to the fancy, than was her father's mansion in its grim reality, as it stood lowering on the street: always by night, when lights were shining from the neighbouring windows, a blot upon its scanty brightness; always by day, a frown upon its never-smiling face.

There were not two dragon sentries keeping ward before the gate of this abode, as in magic legend are usually found on duty over the wronged innocence imprisoned; but besides a glowering visage, with its thin lips parted wickedly, that surveyed all comers from above the archway of the door, there was a monstrous fantasy of rusty iron, curling and twisting like a petrifaction of an arbour over the threshold, budding in spikes and corkscrew points, and bearing, one on either side, two ominous extinguishers, that seemed to say, 'Who enter here, leave light behind!' There were no talismanic characters engraven on the portal, but the house was now so neglected in appearance, that boys chalked the railings and the pavement —particularly round the corner where the side wall was—and drew ghosts on the stable door; and being sometimes driven off by Mr. Towlinson, made portraits of him, in return, with his ears growing out horizontally from under his hat. Noise ceased to be, within the shadow of the roof. The brass band that came into the street once a week, in the morning, never brayed a note in at those windows; but all such company, down to a poor little piping organ of weak intellect, with an imbecile party of automaton dancers, waltzing in and out at folding-doors, fell off from it with one accord, and shunned it as a hopeless place.

The spell upon it was more wasting than the spell that used to set enchanted houses sleeping once upon a time, but left their waking freshness unimpaired.

The passive desolation of disuse was everywhere silently manifest about it. Within doors, curtains, drooping heavily, lost their old folds and shapes, and hung like cumbrous palls. Hecatombs of furniture, still piled and covered up, shrunk like imprisoned and forgotten men, and changed insensibly. Mirrors were dim as with the breath of years. Patterns of carpets faded and became perplexed and faint, like the memory of those years' trifling incidents. Boards, starting at unwonted footsteps, creaked and shook. Keys rusted in the locks of doors. Damp started on the walls, and as the stains came out, the pictures seemed to go in and secrete themselves. Mildew and mould began to lurk in closets. Fungus trees grew in corners of the cellars. Dust accumulated, nobody knew whence nor how; spiders, moths, and grubs were heard of every day. An exploratory black-beetle now and then was found immovable upon the stairs, or in an upper room, as wondering how he got there. Rats began to squeak and scuffle in the night time, through dark galleries they mined behind the paneling.

The dreary magnificence of the state rooms, seen imperfectly by the doubtful light admitted through closed shutters, would have answered well enough for an enchanted abode. Such as the tarnished paws of gilded lions, stealthily put out from beneath their wrappers; the marble lineaments of busts on pedestals, fearfully revealing themselves through veils; the clocks that never told the time, or, if wound up by any chance, told it wrong, and struck unearthly numbers, which are not upon the dial; the accidental tinklings among the pendent lustres, more startling than alarm-bells; the softened sounds and laggard air that made their way among these objects, and a phantom crowd of others, shrouded and hooded, and made spectral of shape. But, besides, there was the great staircase, where the lord of the place so rarely set his foot, and by which his little child had gone up to Heaven. There were other staircases and passages where no one went for weeks together; there were two closed rooms associated with dead members of the family, and with whispered recollections of them; and to all the house but Florence, there was a gentle figure moving through the solitude and gloom, that gave to every lifeless thing a touch of present human interest and wonder.

For Florence lived alone in the deserted house, and day succeeded day, and still she lived alone, and the cold walls looked down upon her with a vacant stare, as if they had a Gorgon-like mind to stare her youth and beauty into stone.

The grass began to grow upon the roof, and in the crevices of the basement paving. A scaly crumbling vegetation sprouted round the window-sills. Fragments of mortar lost their hold upon the insides of the unused chimneys, and came dropping down. The two trees with the smoky trunks were blighted high up, and the withered branches domineered above the leaves. Through the whole building white had turned yellow, yellow nearly black; and since the time when the poor lady died, it had slowly become a dark gap in the long monotonous street.

But Florence bloomed there, like the king's fair daughter in the story. Her books, her music, and her daily teachers, were her only real companions, Susan Nipper and Diogenes excepted: of whom the former, in her attendance on the studies of her young mistress, began to grow quite learned herself, while the latter, softened possibly by the same influences, would lay his head upon the window-ledge, and placidly open and shut his eyes upon the street, all through a summer morning; sometimes pricking up his head to look with great significance after some noisy dog in a cart, who was barking his way along, and sometimes, with an exasperated and unaccountable recollection of his supposed enemy in the neighbourhood, rushing to the door, whence, after a deafening disturbance, he would come jogging back with a ridiculous complacency that belonged to him, and lay his jaw upon the window-ledge again, with the air of a dog who had done a public service.

So Florence lived in her wilderness of a home, within the circle of her innocent pursuits and thoughts, and nothing harmed her. She could go down to her father's rooms now, and think of him, and suffer her loving heart humbly to approach him, without fear of repulse. She could look upon the objects that had surrounded him in his sorrow, and could nestle near his chair, and not dread the glance that she so well remembered. She could render him such little tokens of her duty and service, as putting everything in order for him with her own hands, binding little nosegays for his table, changing them as one by one they withered, and he did not come back, preparing something for him every day, and leaving some timid mark of her presence near his usual seat. To-day, it was a little painted stand for his watch; to-morrow she would be afraid to leave it, and would substitute some other trifle of her making not so likely to attract his eye. Waking in the night, perhaps, she would tremble at the thought of his coming home and angrily rejecting it, and would hurry down with slippered feet and quickly beating heart, and bring it away. At another time, she would only lay her face upon his desk, and leave a kiss there, and a tear.

Still no one knew of this. Unless the household found it out when she was not there—and they all held Mr. Dombey's rooms in awe—it was as deep a secret in her breast as what had gone before it. Florence stole into those rooms at twilight, early in the morning, and at times when meals were served downstairs. And although they were in every nook the better and the brighter for her care, she entered and passed out as quietly as any sunbeam, excepting that she left her light behind.

Shadowy company attended Florence up and down the echoing house, and sat with her in the dismantled rooms. As if her life were an enchanted vision, there arose out of her solitude ministering thoughts, that made it fanciful and unreal. She imagined so often what her life would have been if her father could have loved her and she had been a favourite child, that sometimes, for the moment, she almost believed it was so, and, borne on by the current of that pensive fiction, seemed to remember how they had watched her brother in his grave together; how they had freely shared his heart between them; how they were united in the dear remembrance of him; how they often spoke about him yet; and her kind father, looking at her gently, told her of their common hope and trust in God. At other times she pictured to herself her mother yet alive. And oh the happiness of falling on her neck, and clinging to her with the love and confidence of all her soul! And oh the desolation of the solitary house again, with evening coming on and no one there!

But there was one thought, scarcely shaped out to herself, yet fervent and strong within her, that upheld Florence when she strove and filled her true young heart, so sorely tried, with constancy of purpose. Into her mind, as into all others contending with the great affliction of our mortal nature, there had stolen solemn wonderings and hopes, arising in the dim world beyond the present life, and murmuring, like faint music, of recognition in the far off land between her brother and her mother: of some present consciousness in both of her: some love and commiseration for her: and some knowledge of her as she went her way upon the earth. It was a soothing consolation to Florence to give shelter to these thoughts, until one day—it was soon after she had last seen her father in his own room, late at night—the fancy came upon her, that, in weeping for his alienated heart, she might stir the spirits of the dead against him. Wild, weak, childish, as it may have been to think so, and to tremble at the half-formed thought, it was the impulse of her loving nature; and from that hour Florence strove against the cruel wound in her breast, and tried to think of him whose hand had made it only with hope.

Her father did not know—she held to it from that time—how much she loved him. She was very young, and had no mother, and had never learned, by some fault or misfortune, how to express to him that she loved him. She would be patient, and would try to gain that art in time, and win him to a better knowledge of his only child.

This became the purpose of her life. The morning sun shone down upon the faded house, and found the resolution bright and fresh within the bosom of its solitary mistress. Through all the duties of the day, it animated her; for Florence hoped that the more she knew, and the more accomplished she became, the more glad he would be when he came to know and like her. Sometimes she wondered, with a swelling heart and rising tear, whether she was proficient enough in anything to surprise him when they should become companions. Sometimes she tried to think if there were any kind of knowledge that would bespeak his interest more readily than another. Always: at her books, her music, and her work: in her morning walks, and in her nightly prayers: she had her engrossing aim in view. Strange study for a child, to learn the road to a hard parent's heart.

There were many careless loungers through the street, as the summer evening deepened into night, who glanced across the road at the sombre house, and saw the youthful figure at the window, such a contrast to it, looking upward at the stars as they began to shine, who would have slept the worse if they had known on what design she mused so steadfastly.

The reputation of the mansion as a haunted house, would not have been the gayer with some humble dwellers elsewhere, who were struck by its external gloom in passing and repassing on their daily avocations, and so named it, if they could have read its story in the darkening face. But Florence held her sacred purpose, unsuspected and unaided: and studied only how to bring her father to the understanding that she loved him, and made no appeal against him in any wandering thought.

Thus Florence lived alone in the deserted house, and day succeeded day, and still she lived alone, and the monotonous walls looked down upon her with a stare, as if they had a Gorgon-like intent to stare her youth and beauty into stone.

Susan Nipper stood opposite to her young mistress one morning, as she folded and sealed a note she had been writing: and showed in her looks an approving knowledge of its contents.

'Better late than never, dear Miss Floy,' said Susan, 'and I do say, that even a visit to them old Skettleses will be a God-send.'

'It is very good of Sir Barnet and Lady Skettles, Susan,' returned Florence, with a mild correction of that young lady's familiar mention of the family in question, 'to repeat their invitation so kindly.'

Miss Nipper, who was perhaps the most thorough-going partisan on the face of the earth, and who carried her partisanship into all matters great or small, and perpetually waged war with it against society, screwed up her lips and shook her head as a protest against any recognition of disinterestedness in the Skettleses, and a plea in bar that they would have valuable consideration for their kindness, in the company of Florence.

'They know what they 're about, if ever people did,'

murmured Miss Nipper, drawing in her breath, 'oh! trust them Skettleses for that!'

'I am not very anxious to go to Fulham, Susan, I confess,' said Florence thoughtfully; 'but it will be right to go. I think it will be better.'

'Much better,' interposed Susan, with another emphatic shake of her head.

'And so,' said Florence, 'though I would prefer to have gone when there was no one there, instead of in this vacation time, when it seems there are some young people staying in the house, I have thankfully said yes.'

'For which *I* say, Miss Floy, Oh be joyful!' returned Susan. 'Ah! h—h!'

This last ejaculation, with which Miss Nipper frequently wound up a sentence, at about that epoch of time, was supposed below the level of the hall to have a general reference to Mr. Dombey, and to be expressive of a yearning in Miss Nipper to favour that gentleman with a piece of her mind. But she never explained it; and it had, in consequence, the charm of mystery, in addition to the advantage of the sharpest expression.

'How long it is before we have any news of Walter, Susan!' observed Florence, after a moment's silence.

'Long indeed, Miss Floy!' replied her maid. 'And Perch said, when he came just now to see for letters—but what signifies what *he* says!' exclaimed Susan, reddening and breaking off. 'Much *he* knows about it!'

Florence raised her eyes quickly, and a flush overspread her face.

'If I hadn't,' said Susan Nipper, evidently struggling with some latent anxiety and alarm, and looking full at her young mistress, while endeavouring to work herself into a state of resentment with the unoffending Mr. Perch's image, 'if I hadn't more manliness than that insipidest of his sex, I 'd never take pride in my hair again, but turn it up behind my ears, and wear coarse caps, without a bit of border, until death released me from my insignificance. I may not be a Amazon, Miss Floy, and wouldn't so demean myself by such disfigurement, but anyways I 'm not a giver up, I hope.'

'Give up! What?' cried Florence, with a face of terror.

'Why, nothing, miss,' said Susan. 'Good gracious, nothing! It 's only that wet curl-paper of a man Perch, that any one might almost make away with, with a touch, and really it would be a blessed event for all parties if some one *would* take pity on him, and would have the goodness!'

'Does he give up the ship, Susan?' inquired Florence, very pale.

'No, miss,' returned Susan, 'I should like to see him make so bold as do it to my face! No, miss, but he goes on about some bothering ginger that Mr. Walter was to send to Mrs. Perch, and shakes his dismal head, and says he hopes it may be coming; anyhow, he says, it can't come now in time for the intended occasion, but may do for next, which really,' said Miss Nipper, with aggravated scorn, 'puts me out of patience with the man, for though I can bear a great deal, I am not a camel, neither am I,' added Susan, after a moment's consideration, 'if I know myself, a dromedary neither.'

'What else does he say, Susan?' inquired Florence, earnestly. 'Won't you tell me?'

'As if I wouldn't tell you anything, Miss Floy, and everything!' said Susan. 'Why, miss, he says that there begins to be a general talk about the ship, and that they have never had a ship on that voyage half so long unheard of, and that the captain's wife was at the office yesterday, and seemed a little put out about it, but any one could say that, we knew nearly that before.'

'I must visit Walter's uncle,' said Florence, hurriedly, 'before I leave home. I will go and see him this morning. Let us walk there, directly, Susan.'

Miss Nipper having nothing to urge against the proposal, but being perfectly acquiescent, they were soon equipped, and in the streets, and on their way towards the little midshipman.

The state of mind in which poor Walter had gone to Captain Cuttle's, on the day when Brogley the broker came into possession, and when there seemed to him to be an execution in the very steeples, was pretty much the same as that in which Florence now took her way to uncle Sol's; with this difference, that Florence suffered the added pain of thinking that she had been, perhaps, the innocent occasion of involving Walter in peril, and all to whom he was dear, herself included, in an agony of suspense. For the rest, uncertainty and danger seemed written upon everything. The weathercocks on spires and housetops were mysterious with hints of stormy wind, and pointed, like so many ghostly fingers, out to dangerous seas, where fragments of great wrecks were drifting, perhaps, and helpless men were rocked upon them into a sleep as deep as the unfathomable waters. When Florence came into the City, and passed gentlemen who were talking together, she dreaded to hear them speaking of the ship, and saying it was lost. Pictures and prints of vessels fighting with the rolling waves filled her with alarm. The smoke and clouds, though moving gently, moved too fast for her apprehensions, and made her fear there was a tempest blowing at that moment on the ocean.

Susan Nipper may or may not have been affected similarly, but having her attention much engaged in struggles with boys, whenever there was any press of people—for, between that grade of human kind and herself, there was some natural animosity that invariably broke out, whenever they came together—it would seem that she had not much leisure on the road for intellectual operations.

Arriving in good time abreast of the wooden midshipman on the opposite side of the way, and waiting for an opportunity to cross the street, they were a little surprised at first to see, at the instrument-maker's door, a round-headed lad, with his chubby face addressed towards the sky, who, as they looked at him, suddenly thrust into his capacious mouth two fingers of each hand, and with the assistance of that machinery whistled, with astonishing shrillness, to some pigeons at a considerable elevation in the air.

'Mrs. Richards's eldest, miss!' said Susan, 'and the worrit of Mrs. Richards's life!'

As Polly had been to tell Florence of the resuscitated prospects of her son and heir, Florence was prepared for the meeting: so, a favourable moment presenting itself, they both hastened across, without any further contemplation of Mrs. Richards's bane. That sporting character, unconscious of their approach, again whistled with his utmost might, and then yelled in a rapture of excitement, 'Strays! Whoo-oop! Strays!' which identification had such an affect upon the conscience-stricken pigeons, that instead of going direct to some town in the North of England, as appeared to have been their original intention, they began to wheel and falter; whereupon

Mrs. Richards's first-born pierced them with another whistle, and again yelled, in a voice that rose above the turmoil of the street, 'Strays! Whoo-oop! Strays!'

From this transport, he was abruptly recalled to terrestrial objects, by a poke from Miss Nipper, which sent him into the shop.

'Is this the way you show your penitence, when Mrs. Richards has been fretting for you months and months!' said Susan, following the poke. 'Where 's Mr. Gills?'

Rob, who smoothed his first rebellious glance at Miss Nipper when he saw Florence following, put his knuckles to his hair, in honour of the latter, and said to the former, that Mr. Gills was out.

'Fetch him home,' sad Miss Nipper, with authority, 'and say that my young lady's here.'

'I don't know where he 's gone,' said Rob.

'Is *that* your penitence?' cried Susan, with stinging sharpness.

'Why how can I go and fetch him when I don't know where to go?' whimpered the baited Rob. 'How can you be so unreasonable?'

'Did Mr. Gills say when he should be home?' asked Florence.

'Yes, miss,' replied Rob, with another application of his knuckles to his hair. 'He said he should be home early in the afternoon; in about a couple of hours from now, miss.'

'Is he very anxious about his nephew?' inquired Susan.

'Yes, miss,' returned Rob, preferring to address himself to Florence and slighting Nipper; 'I should say he was very much so. He ain't indoors, miss, not a quarter of an hour together. He can't settle in one place five minutes. He goes about, like a—just like a stray,' said Rob, stooping to get a glimpse of the pigeons through the window, and checking himself, with his fingers half-way to his mouth, on the verge of another whistle.

'Do you know a friend of Mr. Gills, called Captain Cuttle?' inquired Florence, after a moment's reflection.

'Him with a book, miss?' rejoined Rob, with an illustrative twist of his left hand. 'Yes, miss. He was here the day before yesterday.'

'Has he not been here since?' asked Susan.

'No, miss,' returned Rob, still addressing his reply to Florence.

'Perhaps Walter's uncle has gone there, Susan,' observed Florence, turning to her.

'To Captain Cuttle's, miss?' interposed Rob, 'no, he's not gone there, miss. Because he left particular word that if Captain Cuttle called, I should tell him how surprised he was, not to have seen him yesterday, and should make him stop till he came back.'

'Do you know where Captain Cuttle lives?' asked Florence.

Rob replied in the affirmative, and turning to a greasy parchment book on the shop desk, read the address aloud.

Florence again turned to her maid and took counsel with her in a low voice, while Rob the round-eyed, mindful of his patron's secret charge, looked on and listened. Florence proposed that they should go to Captain Cuttle's house; hear from his own lips, what he thought of the absence of any tidings of the Son and Heir; and bring him, if they could, to comfort uncle Sol. Susan at first objected slightly, on the score of distance; but a hackney-coach being mentioned by her mistress, withdrew that opposition, and gave in her assent. There were some minutes of discussion between them before they came to this conclusion, during which the staring Rob paid close attention to both speakers, and inclined his ear to each by turns, as if he were appointed arbitrator of the arguments.

In fine, Rob was despatched for a coach, the visitors keeping shop meanwhile; and when he brought it, they got into it, leaving word for uncle Sol that they would be sure to call again, on their way back. Rob having stared after the coach until it was as invisible as the pigeons had now become, sat down behind the desk with a most assiduous demeanour; and in order that he might forget nothing of what had transpired, made notes of it on various small scraps of paper, with a vast expenditure of ink. There was no danger of these documents betraying anything, if accidentally lost; for long before a word was dry, it became as profound a mystery to Rob, as if he had had no part whatever in its production.

While he was yet busy with these labours, the hackney-coach, after encountering unheard-of-difficulties from swivel-bridges, soft roads, impassable canals, caravans of casks, settlements of scarlet-beans and little wash-houses, and many such obstacles abounding in that country, stopped at the corner of Brig Place. Alighting here, Florence and Susan Nipper walked down the street, and sought out the abode of Captain Cuttle.

It happened by evil chance to be one of Mrs. MacStinger's great cleaning days. On these occasions, Mrs. MacStinger was knocked up by the policeman at a quarter before three in the morning, and rarely succumbed before twelve o'clock next night. The chief object of this institution appeared to be, that Mrs. MacStinger should move all the furniture into the back garden at early dawn, walk about the house in pattens all day, and move the furniture back again after dark. These ceremonies greatly fluttered those doves the young MacStingers, who were not only unable at such times to find any resting-place for the soles of their feet, but generally came in for a good deal of pecking from the maternal bird during the progress of solemnities.

At the moment when Florence and Susan Nipper presented themselves at Mrs. MacStinger's door, that worthy but redoubtable female was in the act of conveying Alexander MacStinger, aged two years and three months, along the passage for forcible deposition in a sitting posture on the street pavement; Alexander being black in the face with holding his breath after punishment, and a cool paving-stone being usually found to act as a powerful restorative in such cases.

The feelings of Mrs. MacStinger, as a woman and a mother, were outraged by the look of pity for Alexander which she observed on Florence's face. Therefore, Mrs. MacStinger asserting those finest emotions of our nature, in preference to weakly gratifying her curiosity, shook and buffeted Alexander both before and during the application of the paving-stone, and took no further notice of the strangers.

'I beg your pardon, ma'am,' said Florence, when the child had found his breath again, and was using it. 'Is this Captain Cuttle's house?'

'No,' said Mrs. MacStinger.

'Not Number Nine?' asked Florence hesitating.

'Who said it wasn't Number Nine?' said Mrs. MacStinger.

Susan Nipper instantly struck in, and begged to inquire what Mrs. MacStinger meant by that, and if she knew whom she was talking to.

Mrs. MacStinger in retort, looked at her all over.

'What do *you* want with Captain Cuttle, I should wish to know?' said Mrs. MacStinger.

'Should you? Then I 'm sorry that you won't be satisfied,' returned Miss Nipper.

'Hush, Susan! If you please!' said Florence. 'Perhaps you can have the goodness to tell us where Captain Cuttle lives, ma'am, as he don't live here.'

'Who says he don't live here?' retorted the implacable MacStinger. 'I said it wasn't Cap'en Cuttle's house—and it ain't his house—and forbid it, that it ever should be his house—for Cap'en Cuttle don't know how to keep a house—and don't deserve to have a house—it 's *my* house—and when I let the upper floor to Cap'en Cuttle, oh I do a thankless thing, and cast pearls before swine!'

Mrs. MacStinger pitched her voice for the upper windows in offering these remarks, and cracked off each clause sharply by itself as if from a rifle possessing an infinity of barrels. After the last shot, the captain's voice was heard to say, in feeble remonstrance from his own room, 'Steady below!'

'Since you want Cap'en Cuttle, there he is!' said Mrs. MacStinger, with an angry motion of her hand. On Florence making bold to enter, without any more parley, and on Susan following, Mrs. MacStinger recommenced her pedestrian exercise in pattens, and Alexander MacStinger (still on the paving-stone), who had stopped in his crying to attend to the conversation, began to wail again, entertaining himself during that dismal performance, which was quite mechanical, with a general survey of the prospect, terminating in the hackney-coach.

The captain in his own apartment was sitting with his hands in his pockets and his legs drawn up under his chair, on a very small desolate island, lying about midway in an ocean of soap and water. The captain's windows had been cleaned, the walls had been cleaned, the stove had been cleaned, and everything, the stove excepted, was wet, and shining with soft soap and sand: the smell of which drysaltery impregnated the air. In the midst of the dreary scene, the captain, cast away upon his island, looked round on the waste of waters with a rueful countenance, and seemed waiting for some friendly bark to come that way, and take him off.

But when the captain, directing his forlorn visage towards the door, saw Florence appear with her maid, no words can describe his astonishment. Mrs. MacStinger's eloquence having rendered all other sounds but imperfectly distinguishable, he had looked for no rarer visitor than the potboy or the milkman; wherefore, when Florence appeared, and coming to the confines of the island, put her hand in his, the captain stood up, aghast, as if he supposed her, for the moment, to be some young member of the Flying Dutchman's family.

Instantly recovering his self-possession, however, the captain's first care was to place her on dry land, which he happily accomplished, with one motion of his arm. Issuing forth, then, upon the main, Captain Cuttle took Miss Nipper round the waist, and bore her to the island also. Captain Cuttle, then, with great respect and admiration, raised the hand of Florence to his lips, and standing off a little (for the island was not large enough for three), beamed on her from the soap and water like a new description of Triton.

'You are amazed to see us, I am sure,' said Florence, with a smile.

The inexpressibly gratified captain kissed his hook

in reply, and growled, as if a choice and delicate compliment were included in the words, 'Stand by! Stand by!'

'But I couldn't rest,' said Florence, 'without coming to ask you what you think about dear Walter—who is my brother now—and whether there is anything to fear, and whether you will not go and console his poor uncle every day, until we have some intelligence of him?'

At these words Captain Cuttle, as by an involuntary gesture, clapped his hand to his head, on which the hard glazed hat was not, and looked discomfited.

'Have you any fears for Walter's safety?' inquired Florence, from whose face the captain (so enraptured he was with it) could not take his eyes: while she, in her turn, looked earnestly at him, to be assured of the sincerity of his reply.

'No, Heart's Delight,' said Captain Cuttle, 'I am not afeard. Wal'r is a lad as 'll go through a deal o' hard weather. Wal'r is a lad as 'll bring as much success to that 'ere brig as a lad is capable on. Wal'r,' said the captain, his eyes glistening with the praise of his young friend, and his hook raised to announce a beautiful quotation, 'is what you may call a out'ard and visible sign of a in'ard and spirited grasp, and when found make a note of.'

Florence, who did not quite understand this, though the captain evidently thought it full of meaning, and highly satisfactory, mildly looked to him for something more.

'I am not afeard, my Heart's Delight,' resumed the captain. 'There 's been most uncommon bad weather in them latitudes, there 's no denyin', and they have drove and drove and been beat off, may be t' other side the world. But the ship 's a good ship, and the lad 's a good lad; and it ain't easy, thank the Lord,' the captain made a little bow, 'to break up hearts of oak, whether they 're in brigs or buzzums. Here we have 'em both ways, which is bringing it up with a round turn, and so I ain't a bit afeard as yet.'

'As yet?' repeated Florence.

'Not a bit,' returned the captain, kissing his iron hand; 'and afore I begin to be, my Heart's Delight, Wal'r will have wrote home from the island, or from some port or another, and made all taut and shipshape. And with regard to old Sol Gills,' here the captain became solemn, 'who I 'll stand by, and not desert until death doe us part, and when the stormy winds do blow, do blow, do blow—overhaul the Catechism,' said the captain parenthetically, 'and there you 'll find them expressions—if it would console Sol Gills to have the opinion of a seafaring man as has got a mind equal to any undertaking that he puts it alongside of, and as was all but smashed in his 'prenticeship, and of which the name is Bunsby, that 'ere man shall give him such an opinion in his own parlour as 'll stun him. Ah!' said Captain Cuttle, vauntingly, 'as much as if he 'd gone and knocked his head again a door!'

'Let us take this gentleman to see him, and let us hear what he says,' cried Florence. 'Will you go with us now? We have a coach here.'

Again the captain clapped his hand to his head, on which the hard glazed hat was not, and looked discomfited. But at this instant a most remarkable phenomenon occurred. The door opening, without any note of preparation, and apparently of itself, the hard glazed hat in question skimmed into the room like a bird, and alighted heavily at the captain's feet. The door then shut as violently as it had opened, and nothing ensued in explanation of the prodigy.

Captain Cuttle picked up his hat, and having turned it over with a look of interest and welcome, began to polish it on his sleeve. While doing so, the captain eyed his visitors intently, and said in a low voice—

'You see I should have bore down on Sol Gills yesterday, and this morning, but she—she took it away and kep it. That 's the long and short of the subject.'

'Who did, for goodness' sake?' asked Susan Nipper.

'The lady of the house, my dear,' returned the captain, in a gruff whisper, and making signals of secrecy. 'We had some words about the swabbing of these here planks,—and she—in short,' said the captain, eyeing the door, and relieving himself with a long breath, 'she stopped my liberty.'

'Oh! I wish she had me to deal with!' said Susan, reddening with the energy of the wish. 'I 'd stop her!'

'Would you, do you think, my dear?' rejoined the captain, shaking his head doubtfully, but regarding the desperate courage of the fair aspirant with obvious admiration. 'I don't know. It 's difficult navigation. She 's very hard to carry on with, my dear. You never can tell how she 'll head, you see. She 's full one minute, and round upon you next. And when she *is* a tartar,' said the captain, with the perspiration breaking out upon his forehead—. There was nothing but a whistle emphatic enough for the conclusion of the sentence, so the captain whistled tremulously. After which he again shook his head, and recurring to his admiration of Miss

Nipper's devoted bravery, timidly repeated, 'Would you, do you think, my dear?'

Susan only replied with a bridling smile, but that was so very full of defiance, that there is no knowing how long Captain Cuttle might have stood entranced in its contemplation, if Florence in her anxiety had not again proposed their immediately resorting to the oracular Bunsby. Thus reminded of his duty, Captain Cuttle put on the glazed hat firmly, took up another knobby stick, with which he had supplied the place of that one given to Walter, and offering his arm to Florence, prepared to cut his way through the enemy.

It turned out, however, that Mrs. MacStinger had already changed her course, and that she headed, as the captain had remarked she often did, in quite a new direction. For when they got downstairs, they found that exemplary woman beating the mats on the door-steps, with Alexander, still upon the paving-stone, dimly looming through a fog of dust; and so absorbed was Mrs. MacStinger in her household occupation, that when Captain Cuttle and his visitors passed, she beat the harder, and neither by word nor gesture showed any consciousness of their vicinity. The captain was so well pleased with this easy escape—although the effect of the door-mats on him was like a copious administration of snuff, and made him sneeze until the tears ran down his face—that he could hardly believe his good fortune; but more than once, between the door and the hackney-coach, looked over his shoulder, with an obvious apprehension of Mrs. MacStinger's giving chase yet.

However they got to the corner of Brig Place without any molestation from that terrible fire-ship; and the captain mounting the coach-box—for his gallantry would not allow him to ride inside with the ladies, though besought to do so—piloted the driver on his course for Captain Bunsby's vessel, which was called the Cautious Clara, and was lying hard by Ratcliffe.

Arrived at the wharf off which this great commander's ship was jammed in among some five hundred companions, whose tangled rigging looked like monstrous cobwebs half swept down, Captain Cuttle appeared at the coach-window, and invited Florence and Miss Nipper to accompany him on board; observing that Bunsby was to the last degree soft-hearted in respect of ladies, and that nothing would so much tend to bring his expansive intellect into a state of harmony as their presentation to the Cautious Clara.

Florence readily consented; and the captain, taking her little hand in his prodigious palm, led her, with a mixed expression of patronage, paternity, pride, and ceremony, that was pleasant to see, over several very dirty decks, until, coming to the Clara, they found that cautious craft (which lay outside the tier) with her gangway removed, and half a dozen feet of river interposed between herself and her nearest neighbour. It appeared, from Captain Cuttle's explanation, that the great Bunsby, like himself, was cruelly treated by his landlady, and that when her usage of him for the time being was so hard that he could bear it no longer, he set this gulf between them as a last resource.

'Clara a-hoy!' cried the captain, putting a hand to each side of his mouth.

'A-hoy!' cried a boy, like the captain's echo, tumbling up from below.

'Bunsby aboard?' cried the captain, hailing the boy in a stentorian voice, as if he were half a mile off instead of two yards.

'Aye, aye!' cried the boy, in the same tone.

The boy then shoved out a plank to Captain Cuttle, who adjusted it carefully, and led Florence across: returning presently for Miss Nipper. So they stood upon the deck of the Cautious Clara, in whose standing rigging, divers fluttering articles of dress were curing, in company with a few tongues and some mackerel.

Immediately there appeared, coming slowly up above the bulk-head of the cabin, another bulk-head—human, and very large—with one stationary eye in the mahogany face, and one revolving one, on the principle of some lighthouses. This head was decorated with shaggy hair, like oakum, which had no governing inclination towards the north, east, west, or south, but inclined to all four quarters of the compass, and to every point upon it. The head was followed by a perfect desert of chin, and by a shirt-collar and neckerchief, and by a dreadnought pilot-coat, and by a pair of dreadnought pilot-trousers, whereof the waistband was so very broad and high, that it became a succedaneum for a waistcoat: being ornamented near the wearer's breast-bone with some massive wooden buttons, like backgammon men. As the lower portions of these pantaloons became revealed, Bunsby stood confessed: his hands in their pockets, which were of vast size; and his gaze directed, not to Captain Cuttle or the ladies, but the mast-head.

The profound appearance of this philosopher, who was bulky and strong, and on whose extremely red face an expression of taciturnity sat enthroned, not inconsistent with his character, in which that quality was proudly conspicuous, almost daunted Captain Cuttle, though on familiar terms with him. Whispering to Florence that Bunsby had never in his life expressed surprise, and was considered not to know what it meant, the captain watched him as he eyed his mast-head, and afterwards swept the horizon; and when the revolving eye seemed to be coming round in his direction, said—

'Bunsby, my lad, how fares it?'

A deep, gruff, husky utterance, which seemed to have no connection with Bunsby, and certainly had not the least effect upon his face, replied, 'Aye, aye, shipmet, how goes it?' At the same time Bunsby's right hand and arm, emerging from a pocket, shook the captain's, and went back again.

'Bunsby,' said the captain, striking home at once, 'here you are; a man of mind, and a man as can give an opinion. Here 's a young lady as wants to take that opinion, in regard of my friend Wal'r; likewise my t 'other friend, Sol Gills, which is a character for you to come within hail of, being a man of science, which is the mother of inwention, and knows no law. Bunsby, will you wear, to oblige me, and come along with us?'

The great commander, who seemed by the expression of his visage to be always on the look-out for something in the extremest distance, and to have no ocular knowledge of anything within ten miles, made no reply whatever.

'Here is a man,' said the captain, addressing himself to his fair auditors, and indicating the commander with his outstretched hook, 'that has fell down more than any man alive; that has had more accidents happen to his own self than the Seamen's Hospital to all hands; that took as many spars and bars and bolts about the outside of his head when he was young, as you 'd want a order for on Chatham-yard to build a pleasure-yacht with; and yet that got his opinions in that way, it 's my belief, for there an't nothing like 'em afloat or ashore.'

The stolid commander appeared, by a very slight vibration in his elbows, to express some satisfaction in this encomium; but if his face had been as distant as his gaze was, it could hardly have enlightened the beholders less in reference to anything that was passing in his thoughts.

'Shipmet,' said Bunsby, all of a sudden, and stooping down to look out under some interposing spar, 'what 'll the ladies drink?'

Captain Cuttle, whose delicacy was shocked by such an inquiry in connection with Florence, drew the sage aside, and seeming to explain in his ear, accompanied him below; where, that he might not take offence, the captain drank a dram himself, which Florence and Susan, glancing down the open skylight, saw the sage, with difficulty finding room for himself between his berth and a very little brass fireplace, serve out for self and friend. They soon reappeared on deck, and Captain Cuttle, triumphing in the success of his enterprise, conducted Florence back to the coach, while Bunsby followed, escorting Miss Nipper, whom he hugged upon the way (much to that young lady's indignation) with his pilot-coated arm, like a blue bear.

The captain put his oracle inside, and gloried so much in having secured him, and having got that mind into a hackney-coach, that he could not refrain from often peeping in at Florence through the little window behind the driver, and testifying his delight in smiles, and also in taps upon his forehead, to hint to her that the brain of Bunsby was hard at it. In the meantime, Bunsby, still hugging Miss Nipper (for his friend, the captain, had not exaggerated the softness of his heart), uniformly preserved his gravity of deportment, and showed no other consciousness of her or anything.

Uncle Sol, who had come home, received them at the door, and ushered them immediately into the little back-parlour: strangely altered by the absence of Walter. On the table, and about the room, were the charts and maps on which the heavy-hearted instrument-maker had again and again tracked the missing vessel across the sea, and on which, with a pair of compasses that he still had in his hand, he had been measuring, a minute before, how far she must have driven, to have driven here or there: and trying to demonstrate that a long time must elapse before hope was exhausted.

'Whether she can have run,' said uncle Sol, looking wistfully over the chart; 'but no, that 's almost impossible. Or whether she can have been forced by stress of weather,—but that 's not reasonably likely. Or whether there is any hope she so far changed her course as—but even I can hardly hope that!' With such broken suggestions, poor old uncle Sol roamed over the great sheet before him, and could not find a speck of hopeful probability in it large enough to set one small point of the compasses upon.

Florence saw immediately—it would have been difficult to help seeing—that there was a singular indescribable change in the old man, and that while his manner was far more restless and unsettled than usual, there was yet a curious, contradictory decision in it, that perplexed her very much. She fancied once that he spoke wildly, and at random; for on her saying she regretted not to have seen him when she had been there before that morning, he at first replied that he had been to see her, and directly afterwards seemed to wish to recall that answer.

'You have been to see me?' said Florence. 'To-day?'

'Yes, my dear young lady,' returned uncle Sol, looking at her and away from her in a confused manner. 'I wished to see you with my own eyes, and to hear you with my own ears, once more before—' There he stopped.

'Before when? Before what?' said Florence, putting her hand upon his arm.

'Did I say "before"?' replied old Sol. 'If I did, I must have meant before we should have news of my dear boy.'

'You are not well,' said Florence, tenderly. 'You have been so very anxious. I am sure you are not well.'

'I am as well,' returned the old man, shutting up his right hand, and holding it out to show her: 'as well and firm as any man at my time of life can hope to be. See! It 's steady. Is its master not as capable of resolution and fortitude as many a younger man? I think so. We shall see.'

There was that in his manner more than in his words, though they remained with her too, which impressed Florence so much, that she would have confided her uneasiness to Captain Cuttle at that moment, if the captain had not seized that moment for expounding the state of circumstances on which the opinion of the sagacious Bunsby was requested, and entreating that profound authority to deliver the same.

Bunsby, whose eye continued to be addressed to somewhere about the half-way house between London and Gravesend, two or three times put out his rough right arm, as seeking to wind it for inspiration round the fair form of Miss Nipper; but that young female having withdrawn herself, in displeasure, to the opposite side of the table, the soft heart of the commander of the Cautious Clara met with no response to its impulses. After sundry failures in this wise, the commander, addressing himself to nobody, thus spake; or rather the voice within him said of its own accord, and quite independent of himself, as if he were possessed by a gruff spirit—

'My name 's Jack Bunsby!'

'He was christened John,' cried the delighted Captain Cuttle. 'Hear him!'

'And what I says,' pursued the voice, after some deliberation, 'I stands to.'

The captain, with Florence on his arm, nodded at the auditory, and seemed to say, 'Now he 's coming out. This is what I meant when I brought him.'

'Whereby,' proceeded the voice, 'why not? If so, what odds? Can any man say otherwise? No. Awast then!'

When it had pursued its train of argument to this point, the voice stopped, and rested. It then proceeded very slowly, thus—

'Do I believe that this here Son and Heir 's gone down, my lads? Mayhap. Do I say so? Which? If a skipper stands out by Sen' George's Channel, making for the Downs, what 's right ahead of him? The Goodwins. He isn't forced to run upon the Goodwins, but he may. The bearings of this observation lays in the application on it. That an't no part of my duty. Awast then, keep a bright lookout for'ard, and good luck to you!'

The voice here went out of the back-parlour and into the street, taking the commander of the Cautious Clara with it, and accompanying him on board again with all convenient expedition, where he immediately turned in, and refreshed his mind with a nap.

SOLEMN REFERENCE IS MADE TO MR. BUNSBY.

The students of the sage's precepts, left to their own application of his wisdom upon a principle which was the main leg of the Bunsby tripod, as it is perchance of some other oracular stools—looked upon one another in a little uncertainty; while Rob the Grinder, who had taken the innocent freedom of peering in, and listening, through the skylight in the roof, came softly down from the leads, in a state of very dense confusion. Captain Cuttle, however, whose admiration of Bunsby was, if possible, enhanced by the splendid manner in which he had justified his reputation and come through this solemn reference, proceeded to explain that Bunsby meant nothing but confidence; that Bunsby had no misgivings; and that such an opinion as that man had given, coming from such a mind as his, was Hope's own anchor, with good roads to cast it in. Florence endeavoured to believe that the captain was right; but the Nipper, with her arms tight folded, shook her head in resolute denial, and had no more trust in Bunsby than in Mr. Perch himself.

The philosopher seemed to have left uncle Sol pretty much where he had found him, for he still went roaming about the watery world, compasses in hand, and discovering no rest for them. It was in pursuance of a whisper in his ear from Florence, while the old man was absorbed in this pursuit, that Captain Cuttle laid his heavy hand upon his shoulder.

'What cheer, Sol Gills?' cried the captain, heartily.

'But so-so, Ned,' returned the instrument-maker. 'I have been remembering, all this afternoon, that on the very day when my boy entered Dombey's house and came home late to dinner, sitting just there where you stand, we talked of storm and shipwreck, and I could hardly turn him from the subject.'

But meeting the eyes of Florence, which were fixed with earnest scrutiny upon his face, the old man stopped and smiled.

'Stand by, old friend!' cried the captain. 'Look alive! I tell you what, Sol Gills; arter I 've convoyed Heart's Delight safe home,' here the captain kissed his hook to Florence, 'I 'll come back and take you in tow for the rest of this blessed day. You 'll come and eat your dinner along with me, Sol, somewheres or another.'

'Not to-day, Ned!' said the old man quickly, and appearing to be unaccountably startled by the proposition. 'Not to-day. I couldn't do it!'

'Why not?' returned the captain, gazing at him in astonishment.

'I—I have so much to do. I—I mean to think of, and arrange. I couldn't do it, Ned, indeed. I must go out again, and be alone, and turn my mind to many things to-day.'

The captain looked at the instrument-maker, and looked at Florence, and again at the instrument-maker. 'To-morrow, then,' he suggested, at last.

'Yes, yes. To-morrow,' said the old man. 'Think of me to-morrow. Say to-morrow.'

'I shall come here early, mind, Sol Gills,' stipulated the captain.

'Yes, yes. The first thing to-morrow morning,' said old Sol: 'and now good-bye, Ned Cuttle, and God bless you!'

Squeezing both the captain's hands, with uncommon fervour, as he said it, the old man turned to Florence, folded hers in his own, and put them to his lips; then hurried her out to the coach with very singular precipitation. Altogether, he made such an effect on Captain Cuttle that the captain lingered behind, and instructed Rob to be particularly gentle and attentive to his master until the morning: which injunction he strengthened with the pavement of one shilling down, and the promise of another sixpence before noon next day. This kind office performed, Captain Cuttle, who considered himself the natural and lawful body-guard of Florence, mounted the box with a mighty sense of his trust, and escorted her home. At parting, he assured her that he would stand by Sol Gills, close and true; and once again inquired of Susan Nipper, unable to forget her gallant words in reference to Mrs. MacStinger, 'Would you, do you think, my dear, though?'

When the desolate house had closed upon the two, the captain's thoughts reverted to the old instrument-maker, and he felt uncomfortable. Therefore, instead of going home, he walked up and down the street several times, and, eking out his leisure until evening, dined late at a certain angular little tavern in the City, with a public parlour like a wedge, to which glazed hats much resorted. The captain's principal intention was to pass Sol Gills's after dark, and look in through the window: which he did. The parlour door stood open, and he could see his old friend writing busily and steadily at the table within, while the little midshipman, already sheltered from the night dews, watched him from the counter; under which Rob the Grinder made his own bed, preparatory to shutting the shop. Reassured by the tranquillity that reigned within the precincts of the wooden mariner, the captain headed for Brig Place, resolving to weigh anchor betimes in the morning.

## CHAPTER XXIV

### THE STUDY OF A LOVING HEART

Sir Barnet and Lady Skettles, very good people, resided in a pretty villa at Fulham, on the banks of the Thames; which was one of the most desirable residences in the world when a rowing-match happened to be going past, but had its little inconveniences at other times, among which may be enumerated the occasional appearance of the river in the drawing-room, and the contemporaneous disappearance of the lawn and shrubbery.

Sir Barnet Skettles expressed his personal consequence chiefly through an antique gold snuff-box, and a ponderous silk pocket-handkerchief, which he had an imposing manner of drawing out of his pocket like a banner, and using with both hands at once. Sir Barnet's object in life was constantly to extend the range of his acquaintance. Like a heavy body dropped into water—not to disparage so worthy a gentleman by the comparison—it was in the nature of things that Sir Barnet must spread an ever-widening circle about him, until there was no room left. Or, like a sound in air, the vibration of which, according to the speculation of an ingenious modern philosopher, may go on travelling for ever through the interminable fields of space, nothing but coming to the end of his moral tether could stop Sir Barnet Skettles in his voyage of discovery through the social system.

Sir Barnet was proud of making people acquainted with people. He liked the thing for its own sake, and it advanced his favourite object too. For example, if Sir Barnet had the good fortune to get hold of a raw recruit, or a country gentleman, and ensnared him to his hospitable villa, Sir Barnet would say to him, on the morning after his arrival, 'Now, my dear sir, is there anybody you would like to know? Who is there you would wish to meet? Do you take any interest in writing people, or in painting, or sculpturing people, or in acting people, or in anything of that sort?' Possibly the patient answered yes, and mentioned somebody, of whom Sir Barnet had no more personal knowledge than of Ptolemy the Great. Sir Barnet replied, that nothing on earth was easier, as he knew him very well: immediately called on the aforesaid somebody, left his card, wrote a short note, 'My dear sir—penalty of your eminent position—friend at my house naturally desirous—Lady Skettles and myself participate—trust that genius being superior to ceremonies, you will do us the distinguished favour of giving us the pleasure,' etc., etc.—and so killed a brace of birds with one stone, dead as doornails.

With the snuff-box and banner in full force, Sir Barnet Skettles propounded his usual inquiry to Florence on the first morning of her visit. When Florence thanked him, and said there was no one in particular whom she desired to see, it was natural she should think with a pang, of poor lost Walter. When Sir Barnet Skettles, urging his kind offer, said, 'My dear Miss Dombey, are you sure you can remember no one whom your good papa—to whom I beg you to present the best compliments of myself and Lady Skettles when you write—might wish you to know?' it was natural, perhaps, that her poor head should droop a little, and that her voice should tremble as it softly answered in the negative.

Skettles Junior, much stiffened as to his cravat, and sobered down as to his spirits, was at home for the holidays, and appeared to feel himself aggrieved by the solicitude of his excellent mother that he should be attentive to Florence. Another and a deeper injury under which the soul of young Barnet chafed, was the company of Doctor and Mrs. Blimber, who had been invited on a visit to the paternal roof-tree, and of whom the young gentleman often said he would have preferred their passing the vacation at Jericho.

'Is there anybody *you* can suggest, now, Doctor Blimber?' said Sir Barnet Skettles, turning to that gentleman.

'You are very kind, Sir Barnet,' returned Doctor Blimber. 'Really I am not aware that there is, in particular. I like to know my fellow-men in general, Sir Barnet. What does Terence say? Any one who is the parent of a son is interesting to *me*.'

'Has Mrs. Blimber any wish to see any remarkable person?' asked Sir Barnet, courteously.

Mrs. Blimber replied, with a sweet smile and a shake of her sky-blue cap, that if Sir Barnet could have made her known to Cicero, she would have troubled him; but such an introduction not being feasible, and she already enjoying the friendship of himself and his amiable lady, and possessing with the Doctor her husband their joint confidence in regard to their dear son—here young Barnet was observed to curl his nose—she asked no more.

Sir Barnet was fain, under these circumstances, to content himself for the time with the company assembled. Florence was glad of that; for she had a study to pursue among them, and it lay too near her heart, and was too precious and momentous, to yield to any other interest.

There were some children staying in the house. Children who were as frank and happy with fathers and with mothers as those rosy faces opposite home.

Children who had no restraint upon their love, and freely showed it. Florence sought to learn their secret; sought to find out what it was she had missed; what simple art they knew, and she knew not; how she could be taught by them to show her father that she loved him, and to win his love again.

Many a day did Florence thoughtfully observe these children. On many a bright morning did she leave her bed when the glorious sun rose, and walking up and down upon the river's bank, before any one in the house was stirring, look up at the windows of their rooms, and think of them, asleep, so gently tended and affectionately thought of. Florence would feel more lonely then, than in the great house all alone; and would think sometimes that she was better there than here, and that there was greater peace in hiding herself than in mingling with others of her age, and finding how unlike them all she was. But attentive to her study, though it touched her to the quick at every little leaf she turned in the hard book, Florence remained among them, and tried, with patient hope, to gain the knowledge that she wearied for.

Ah! how to gain it! how to know the charm in its beginning! There were daughters here, who rose up in the morning, and lay down to rest at night, possessed of fathers' hearts already. They had no repulse to overcome, no coldness to dread, no frown to smooth away. As the morning advanced, and the windows opened one by one, and the dew began to dry upon the flowers and grass, and youthful feet began to move upon the lawn, Florence, glancing round at the bright faces, thought what was there she could learn from these children? It was too late to learn from them; each could approach her father fearlessly, and put up her lips to meet the ready kiss, and wind her arm about the neck that bent down to caress her. *She* could not begin by being so bold. Oh! could it be that there was less and less hope as she studied more and more!

She remembered well, that even the old woman who had robbed her when a little child—whose image and whose house, and all she had said and done, were stamped upon her recollection, with the enduring sharpness of a fearful impression made at that early period of life—had spoken fondly of her daughter, and how terribly even she had cried out in the pain of hopeless separation from her child. But her own mother, she would think again, when she recalled this, had loved her well. Then, sometimes, when her thoughts reverted swiftly to the void between herself and her father, Florence would tremble, and the tears would start upon her face, as she pictured to herself her mother living on, and coming also to dislike her, because of her wanting the unknown grace that should conciliate that father naturally, and had never done so from the cradle. She knew that this imagination did wrong to her mother's memory, and had no truth in it, or base to rest upon; and yet she tried so hard to justify him, and to find the whole blame in herself, that she could not resist its passing, like a wild cloud, through the distance of her mind.

There came among the other visitors, soon after Florence, one beautiful girl, three or four years younger than she, who was an orphan child, and who was accompanied by her aunt, a grey-haired lady, who spoke much to Florence, and who greatly liked (but that they all did) to hear her sing of an evening, and would always sit near her at that time, with motherly interest. They had only been two days in the house, when Florence, being in an arbour in the garden one warm morning, musingly observant of a youthful group upon the turf, through some intervening boughs, and wreathing flowers for the head of one little creature among them who was the pet and plaything of the rest, heard this same lady and her niece, in pacing up and down a sheltered nook close by, speak of herself.

'Is Florence an orphan like me, aunt?' said the child.

'No, my love. She has no mother, but her father is living.'

'Is she in mourning for her poor mamma, now?' inquired the child quickly.

'No; for her only brother.'

'Has she no other brother?'

'None.'

'No sister?'

'None.'

'I am very, very sorry!' said the little girl.

As they stopped soon afterwards to watch some boats, and had been silent in the meantime, Florence, who had risen when she heard her name, and had gathered up her flowers to go and meet them, that they might know of her being within hearing, resumed her seat and work, expecting to hear no more; but the conversation recommenced next moment.

'Florence is a favourite with every one here, and deserves to be, I am sure,' said the child, earnestly. 'Where is her papa?'

The aunt replied, after a moment's pause, that she did not know. Her tone of voice arrested Florence, who had started from her seat again; and held her fastened to the spot, with her work hastily caught up to her bosom, and her two hands saving it from being scattered on the ground.

'He is in England, I hope, aunt?' said the child.

'I believe so. Yes; I know he is, indeed.'

'Has he ever been here?'

'I believe not. No.'

'Is he coming here to see her?'

'I believe not.'

'Is he lame, or blind, or ill, aunt?' asked the child.

The flowers that Florence held to her breast began to fall when she heard those words, so wonderingly spoken. She held them closer; and her face hung down upon them.

'Kate,' said the lady, after another moment of silence, 'I will tell you the whole truth about Florence as I have heard it, and believe it to be. Tell no one else, my dear, because it may be little known here, and your doing so would give her pain.'

'I never will!' exclaimed the child.

'I know you never will,' returned the lady. 'I can trust you as myself. I fear then, Kate, that Florence's father cares little for her, very seldom sees her, and never was kind to her in her life, and now quite shuns her and avoids her. She would love him dearly if he would suffer her, but he will not—though for no fault of hers; and she is greatly to be loved and pitied by all gentle hearts.'

More of the flowers that Florence held, fell scattering on the ground; those that remained were wet, but not with dew; and her face dropped upon her laden hands.

'Poor Florence! Dear, good Florence!' cried the child.

'Do you know why I have told you this, Kate?' said the lady.

'That I may be very kind to her, and take great care to try to please her. Is that the reason, aunt?'

'Partly,' said the lady, 'but not all. Though we see her so cheerful; with a pleasant smile for every one; ready to oblige us all, and bearing her part in every amusement here: she can hardly be quite happy, do you think she can, Kate?'

'I am afraid not,' said the little girl.

'And you can understand,' pursued the lady, 'why her observation of children who have parents who are fond of them, and proud of them—like many here, just now—should make her sorrowful in secret?'

'Yes, dear aunt,' said the child, 'I understand that very well. Poor Florence!'

More flowers strayed upon the ground, and those she yet held to her breast trembled as if a wintry wind were rustling them.

'My Kate,' said the lady, whose voice was serious, but very calm and sweet, and had so impressed Florence from the first moment of her hearing it, 'of all the youthful people here, you are her natural and harmless friend; you have not the innocent means, that happier children have—'

'There are none happier, aunt!' exclaimed the child, who seemed to cling about her.

—'As other children have, dear Kate, of reminding her of her misfortune. Therefore I would have you, when you try to be her little friend, try all the more for that, and feel that the bereavement you sustained —thank Heaven! before you knew its weight—gives you claim and hold upon poor Florence.'

'But I am not without a parent's love, aunt, and I never have been,' said the child, 'with you.'

'However that may be, my dear,' returned the lady, 'your misfortune is a lighter one than Florence's; for not an orphan in the wide world can be so deserted as the child who is an outcast from a living parent's love.'

The flowers were scattered on the ground like dust; the empty hands were spread upon the face; and orphaned Florence, shrinking down upon the ground, wept long and bitterly.

But true of heart and resolute in her good purpose, Florence held to it as her dying mother held by her upon the day that gave Paul life. He did not know how much she loved him. However long the time in coming, and however slow the interval, she must try to bring that knowledge to her father's heart one day or other. Meantime she must be careful in no thoughtless word, or look, or burst of feeling awakened by any chance circumstance, to complain against him, or to give occasion for these whispers to his prejudice.

Even in the response she made the orphan child, to whom she was attracted strongly, and whom she had such occasion to remember, Florence was mindful of him. If she singled her out too plainly (Florence thought) from among the rest, she would confirm—in one mind certainly: perhaps in more—the belief that he was cruel and unnatural. Her own delight was no set-off to this. What she had overheard was a reason, not for soothing herself, but for saving him; and Florence did it, in pursuance of the study of her heart.

She did so always. If a book were read aloud, and there were anything in the story that pointed at an unkind father, she was in pain for their application of it to him; not for herself. So with any trifle of an interlude that was acted, or picture that was shown, or game that was played, among them. The occasions for such tenderness towards him were so many, that her mind misgave her often, it would indeed be better to go back to the old house, and live again within the shadow of its dull walls, undisturbed. How few who saw sweet Florence, in her spring of womanhood, the modest little queen of those small revels, imagined what a load of sacred care lay heavy in her breast! How few of those who stiffened in her father's freezing atmosphere, suspected what a heap of fiery coals was piled upon his head!

Florence pursued her study patiently, and, failing to acquire the secret of the nameless grace she sought, among the youthful company who were assembled in the house, often walked out alone, in the early morning among the children of the poor. But still she found them all too far advanced to learn from. They had won their household places long ago, and did not stand without, as she did, with a bar across the door.

There was one man whom she several times observed at work very early, and often with a girl of about her own age seated near him. He was a very poor man, who seemed to have no regular employment, but now went roaming about the banks of the river when the tide was low, looking out for bits and scraps in the mud; and now worked at the unpromising little patch of garden-ground before his cottage; and now tinkered up a miserable old boat that belonged to him; or did some job of that kind for a neighbour, as chance occurred. Whatever the man's labour, the girl was never employed; but sat, when she was with him, in a listless, moping state, and idle.

Florence had often wished to speak to this man; yet she had never taken courage to do so, as he made no movement towards her. But one morning when she happened to come upon him suddenly, from a by-path among some pollard willows which terminated in the little shelving piece of stony ground that lay between his dwelling and the water, where he was bending over a fire he had made to caulk the old boat which was lying bottom upwards, close by, he raised his head at the sound of her footstep, and gave her Good morning.

'Good morning,' said Florence, approaching nearer, 'you are at work early.'

'I'd be glad to be often at work earlier, miss, if I had work to do.'

'Is it so hard to get?' asked Florence.

'*I* find it so,' replied the man.

Florence glanced to where the girl was sitting, drawn together, with her elbows on her knees, and her chin on her hands, and said—

'Is that your daughter?'

He raised his head quickly, and looking towards the girl with a brightened face, nodded to her, and said 'Yes.' Florence looked towards her too, and gave her a kind salutation; the girl muttered something in return, ungraciously and sullenly.

'Is she in want of employment also?' said Florence.

The man shook his head. 'No, miss,' he said. 'I work for both.'

'Are there only you two, then?' inquired Florence.

'Only us two,' said the man. 'Her mother has been dead these ten year. Martha!' (he lifted up his head again, and whistled to her,) 'won't you say a word to the pretty young lady?'

The girl made an impatient gesture with her cowering shoulders, and turned her head another way. Ugly, misshapen, peevish, ill-conditioned, ragged, dirty—but beloved! Oh, yes! Florence had seen her father's look towards her, and she knew whose look it had no likeness to.

'I'm afraid she's worse this morning, my poor girl!' said the man, suspending his work, and contemplating his ill-favoured child, with a compassion that was the more tender for being rough.

'She is ill, then!' said Florence.

The man drew a deep sigh. 'I don't believe my Martha's had five short days' good health,' he answered, looking at her still, 'in as many long years.'

'Aye! and more than that, John,' said a neighbour, who had come down to help him with the boat.

'More than that, you say, do you?' cried the other, pushing back his battered hat, and drawing his hand across his forehead. 'Very like. It seems a long, long time.'

'And the more the time,' pursued the neighbour, 'the more you 've favoured and humoured her, John, till she 's got to be a burden to herself, and everybody else.'

'Not to me,' said her father, falling to his work again. 'Not to me.'

Florence could feel—who better?—how truly he spoke. She drew a little closer to him, and would have been glad to touch his rugged hand, and thank him for his goodness to the miserable object that he looked upon with eyes so different from any other man's.

'Who would favour my poor girl—to call it favouring—if *I* didn't?' said the father.

'Aye, aye,' cried the neighbour. 'In reason, John. But you! You rob yourself to give to her. You bind yourself hand and foot on her account. You make your life miserable along of her. And what does *she* care? You don't believe she knows it?'

The father lifted up his head again, and whistled to her. Martha made the same impatient gesture with her crouching shoulders, in reply; and he was glad and happy.

'Only for that, miss,' said the neighbour, with a smile, in which there was more of secret sympathy than he expressed; 'only to get that, he never lets her out of his sight!'

'Because the day 'll come, and has been coming a

long while,' observed the other, bending low over his work, 'when to get half as much from that unfort'nate child of mine—to get the trembling of a finger, or the waving of a hair—would be to raise the dead.'

Florence softly put some money near his hand, on the old boat, and left him.

And now Florence began to think, if she were to fall ill, if she were to fade like her dear brother, would he then know that she had loved him; would she then grow dear to him; would he come to her bedside, when she was weak and dim of sight, and take her into his embrace, and cancel all the past? Would he so forgive her, in that changed condition, for not having been able to lay open her childish heart to him, as to make it easy to relate with what emotions she had gone out of his room that night; what she had meant to say if she had had the courage; and how she had endeavoured, afterwards, to learn the way she never knew in infancy?

Yes, she thought if she were dying, he would relent. She thought, that if she lay, serene and not unwilling to depart, upon the bed that was curtained round with recollections of their darling boy, he would be touched home, and would say, 'Dear Florence, live for me, and we will love each other as we might have done, and be as happy as we might have been these many years!' She thought that if she heard such words from him, and had her arms clasped round him, she could answer with a smile, 'It is too late for anything but this; I never could be happier, dear father!' and so leave him, with a blessing on her lips.

The golden water she remembered on the wall, appeared to Florence, in the light of such reflections, only as a current flowing on to rest, and to a region where the dear ones, gone before, were waiting, hand in hand; and often when she looked upon the darker river rippling at her feet, she thought with awful wonder, but not terror, of that river which her brother had so often said was bearing him away.

The father and his sick daughter were yet fresh in Florence's mind, and, indeed, that incident was not a week old, when Sir Barnet and his lady going out walking in the lanes one afternoon, proposed to her to bear them company. Florence readily consenting, Lady Skettles ordered out young Barnet as a matter of course. For nothing delighted Lady Skettles so much, as beholding her eldest son with Florence on his arm.

Barnet, to say the truth, appeared to entertain an opposite sentiment on the subject, and on such occasions frequently expressed himself audibly, though indefinitely, in reference to 'a parcel of girls.' As it was not easy to ruffle her sweet temper, however, Florence generally reconciled the young gentleman to his fate after a few minutes, and they strolled on amicably: Lady Skettles and Sir Barnet following, in a state of perfect complacency and high gratification.

This was the order of procedure on the afternoon in question: and Florence had almost succeeded in overruling the present objections of Skettles Junior to his destiny, when a gentleman on horseback came riding by, looked at them earnestly as he passed, drew in his rein, wheeled round, and came riding back again, hat in hand.

The gentleman had looked particularly at Florence; and when the little party stopped, on his riding back, he bowed to her, before saluting Sir Barnet and his lady. Florence had no remembrance of having ever seen him, but she started involuntarily when he came near her, and drew back.

'My horse is perfectly quiet, I assure you,' said the gentleman.

It was not that, but something in the gentleman himself—Florence could not have said what—that made her recoil as if she had been stung.

'I have the honour to address Miss Dombey, I believe?' said the gentleman, with a most persuasive smile. On Florence inclining her head, he added, 'My name is Carker. I can hardly hope to be remembered by Miss Dombey, except by name. Carker.'

Florence, sensible of a strange inclination to shiver, though the day was hot, presented him to her host and hostess; by whom he was very graciously received.

'I beg pardon,' said Mr. Carker, 'a thousand times! But I am going down to-morrow morning to Mr. Dombey, at Leamington, and if Miss Dombey can intrust me with any commission, need I say how *very* happy I shall be?'

Sir Barnet immediately divining that Florence would desire to write a letter to her father, proposed to return, and besought Mr. Carker to come home and dine in his riding gear. Mr. Carker had the misfortune to be engaged to dinner, but if Miss Dombey wished to write, nothing would delight him more than to accompany them back, and to be her faithful slave in waiting as long as she pleased. As he said this with his widest smile, and bent down close to her to pat his horse's neck, Florence meeting his eyes, saw, rather than heard him say, 'There is no news of the ship!'

Confused, frightened, shrinking from him, and not even sure that he had said those words, for he seemed to have shown them to her in some extraordinary manner through his smile, instead of uttering them, Florence faintly said that she was obliged to him, but she would not write; she had nothing to say.

'Nothing to send, Miss Dombey?' said the man of teeth.

'Nothing,' said Florence, 'but my—but my dear love—if you please.'

Disturbed as Florence was, she raised her eyes to his face with an imploring and expressive look, that plainly besought him, if he knew—which he as plainly did—that any message between her and her father was an uncommon charge, but that one most of all, to spare her. Mr. Carker smiled and bowed low, and being charged by Sir Barnet with the best compliments of himself and Lady Skettles, took his leave and rode away: leaving a favourable impression on that worthy couple. Florence was seized with such a shudder as he went, that Sir Barnet, adopting the popular superstition, supposed somebody was passing over her grave. Mr. Carker, turning a corner, on the instant, looked back, and bowed, and disappeared, as if he rode off to the churchyard straight, to do it.

## CHAPTER XXV

### STRANGE NEWS OF UNCLE SOL

Captain Cuttle, though no sluggard, did not turn out so early on the morning after he had seen Sol Gills, through the shop-window, writing in the parlour, with the midshipman upon the counter, and Rob the Grinder making up his bed below it, but that the clocks struck six as he raised himself on his elbow, and took a survey of his little chamber. The captain's eyes must have done severe duty, if he usually opened them as wide awaking as he did that morning; and were but roughly rewarded for their vigilance, if he generally rubbed them half as hard. But the occasion was no common one, for Rob the Grinder had certainly never stood in the doorway of Captain Cuttle's bedroom before, and in it he stood then, panting at the captain, with a flushed and touzled air of bed about him, that greatly heightened both his colour and expression.

'Holloa!' roared the captain. 'What 's the matter?'

Before Rob could stammer a word in answer, Captain Cuttle turned out, all in a heap, and covered the boy's mouth with his hand.

'Steady, my lad,' said the captain, 'don't ye speak a word to me as yet!'

The captain, looking at his visitor in great consternation, gently shouldered him into the next room, after laying this injunction upon him; and disappearing for a few moments, forthwith returned in the blue suit. Holding up his hand in token of the injunction not yet being taken off, Captain Cuttle walked up to the cupboard, and poured himself out a dram; a counterpart of which he handed to the messenger. The captain then stood himself up in a corner, against the wall, as if to forestall the possibility of being knocked backwards by the communication that was to be made to him; and having swallowed his liquor with his eyes fixed on the messenger, and his face as pale as his face could be, requested him to 'heave ahead.'

'Do you mean, tell you, captain?' asked Rob, who had been greatly impressed by these precautions.

'Aye!' said the captain.

'Well, sir,' said Rob, 'I ain't got much to tell. But look here!'

Rob produced a bundle of keys. The captain surveyed them, remained in his corner, and surveyed the messenger.

'And look here!' pursued Rob.

The boy produced a sealed packet, which Captain Cuttle stared at as he had stared at the keys.

'When I woke this morning, captain,' said Rob, 'which was about a quarter after five, I found these on my pillow. The shop-door was unbolted and unlocked, and Mr. Gills gone.'

'Gone!' roared the captain.

'Flowed, sir,' returned Rob.

The captain's voice was so tremendous, and he came out of his corner with such way on him, that Rob retreated before him into another corner: holding out the keys and packet, to prevent himself from being run down.

'"For Captain Cuttle," sir,' cried Rob, 'is on the keys, and on the packet too. Upon my word and honour, Captain Cuttle, I don't know anything more about it. I wish I may die if I do! Here 's a sitiwation for a lad that 's just got a sitiwation,' cried the unfortunate Grinder, screwing his cuff into his face: 'his master bolted with his place, and him blamed for it!'

These lamentations had reference to Captain Cuttle's gaze, or rather glare, which was full of vague suspicions, threatenings, and denunciations. Taking the proffered packet from his hand, the captain opened it and read as follows:—

'"My dear Ned Cuttle. Enclosed is my will!"' The captain turned it over, with a doubtful look—'"and Testament."—Where's the Testament?' said the captain, instantly impeaching the ill-fated Grinder. 'What have you done with that, my lad?'

'*I* never see it,' whimpered Rob. 'Don't keep on

suspecting an innocent lad, captain. *I* never touched the Testament.'

Captain Cuttle shook his head, implying that somebody must be answerable for it; and gravely proceeded—

'"Which don't break open for a year, or until you have decisive intelligence of my dear Walter, who is dear to you, Ned, too, I am sure."' The captain paused and shook his head in some emotion; then, as a re-establishment of his dignity in this trying position, looked with exceeding sternness at the Grinder. '"If you should never hear of me, or see me more, Ned, remember an old friend as he will remember you to the last—kindly; and at least until the period I have mentioned has expired, keep a home in the old place for Walter. There are no debts, the loan from Dombey's house is paid off, and all my keys I send with this. Keep this quiet, and make no inquiry for me; it is useless. So no more, dear Ned, from your true friend, Solomon Gills."' The captain took a long breath, and then read these words, written below; '"The boy Rob, well recommended, as I told you, from Dombey's house. If all else should come to the hammer, take care, Ned, of the little midshipman."'

To convey to posterity any idea of the manner in which the captain, after turning this letter over and over, and reading it a score of times, sat down in his chair, and held a court-martial on the subject in his own mind, would require the united genius of all the great men, who, discarding their own untoward days, have determined to go down to posterity, and have never got there. At first the captain was too much confounded and distressed to think of anything but the letter itself; and even when his thoughts began to glance upon the various attendant facts, they might, perhaps, as well have occupied themselves with their former theme, for any light they reflected on them. In this state of mind, Captain Cuttle having the Grinder before the court, and no one else, found it a great relief to decide, generally, that he was an object of suspicion: which the captain so clearly expressed in his visage, that Rob remonstrated.

'Oh, don't, captain!' cried the Grinder. 'I wonder how you can! what have I done to be looked at, like that?'

'My lad,' said Captain Cuttle, 'don't you sing out afore you 're hurt. And don't you commit yourself, whatever you do.'

'I haven't been and committed nothing, captain!' answered Rob.

'Keep her free, then,' said the captain, impressively, 'and ride easy.'

With a deep sense of the responsibility imposed upon him, and the necessity of thoroughly fathoming this mysterious affair, as became a man in his relations with the parties, Captain Cuttle resolved to go down and examine the premises, and to keep the Grinder with him. Considering that youth as under arrest at present, the captain was in some doubt whether it might not be expedient to handcuff him, or tie his ankles together, or attach a weight to his legs; but not being clear as to the legality of such formalities, the captain decided merely to hold him by the shoulder all the way, and knock him down if he made any objection.

However, he made none, and consequently got to the instrument-maker's house without being placed under any more stringent restraint. As the shutters were not yet taken down, the captain's first care was to have the shop opened; and when the daylight was freely admitted, he proceeded, with its aid, to further investigation.

The captain's first care was to establish himself in a chair in the shop, as president of the solemn tribunal that was sitting within him; and to require Rob to lie down in his bed under the counter, show exactly where he discovered the keys and packet when he awoke, how he found the door when he went to try it, how he started off to Brig Place—cautiously preventing the latter imitation from being carried farther than the threshold—and so on to the end of the chapter. When all this had been done several times, the captain shook his head and seemed to think the matter had a bad look.

Next, the captain, with some indistinct idea of finding a body, instituted a strict search over the whole house; groping in the cellars with a lighted candle, thrusting his hook behind doors, bringing his head into violent contact with beams, and covering himself with cobwebs. Mounting up to the old man's bedroom, they found that he had not been in bed on the previous night, but had merely lain down on the coverlet, as was evident from the impression yet remaining there.

'And *I* think, captain,' said Rob, looking round the room, 'that when Mr. Gills was going in and out so often, these last few days, he was taking little things away, piecemeal, not to attract attention.'

'Aye!' said the captain, mysteriously. 'Why so, my lad?'

'Why,' returned Rob, looking about, 'I don't see his shaving tackle. Nor his brushes, captain. Nor no shirts. Nor yet his shoes.'

As each of these articles was mentioned, Captain Cuttle took particular notice of the corresponding department of the Grinder, lest he should appear to have been in recent use, or should prove to be in present possession thereof. But Rob had no occasion to shave, certainly was not brushed, and wore the clothes he had worn for a long time past, beyond all possibility of mistake.

'And what should you say,' said the captain—'not committing yourself—about his time of sheering off? Hey?'

'Why, I think, captain,' returned Rob, 'that he must have gone pretty soon after I began to snore.'

'What o'clock was that?' said the captain, prepared to be very particular about the exact time.

'How can I tell, captain!' answered Rob. 'I only know that I 'm a heavy sleeper at first, and a light one towards morning; and if Mr. Gills had come through the shop near daybreak, though ever so much on tip-toe, I 'm pretty sure I should have heard him shut the door at all events.'

On mature consideration of this evidence, Captain Cuttle began to think that the instrument-maker must have vanished of his own accord; to which logical conclusion he was assisted by the letter addressed to himself, which, as being unquestionably in the old man's handwriting, would seem, with no great forcing, to bear the construction, that he arranged of his own will, to go, and so went. The captain had next to consider where and why? and as there was no way whatsoever that he saw to the solution of the first difficulty, he confined his meditations to the second.

Remembering the old man's curious manner, and the farewell he had taken of him; unaccountably fervent at the time, but quite intelligible now: a terrible apprehension strengthened on the captain, that, overpowered by his anxieties and regrets for Walter, he had been driven to commit suicide. Unequal to the wear and tear of daily life, as he had often professed himself to be, and shaken as he no doubt was by the uncertainty and deferred hope he had undergone, it seemed no violently strained misgiving, but only too probable.

Free from debt, and with no fear for his personal liberty, or the seizure of his goods, what else but such a state of madness could have hurried him away alone and secretly? As to his carrying some apparel with him, if he had really done so—and they were not even sure of that—he might have done so, the captain argued, to prevent inquiry, to distract attention from his probable fate, or to ease the very mind that was now revolving all these possibilities. Such, reduced into plain language, and condensed within a small compass, was the final result and substance of Captain Cuttle's deliberations: which took a long time to arrive at this pass, and were, like some more public deliberations, very discursive and disorderly.

Dejected and despondent in the extreme, Captain Cuttle felt it just to release Rob from the arrest in which he had placed him, and to enlarge him, subject to a kind of honourable inspection which he still resolved to exercise; and having hired a man, from Brogley the broker, to sit in the shop during their absence, the captain, taking Rob with him, issued forth upon a dismal quest after the mortal remains of Solomon Gills.

Not a station-house or bone-house, or work-house in the metropolis escaped a visitation from the hard glazed hat. Along the wharves, among the shipping on the bank-side, up the river, down the river, here, there, everywhere, it went gleaming where men were thickest, like the hero's helmet in an epic battle. For a whole week the captain read of all the found and missing people in all the newspapers and handbills, and went forth on expeditions at all hours of the day to identify Solomon Gills, in poor little ship-boys who had fallen overboard, and in tall foreigners with dark beards who had taken poison—'to make sure,' Captain Cuttle said, 'that it warn't him.' It is a sure thing that it never was, and that the good captain had no other satisfaction.

Captain Cuttle at last abandoned these attempts as hopeless, and set himself to consider what was to be done next. After several new perusals of his poor friend's letter, he considered that the maintenance of 'a home in the old place for Walter' was the primary duty imposed upon him. Therefore, the captain's decision was, that he would keep house on the premises of Solomon Gills himself, and would go into the instrument-business, and see what came of it.

But as this step involved the relinquishment of his apartments at Mrs. MacStinger's, and he knew that resolute woman would never hear of his deserting them, the captain took the desperate determination of running away.

'Now, look ye here, my lad,' said the captain to Rob, when he had matured this notable scheme, 'to-morrow, I shan't be found in this here roadstead till night—not till arter midnight p'rhaps. But you keep watch till you hear me knock, and the moment you do, turn-to, and open the door.'

'Very good, captain,' said Rob.

'You'll continue to be rated on this here books,' pursued the captain, condescendingly, 'and I don't say but what you may get promotion, if you and me should pull together with a will. But the moment you hear me knock to-morrow night, whatever time it is, turn-to and show yourself smart with the door.'

'I'll be sure to do it, captain,' replied Rob.

'Because you understand,' resumed the captain,

coming back again to enforce this charge upon his mind, 'there may be, for anything I can say, a chase; and I might be took while I was waiting, if you didn't show yourself smart with the door.'

Rob again assured the captain that he would be prompt and wakeful; and the captain having made this prudent arrangement, went home to Mrs. MacStinger's for the last time.

The sense the captain had of its being the last time, and of the awful purpose hidden beneath his blue waistcoat, inspired him with such a mortal dread of Mrs. MacStinger, that the sound of that lady's foot downstairs at any time of the day, was sufficient to throw him into a fit of trembling. It fell out, too, that Mrs. MacStinger was in a charming temper—mild and placid as a house-lamb; and Captain Cuttle's conscience suffered terrible twinges, when she came up to inquire if she could cook him nothing for his dinner.

'A nice small kidney-pudding now, Cap'en Cuttle,' said his landlady: 'or a sheep's heart. Don't mind my trouble.'

'No thank 'ee, ma'am,' returned the captain.

'Have a roast fowl,' said Mrs. MacStinger, 'with a bit of weal stuffing and some egg sauce. Come, Cap'en Cuttle! Give yourself a little treat!'

'No thank 'ee, ma'am,' returned the Captain very humbly.

'I 'm sure you 're out of sorts, and want to be stimulated,' said Mrs. MacStinger. 'Why not have, for once in a way, a bottle of sherry wine?'

'Well, ma'am,' rejoined the captain, 'if you 'd be so good as take a glass or two, I think I would try that. Would you do me the favour, ma'am,' said the captain, torn to pieces by his conscience, 'to accept a quarter's rent ahead?'

'And why so, Cap'en Cuttle?' retorted Mrs. MacStinger—sharply, as the captain thought.

The captain was frightened to death. 'If you would, ma'am,' he said with submission, 'it would oblige me. I can't keep my money very well. It pays itself out. I should take it kind if you 'd comply.'

'Well, Cap'en Cuttle,' said the unconscious MacStinger, rubbing her hands, 'you can do as you please. It 's not for me, with my family, to refuse, no more than it is to ask.'

'And would you, ma'am,' said the captain, taking down the tin canister in which he kept his cash, from the top shelf of the cupboard, 'be so good as offer eighteenpence a-piece to the little family all round? If you could make it convenient, ma'am, to pass the word presently for them children to come for'ard, in a body, I should be glad to see 'em.'

These innocent MacStingers were so many daggers to the captain's breast, when they appeared in a swarm, and tore at him with the confiding trustfulness he so little deserved. The eye of Alexander MacStinger, who had been his favourite, was insupportable to the captain; the voice of Juliana MacStinger, who was the picture of her mother, made a coward of him.

Captain Cuttle kept up appearances, nevertheless, tolerably well, and for an hour or two was very hardly used and roughly handled by the young MacStingers; who in their childish frolics, did a little damage also to the glazed hat, by sitting in it, two at a time, as in a nest, and drumming on the inside of the crown with their shoes. At length the captain sorrowfully dismissed them: taking leave of these cherubs with the poignant remorse and grief of a man who was going to execution.

In the silence of night, the captain packed up his heavier property in a chest, which he locked, intending to leave it there, in all probability for ever, but on the forlorn chance of one day finding a man sufficiently bold and desperate to come and ask for it. Of his lighter necessaries, the captain made a bundle; and disposed his plate about his person, ready for flight. At the hour of midnight, when Brig Place was buried in slumber, and Mrs. MacStinger was lulled in sweet oblivion, with her infants around her, the guilty captain, stealing down on tiptoe, in the dark, opened the door, closed it softly after him, and took to his heels.

Pursued by the image of Mrs. MacStinger springing out of bed, and, regardless of costume, following and bringing him back; pursued also by a consciousness of his enormous crime; Captain Cuttle held on at a great pace, and allowed no grass to grow under his feet, between Brig Place and the instrument-maker's door. It opened when he knocked—for Rob was on the watch—and when it was bolted and locked behind him, Captain Cuttle felt comparatively safe.

'Whew!' cried the captain, looking round him, 'it 's a breather!'

'Nothing the matter, is there, captain?' cried the gaping Rob.

'No, no!' said Captain Cuttle, after changing colour, and listening to a passing footstep in the street. 'But mind ye, my lad; if any lady, except either of them two as you see t' other day, ever comes and asks for Cap'en Cuttle, be sure to report no person of that name known, nor never heard of here; observe them orders, will you?'

'I 'll take care, captain,' returned Rob.

'You might say—if you liked,' hesitated the captain, 'that you 'd read in the paper that a cap'en of that name was gone to Australia, emigrating, along with a whole ship's complement of people as had all swore never to come back no more.'

Rob nodded his understanding of these instructions; and Captain Cuttle promising to make a man of him, if he obeyed orders, dismissed him, yawning, to his bed under the counter, and went aloft to the chamber of Solomon Gills.

What the captain suffered next day, whenever a bonnet passed, or how often he darted out of the shop to elude imaginary MacStingers, and sought safety in the attic, cannot be told. But to avoid the fatigues attendant on this means of self-preservation, the captain curtained the glass door of communication between the shop and parlour, on the inside, fitted a key to it from the bunch that had been sent to him: and cut a small hole of espial in the wall. The advantage of this fortification is obvious. On a bonnet appearing, the captain instantly slipped into his garrison, locked himself up, and took a secret observation of the enemy. Finding it a false alarm, the captain instantly slipped out again. And the bonnets in the street were so very numerous, and alarms were so inseparable from their appearance, that the captain was almost incessantly slipping in and out all day long.

Captain Cuttle found time, however, in the midst of this fatiguing service, to inspect the stock; in connection with which he had the general idea (very laborious to Rob) that too much friction could not be bestowed upon it, and that it could not be made too bright. He also ticketed a few attractive looking articles at a venture, at prices ranging from ten shillings to fifty pounds, and exposed them in the window to the great astonishment of the public.

After effecting these improvements, Captain Cuttle, surrounded by the instruments, began to feel scientific: and looked up at the stars at night, through the skylight, when he was smoking his pipe in the little back-parlour before going to bed, as if he had established a kind of property in them. As a tradesman in the City, too, he began to have an interest in the Lord Mayor, and the Sheriffs, and in Public Companies; and felt bound to read the quotations of the Funds every day, though he was unable to make out, on any principle of navigation, what the figures meant, and could have very well dispensed with the fractions. Florence, the captain waited on, with his strange news of uncle Sol, immediately after taking possession of the midshipman; but she was away from home. So the captain sat himself down in his altered station of life, with no company but Rob the Grinder; and losing count of time, as men do when great changes come upon them, thought musingly of Walter, and of Solomon Gills, and even of Mrs. MacStinger herself, as among the things that had been.

## CHAPTER XXVI

### SHADOWS OF THE PAST AND FUTURE

'Your most obedient, sir,' said the major. 'Damme, sir, a friend of my friend Dombey's is a friend of mine, and I 'm glad to see you!'

'I am infinitely obliged, Carker,' explained Mr. Dombey, 'to Major Bagstock, for his company and conversation. Major Bagstock has rendered me great service, Carker.'

Mr. Carker the manager, hat in hand, just arrived at Leamington, and just introduced to the major, showed the major his whole double range of teeth, and trusted he might take the liberty of thanking him with all his heart for having effected so great an improvement in Mr. Dombey's looks and spirits.

'By Gad, sir,' said the major, in reply, 'there are no thanks due to me, for it 's a give and take affair. A great creature like our friend Dombey, sir,' said the major, lowering his voice, but not lowering it so much as to render it inaudible to that gentleman, 'cannot help improving and exalting his friends. He strengthens and invigorates a man, sir, does Dombey, in his moral nature.'

Mr. Carker snapped at the expression. In his moral nature. Exactly. The very words he had been on the point of suggesting.

'But when my friend Dombey, sir,' added the major, 'talks to you of Major Bagstock, I must crave leave to set him and you right. He means plain Joe, sir — Joey B.— Josh. Bagstock — Joseph — rough and tough Old J., sir. At your service.'

Mr. Carker's excessively friendly inclinations towards the major, and Mr. Carker's admiration of his roughness, toughness, and plainness, gleamed out of every tooth in Mr. Carker's head.

'And now, sir,' said the major, 'you and Dombey have the devil's own amount of business to talk over.'

'By no means, major,' observed Mr. Dombey.

'Dombey,' said the major, defiantly, 'I know better; a man of your mark—the Colossus of commerce—is not to be interrupted. Your moments are precious. We shall meet at dinner-time. In the interval, old Joseph will be scarce. The dinner hour is a sharp seven, Mr. Carker.'

With that, the major, greatly swollen as to his face, withdrew; but immediately putting in his head at the door again, said—

'I beg your pardon. Dombey, have you any message to 'em?'

Mr. Dombey in some embarrassment, and not without a glance at the courteous keeper of his business confidence, intrusted the major with his compliments.

'By the Lord, sir,' said the major, 'you must make it something warmer than that, or Old Joe will be far from welcome.'

'Regards then, if you will, major,' returned Mr. Dombey.

'Damme, sir,' said the major, shaking his shoulders and his great cheeks jocularly: 'make it something warmer than that.'

'What you please, then, major,' observed Mr. Dombey.

'Our friend is sly, sir, sly, sir, de-vilish sly,' said the major, staring round the door at Carker. 'So is Bagstock.' But stopping in the midst of a chuckle, and drawing himself up to his full height, the major solemnly exclaimed, as he struck himself on the chest, 'Dombey! I envy your feelings. God bless you!' and withdrew.

'You must have found the gentleman a great resource,' said Carker, following him with his teeth.

'Very great indeed,' said Mr. Dombey.

'He has friends here, no doubt,' pursued Carker. 'I perceive, from what he has said, that you go into society here. Do you know,' smiling horribly, 'I am so very glad that you go into society!'

Mr. Dombey acknowledged this display of interest on the part of his second in command, by twirling his watch-chain, and slightly moving his head.

'You were formed for society,' said Carker. 'Of all the men I know, you are the best adapted, by nature and by position, for society. Do you know

I have been frequently amazed that you should have held it at arm's length so long!'

'I have had my reasons, Carker. I have been alone, and indifferent to it. But you have great social qualifications yourself, and are the more likely to have been surprised.'

'Oh! *I!*' returned the other, with ready self-disparagement. 'It 's quite another matter in the case of a man like me. I don't come into comparison with *you.*'

Mr. Dombey put his hand to his neckcloth, settled his chin in it, coughed, and stood looking at his faithful friend and servant for a few moments in silence.

'I shall have the pleasure, Carker,' said Mr. Dombey at length: making as if he swallowed something a little too large for his throat: 'to present you to my—to the major's friends. Highly agreeable people.'

'Ladies among them, I presume?' insinuated the smooth manager.

'They are all—that is to say, they are both—ladies,' replied Mr. Dombey.

'Only two?' smiled Carker.

'They are only two. I have confined my visits to their residence, and have made no other acquaintance here.'

'Sisters, perhaps?' quoth Carker.

'Mother and daughter,' replied Mr. Dombey.

As Mr. Dombey dropped his eyes, and adjusted his neckcloth again, the smiling face of Mr. Carker the manager became in a moment, and without any stage of transition, transformed into a most intent and frowning face, scanning his closely, and with an ugly sneer. As Mr. Dombey raised his eyes, it changed back, no less quickly, to its old expression, and showed him every gum of which it stood possessed.

'You are very kind,' said Carker, 'I shall be delighted to know them. Speaking of daughters, I have seen Miss Dombey.'

There was a sudden rush of blood to Mr. Dombey's face.

'I took the liberty of waiting on her,' said Carker, 'to inquire if she could charge me with any little commission. I am not so fortunate as to be the bearer of any but her—but her dear love.'

Wolf's face that it was then, with even the hot tongue revealing itself through the stretched mouth, as the eyes encountered Mr. Dombey's!

'What business intelligence is there?' inquired the latter gentleman, after a silence, during which Mr. Carker had produced some memoranda and other papers.

'There is very little,' returned Carker. 'Upon the whole we have not had our usual good fortune of late, but that is of little moment to you. At Lloyd's, they give up the Son and Heir for lost. Well, she was insured, from her keel to her masthead.'

'Carker,' said Mr. Dombey, taking a chair near him, 'I cannot say that young man Gay, ever impressed me favourably—'

'Nor me,' interposed the manager.

'But I wish,' said Mr. Dombey, without heeding the interruption, 'he had never gone on board that ship. I wish he had never been sent out.'

'It is a pity you didn't say so, in good time, is it not?' retorted Carker, coolly. 'However, I think it 's all for the best. I really think it 's all for the best. Did I mention that there was something like a little confidence between Miss Dombey and myself?'

'No,' said Mr. Dombey, sternly.

'I have no doubt,' returned Mr. Carker, after an impressive pause, 'that wherever Gay is, he is much better where he is than at home here. If I were, or could be, in your place, I should be satisfied of that. I am quite satisfied of it myself. Miss Dombey is confiding and young—perhaps hardly proud enough, for your daughter—if she have a fault. Not that that is much though, I am sure. Will you check these balances with me?'

Mr. Dombey leaned back in his chair, instead of bending over the papers that were laid before him, and looked the manager steadily in the face. The manager, with his eyelids slightly raised, affected to be glancing at his figures, and to await the leisure of his principal. He showed that he affected this, as if from great delicacy, and with a design to spare Mr. Dombey's feelings; and the latter, as he looked at him, was cognisant of his intended consideration, and felt that but for it, this confidential Carker would have said a great deal more, which he, Mr. Dombey, was too proud to ask for. It was his way in business, often. Little by little, Mr. Dombey's gaze relaxed, and his attention became diverted to the papers before him; but while busy with the occupation they afforded him, he frequently stopped, and looked at Mr. Carker again. Whenever he did so, Mr. Carker was demonstrative, as before, in his delicacy, and impressed it on his great chief more and more.

While they were thus engaged; and under the skilful culture of the manager, angry thoughts in reference to poor Florence brooded and bred in Mr. Dombey's breast, usurping the place of the cold dislike that generally reigned there; Major Bagstock, much admired by the old ladies of Leamington, and followed by the native, carrying the usual amount of light baggage, straddled along the shady side of the way, to make a morning call on Mrs. Skewton. It being mid-day when the major reached the bower of Cleopatra, he had the good fortune to find his princess on her usual sofa, languishing over a cup of coffee, with the room so darkened and shaded for her more luxurious repose, that Withers, who was in attendance on her, loomed like a phantom page.

'What insupportable creature is this, coming in!' said Mrs. Skewton. 'I cannot bear it. Go away, whoever you are!'

'You have not the heart to banish J. B., ma'am!' said the major, halting midway, to remonstrate, with his cane over his shoulder.

'Oh it's you, is it? On second thoughts, you may enter,' observed Cleopatra.

The major entered accordingly, and advancing to the sofa pressed her charming hand to his lips.

'Sit down,' said Cleopatra, listlessly waving her fan, 'a long way off. Don't come too near me, for I am frightfully faint and sensitive this morning, and you smell of the sun. You are absolutely tropical.'

'By George, ma'am,' said the major, 'the time has been when Joseph Bagstock has been grilled and blistered by the sun; the time was, when he was forced, ma'am, into such full blow, by high hothouse heat in the West Indies, that he was known as the Flower. A man never heard of Bagstock, ma'am, in those days; he heard of the Flower—the Flower of Ours. The Flower may have faded, more or less, ma'am,' observed the major, dropping into a much nearer chair than had been indicated by his cruel divinity, 'but it is a tough plant yet, and constant as the evergreen.'

Here the major, under cover of the dark room, shut up one eye, rolled his head like a harlequin, and, in his great self-satisfaction, perhaps went nearer to the confines of apoplexy than he had ever gone before.

'Where is Mrs. Granger?' inquired Cleopatra of her page.

Withers believed she was in her own room.

'Very well,' said Mrs. Skewton. 'Go away, and shut the door. I am engaged.'

As Withers disappeared, Mrs. Skewton turned her head languidly towards the major, without otherwise moving, and asked him how his friend was?

'Dombey, ma'am,' returned the major, with a facetious gurgling in his throat, 'is as well as a man in his condition *can* be. His condition is a desperate one, ma'am. He is touched, is Dombey! Touched!' cried the major. 'He is bayonetted through the body.'

Cleopatra cast a sharp look at the major, that contrasted forcibly with the affected drawl in which she presently said—

'Major Bagstock, although I know but little of the world,—nor can I really regret my inexperience, for I fear it is a false place, full of withering conventionalities: where nature is but little regarded, and where the music of the heart, and the gushing of the soul, and all that sort of thing, which is so truly poetical, is seldom heard,—I cannot misunderstand your meaning. There is an allusion to Edith—to my extremely dear child,' said Mrs. Skewton, tracing the outline of her eyebrows with her forefinger, 'in your words, to which the tenderest of chords vibrates excessively!'

'Bluntness, ma'am,' returned the major, 'has ever been the characteristic of the Bagstock breed. You are right. Joe admits it.'

'And that allusion,' pursued Cleopatra, 'would involve one of the most—if not positively *the* most—touching, and thrilling, and sacred emotions of which our sadly-fallen nature is susceptible, I conceive.'

The major laid his hand upon his lips, and wafted a kiss to Cleopatra, as if to identify the emotion in question.

'I feel that I am weak. I feel that I am wanting in that energy, which should sustain a mamma: not to say a parent: on such a subject,' said Mrs. Skewton, trimming her lips with the laced edge of her pocket-handkerchief; 'but I can hardly approach a topic so excessively momentous to my dearest Edith without a feeling of faintness. Nevertheless, bad man, as you have boldly remarked upon it, and as it has occasioned me great anguish': Mrs. Skewton touched her left side with her fan: 'I will not shrink from my duty.'

The major, under cover of the dimness, swelled, and swelled, and rolled his purple face about, and winked his lobster eye, until he fell into a fit of wheezing, which obliged him to rise and take a turn or two about the room, before his fair friend could proceed.

'Mr. Dombey,' said Mrs. Skewton, when she at length resumed, 'was obliging enough, now many weeks ago, to do us the honour of visiting us here; in company, my dear major, with yourself. I acknowledge—let me be open—that it is my failing to be the creature of impulse, and to wear my heart, as it were, outside. I know my failing full well. My enemy cannot know it better. But I am not penitent; I would rather not be frozen by the heartless world, and am content to bear this imputation justly.'

Mrs. Skewton arranged her tucker, pinched her wiry throat to give it a soft surface, and went on, with great complacency.

'It gave me (my dearest Edith too, I am sure) infinite pleasure to receive Mr. Dombey. As a friend of yours, my dear major, we were naturally disposed to be prepossessed in his favour, and I fancied that

I observed an amount of heart in Mr. Dombey, that was excessively refreshing.'

'There is devilish little heart in Dombey now, ma'am,' said the major.

'Wretched man!' cried Mrs. Skewton, looking at him languidly, 'pray be silent.'

'J. B. is dumb, ma'am,' said the major.

'Mr. Dombey,' pursued Cleopatra, smoothing the rosy hue upon her cheeks, 'accordingly repeated his visit; and possibly finding some attraction in the simplicity and primitiveness of our tastes—for there is always a charm in nature—it is so very sweet—became one of our little circle every evening. Little did I think of the awful responsibility into which I plunged when I encouraged Mr. Dombey—to—'

'To beat up these quarters, ma'am,' suggested Major Bagstock.

'Coarse person!' said Mrs. Skewton, 'you anticipate my meaning, though in odious language.'

Here Mrs. Skewton rested her elbow on the little table at her side, and suffering her wrist to droop in what she considered a graceful and becoming manner, dangled her fan to and fro, and lazily admired her hand while speaking.

'The agony I have endured,' she said mincingly, 'as the truth has by degrees dawned upon me, has been too exceedingly terrific to dilate upon. My whole existence is bound up in my sweetest Edith; and to see her change from day to day—my beautiful pet, who has positively garnered up her heart since the death of that most delightful creature, Granger—is the most affecting thing in the world.'

Mrs. Skewton's world was not a very trying one, if one might judge of it by the influence of its most affecting circumstance upon her; but this by the way.

'Edith,' simpered Mrs. Skewton, 'who is the perfect pearl of my life, is said to resemble me. I believe we *are* alike.'

'There is one man in the world who never will admit that any one resembles you, ma'am,' said the major; 'and that man's name is old Joe Bagstock.'

Cleopatra made as if she would brain the flatterer with her fan, but relenting, smiled upon him and proceeded—

'If my charming girl inherits any advantages from me, wicked one!': the major was the wicked one: 'she inherits also my foolish nature. She has great force of character—mine has been said to be immense, though I don't believe it—but once moved, she is susceptible and sensitive to the last extent. What are my feelings when I see her pining! They destroy me.'

The major advancing his double chin, and pursing up his blue lips into a soothing expression, affected the profoundest sympathy.

'The confidence,' said Mrs. Skewton, 'that has subsisted between us—the free development of soul, and openness of sentiment—is touching to think of. We have been more like sisters than mamma and child.'

'J. B.'s own sentiment,' observed the major, 'expressed by J. B. fifty thousand times!'

'Do not interrupt, rude man!' said Cleopatra. 'What are my feelings, then, when I find that there is one subject avoided by us! That there is a what 's-his-name—a gulf—opened between us. That my own artless Edith is changed to me! They are of the most poignant description, of course.'

The major left his chair, and took one nearer to the little table.

'From day to day I see this, my dear major,' proceeded Mrs. Skewton. 'From day to day I feel this. From hour to hour I reproach myself for that excess of faith and trustfulness which has led to such distressing consequences; and almost from minute to minute, I hope that Mr. Dombey may explain himself, and relieve the torture I undergo, which is extremely wearing. But nothing happens, my dear major; I am the slave of remorse—take care of the coffee cup; you are so very awkward—my darling Edith is an altered being; and I really don't see what is to be done, or what good creature I can advise with.'

Major Bagstock, encouraged perhaps by the softened and confidential tone into which Mrs. Skewton, after several times lapsing into it for a moment, seemed now to have subsided for good, stretched out his hand across the little table, and said with a leer—

'Advise with Joe, ma'am.'

'Then, you aggravating monster,' said Cleopatra, giving one hand to the major, and tapping his knuckles with her fan, which she held in the other: 'why don't you talk to me? you know what I mean. Why don't you tell me something to the purpose?'

The major laughed, and kissed the hand she had bestowed upon him, and laughed again, immensely.

'Is there as much heart in Mr. Dombey as I gave him credit for?' languished Cleopatra, tenderly. 'Do you think he is in earnest, my dear major? Would you recommend his being spoken to, or his being left alone? Now tell me, like a dear man, what you would advise.'

'Shall we marry him to Edith Granger, ma'am?' chuckled the major, hoarsely.

'Mysterious creature!' returned Cleopatra, bringing her fan to bear upon the major's nose. 'How can *we* marry him?'

'Shall we marry him to Edith Granger, ma'am, I say?' chuckled the major again.

Mrs. Skewton returned no answer in words, but smiled upon the major with so much archness and vivacity, that that gallant officer considering himself challenged, would have imprinted a kiss on her exceedingly red lips, but for her interposing the fan with a very winning and juvenile dexterity. It might have been in modesty; it might have been in apprehension of some danger to their bloom.

'Dombey, ma'am,' said the major, 'is a great catch.'

'Oh, mercenary wretch!' cried Cleopatra, with a little shriek, 'I am shocked.'

'And Dombey, ma'am,' pursued the major, thrusting forward his head, and distending his eyes, 'is in earnest. Joseph says it; Bagstock knows it; J. B. keeps him to the mark. Leave Dombey to himself, ma'am. Dombey is safe, ma'am. Do as you have done; do no more; and trust to J. B. for the end.'

'You really think so, my dear major?' returned Cleopatra, who had eyed him very cautiously, and very searchingly, in spite of her listless bearing.

'Sure of it, ma'am,' rejoined the major. 'Cleopatra the peerless, and her Antony Bagstock, will often speak of this, triumphantly, when sharing the elegance and wealth of Edith Dombey's establishment. Dombey's right-hand man, ma'am,' said the major, stopping abruptly in a chuckle, and becoming serious, 'has arrived.'

'This morning?' said Cleopatra.

'This morning, ma'am,' returned the major. 'And Dombey's anxiety for his arrival, ma'am, is to be referred—take J. B.'s word for this; for Joe is de-vilish sly'—the major tapped his nose, and screwed up one of his eyes tight: which did not enhance his native beauty—'to his desire that what is in the wind should become known to him, without Dombey's telling and consulting him. For Dombey is as proud, ma'am,' said the major, 'as Lucifer.'

'A charming quality,' lisped Mrs. Skewton; 'reminding one of dearest Edith.'

'Well, ma'am,' said the major. 'I have thrown out hints already, and the right-hand man understands 'em; and I 'll throw out more, before the day is done. Dombey projected this morning a ride to Warwick Castle, and to Kenilworth, to-morrow, to be preceded by a breakfast with us. I undertook the delivery of this invitation. Will you honour us so far, ma'am?' said the major, swelling with shortness of breath and slyness, as he produced a note, addressed to the Honourable Mrs. Skewton, by favour of Major Bagstock, wherein hers ever faithfully, Paul Dombey, besought her and her amiable and accomplished daughter to consent to the proposed excursion; and in a postscript unto which, the same ever faithfully Paul Dombey entreated to be recalled to the remembrance of Mrs. Granger.

'Hush!' said Cleopatra, suddenly, 'Edith!'

The loving mother can scarcely be described as resuming her insipid and affected air when she made this exclamation; for she had never cast it off; nor was it likely that she ever would or could, in any other place than in the grave. But hurriedly dismissing whatever shadow of earnestness, or faint confession of a purpose, laudable or wicked, that her face, or voice, or manner, had, for the moment, betrayed, she lounged upon the couch, her most insipid and most languid self again, as Edith entered the room.

Edith, so beautiful and stately, but so cold and so repelling. Who, slightly acknowledging the presence of Major Bagstock, and directing a keen glance at her mother, drew back the curtain from a window, and sat down there, looking out.

'My dearest Edith,' said Mrs. Skewton, 'where on earth have you been? I have wanted you, my love, most sadly.'

'You said you were engaged, and I stayed away,' she answered, without turning her head.

'It was cruel to old Joe, ma'am,' said the major in his gallantry.

'It was very cruel, I know,' she said, still looking out—and said with such calm disdain, that the major was discomfited, and could think of nothing in reply.

'Major Bagstock, my darling Edith,' drawled her mother, 'who is generally the most useless and disagreeable creature in the world: as you know—'

'It is surely not worth while, mamma,' said Edith, looking round, 'to observe these forms of speech. We are quite alone. We know each other.'

The quiet scorn that sat upon her handsome face—a scorn that evidently lighted on herself, no less than them—was so intense and deep, that her mother's simper, for the instant, though of a hardy constitution, drooped before it.

'My darling girl,' she began again.

'Not woman yet?' said Edith, with a smile.

'How very odd you are to-day, my dear! Pray let me say, my love, that Major Bagstock has brought the kindest of notes from Mr. Dombey, proposing that we should breakfast with him to-morrow, and ride to Warwick and Kenilworth. Will you go, Edith?'

'Will I go!' she repeated, turning very red, and breathing quickly as she looked round at her mother.

'I knew you would, my own,' observed the latter carelessly. 'It is, as you say, quite a form to ask. Here is Mr. Dombey's letter, Edith.'

'Thank you. I have no desire to read it,' was her answer.

'Then perhaps I had better answer it myself,' said

JOE B. IS SLY, SIR; DEVILISH SLY.

Mrs. Skewton, 'though I had thought of asking *you* to be my secretary, darling.' As Edith made no movement and no answer, Mrs. Skewton begged the major to wheel her little table nearer, and to set open the desk it contained, and to take out pen and paper for her; all which congenial offices of gallantry the major discharged, with much submission and devotion.

'Your regards, Edith, my dear?' said Mrs. Skewton, pausing, pen in hand, at the postscript.

'What you will, mamma,' she answered, without turning her head, and with supreme indifference.

Mrs. Skewton wrote what she would, without seeking for any more explicit directions, and handed her letter to the major, who receiving it as a precious charge, made a show of laying it near his heart, but was fain to put it in the pocket of his pantaloons on account of the insecurity of his waistcoat. The major then took a very polished and chivalrous farewell of both ladies, which the elder one acknowledged in her usual manner, while the younger, sitting with her face addressed to the window, bent her head so slightly that it would have been a greater compliment to the major to have made no sign at all, and to have left him to infer that he had not been heard or thought of.

'As to alteration in her, sir,' mused the major on his way back; on which expedition—the afternoon being sunny and hot—he ordered the native and the light baggage to the front, and walked in the shadow of that expatriated prince: 'as to alteration, sir, and pining, and so forth, that won't go down with Joseph Bagstock. None of that, sir. It won't do here. But as to there being something of a division between 'em—or a gulf as the mother calls it—damme, sir, that seems true enough. And it's odd enough! Well, sir!' panted the major, 'Edith Granger and Dombey are well matched; let 'em fight it out! Bagstock backs the winner!'

The major, by saying these latter words aloud, in the vigour of his thoughts, caused the unhappy native to stop, and turn round, in the belief that he was personally addressed. Exasperated to the last degree by this act of insubordination, the major (though he was swelling with enjoyment of his own humour, at the moment of its occurrence) instantly thrust his cane among the native's ribs, and continued to stir him up, at short intervals, all the way to the hotel.

Nor was the major less exasperated as he dressed for dinner, during which operation the dark servant underwent the pelting of a shower of miscellaneous objects, varying in size from a boot to a hairbrush, and including everything that came within his master's reach. For the major plumed himself on having the native in a perfect state of drill, and visited the least departure from strict discipline with this kind of fatigue duty. Add to this, that he maintained the native about his person as a counter-irritant against the gout, and all other vexations, mental as well as bodily; and the native would appear to have earned his pay—which was not large.

At length, the major having disposed of all the missiles that were convenient to his hand, and having called the native so many new names as must have given him great occasion to marvel at the resources of the English language, submitted to have his cravat put on; and being dressed, and finding himself in a brisk flow of spirits after this exercise, went downstairs to enliven 'Dombey' and his right-hand man.

Dombey was not yet in the room, but the right-hand man was there, and his dental treasures were, as usual, ready for the major.

'Well, sir!' said the major. 'How have you passed the time since I had the happiness of meeting you? Have you walked at all?'

'A saunter of barely half an hour's duration,' returned Carker. 'We have been so much occupied.'

'Business, eh?' said the major.

'A variety of little matters necessary to be gone through,' replied Carker. 'But do you know—this is quite unusual with me, educated in a distrustful school, and who am not generally disposed to be communicative,' he said, breaking off, and speaking in a charming tone of frankness—'but I feel quite confidential with you, Major Bagstock.'

'You do me honour, sir,' returned the major. 'You may be.'

'Do you know, then,' pursued Carker, 'that I have not found my friend—*our* friend, I ought rather to call him—'

'Meaning Dombey, sir?' cried the major. 'You see me, Mr. Carker, standing here! J. B.?'

He was puffy enough to see, and blue enough; and Mr. Carker intimated that he had that pleasure.

'Then you see a man, sir, who would go through fire and water to serve Dombey,' returned Major Bagstock.

Mr. Carker smiled, and said he was sure of it. 'Do you know, Major,' he proceeded: 'to resume where I left off: that I have not found our friend so attentive to business to-day, as usual?'

'No?' observed the delighted major.

'I have found him a little abstracted, and with his attention disposed to wander,' said Carker.

'By Jove, sir,' cried the major, 'there 's a lady in the case.'

'Indeed, I begin to believe there really is,' returned Carker; 'I thought you might be jesting when you seemed to hint at it; for I know you military men—'

The major gave the horse's cough, and shook his head and shoulders, as much as to say, 'Well! we *are* gay dogs, there 's no denying.' He then seized Mr. Carker by the button-hole, and with starting eyes whispered in his ear, that she was a woman of extraordinary charms, sir. That she was a young widow, sir. That she was of a fine family, sir. That Dombey was over head and ears in love with her, sir, and that it would be a good match on both sides; for she had beauty, blood, and talent, and Dombey had fortune; and what more could any couple have? Hearing Mr. Dombey's footsteps without, the major cut himself short by saying, that Mr. Carker would see her to-morrow morning, and would judge for himself; and between his mental excitement, and the exertion of saying all this in wheezy whispers, the major sat gurgling in the throat and watering at the eyes, until dinner was ready.

The major, like some other noble animals, exhibited himself to great advantage at feeding time. On this occasion, he shone resplendent at one end of the table, supported by the milder lustre of Mr. Dombey at the other; while Carker on one side lent his ray to either light, or suffered it to merge into both, as occasion arose.

During the first course or two, the major was usually grave; for the native, in obedience to general orders, secretly issued, collected every sauce and cruet round him, and gave him a great deal to do, in taking out the stoppers, and mixing up the contents in his plate. Besides which, the native had private zests and flavours on a side-table, with which the major daily scorched himself; to say nothing of strange machines out of which he spirited unknown liquids into the major's drink. But on this occasion, Major Bagstock, even amidst these many occupations, found time to be social; and his sociality consisted in excessive slyness for the behoof of Mr. Carker, and the betrayal of Mr. Dombey's state of mind.

'Dombey,' said the major, 'you don't eat; what 's the matter?'

'Thank you,' returned that gentleman, 'I am doing very well; I have no great appetite to-day.'

'Why, Dombey, what 's become of it?' asked the major. 'Where 's it gone? You haven't left it with our friends, I 'll swear, for I can answer for their having none to-day at luncheon. I can answer for one of 'em, at least: I won't say which.'

Then the major winked at Carker, and became so frightfully sly, that his dark attendant was obliged to pat him on the back, without orders, or he would probably have disappeared under the table.

In a later stage of the dinner: that is to say, when the native stood at the major's elbow ready to serve the first bottle of champagne; the major became still slyer.

'Fill this to the brim, you scoundrel,' said the major, holding up his glass. 'Fill Mr. Carker's to the brim too. And Mr. Dombey's too. By Gad, gentlemen,' said the major, winking at his new friend, while Mr. Dombey looked into his plate with a conscious air, 'we 'll consecrate this glass of wine to a divinity whom Joe is proud to know, and at a distance humbly and reverently to admire. Edith,' said the major, 'is her name; angelic Edith!'

'To angelic Edith!' cried the smiling Carker.

'Edith, by all means,' said Mr. Dombey.

The entrance of the waiters with new dishes caused the major to be slyer yet, but in a more serious vein. 'For though among ourselves, Joe Bagstock mingles jest and earnest on this subject, sir,' said the major, laying his finger on his lips, and speaking half apart to Carker, 'he holds that name too sacred to be made the property of these fellows, or of any fellows. Not a word, sir, while they are here!'

This was respectful and becoming on the major's part, and Mr. Dombey plainly felt it so. Although embarrassed in his own frigid way, by the major's allusions, Mr. Dombey had no objection to such rallying, it was clear, but rather courted it. Perhaps the major had been pretty near the truth, when he had divined that morning that the great man who was too haughty formally to consult with, or confide in his prime minister, on such a matter, yet wished him to be fully possessed of it. Let this be how it may, he often glanced at Mr. Carker while the major plied his light artillery, and seemed watchful of its effect upon him.

But the major, having secured an attentive listener, and a smiler who had not his match in all the world—'in short, a de-vilish intelligent and agreeable fellow,' as he often afterwards declared—was not going to let him off with a little slyness personal to Mr. Dombey. Therefore, on the removal of the cloth, the major developed himself as a choice spirit in the broader and more comprehensive range of narrating regimental stories, and cracking regimental jokes, which he did with such prodigal exuberance, that Carker was (or feigned to be) quite exhausted with laughter and admiration: while Mr. Dombey looked on over his starched cravat, like the major's proprietor, or like a stately showman who was glad to see his bear dancing well.

When the major was too hoarse with meat and drink, and the display of his social powers, to render himself intelligible any longer, they adjourned to coffee. After which, the major inquired of Mr.

Carker the manager, with little apparent hope of an answer in the affirmative, if he played picquet.

'Yes, I play picquet a little,' said Mr. Carker.

'Backgammon, perhaps?' observed the major, hesitating.

'Yes, I play backgammon a little too,' replied the man of teeth.

'Carker plays at all games, I believe,' said Mr. Dombey, laying himself on a sofa like a man of wood without a hinge or a joint in him; 'and plays them well.'

In sooth, he played the two in question, to such perfection, that the major was astonished, and asked him, at random, if he played chess.

'Yes, I play chess a little,' answered Carker. 'I have sometimes played, and won a game—it 's a mere trick—without seeing the board.'

'By Gad, sir!' said the major, staring, 'you are a contrast to Dombey, who plays nothing.'

'Oh! *He!*' returned the manager. '*He* has never had occasion to acquire such little arts. To men like me, they are sometimes useful. As at present, Major Bagstock, when they enable me to take a hand with you.'

It might be only the false mouth, so smooth and wide; and yet there seemed to lurk beneath the humility and subserviency of this short speech, a something like a snarl; and, for a moment, one might have thought that the white teeth were prone to bite the hand they fawned upon. But the major thought nothing about it; and Mr. Dombey lay meditating with his eyes half shut, during the whole of the play, which lasted until bed-time.

By that time, Mr. Carker, though the winner, had mounted high into the major's good opinion, insomuch that when he left the major at his own room before going to bed, the major as a special attention, sent the native—who always rested on a mattress spread upon the ground at his master's door—along the gallery, to light him to his room in state.

There was a faint blur on the surface of the mirror in Mr. Carker's chamber, and its reflection was, perhaps, a false one. But it showed, that night, the image of a man, who saw, in his fancy, a crowd of people slumbering on the ground at his feet, like the poor native at his master's door: who picked his way among them: looking down, maliciously enough: but trod upon no upturned face—as yet.

## CHAPTER XXVII

### DEEPER SHADOWS

Mr. Carker the manager rose with the lark, and went out, walking in the summer day. His meditations—and he meditated with contracted brows while he strolled along—hardly seemed to soar as high as the lark, or to mount in that direction; rather they kept close to their nest upon the earth, and looked about, among the dust and worms. But there was not a bird in the air, singing unseen, farther beyond the reach of human eye than Mr. Carker's thoughts. He had his face so perfectly under control, that few could say more, in distinct terms, of its expression, than that it smiled or that it pondered. It pondered now, intently. As the lark rose higher, he sank deeper in thought. As the lark poured out her melody clearer and stronger, he fell into a graver and profounder silence. At length, when the lark came headlong down, with an accumulating stream of song, and dropped among the green wheat near him, rippling in the breath of the morning like a river, he sprang up from his reverie, and looked round with a sudden smile, as courteous and as soft as if it had had numerous observers to propitiate; nor did he relapse, after being thus awakened; but clearing his face, like one who bethought himself that it might otherwise wrinkle and tell tales, went smiling on, as if for practice.

Perhaps with an eye to first impressions, Mr. Carker was very carefully and trimly dressed, that morning. Though always somewhat formal, in his dress, in imitation of the great man whom he served, he stopped short of the extent of Mr. Dombey's stiffness; at once perhaps because he knew it to be ludicrous, and because in doing so he found another means of expressing his sense of the difference and distance between them. Some people quoted him indeed, in this respect, as a pointed commentary, and not a flattering one, on his icy patron—but the world is prone to misconstruction, and Mr. Carker was not accountable for its bad propensity.

Clean and florid: with his light complexion, fading as it were, in the sun, and his dainty step enhancing the softness of the turf: Mr. Carker the manager strolled about meadows, and green lanes, and glided among avenues of trees, until it was time to return to breakfast. Taking a nearer way back, Mr. Carker pursued it, airing his teeth, and said aloud as he did so, 'Now to see the second Mrs. Dombey!'

He hath strolled beyond the town, and re-entered it by a pleasant walk, where there was a deep shade of leafy trees, and where there were a few benches here and there for those who chose to rest. It not being a place of general resort at any hour, and wearing at that time of the still morning the air of being quite deserted and retired, Mr. Carker had it, or thought he had it, all to himself. So, with the whim of an idle man, to whom there yet remained twenty minutes for reaching a destination easily accessible in ten, Mr. Carker threaded the great boles of the trees, and went passing in and out, before this one and behind that, weaving a chain of footsteps on the dewy ground.

But he found he was mistaken in supposing there was no one in the grove, for as he softly rounded the trunk of one large tree, on which the obdurate bark was knotted and over-lapped like the hide of a rhinoceros or some kindred monster of the ancient days before the Flood, he saw an unexpected figure sitting on a bench near at hand, about which, in another moment, he would have wound the chain he was making.

It was that of a lady, elegantly dressed and very handsome, whose dark proud eyes were fixed upon the ground, and in whom some passion or struggle was raging. For as she sat looking down, she held a corner of her under-lip within her mouth, her bosom heaved, her nostril quivered, her head trembled, indignant tears were on her cheek, and her foot was set upon the moss as though she would have crushed it into nothing. And yet almost the salf-same glance that showed him this, showed him the self-same lady rising with a scornful air of weariness and lassitude, and turning away with nothing expressed in face or figure but careless beauty and imperious disdain.

A withered and very ugly old woman, dressed not so much like a gipsy as like any of that medley race of vagabonds who tramp about the country, begging, and stealing, and tinkering, and weaving rushes, by turns, or all together, had been observing the lady, too; for, as she rose, this second figure strangely confronting the first, scrambled up from the ground—out of it, it almost appeared—and stood in the way.

'Let me tell your fortune, my pretty lady,' said the old woman, munching with her jaws, as if the Death's head beneath her yellow skin were impatient to get out.

'I can tell it for myself,' was the reply.

'Aye, aye, pretty lady; but not right. You didn't tell it right when you were sitting there. I see you! Give me a piece of silver, pretty lady, and I'll tell your fortune true. There's riches, pretty lady, in your face.'

'I know,' returned the lady, passing her with a dark smile, and a proud step. 'I knew it before.'

'What! You won't give me nothing?' cried the old woman. 'You won't give me nothing to tell your fortune, pretty lady? How much will you give me *not* to tell it, then? Give me something, or I'll call it after you!' croaked the old woman, passionately.

Mr. Carker, whom the lady was about to pass close, slinking against his tree as she crossed to gain the path, advanced so as to meet her, and pulling off his hat as she went by, bade the old woman hold her peace. The lady acknowledged his interference with an inclination of the head, and went her way.

'You give me something then, or I'll call it after her!' screamed the old woman, throwing up her arms, and pressing forward against his outstretched hand. 'Or come,' she added, dropping her voice suddenly, looking at him earnestly, and seeming in a moment to forget the object of her wrath, 'give me something, or I'll call it after *you!*'

'After *me,* old lady!' returned the manager, putting his hand in his pocket.

'Yes,' said the woman, steadfast in her scrutiny, and holding out her shrivelled hand. '*I* know!'

'What do you know?' demanded Carker, throwing

her a shilling. 'Do you know who the handsome lady is?'

Munching like that sailor's wife of yore, who had chestnuts in her lap, and scowling like the witch who asked for some in vain, the old woman picked the shilling up, and going backwards, like a crab, or like a heap of crabs: for her alternately expanding and contracting hands might have represented two of that species, and her creeping face, some half a dozen more: crouched on the veinous root of an old tree, pulled out a short black pipe from within the crown of her bonnet, lighted it with a match, and smoked in silence, looking fixedly at her questioner.

Mr. Carker laughed, and turned upon his heel.

'Good!' said the old woman. 'One child dead, and one child living: one wife dead, and one wife coming. Go and meet her!'

In spite of himself, the manager looked round again, and stopped. The old woman, who had not removed her pipe, and was munching and mumbling while she smoked, as if in conversation with an invisible familiar, pointed with her finger in the direction he was going, and laughed.

'What was that you said, Beldamite?' he demanded.

The woman mumbled, and chattered, and smoked, and still pointed before him; but remained silent. Muttering a farewell that was not complimentary, Mr. Carker pursued his way; but as he turned out of that place, and looked over his shoulder at the root of the old tree, he could yet see the finger pointing before him, and thought he heard the woman screaming, 'Go and meet her!'

Preparations for a choice repast were completed, he found, at the hotel; and Mr. Dombey, and the major, and the breakfast, were awaiting the ladies.

Individual constitution has much to do with the development of such facts, no doubt; but in this case, appetite carried it hollow over the tender passion; Mr. Dombey being very cool and collected, and the major fretting and fuming in a state of violent heat and irritation. At length the door was thrown open by the native, and, after a pause, occupied by her languishing along the gallery, a very blooming, but not very youthful lady, appeared.

'My dear Mr. Dombey,' said the lady, 'I am afraid we are late, but Edith has been out already looking for a favourable point of view for a sketch, and kept me waiting for her. Falsest of majors,' giving him her little finger, 'how do you do?'

'Mrs. Skewton,' said Mr. Dombey, 'let me gratify my friend Carker': Mr. Dombey unconsciously emphasised the word friend, as saying 'no really; I do allow him to take credit for that distinction'; 'by presenting him to you. You have heard me mention Mr. Carker.'

'I am charmed, I am sure,' said Mrs. Skewton, graciously.

Mr. Carker was charmed, of course. Would he have been more charmed on Mr. Dombey's behalf, if Mrs. Skewton had been (as he at first supposed her) the Edith whom they had toasted overnight?

'Why, where for Heaven's sake, is Edith?' exclaimed Mrs. Skewton, looking round. 'Still at the door, giving Withers orders about the mounting of those drawings! My dear Mr. Dombey, will you have the kindness—'

Mr. Dombey was already gone to seek her. Next moment he returned, bearing on his arm the same elegantly dressed and very handsome lady whom Mr. Carker had encountered underneath the trees.

'Carker—' began Mr. Dombey. But their recognition of each other was so manifest, that Mr. Dombey stopped surprised.

'I am obliged to the gentleman,' said Edith, with a stately bend, 'for sparing me some annoyance from an importunate beggar just now.'

'I am obliged to my good fortune,' said Mr. Carker, bowing low, 'for the opportunity of rendering so slight a service to one whose servant I am proud to be.'

As her eye rested on him for an instant, and then lighted on the ground, he saw in its bright and searching glance a suspicion that he had not come up at the moment of his interference, but had secretly observed her sooner. As he saw that, she saw in *his* eye that her distrust was not without foundation.

'Really,' cried Mrs. Skewton, who had taken this opportunity of inspecting Mr. Carker through her glass, and satisfying herself (as she lisped audibly to the major) that he was all heart; 'really now, this is one of the most enchanting coincidences that I ever heard of. The idea! My dearest Edith, there is such an obvious destiny in it, that really one might almost be induced to cross one's arms upon one's frock, and say, like those wicked Turks, there is no What's-his-name but Thingummy, and What-you-may-call-it is his prophet!'

Edith deigned no revision of this extraordinary quotation from the Koran, but Mr. Dombey felt it necessary to offer a few polite remarks.

'It gives me great pleasure,' said Mr. Dombey, with cumbrous gallantry, 'that a gentleman so nearly connected with myself as Carker is, should have had the honour and happiness of rendering the least assistance to Mrs. Granger.' Mr. Dombey bowed to her. 'But it gives me some pain, and it occasions me to be really envious of Carker'; he unconsciously laid stress on these words, as sensible that they must appear to involve a very surprising proposition; 'envious of Carker, that I had not that honour and that happiness myself.' Mr. Dombey bowed again. Edith, saving for a curl of her lip, was motionless.

'By the Lord, sir,' cried the major, bursting into speech at sight of the waiter, who was come to announce breakfast, 'it 's an extraordinary thing to me that no one can have the honour and happiness of shooting all such beggars through the head without being brought to book for it. But here 's an arm for Mrs. Granger if she 'll do J. B. the honour to accept it; and the greatest service Joe can render you, ma'am, just now, is, to lead you in to table!'

With this, the major gave his arm to Edith; Mr. Dombey led the way with Mrs. Skewton; Mr. Carker went last, smiling on the party.

'I am quite rejoiced, Mr. Carker,' said the lady-mother, at breakfast, after another approving survey of him through her glass, 'that you have timed your visit so happily, as to go with us to-day. It is the most enchanting expedition!'

'Any expedition would be enchanting in such society,' returned Carker; 'but I believe it is, in itself, full of interest.'

'Oh!' cried Mrs. Skewton, with a faded little scream of rapture, 'the Castle is charming!—associations of the Middle Ages—and all that—which is so truly exquisite. Don't you dote upon the Middle Ages, Mr. Carker?'

'Very much, indeed,' said Mr. Carker.

'Such charming times!' cried Cleopatra. 'So full of faith! So vigorous and forcible! So picturesque! So perfectly removed from commonplace! Oh dear! If they would only leave us a little more of the poetry of existence in these terrible days!'

Mrs. Skewton was looking sharp after Mr. Dombey all the time she said this, who was looking at Edith: who was listening, but who never lifted up her eyes.

'We are dreadfully real, Mr. Carker,' said Mrs. Skewton; 'are we not?'

Few people had less reason to complain of their reality than Cleopatra, who had as much that was false about her as could well go to the composition of anybody with a real individual existence. But Mr. Carker commiserated our reality nevertheless, and agreed that we were very hardly used in that regard.

'Pictures at the Castle, quite divine!' said Cleopatra. 'I hope you dote upon pictures?'

'I assure you, Mrs. Skewton,' said Mr. Dombey, with solemn encouragement of his manager, 'that Carker has a very good taste for pictures; quite a natural power of appreciating them. He is a very creditable artist himself. He will be delighted, I am sure, with Mrs. Granger's taste and skill.'

'Damme, sir!' cried Major Bagstock, 'my opinion is, that you 're the admirable Carker, and can do anything.'

'Oh!' smiled Carker, with humility, 'you are much too sanguine, Major Bagstock. I can do very little. But Mr. Dombey is so generous in his estimation of any trivial accomplishment a man like myself may find it almost necessary to acquire, and to which, in his very different sphere, he is far superior, that—' Mr. Carker shrugged his shoulders, deprecating further praise, and said no more.

All this time, Edith never raised her eyes, unless to

glance towards her mother when that lady's fervent spirit shone forth in words. But as Carker ceased, she looked at Mr. Dombey for a moment. For a moment only; but with a transient gleam of scornful wonder on her face, not lost on one observer, who was smiling round the board.

Mr. Dombey caught the dark eye-lash in its descent, and took the opportunity of arresting it.

'You have been to Warwick often, unfortunately?' said Mr. Dombey.

'Several times.'

'The visit will be tedious to you, I am afraid.'

'Oh no; not at all.'

'Ah! You are like your cousin Feenix, my dearest Edith,' said Mrs. Skewton. 'He has been to Warwick Castle fifty times, if he has been there once; yet if he came to Leamington to-morrow—I wish he would, dear angel!—he would make his fifty-second visit next day.'

'We are all enthusiastic, are we not, mamma?' said Edith, with a cold smile.

'Too much so, for our peace, perhaps, my dear,' returned her mother; 'but we won't complain. Our own emotions are our recompense. If, as your cousin Feenix says, the sword wears out that what 's-its-name—'

'The scabbard, perhaps,' said Edith.

'Exactly—a little too fast, it is because it is bright and glowing, you know, my dearest love.'

Mrs. Skewton heaved a gentle sigh, supposed to cast a shadow on the surface of that dagger of lath, whereof her susceptible bosom was the sheath: and leaning her head on one side, in the Cleopatra manner, looked with pensive affection on her darling child.

Edith had turned her face towards Mr. Dombey

when he first addressed her, and had remained in that attitude, while speaking to her mother, and while her mother spoke to her, as though offering him her attention, if he had anything more to say. There was something in the manner of this simple courtesy: almost defiant, and giving it the character of being rendered on compulsion, or as a matter of traffic to which she was a reluctant party: again not lost upon that same observer who was smiling round the board. It set him thinking of her as he had first seen her, when she had believed herself to be alone among the trees.

Mr. Dombey having nothing else to say, proposed—the breakfast being now finished, and the major gorged, like any boa constrictor—that they should start. A barouche being in waiting, according to the orders of that gentleman, the two ladies, the major and himself, took their seats in it; the native and the wan page mounted the box, Mr. Towlinson being left behind; and Mr. Carker, on horseback, brought up the rear.

Mr. Carker cantered behind the carriage, at the distance of a hundred yards or so, and watched it, during all the ride, as if he were a cat, indeed, and its four occupants, mice. Whether he looked to one side of the road, or to the other—over distant landscape, with its smooth undulations, windmills, corn, grass, bean-fields, wild-flowers, farm-yards, hay-ricks, and the spire among the wood—or upwards in the sunny air, where butterflies were sporting round his head, and birds were pouring out their songs—or downward, where the shadows of the branches interlaced, and made a trembling carpet on the road—or onward, where the overhanging trees formed aisles and arches, dim with the softened light that steeped through leaves—one corner of his eye was ever on the formal head of Mr. Dombey, addressed towards him, and the feather in the bonnet, drooping so neglectfully and scornfully between them; much as he had seen the haughty eyelids droop; not least so, when the face met that now fronting it. Once, and once only, did his wary glance release these objects; and that was, when a leap over a low hedge, and a gallop across a field, enabled him to anticipate the carriage coming by the road, and to be standing ready, at the journey's end, to hand the ladies out. Then, and but then, he met her glance for an instant in her first surprise; but when he touched her, in alighting, with his soft white hand, it over-looked him altogether as before.

Mrs. Skewton was bent on taking charge of Mr. Carker herself, and showing him the beauties of the Castle. She was determined to have his arm, and the major's too. It would do that incorrigible creature: who was the most barbarous infidel in point of poetry: good to be in such company. This chance arrangement left Mr. Dombey at liberty to escort Edith: which he did, stalking before them through the apartments with a gentlemanly solemnity.

'Those darling bygone times, Mr. Carker,' said Cleopatra, 'with their delicious fortresses, and their dear old dungeons, and their delightful places of torture, and their romantic vengeances, and their picturesque assaults and sieges, and everything that makes life truly charming! How dreadfully we have degenerated!'

'Yes, we have fallen off deplorably,' said Mr. Carker.

The peculiarity of their conversation was, that Mrs. Skewton, in spite of her ecstasies, and Mr. Carker, in spite of his urbanity, were both intent on watching Mr. Dombey and Edith. With all their conversational endowments, they spoke somewhat distractedly, and a random in consequence.

'We have no faith left, positively,' said Mrs. Skewton advancing her shrivelled ear; for Mr. Dombey was saying something to Edith. 'We have no faith in the dear old barons, who were the most delightful creatures—or in the dear old priests, who were the most warlike of men—or even in the days of that inestimable Queen Bess, upon the wall there, which were so extremely golden. Dear creature! She was all heart! And that charming father of hers! I hope you dote on Harry the Eighth!'

'I admire him very much,' said Carker.

'So bluff!' cried Mrs. Skewton, 'wasn't he? So burly. So truly English. Such a picture, too, he makes, with his dear little peepy eyes, and his benevolent chin!'

'Ah, ma'am!' said Carker, stopping short; 'but if you speak of pictures, there 's a composition! What gallery in the world can produce the counterpart of that!'

As the smiling gentleman thus spake, he pointed through a doorway to where Mr. Dombey and Edith were standing alone in the centre of another room.

They were not interchanging a word or a look. Standing together, arm in arm, they had the appearance of being more divided than if seas had rolled between them. There was a difference even in the pride of the two, that removed them farther from each other, than if one had been the proudest and the other the humblest specimen of humanity in all creation. He, self-important, unbending, formal, austere. She, lovely and graceful in an uncommon degree, but totally regardless of herself and him and everything around, and spurning her own attractions with her haughty brow and lip, as if they were a badge or livery she hated. So unmatched were they, and opposed, so forced and linked together by a chain which adverse hazard and mischance had forged: that fancy might have imagined the pictures on the walls around them, startled by the unnatural conjunction, and observant of it in their several expressions. Grim knights and warriors looked scowling on them. A churchman, with his hand upraised, denounced the mockery of such a couple coming to God's altar. Quiet waters in landscapes, with the sun reflected in their depths, asked, if better means of escape were not at hand, was there no drowning left?' Ruins cried, 'Look here, and see what We are, wedded to uncongenial Time!' Animals, opposed by nature, worried one another, as a moral to them. Loves and Cupids took to flight afraid, and Martyrdom had no such torment in its painted history of suffering.

Nevertheless, Mrs. Skewton was so charmed by the sight to which Mr. Carker invoked her attention, that she could not refrain from saying, half aloud, how sweet, how very full of soul it was! Edith, overhearing, looked round, and flushed indignant scarlet to her hair.

'My dearest Edith knows I was admiring her!' said Cleopatra, tapping her, almost timidly, on the back with her parasol. 'Sweet pet!'

Again Mr. Carker saw the strife he had witnessed so unexpectedly among the trees. Again he saw the haughty languor and indifference come over it, and hide it like a cloud.

She did not raise her eyes to him; but with a slight peremptory motion of them, seemed to bid her mother come near. Mrs. Skewton thought it expedient to understand the hint, and advancing quickly, with her two cavaliers, kept near her daughter from that time.

Mr. Carker now, having nothing to distract his attention, began to discourse upon the pictures, and to select the best, and point them out to Mr. Dombey: speaking with his usual familiar recognition of Mr. Dombey's greatness, and rendering homage by adjusting his eye-glass for him, or finding out the right place in his catalogue, or holding his stick, or the like. These services did not so much originate with Mr. Carker, in truth, as with Mr. Dombey himself, who was apt to assert his chieftainship by saying, with subdued authority, and in an easy way—for him—'Here, Carker, have the goodness to assist me, will you?' which the smiling gentleman always did with pleasure.

They made the tour of the pictures, the walls, crow's nest, and so forth; and as they were still one little party, and the major was rather in the shade: being sleepy during the process of digestion: Mr. Carker became communicative and agreeable. At first, he addressed himself for the most part to Mrs. Skewton; but as that sensitive lady was in such ecstasies with the works of art, after the first quarter of an hour, that she could do nothing but yawn (they were such perfect inspirations, she observed as a reason for that mark of rapture), he transferred his attentions to Mr. Dombey. Mr. Dombey said little beyond an occasional 'Very true, Carker,' or 'Indeed, Carker,' but he tacitly encouraged Carker to proceed, and inwardly approved of his behaviour very much: deeming it as well that somebody should talk, and thinking that his remarks, which were, as one might say, a branch of the parent establishment, might amuse Mrs. Granger. Mr. Carker, who possessed an excellent discretion, never took the liberty of addressing that lady, direct; but she seemed to listen, though she never looked at him; and once or twice, when he was emphatic in his peculiar humility, the twilight smile stole over her face, not as a light, but as a deep black shadow.

Warwick Castle being at length pretty well exhausted, and the major very much so: to say nothing of Mrs. Skewton, whose peculiar demonstrations of delight had become very frequent indeed: the carriage was again put in requisition, and they rode to several admired points of view in the neighbourhood. Mr. Dombey ceremoniously observed of one of these, that a sketch, however slight, from the fair hand of Mrs. Granger, would be a remembrance to him of that agreeable day: though he wanted no artificial remembrance, he was sure (here Mr. Dombey made another of his bows), which he must always highly value. Withers the lean having Edith's sketch-book under his arm, was immediately called upon by Mrs. Skewton to produce the same: and the carriage stopped, that Edith might make the drawing, which Mr. Dombey was to put away among his treasures.

'But I am afraid I trouble you too much,' said Mr. Dombey.

'By no means. Where would you wish it taken from?' she answered, turning to him with the same enforced attention as before.

Mr. Dombey, with another bow, which cracked the starch in his cravat, would beg to leave that to the artist.

'I would rather you chose for yourself,' said Edith.

'Suppose then,' said Mr. Dombey, 'we say from here. It appears a good spot for the purpose, or—Carker, what do *you* think?'

There happened to be in the foreground, at some little distance, a grove of trees, not unlike that in which Mr. Carker had made his chain of footsteps in the morning, and with a seat under one tree, greatly resembling, in the general character of its situation, the point where his chain had broken.

'Might I venture to suggest to Mrs. Granger,' said Carker, 'that that is an interesting—almost a curious—point of view?'

She followed the direction of his riding-whip with her eyes, and raised them quickly to his face. It was the second glance they had exchanged since their introduction; and would have been exactly like the first, but that its expression was plainer.

'Will you like that?' said Edith to Mr. Dombey.

'I shall be charmed,' said Mr. Dombey to Edith.

Therefore the carriage was driven to the spot where Mr. Dombey was to be charmed; and Edith, without moving from her seat, and opening her sketch-book with her usual proud indifference, began to sketch.

'My pencils are all pointless,' she said, stopping and turning them over.

'Pray allow me,' said Mr. Dombey. 'Or Carker will do it better, as he understands these things. Carker, have the goodness to see to these pencils for Mrs. Granger.'

Mr. Carker rode up close to the carriage-door on Mrs. Granger's side, and letting the rein fall on his horse's neck, took the pencils from her hand with a smile and a bow, and sat in the saddle leisurely mending them. Having done so, he begged to be allowed to hold them, and to hand them to her as they were required; and thus Mr. Carker, with many commendations of Mrs. Granger's extraordinary skill—especially in trees—remained close at her side, looking over the drawing as she made it. Mr. Dombey in the meantime stood bolt upright in the carriage like a highly respectable ghost, looking on too; while Cleopatra and the major dallied as two ancient doves might do.

'Are you satisfied with that, or shall I finish it a little more?' said Edith, showing the sketch to Mr. Dombey.

Mr. Dombey begged that it might not be touched; it was perfection.

'It is most extraordinary,' said Carker, bringing every one of his red gums to bear upon his praise. 'I was not prepared for anything so beautiful, and so unusual altogether.'

This might have applied to the sketcher no less than to the sketch; but Mr. Carker's manner was openness itself—not as to his mouth alone, but as to his whole spirit. So it continued to be while the drawing was laid aside for Mr. Dombey, and while the sketching materials were put up; then he handed in the pencils (which were received with a distant acknowledgment of his help, but without a look), and tightening his rein, fell back, and followed the carriage again.

Thinking, perhaps, as he rode, that even this trivial sketch had been made and delivered to its owner, as if it had been bargained for and bought. Thinking, perhaps, that although she had assented with such perfect readiness to his request, her haughty face, bent over the drawing, or glancing at the distant objects represented in it, had been the face of a proud woman, engaged in a sordid and miserable transaction. Thinking, perhaps, of such things: but smiling certainly, and while he seemed to look about him freely, in enjoyment of the air and exercise, keeping always that sharp corner of his eye upon the carriage.

A stroll among the haunted ruins of Kenilworth, and more rides to more points of view; most of which,

Mrs. Skewton reminded Mr. Dombey, Edith had already sketched, as he had seen in looking over her drawings: brought the day's expedition to a close. Mrs. Skewton and Edith were driven to their own lodgings; Mr. Carker was graciously invited by Cleopatra to return thither with Mr. Dombey and the major, in the evening, to hear some of Edith's music; and the three gentlemen returned to their hotel to dinner.

The dinner was the counterpart of yesterday's, except that the major was twenty-four hours more triumphant and less mysterious. Edith was toasted again. Mr. Dombey was again agreeably embarrassed. And Mr. Carker was full of interest and praise.

There were no other visitors at Mrs. Skewton's. Edith's drawings were strewn about the room, a little more abundantly than usual perhaps; and Withers, the wan page, handed round a little stronger tea. The harp was there; the piano was there; and Edith sang and played. But even the music was played by Edith to Mr. Dombey's order, as it were, in the same uncompromising way. As thus.

'Edith, my dearest love,' said Mrs. Skewton, half an hour after tea, 'Mr. Dombey is dying to hear you, I know.'

'Mr. Dombey has life enough left to say so for himself, mamma, I have no doubt.'

'I shall be immensely obliged,' said Mr. Dombey.

'What do you wish?'

'Piano?' hesitated Mr. Dombey.

'Whatever you please. You have only to choose.'

Accordingly, she began with the piano. It was the same with the harp; the same with her singing; the same with the selection of the pieces that she sang and played. Such frigid and constrained, yet prompt and pointed acquiescence with the wishes he imposed upon her, and on no one else, was sufficiently remarkable to penetrate through all the mysteries of picquet, and impress itself on Mr. Carker's keen attention. Nor did he lose sight of the fact that Mr. Dombey was evidently proud of his power, and liked to show it.

Nevertheless, Mr. Carker played so well—some games with the major, and some with Cleopatra, whose vigilance of eye in respect of Mr. Dombey and Edith no lynx could have surpassed—that he even heightened his position in the lady-mother's good graces; and when on taking leave he regretted that he would be obliged to return to London next morning, Cleopatra trusted: community of feeling not being met with every day: that it was far from being the last time they would meet.

'I hope so,' said Mr. Carker, with an expressive look at the couple in the distance, as he drew towards the door, following the major. 'I think so.'

Mr. Dombey, who had taken a stately leave of Edith, bent, or made some approach to bend, over Cleopatra's couch, and said, in a low voice—

'I have requested Mrs. Granger's permission to call on her to-morrow morning—for a purpose—and she has appointed twelve o'clock. May I hope to have the pleasure of finding you at home, madam, afterwards?'

Cleopatra was so much fluttered and moved, by hearing this, of course, incomprehensible speech, that she could only shut her eyes, and shake her head, and give Mr. Dombey her hand; which Mr. Dombey, not exactly knowing what to do with, dropped.

'Dombey, come along!' cried the major, looking in at the door. 'Damme, sir, old Joe has a great mind to propose an alteration in the name of the Royal

Hotel, and that it should be called the Three Jolly Bachelors, in honour of ourselves and Carker.' With this the major slapped Mr. Dombey on the back, and winking over his shoulder at the ladies, with a frightful tendency of blood to the head, and carried him off.

Mrs. Skewton reposed on her sofa, and Edith sat apart, by her harp, in silence. The mother, trifling with her fan, looked stealthily at the daughter more than once, but the daughter, brooding gloomily with downcast eyes, was not to be disturbed.

Thus they remained for a long hour, without a word, until Mrs. Skewton's maid appeared, according to custom, to prepare her gradually for night. At night, she should have been a skeleton, with dart and hour-glass, rather than a woman, this attendant; for her touch was as the touch of Death. The painted object shrivelled underneath her hand; the form collapsed, the hair dropped off, the arched dark eyebrows changed to scanty tufts of grey; the pale lips shrunk, the skin became cadaverous and loose; an old, worn, yellow nodding woman, with red eyes, alone remained in Cleopatra's place, huddled up, like a slovenly bundle, in a greasy flannel gown.

The very voice was changed, as it addressed Edith, when they were alone again.

'Why don't you tell me,' it said, sharply, 'that he is coming here to-morrow by appointment?'

'Because you know it,' returned Edith, 'mother.'

The mocking emphasis she laid on that one word!

'You know he has bought me,' she resumed. 'Or that he will, to-morrow. He has considered of his bargain; he has shown it to his friend; he is even rather proud of it; he thinks that it will suit him, and may be had sufficiently cheap; and he will buy to-morrow. God, that I have lived for this, and that I feel it!'

Compress into one handsome face the conscious self-abasement, and the burning indignation of a hundred women, strong in passion and in pride; and there it hid itself with two white shuddering arms.

'What do you mean?' returned the angry mother. 'Haven't you from a child—'

'A child!' said Edith, looking at her, 'when was I a child! What childhood did you ever leave to me? I was a woman—artful, designing, mercenary, laying snares for men—before I knew myself, or you, or even understood the base and wretched aim of every new display I learnt. You gave birth to a woman. Look upon her. She is in her pride to-night.'

And as she spoke, she struck her hand upon her beautiful bosom, as though she would have beaten down herself.

'Look at me,' she said, 'who have never known what it is to have an honest heart, and love. Look at me, taught to scheme and plot when children play; and married in my youth—an old age of design—to one for whom I had no feeling but indifference. Look at me, whom he left a widow, dying before his inheritance descended to him—a judgment on you! well deserved!—and tell me what has been my life for ten years since.'

'We have been making every effort to endeavour to secure to you a good establishment,' rejoined her mother. 'That has been your life. And now you have got it.'

'There is no slave in a market: there is no horse in a fair: so shown and offered and examined and paraded, mother, as I have been, for ten shameful years,' cried Edith, with a burning brow, and the same bitter emphasis on the one word. 'Is it not so? Have I been made the byword of all kinds of men? Have fools, have profligates, have boys, have dotards, dangled after me, and one by one rejected me, and fallen off, because you were too plain with all your cunning: yes, and too true, with all those false pretences: until we have almost come to be notorious? The licence of look and touch,' she said, with flashing eyes, 'have I submitted to it, in half the places of resort upon the map of England. Have I been hawked and vended here and there, until the last grain of self-respect is dead within me, and I loathe myself? Has *this* been my late childhood? I had none before. Do not tell me that I had, to-night, of all nights in my life!'

'You might have been well married,' said her mother, 'twenty times at least, Edith, if you had given encouragement enough.'

'No! Who takes me, refuse that I am, and as I well deserve to be,' she answered, raising her head, and trembling in her energy of shame and stormy pride, 'shall take me, as this man does, with no art of mine put forth to lure him. He sees me at the auction, and he thinks it well to buy me. Let him! When he came to view me—perhaps to bid—he required to see the roll of my accomplishments. I gave it to him. When he would have me show one of them, to justify his purchase to his men, I require of him to say which he demands, and I exhibit it. I will do no more. He makes the purchase of his own will, and with his own sense of its worth, and the power of his money; and I hope it may never disappoint him. *I* have not vaunted and pressed the bargain; neither have you, so far as I have been able to prevent you.'

'You talk strangely to-night, Edith, to your own mother.'

'It seems so to me; stranger to me than you,' said Edith. 'But my education was completed long ago. I am too old now, and have fallen too low, by degrees, to take a new course, and to stop yours, and to help myself. The germ of all that purifies a woman's breast, and makes it true and good, has never stirred in mine, and I have nothing else to sustain me when I despise myself.' There had been a touching sadness in her voice, but it was gone, when she went on to say, with a curled lip, 'So, as we are genteel and poor, I am content that we should be made rich by these means; all I say, is, I have kept the only purpose I have had the strength to form—I had almost said the power, with you at my side, mother—and have not tempted this man on.'

'This man! You speak,' said her mother, 'as if you hated him.'

'And you thought I loved him, did you not?' she answered, stopping on her way across the room, and looking round. 'Shall I tell you,' she continued, with her eyes fixed on her mother, 'who already knows us thoroughly, and reads us right, and before whom I have even less of self-respect or confidence than before my own inward self; being so much degraded by his knowledge of me?'

'This is an attack, I suppose,' returned her mother coldly, 'on poor, unfortunate what 's-his-name—Mr. Carker! Your want of self-respect and confidence, my dear, in reference to that person (who is very agreeable, it strikes me), is not likely to have much effect on your establishment. Why do you look at me so hard? Are you ill?'

Edith suddenly let fall her face, as if it had been

stung, and while she pressed her hands upon it, a terrible tremble crept over her whole frame. It was quickly gone; and with her usual step, she passed out of the room.

The maid who should have been a skeleton, then reappeared, and giving one arm to her mistress, who appeared to have taken off her manner with her charms, and to have put on paralysis with her flannel gown, collected the ashes of Cleopatra, and carried them away in the other, ready for to-morrow's revivification.

# CHAPTER XXVIII

## ALTERATIONS

'So the day has come at length, Susan,' said Florence to the excellent Nipper, 'when we are going back to our quiet home!'

Susan drew in her breath with an amount of expression not easily described, and further relieving her feelings with a smart cough, answered, 'Very quiet indeed, Miss Floy, no doubt. Excessive so.'

'When I was a child,' said Florence, thoughtfully, and after musing for some moments, 'did you ever see that gentleman who has taken the trouble to ride down here to speak to me, now three times—three times, I think, Susan?'

'Three times, miss,' returned the Nipper. 'Once when you was out walking with them Sket—'

Florence gently looked at her, and Miss Nipper checked herself.

'With Sir Barnet and his lady, I mean to say, miss, and the young gentleman. And two evenings since then.'

'When I was a child, and when company used to come to visit papa, did you ever see that gentleman at home, Susan?' asked Florence.

'Well, miss,' returned her maid, after considering, 'I really couldn't say I ever did. When your poor dear ma died, Miss Floy, I was very new in the family, you see, and *my* element': the Nipper bridled, as opining that her merits had been always designedly extinguished by Mr. Dombey: 'was the floor below the attics.'

'To be sure,' said Florence, still thoughtfully; 'you are not likely to have known who came to the house. I quite forgot.'

'Not, miss, but what we talked about the family and visitors,' said Susan, 'and but what I heard much said, although the nurse before Mrs. Richards *did* make unpleasant remarks when I was in company, and hint at "little pitchers," but that could only be attributed, poor thing,' observed Susan, with composed forbearance, 'to habits of intoxication, for which she was required to leave, and did.'

Florence, who was seated at her chamber window, with her face resting on her hand, sat looking out, and hardly seemed to hear what Susan said, she was so lost in thought.

'At all events, miss,' said Susan, 'I remember very well that this same gentleman, Mr. Carker, was almost, if not quite, as great a gentleman with your papa then, as he is now. It used to be said in the house then, miss, that he was at the head of all your pa's affairs in the City, and managed the whole, and that your pa minded him more than anybody, which, begging your pardon, Miss Floy, he might easy do, for he never minded anybody else. I knew that, "pitcher" as I might have been.'

Susan Nipper, with an injured remembrance of the

nurse before Mrs. Richards, emphasised 'pitcher' strongly.

'And that Mr. Carker has not fallen off, miss,' she pursued, 'but has stood his ground, and kept his credit with your pa, I know from what is always said among our people by that Perch, whenever he comes to the house; and though he 's the weakest weed in the world, Miss Floy, and no one can have a moment's patience with the man, he knows what goes on in the City tolerable well, and says that your pa does nothing without Mr. Carker, and leaves all to Mr. Carker, and acts according to Mr. Carker, and has Mr. Carker always at his elbow, and I do believe that he believes (that washiest of Perches!) that after your pa, the Emperor of India is the child unborn to Mr. Carker.'

Not a word of this was lost on Florence, who, with an awakened interest in Susan's speech, no longer gazed abstractedly on the prospect without, but looked at her, and listened with attention.

'Yes, Susan,' she said, when that young lady had concluded. 'He is in papa's confidence, and is his friend, I am sure.'

Florence's mind ran high on this theme, and had done for some days. Mr. Carker, in the two visits with which he had followed up his first one, had assumed a confidence between himself and her—a right on his part to be mysterious and stealthy, in telling her that the ship was still unheard of—a kind of mildly restrained power and authority over her—that made her wonder, and caused her great uneasiness. She had no means of repelling it, or of freeing herself from the web he was gradually winding about her; for that would have required some art and knowledge of the world, opposed to such address as his; and Florence had none. True, he had said no more to her than that there was no news of the ship, and that he feared the worst; but how he came to know that she was interested in the ship, and why he had no right to signify his knowledge to her, so insidiously and darkly, troubled Florence very much.

This conduct on the part of Mr. Carker, and her habit of often considering it with wonder and uneasiness, began to invest him with an uncomfortable fascination in Florence's thoughts. A more distinct remembrance of his features, voice, and manner; which she sometimes courted as a means of reducing him to the level of a real personage, capable of exerting no greater charm over her than another: did not remove the vague impression. And yet he never frowned, or looked upon her with an air of dislike or animosity, but was always smiling and serene.

Again, Florence in pursuit of her strong purpose with reference to her father, and her steady resolution to believe that she was herself unwittingly to blame for their so cold and distant relations, would recall to mind that this gentleman was his confidential friend, and would think, with an anxious heart, could her struggling tendency to dislike and fear him be a part of that misfortune in her, which had turned her father's love adrift, and left her so alone? She dreaded that it might be; sometimes believed it was: then she resolved that she would try to conquer this wrong feeling; persuaded herself that she was honoured and encouraged by the notice of her father's friend; and hoped that patient observation of him and trust in him would lead her bleeding feet along that stony road which ended in her father's heart.

Thus, with no one to advise her—for she could advise with no one without seeming to complain against him—gentle Florence tossed on an uneasy sea of doubt and hope; and Mr. Carker, like a scaly monster of the deep, swam down below, and kept his shining eye upon her.

Florence had a new reason in all this for wishing to be at home again. Her lonely life was better suited to her course of timid hope and doubt; and she feared sometimes, that in her absence she might miss some hopeful chance of testifying her affection for her father. Heaven knows, she might have set her mind at rest, poor child! on this last point; but her slighted love was fluttering within her, and, even in her sleep, it flew away in dreams, and nestled, like a wandering bird come home, upon her father's neck.

Of Walter she thought often. Ah! how often, when the night was gloomy, and the wind was blowing round the house! But hope was strong in her breast. It is so difficult for the young and ardent, even with such experience as hers, to imagine youth and ardour quenched like a weak flame, and the bright day of life merging into night, at noon, that hope was strong yet. Her tears fell frequently for Walter's sufferings; but rarely for his supposed death, and never long.

She had written to the old instrument-maker, but had received no answer to her note: which indeed required none. Thus matters stood with Florence on the morning when she was going home, gladly, to her old secluded life.

Doctor and Mrs. Blimber, accompanied (much against his will) by their valued charge, Master Barnet, were already gone back to Brighton, where that young gentleman and his fellow-pilgrims to Parnassus were then, no doubt, in the continual resumption of their studies. The holiday time was past and over; most of the juvenile guests at the villa had taken their departure; and Florence's long visit was come to an end.

There was one guest, however, albeit not resident within the house, who had been very constant in his attention to the family, and who still remained devoted to them. This was Mr. Toots, who after renewing, some weeks ago, the acquaintance he had had the happiness of forming with Skettles Junior, on the night when he burst the Blimberian bonds and soared into freedom with his ring on, called regularly every other day, and left a perfect pack of cards at the hall-door; so many indeed, that the ceremony was quite a deal on the part of Mr. Toots, and a hand at whist on the part of the servant.

Mr. Toots, likewise, with the bold and happy idea of preventing the family from forgetting him (but there is reason to suppose that this expedient originated in the teeming brain of the Chicken), had established a six-oared cutter, manned by aquatic friends of the Chicken's and steered by that illustrious character in person, who wore a bright red fireman's coat for the purpose, and concealed the perpetual black eye with which he was afflicted, beneath a green shade. Previous to the institution of this equipage, Mr. Toots sounded the Chicken on a hypothetical case, as, supposing the Chicken to be enamoured of a young lady named Mary, and to have conceived the intention of starting a boat of his own, what would he call that boat? The Chicken replied, with divers strong asseverations, that he would either christen it Poll or The Chicken's Delight. Improving on this idea, Mr. Toots, after deep study and the exercise of much invention, resolved to call his boat The Toots's Joy, as a delicate compliment to Florence, of which no man knowing the parties, could possibly miss the appreciation.

Stretched on a crimson cushion in his gallant bark, with his shoes in the air, Mr. Toots, in the exercise of his project, had come up the river, day after day, and week after week, and had flitted to and fro, near Sir Barnet's garden, and had caused his crew to cut across and across the river at sharp angles, for his better exhibition to any lookers-out from Sir Barnet's windows, and had had such evolutions performed by The Toots's Joy as had filled all the neighbouring part of the water-side with astonishment. But whenever he saw any one in Sir Barnet's garden on the brink of the river, Mr. Toots always feigned to be passing there, by a combination of coincidences of the most singular and unlikely description.

'How are you, Toots?' Sir Barnet would say, waving his hand from the lawn, while the artful Chicken steered close in shore.

'How de do, Sir Barnet?' Mr. Toots would answer. 'What a surprising thing that I should see *you* here!'

Mr. Toots in his sagacity, always said this, as if instead of that being Sir Barnet's house, it were some deserted edifice on the banks of the Nile, or Ganges.

'I never was so surprised!' Mr. Toots would exclaim.—'Is Miss Dombey there?'

Whereupon Florence would appear, perhaps.

'Oh, Diogenes is quite well, Miss Dombey,' Mr. Toots would cry. 'I called to ask this morning.'

'Thank you very much!' the pleasant voice of Florence would reply.

'Won't you come ashore, Toots?' Sir Barnet would say then. 'Come! you 're in no hurry. Come and see us.'

'Oh it 's of no consequence, thank you!' Mr. Toots would blushingly rejoin. 'I thought Miss Dombey might like to know, that 's all. Good-bye!' And poor Mr. Toots, who was dying to accept the invitation, but hadn't the courage to do it, signed to the Chicken, with an aching heart, and away went the Joy, cleaving the water like an arrow.

The Joy was lying in a state of extraordinary splendour, at the garden steps, on the morning of Florence's departure. When she went downstairs to take leave, after her talk with Susan, she found Mr. Toots awaiting her in the drawing-room.

'Oh, how de do, Miss Dombey?' said the stricken Toots, always dreadfully disconcerted when the desire of his heart was gained, and he was speaking to her; 'thank you, I'm very well indeed, I hope you 're the same, so was Diogenes yesterday.'

'You are very kind,' said Florence.

'Thank you, it 's of no consequence,' retorted Mr. Toots. 'I thought perhaps you wouldn't mind, in this fine weather, coming home by water, Miss Dombey. There 's plenty of room in the boat for your maid.'

'I am very much obliged to you,' said Florence, hesitating. 'I really am—but I would rather not.'

'Oh, it 's of no consequence,' retorted Mr. Toots. 'Good morning!'

'Won't you wait and see Lady Skettles?' asked Florence, kindly.

'Oh no, thank you,' returned Mr. Toots, 'it 's of no consequence at all.'

So shy was Mr. Toots on such occasions, and so flurried! But Lady Skettles entering at the moment, Mr. Toots was suddenly seized with a passion for asking her how she did, and hoping she was very well; nor could Mr. Toots by any possibility leave off shaking hands with her, until Sir Barnet appeared: to whom he immediately clung with the tenacity of desperation.

'We are losing, to-day, Toots,' said Sir Barnet, turning towards Florence, 'the light of our house, I assure you.'

'Oh, it 's of no conseq— I mean yes, to be sure,' faltered the embarrassed Toots. 'Good morning!'

Notwithstanding the emphatic nature of this farewell, Mr. Toots, instead of going away, stood leering about him, vacantly. Florence, to relieve him, bade adieu, with many thanks, to Lady Skettles, and gave her arm to Sir Barnet.

'May I beg of you, my dear Miss Dombey,' said her host, as he conducted her to the carriage, 'to present my best compliments to your dear papa?'

It was distressing to Florence to receive the commission, for she felt as if she were imposing on Sir Barnet, by allowing him to believe that a kindness rendered to her, was rendered to her father. As she could not explain, however, she bowed her head and thanked him; and again she thought that the dull home, free from such embarrassments, and such reminders of her sorrow, was her natural and best retreat.

Such of her late friends and companions as were yet remaining at the villa, came running from within, and from the garden to say good-bye. They were all attached to her, and very earnest in taking leave of her. Even the household were sorry for her going, and the servants came nodding and curtseying round the carriage door. As Florence looked round on the kind faces, and saw among them those of Sir Barnet and his lady, and of Mr. Toots, who was chuckling and staring at her from a distance, she was reminded of the night when Paul and she had come from Doctor Blimber's: and when the carriage drove away, her face was wet with tears.

Sorrowful tears. but tears of consolation, too; for

all the softer memories connected with the dull old house to which she was returning made it dear to her, as they rose up. How long it seemed since she had wandered through the silent rooms: since she had last crept, softly and afraid, into those her father occupied: since she had felt the solemn but yet soothing influence of the beloved dead in every action of her daily life! This new farewell reminded her, besides, of her parting with poor Walter: of his looks and words that night: and of the gracious blending she had noticed in him, of tenderness for those he left behind, with courage and high spirit. His little history was associated with the old house too, and gave it a new claim and hold upon her heart.

Even Susan Nipper softened towards the home of so many years, as they were on their way towards it. Gloomy as it was, and rigid justice as she rendered to its gloom, she forgave it a great deal. 'I shall be glad to see it again, I don't deny, miss,' said the Nipper. 'There ain't much in it to boast of, but I wouldn't have it burnt or pulled down, neither!'

'You'll be glad to go through the old rooms, won't you, Susan?' said Florence, smiling.

'Well, miss,' returned the Nipper, softening more and more towards the house, as they approached it nearer, 'I won't deny but what I shall, though I shall hate 'em again to-morrow, very likely.'

Florence felt that, for her, there was greater peace within it than elsewhere. It was better and easier to keep her secret shut up there, among the tall dark walls, than to carry it abroad into the light, and try to hide it from a crowd of happy eyes. It was better to pursue the study of her loving heart, alone, and find no new discouragements in loving hearts about her. It was easier to hope, and pray, and love on, all uncared for, yet with constancy and patience, in the tranquil sanctuary of such remembrances: although it mouldered, rusted, and decayed about her: than in a new scene, let its gaiety be what it would. She welcomed back her old enchanted dream of life, and longed for the old dark door to close upon her, once again.

Full of such thoughts, they turned into the long and sombre street. Florence was not on that side of the carriage which was nearest to her home, and as the distance lessened between them and it, she looked out of her window for the children over the way.

She was thus engaged, when an exclamation from Susan caused her to turn quickly round.

'Why, gracious me!' cried Susan, breathless, 'where 's our house!'

'Our house!' said Florence.

Susan, drawing in her head from the window, thrust it out again, drew it in again as the carriage stopped, and stared at her mistress in amazement.

There was a labyrinth of scaffolding raised all round the house from the basement to the roof. Loads of bricks and stones, and heaps of mortar, and piles of wood, blocked up half the width and length of the broad street at the side. Ladders were raised against the walls: labourers were climbing up and down; men were at work upon the steps of the scaffolding; painters and decorators were busy inside; great rolls of ornamental paper were being delivered from a cart at the door; an upholsterer's waggon also stopped the way; no furniture was to be seen through the gaping and broken windows in any of the rooms; nothing but workmen, and the implements of their several trades, swarming from the kitchens to the garrets. Inside and outside alike: bricklayers, painters, carpenters, masons: hammer, hod, brush, pickaxe, saw, and trowel: all at work together, in full chorus.

Florence descended from the coach, half doubting if it were, or could be the right house, until she recognised Towlinson, with a sunburnt face, standing at the door to receive her.

'There is nothing the matter?' inquired Florence.

'Oh no, miss.'

'There are great alterations going on.'

'Yes, miss, great alterations,' said Towlinson.

Florence passed him as if she were in a dream, and hurried upstairs. The garish light was in the long-darkened drawing-room, and there were steps and platforms, and men in paper caps, in the high places. Her mother's picture was gone with the rest of the moveables, and on the mark where it had been, was scrawled in chalk, 'this room in-panel. Green and gold.' The staircase was a labyrinth of posts and planks like the outside of the house, and a whole Olympus of plumbers and glaziers was reclining in various attitudes, on the skylight. Her own room was not yet touched within, but there were beams and boards raised against it without, baulking the daylight. She went up swiftly to that other bedroom, where the little bed was; and a dark giant of a man with a pipe in his mouth, and his head tied up in a pocket-handkerchief, was staring in at the window.

It was here that Susan Nipper, who had been in quest of Florence, found her, and said, would she go downstairs to her papa, who wished to speak to her.

'At home! and wishing to speak to me!' cried Florence, trembling.

Susan, who was infinitely wore distraught than Florence herself, repeated her errand; and Florence, pale and agitated, hurried down again, without a moment's hesitation. She thought upon the way down, would she dare to kiss him? The longing of her heart resolved her, and she thought she would.

Her father might have heard that heart beat, when it came into his presence. One instant, and it would have beat against his breast—

But he was not alone. There were two ladies there; and Florence stopped. Striving so hard with her emotion, that if her brute friend Di had not burst in and overwhelmed her with his caresses as a welcome home—at which one of the ladies gave a little scream, and that diverted her attention from herself—she would have swooned upon the floor.

'Florence,' said her father, putting out his hand: so stiffly that it held her off: 'how do you do?'

Florence took the hand between her own and putting it timidly to her lips, yielded to its withdrawal. It touched the door in shutting it, with quite as much endearment as it had touched her.

'What dog is that?' said Mr. Dombey, displeased.

'It is a dog, papa—from Brighton.'

'Well!' said Mr. Dombey; and a cloud passed over his face, for he understood her.

'He is very good-tempered,' said Florence, addressing herself with her natural grace and sweetness to the two lady strangers. 'He is only glad to see me. Pray forgive him.'

She saw in the glance they interchanged, that the lady who had screamed, and who was seated, was old; and that the other lady, who stood near her papa, was very beautiful, and of an elegant figure.

'Mrs. Skewton,' said her father, turning to the first, and holding out his hand, 'this is my daughter Florence.'

'Charming, I am sure,' observed the lady, putting up her glass. 'So natural! My darling Florence, you must kiss me, if you please.'

Florence having done so, turned towards the other lady, by whom her father stood waiting.

'Edith,' said Mr. Dombey, 'this is my daughter Florence. Florence, this lady will soon be your mamma.'

Florence started, and looked up at the beautiful face in a conflict of emotions, among which the tears that name awakened, struggled for a moment with surprise, interest, admiration, and an indefinable sort of fear. Then she cried out, 'Oh, papa, may you be happy! may you be very, very happy all your life!' and then fell weeping on the lady's bosom.

There was a short silence. The beautiful lady, who at first had seemed to hesitate whether or no she should advance to Florence, held her to her breast, and pressed the hand with which she clasped her, close about her waist, as if to reassure her and comfort her. Not one word passed the lady's lips. She bent her head down over Florence, and she kissed her on the cheek, but she said no word.

'Shall we go on through the rooms,' said Mr. Dombey, 'and see how our workmen are doing? Pray allow me, my dear madam.'

He said this in offering his arm to Mrs. Skewton, who had been looking at Florence through her glass, as though picturing to herself what she might be made, by the infusion—from her own copious storehouse, no doubt—of a little more Heart and Nature. Florence was still sobbing on the lady's breast, and holding to her, when Mr. Dombey was heard to say from the conservatory—

'Let us ask Edith. Dear me, where is she?'

'Edith, my dear!' cried Mrs. Skewton, 'where are you? Looking for Mr. Dombey somewhere, I know. We are here, my love.'

The beautiful lady released her hold of Florence, and pressing her lips once more upon her face, withdrew hurriedly, and joined them. Florence remained standing in the same place: happy, sorry, joyful, and in tears, she knew not how, or how long, but all at once: when her new mamma came back, and took her in her arms again.

'Florence,' said the lady, hurriedly, and looking into her face with great earnestness. 'You will not begin by hating me?'

'By hating you, mamma?' cried Florence, winding her arm round her neck, and returning the look.

'Hush! Begin by thinking well of me,' said the beautiful lady. 'Begin by believing that I will try to make you happy, and that I am prepared to love you, Florence. Good-bye. We shall meet again soon. Good-bye. Don't stay here, now.'

Again she pressed her to her breast—she had spoken in a rapid manner, but firmly—and Florence saw her rejoin them in the other room.

And now Florence began to hope that she would learn from her new and beautiful mamma, how to gain her father's love; and in her sleep that night, in her lost old home, her own mamma smiled radiantly upon the hope, and blessed it. Dreaming Florence!

# CHAPTER XXIX

## THE OPENING OF THE EYES OF MRS. CHICK

Miss Tox, all unconscious of any such rare appearances in connection with Mr. Dombey's house, as scaffolding and ladders, and men with their heads tied up in pocket-handkerchiefs, glaring in at the windows like flying genii or strange birds,—having breakfasted one morning at about this eventful period of time, on her customary viands; to wit, one French roll rasped, one egg new laid (or warranted to be), and one little pot of tea, wherein was infused one little silver scoopful of that herb on behalf of Miss Tox, and one little silver scoopful on behalf of the teapot—a flight of fancy in which good housekeepers delight; went upstairs to set forth the Bird Waltz on the harpsichord, to water and arrange the plants, to dust the nick-nacks, and according to her daily custom, to make her little drawing-room the garland of Princess's Place.

Miss Tox endued herself with the pair of ancient gloves, like dead leaves, in which she was accustomed to perform these avocations—hidden from human sight at other times in a table drawer—and went methodically to work; beginning with the Bird Waltz; passing, by a natural association of ideas, to her bird—a very high-shouldered canary, stricken in years, and much rumpled, but a piercing singer, as Princess's Place well knew; taking, next in order, the little china ornaments, paper fly-cages, and so forth; and coming round, in good time, to the plants, which generally required to be snipped here and there with a pair of scissors, for some botanical reason that was very powerful with Miss Tox.

Miss Tox was slow in coming to the plants, this morning. The weather was warm, the wind southerly; and there was a sigh of the summer time in Princess's Place, that turned Miss Tox's thoughts upon the country. The pot-boy attached to the Princess's Arms had come out with a can and trickled water, in a flowing pattern, all over Princess's Place, and it gave the weedy ground a fresh scent—quite a growing scent, Miss Tox said. There was a tiny blink of sun peeping in from the great street round the corner, and the smoky sparrows hopped over it and back again, brightening as they passed: or bathed in it, like a stream, and became glorified sparrows, unconnected with chimneys. Legends in praise of ginger beer, with pictorial representations of thirsty customers submerged in the effervescence, or stunned by the flying corks, were conspicuous in the window of the Princess's Arms. They were making late hay, somewhere out of town; and though the fragrance had a long way to come, and many counter-fragrances to contend with among the dwellings of the poor (may God reward the worthy gentlemen who stickle for the Plague as part and parcel of the wisdom of our ancestors, and who do their little best to keep those dwellings miserable!), yet it was wafted faintly into Princess's Place, whispering of Nature and her wholesome air, as such things will, even unto prisoners and captives, and those who are desolate and oppressed, in very spite of aldermen and knights to boot: at whose sage nod—and how they nod!—the rolling world stands still!

Miss Tox sat down upon the window-seat, and thought of her good papa deceased—Mr. Tox, of the Customs Department of the public service; and of her childhood, passed at a sea-port, among a considerable quantity of cold tar, and some rusticity.

She fell into a softened remembrance of meadows, in old time, gleaming with buttercups, like so many inverted firmaments of golden stars; and how she had made chains of dandelion-stalks for youthful vowers of eternal constancy, dressed chiefly in nankeen; and how soon those fetters had withered and broken.

Sitting on the window-seat, and looking out upon the sparrows and the blink of sun, Miss Tox thought likewise of her good mamma deceased—sister to the owner of the powdered head and pigtail—of her virtues and her rheumatism. And when a man with bulgy legs, and a rough voice, and a heavy basket on his head that crushed his hat into a mere black muffin, came crying flowers down Princess's Place, making his timid little roots of daisies shudder in the vibration of every yell he gave, as though he had been an ogre, hawking little children, summer recollections were so strong upon Miss Tox, that she shook her head, and murmured she would be comparatively old before she knew it—which seemed likely.

In her pensive mood, Miss Tox's thoughts went wandering on Mr. Dombey's track; probably because the major had returned home to his lodgings opposite, and had just bowed to her from his window. What other reason could Miss Tox have for connecting Mr. Dombey with her summer days and dandelion fetters? Was he more cheerful? thought Miss Tox. Was he reconciled to the decrees of fate? Would he ever marry again? and if yes, whom? What sort of person now?

A flush—it was warm weather—overspread Miss Tox's face, as, while entertaining these meditations, she turned her head, and was surprised by the reflection of her thoughtful image in the chimney-glass. Another flush succeeded when she saw a little carriage drive into Princess's Place, and make straight for her own door. Miss Tox arose, took up her scissors hastily, and so coming, at last, to the plants, was very busy with them when Mrs. Chick entered the room.

'How is my sweetest friend?' exclaimed Miss Tox, with open arms.

A little stateliness was mingled with Miss Tox's sweetest friend's demeanour, but she kissed Miss Tox, and said, 'Lucretia, thank you, I am pretty well. I hope you are the same. Hem!'

Mrs. Chick was labouring under a peculiar little monosyllabic cough; a sort of primer, or easy introduction to the art of coughing.

'You call very early, and how kind that is, my dear!' pursued Miss Tox. 'Now, have you breakfasted?'

'Thank you, Lucretia,' said Mrs. Chick, 'I have. I took an early breakfast'—the good lady seemed curious on the subject of Princess's Place, and looked all round it as she spoke, 'with my brother, who has come home.'

'He is better, I trust, my love,' faltered Miss Tox.

'He is greatly better, thank you. Hem!'

'My dear Louisa must be careful of that cough,' remarked Miss Tox.

'It 's nothing,' returned Mrs. Chick. 'It 's merely change of weather. We must expect change.'

'Of weather?' asked Miss Tox, in her simplicity.

'Of everything,' returned Mrs. Chick. 'Of course we must. It 's a world of change. Any one would surprise me very much, Lucretia, and would greatly alter my opinion of their understanding, if they attempted to contradict or evade what is so perfectly evident. Change!' exclaimed Mrs. Chick, with severe philosophy. 'Why, my gracious me, what is there that does *not* change? even the silkworm, who I am sure might be supposed not to trouble itself about such subjects, changes into all sorts of unexpected things continually.'

'My Louisa,' said the mild Miss Tox, 'is ever happy in her illustrations.'

'You are so kind, Lucretia,' returned Mrs. Chick, a little softened, 'as to say so, and to think so, I believe. I hope neither of us may ever have any cause to lessen our opinion of the other, Lucretia.'

'I am sure of it,' returned Miss Tox.

Mrs. Chick coughed as before, and drew lines on the carpet with the ivory end of her parasol. Miss Tox, who had experience of her fair friend, and knew that under the pressure of any slight fatigue or vexation she was prone to a discursive kind of irritability, availed herself of the pause, to change the subject.

'Pardon me, my dear Louisa,' said Miss Tox, 'but have I caught sight of the manly form of Mr. Chick in the carriage?'

'He is there,' said Mrs. Chick, 'but pray leave him there. He has his newspaper, and would be quite contented for the next two hours. Go on with your flowers, Lucretia, and allow me to sit here and rest.'

'My Louisa knows,' observed Miss Tox, 'that between friends like ourselves, any approach to ceremony would be out of the question. Therefore—' Therefore Miss Tox finished the sentence, not in words but action; and putting on her gloves again, which she had taken off, and arming herself once more with her scissors, began to snip and clip among the leaves with microscopic industry.

'Florence has returned home also,' said Mrs. Chick, after sitting silent for some time, with her head on one side, and her parasol sketching on the floor; 'and really Florence is a great deal too old now, to continue to lead that solitary life to which she has been accustomed. Of course she is. There can be no doubt about it. I should have very little respect, indeed, for anybody who could advocate a different opinion. Whatever my wishes might be, I *could not* respect them. We cannot command our feelings to such an extent as that.'

Miss Tox assented, without being particular as to the intelligibility of the proposition.

'If she 's a strange girl,' said Mrs. Chick, 'and if my brother Paul cannot feel perfectly comfortable in her society, after all the sad things that have happened, and all the terrible disappointments that have been undergone, then, what is the reply? That he must make an effort. That he is bound to make an effort. We have always been a family remarkable for effort. Paul is at the head of the family; almost the only representative of it left—for what am I—*I* am of no consequence—'

'My dearest love,' remonstrated Miss Tox.

Mrs. Chick dried her eyes, which were for the moment, overflowing; and proceeded—

'And consequently he is more than ever bound to make an effort. And though his having done so, comes upon me with a sort of shock—for mine is a very weak and foolish nature; which is anything but a blessing I am sure; I often wish my heart was a marble slab, or a paving stone—'

'My sweet Louisa,' remonstrated Miss Tox again.

'Still, it is a triumph to me to know that he is so true to himself, and to his name of Dombey; although, of course, I always knew he would be. I only hope,' said Mrs. Chick, after a pause, 'that she may be worthy of the name too.'

Miss Tox filled a little green watering-pot from a jug, and happening to look up when she had done so, was so surprised by the amount of expression Mrs.

Chick had conveyed into her face, and was bestowing upon her, that she put the little watering-pot on the table for the present, and sat down near it.

'My dear Louisa,' said Miss Tox, 'will it be the least satisfaction to you, if I venture to observe in reference to that remark, that I, as a humble individual, think your sweet niece in every way most promising?'

'What do you mean, Lucretia?' returned Mrs. Chick, with increased stateliness of manner. 'To what remark of mine, my dear, do you refer?'

'Her being worthy of her name, my love,' replied Miss Tox.

'If,' said Mrs. Chick, with solemn patience, 'I have not expressed myself with clearness, Lucretia, the fault of course is mine. There is, perhaps, no reason why I should express myself at all, except the intimacy that has subsisted between us, and which I very much hope, Lucretia—confidently hope—nothing will occur to disturb. Because, why should I do anything else? There is no reason; it would be absurd. But I wish to express myself clearly, Lucretia; and therefore to go back to that remark, I must beg to say that it was not intended to relate to Florence, in any way.'

'Indeed!' returned Miss Tox.

'No,' said Mrs. Chick shortly and decisively.

'Pardon me, my dear,' rejoined her meek friend; 'but I cannot have understood it. I fear I am dull.'

Mrs. Chick looked round the room and over the way; at the plants, at the bird, at the watering-pot, at almost everything within view, except Miss Tox; and finally dropping her glance upon Miss Tox, for a moment on its way to the ground, said, looking meanwhile with elevated eyebrows at the carpet—

'When I speak, Lucretia, of her being worthy of

the name, I speak of my brother Paul's second wife. I believe I have already said, in effect, if not in the very words I now use, that it is his intention to marry a second wife.'

Miss Tox left her seat in a hurry, and returned to her plants; clipping among the stems and leaves, with as little favour as a barber working at so many pauper heads of hair.

'Whether she will be fully sensible of the distinction conferred upon her,' said Mrs. Chick, in a lofty tone, 'is quite another question. I hope she may be. We are bound to think well of one another in this world, and I hope she may be. I have not been advised with myself. If I had been advised with, I have no doubt my advice would have been cavalierly received, and therefore it is infinitely better as it is. I much prefer it as it is.'

Miss Tox, with head bent down, still clipped among the plants. Mrs. Chick, with energetic shakings of her own head from time to time, continued to hold forth, as if in defiance of somebody.

'If my brother Paul had consulted with me, which he sometimes does—or rather, sometimes used to do; for he will naturally do that no more now, and this is a circumstance which I regard as a relief from responsibility,' said Mrs. Chick, hysterically, 'for I thank Heaven I am not jealous—' here Mrs. Chick again shed tears; 'if my brother Paul had come to me, and had said, "Louisa, what kind of qualities would you advise me to look out for, in a wife?" I should certainly have answered, "Paul, you must have family, you must have beauty, you must have dignity, you must have connection." Those are the words I should have used. You might have led me to the block immediately afterwards,' said Mrs. Chick, as if that consequence were highly probable, 'but I should have used them. I should have said, "Paul! You to marry a second time without family! You to marry without beauty! You to marry without dignity! You to marry without connection! There is nobody in the world, not mad, who could dream of daring to entertain such a preposterous idea!"'

Miss Tox stopped clipping; and with her head among the plants, listened attentively. Perhaps Miss Tox thought there was hope in this exordium, and the warmth of Mrs. Chick.

'I should have adopted this course of argument,' pursued the discreet lady, 'because I trust I am not a fool. I make no claim to be considered a person of superior intellect—though I believe some people have been extraordinary enough to consider me so; one so little humoured as I am, would very soon be disabused of any such notion; but I trust I am not a downright fool. And to tell ME,' said Mrs. Chick with ineffable disdain, 'that my brother Paul Dombey could ever contemplate the possibility of uniting himself to anybody—I don't care who'—she was more sharp and emphatic in that short clause than in any other part of her discourse—'not possessing these requisites, would be to insult what understanding I *have* got, as much as if I was to be told that I was born and bred an elephant, which I *may* be told next,' said Mrs. Chick, with resignation. 'It wouldn't surprise me at all. I expect it.'

In the moment's silence that ensued, Miss Tox's scissors gave a feeble clip or two: but Miss Tox's face was still invisible, and Miss Tox's morning gown was agitated. Mrs. Chick looked sideways at her, through the intervening plants, and went on to say, in a tone of bland conviction, and as one dwelling on a point of fact that hardly required to be stated—

'Therefore, of course my brother Paul has done what was to be expected of him, and what anybody might have foreseen he would do, if he entered the marriage state again. I confess it takes me rather by surprise, however gratifying; because when Paul went out of town I had no idea at all that he would form any attachment out of town, and he certainly had no attachment when he left here. However, it seems to be extremely desirable in every point of view. I have no doubt the mother is a most genteel and elegant creature, and I have no right whatever to dispute the policy of her living with them: which is Paul's affair, not mine—and as to Paul's choice, herself, I have only seen her picture yet, but that is beautiful indeed. Her name is beautiful too,' said Mrs. Chick, shaking her head with energy, and arranging herself in her chair; 'Edith is at once uncommon, as it strikes me, and distinguished. Consequently, Lucretia, I have no doubt you will be happy to hear that the marriage is to take place immediately—of course, you will': great emphasis again: 'and that you are delighted with this change in the condition of my brother, who has shown you a great deal of pleasant attention at various times.'

Miss Tox made no verbal answer, but took up the little watering-pot with a trembling hand, and looked vacantly round as if considering what article of furniture would be improved by the contents. The room door opening at this crisis of Miss Tox's feelings, she started, laughed aloud, and fell into the arms of the person entering; happily insensible alike of Mrs. Chick's indignant countenance, and of the major at his window over the way, who had his double-barrelled eye-glass in full action, and whose face and figure were dilated with Mephistophelean joy.

Not so the expatriated native, amazed supporter of Miss Tox's swooning form, who, coming straight upstairs, with a polite inquiry touching Miss Tox's health (in exact pursuance of the major's malicious instructions), had accidentally arrived in the very nick of time to catch the delicate burden in his arms, and to receive the contents of the little watering-pot in his shoe; both of which circumstances, coupled with his consciousness of being closely watched by the wrathful major, who had threatened the usual penalty in regard of every bone in his skin in case of any failure, combined to render him a moving spectacle of mental and bodily distress.

For some moments, this afflicted foreigner remained clasping Miss Tox to his heart, with an energy of action in remarkable opposition to his disconcerted face, while that poor lady trickled slowly down upon him the very last sprinklings of the little watering-pot, as if he were a delicate exotic (which indeed he was), and might be almost expected to blow while the gentle rain descended. Mrs. Chick, at length recovering sufficient presence of mind to interpose, commanded him to drop Miss Tox upon the sofa and withdraw; and the exile promptly obeying, she applied herself to promote Miss Tox's recovery.

But none of that gentle concern which usually characterises the daughters of Eve in their tending of each other; none of that freemasonry in fainting, by which they are generally bound together in a mysterious bond of sisterhood; was visible in Mrs. Chick's demeanour. Rather like the executioner who restores the victim to sensation previous to proceeding with the torture (or was wont to do so, in the good old times for which all true men wear perpetual mourning), did Mrs. Chick administer the smelling-bottle, the slapping on the hands, the dashing of cold water on the face, and the other proved remedies. And when, at length, Miss Tox opened her eyes, and gradually became restored to animation and consciousness, Mrs. Chick drew off as from a criminal, and reversing the precedent of the murdered king of Denmark, regarded her more in anger than in sorrow.

'Lucretia!' said Mrs. Chick. 'I will not attempt to disguise what I feel. My eyes are opened, all at once. I wouldn't have believed this, if a saint had told it to me.'

'I am foolish to give way to faintness,' Miss Tox faltered. 'I shall be better presently.'

'You will be better presently, Lucretia!' repeated Mrs. Chick, with exceeding scorn. 'Do you suppose I am blind? Do you imagine I am in my second childhood? No, Lucretia! I am obliged to you!'

Miss Tox directed an imploring, helpless kind of look towards her friend, and put her handkerchief before her face.

'If any one had told me this yesterday,' said Mrs. Chick, with majesty, 'or even half an hour ago, I should have been tempted, I almost believe, to strike them to the earth. Lucretia Tox, my eyes are opened to you all at once. The scales': here Mrs. Chick cast down an imaginary pair, such as are commonly used in grocers' shops: 'have fallen from my sight. The blindness of my confidence is past, Lucretia. It has been abused and played upon, and evasion is quite out of the question now, I assure you.'

'Oh! to what do you allude so cruelly, my love?' asked Miss Tox, through her tears.

'Lucretia,' said Mrs. Chick, 'ask your own heart.

I must entreat you not to address me by any such familiar terms as you have just used, if you please. I have some self-respect left, though you may think otherwise.'

'Oh, Louisa!' cried Miss Tox. 'How can you speak to me like that?'

'How can I speak to you like that?' retorted Mrs. Chick, who, in default of having any particular argument to sustain herself upon, relied principally on such repetitions for her most withering effects. 'Like that! You may well say like that, indeed!'

Miss Tox sobbed pitifully.

'The idea!' said Mrs. Chick, 'of your having basked at my brother's fireside, like a serpent, and wound yourself, through me, almost into his confidence, Lucretia, that you might, in secret, entertain designs upon him, and dare to aspire to contemplate the possibility of his uniting himself to *you!* Why, it is an idea,' said Mrs. Chick, with sarcastic dignity, 'the absurdity of which almost relieves its treachery.'

'Pray, Louisa,' urged Miss Tox, 'do not say such dreadful things.'

'Dreadful things!' repeated Mrs. Chick. 'Dreadful things! Is it not a fact, Lucretia, that you have just now been unable to command your feelings even before me, whose eyes you had so completely closed?'

'I have made no complaint,' sobbed Miss Tox. 'I have said nothing. If I have been a little overpowered by your news, Louisa, and have ever had any lingering thought that Mr. Dombey was inclined to be particular towards me, surely *you* will not condemn me.'

'She is going to say,' said Mrs. Chick, addressing herself to the whole of the furniture, in a comprehensive glance of resignation and appeal, 'she is going to say—I know it—that I have encouraged her!'

'I don't wish to exchange reproaches, dear Louisa,' sobbed Miss Tox. 'Nor do I wish to complain. But, in my own defence—'

'Yes,' cried Mrs. Chick, looking round the room with a prophetic smile, 'that 's what she 's going to say. I knew it. You had better say it. Say it openly! Be open, Lucretia Tox,' said Mrs. Chick, with desperate sternness, 'whatever you are.'

'In my own defence,' faltered Miss Tox, 'and only in my own defence against your unkind words, my dear Louisa, I would merely ask you if you haven't often favoured such a fancy, and even said it might happen, for anything we could tell?'

'There is a point,' said Mrs. Chick, rising, not as if she were going to stop at the floor, but as if she were about to soar up, high, into her native skies, 'beyond which endurance becomes ridiculous, if not culpable. I can bear much; but not too much. What spell was on me when I came into this house this day, I don't know; but I had a presentiment—a dark presentiment,' said Mrs. Chick, with a shiver, 'that something was going to happen. Well may I have had that foreboding, Lucretia, when my confidence of many years is destroyed in an instant, when my eyes are opened all at once, and when I find you revealed in your true colours. Lucretia, I have been mistaken in you. It is better for us both that this subject should end here. I wish you well, and I shall ever wish you well. But, as an individual who desires to be true to herself in her own poor position, whatever that position may be, or may not be—and as the sister of my brother—and as the sister-in-law of my brother's wife—and as a connection by marriage of my brother's wife's mother—may I be permitted to add, as a Dombey?—I can wish you nothing else but good morning.'

These words, delivered with cutting suavity, tempered and chastened by a lofty air of moral rectitude, carried the speaker to the door. There she inclined her head in a ghostly and statue-like manner, and so withdrew to her carriage, to seek comfort and consolation in the arms of Mr. Chick her lord.

Figuratively speaking, that is to say; for the arms of Mr. Chick were full of his newspaper. Neither did that gentleman address his eyes towards his wife otherwise than by stealth. Neither did he offer any consolation whatever. In short, he sat reading, and humming fag ends of tunes, and sometimes glancing furtively at her without delivering himself of a word, good, bad, or indifferent.

In the meantime Mrs. Chick sat swelling and bridling, and tossing her head, as if she were still repeating that solemn formula of farewell to Lucretia Tox. At length, she said aloud, 'Oh the extent to which her eyes had been opened that day!'

'To which your eyes have been opened, my dear!' repeated Mr. Chick.

'Oh, don't talk to me!' said Mrs. Chick. 'If you can bear to see me in this state, and not ask me what the matter is, you had better hold your tongue for ever.'

'What *is* the matter, my dear?' asked Mr. Chick.

'To think,' said Mrs. Chick, in a state of soliloquy, 'that she should ever have conceived the base idea of connecting herself with our family by a marriage with Paul! To think that when she was playing at horses with that dear child who is now in his grave—I never liked it at the time—she should have been hiding such a double-faced design! I wonder she was never afraid that something would happen to her. She is fortunate if nothing does.'

'I really thought, my dear,' said Mr. Chick slowly,

after rubbing the bridge of his nose for some time with his newspaper, 'that you had gone on the same tack yourself, all along, until this morning; and had thought it would be a convenient thing enough, if it could have been brought about.'

Mrs. Chick instantly burst into tears, and told Mr. Chick that if he wished to trample upon her with his boots, he had better do it.

'But with Lucretia Tox I have done,' said Mrs. Chick, after abandoning herself to her feelings for some minutes, to Mr. Chick's great terror. 'I can bear to resign Paul's confidence in favour of one who, I hope and trust, may be deserving of it, and with whom he has a perfect right to replace poor Fanny if he chooses; I can bear to be informed, in Paul's cool manner, of such a change in his plans, and never to be consulted until all is settled and determined; but deceit I can *not* bear, and with Lucretia Tox I have done. It is better as it is,' said Mrs. Chick, piously; 'much better. It would have been a long time before I could have accommodated myself comfortably with her, after this; and I really don't know, as Paul is going to be very grand, and these are people of condition, that she would have been quite presentable, and might not have compromised myself. There 's a providence in everything; everything works for the best; I have been tried to-day, but, upon the whole, I don't regret it.'

In which Christian spirit, Mrs. Chick dried her eyes, and smoothed her lap, and sat as became a person calm under a great wrong. Mr. Chick, feeling his unworthiness no doubt, took an early opportunity of being set down at a street-corner and walking away, whistling, with his shoulders very much raised, and his hands in his pockets.

While poor excommunicated Miss Tox, who, if she

were a fawner and toad-eater, was at least an honest and a constant one, and had ever borne a faithful friendship towards her impeacher, and had been truly absorbed and swallowed up in devotion to the magnificence of Mr. Dombey—while poor excommunicated Miss Tox watered her plants with her tears, and felt that it was winter in Princess's Place.

## CHAPTER XXX

### THE INTERVAL BEFORE THE MARRIAGE

ALTHOUGH the enchanted house was no more, and the working world had broken into it, and was hammering and crashing and tramping up and down stairs all day long, keeping Diogenes in an incessant paroxysm of barking, from sunrise to sunset—evidently convinced that his enemy had got the better of him at last, and was then sacking the premises in triumphant defiance—there was, at first, no other great change in the method of Florence's life. At night, when the workpeople went away, the house was dreary and deserted again; and Florence, listening to their voices echoing through the hall and staircase as they departed, pictured to herself the cheerful homes to which they were returning, and the children who were waiting for them, and was glad to think that they were merry and well pleased to go.

She welcomed back the evening silence as an old friend, but it came now with an altered face, and looked more kindly on her. Fresh hope was in it. The beautiful lady who had soothed and caressed her, in the very room in which her heart had been so wrung, was a spirit of promise to her. Soft shadows of the bright life dawning, when her father's affection should be gradually won, and all, or much should be restored, of what she had lost on the dark day when a mother's love had faded with a mother's last breath on her cheek, moved about her in the twilight and were welcome company. Peeping at the rosy children her neighbours, it was a new and precious sensation to think that they might soon speak together and know each other; when she would not fear, as of old, to show herself before them, lest they should be grieved to see her in her black dress sitting there alone!

In her thoughts of her new mother, and in the love and trust overflowing her pure heart towards her, Florence loved her own dead mother more and more. She had no fear of setting up a rival in her breast. The new flower sprang from the deep-planted and long-cherished root, she knew. Every gentle word that had fallen from the lips of the beautiful lady, sounded to Florence like an echo of the voice long hushed and silent. How could she love that memory less for living tenderness, when it was her memory of all parental tenderness and love!

Florence was, one day, sitting reading in her room, and thinking of the lady and her promised visit soon—for her book turned on a kindred subject—when, raising her eyes, she saw her standing in the doorway.

'Mamma!' cried Florence, joyfully meeting her. 'Come again!'

'Not mamma yet,' returned the lady, with a serious smile, as she encircled Florence's neck with her arm.

'But very soon to be,' cried Florence.

'Very soon now, Florence; very soon.'

Edith bent her head a little, so as to press the blooming cheek of Florence against her own, and for some few moments remained thus silent. There was something so very tender in her manner, that Florence was even more sensible of it than on the first occasion of their meeting.

She led Florence to a chair beside her, and sat down: Florence looking in her face, quite wondering at its beauty, and willingly leaving her hand in hers.

'Have you been alone, Florence, since I was here last?'

'Oh yes!' smiled Florence, hastily.

She hesitated and cast down her eyes; for her new mamma was very earnest in her look, and the look was intently and thoughtfully fixed upon her face.

'I—I—am used to be alone,' said Florence. 'I don't mind it at all. Di and I pass whole days together, sometimes.' Florence might have said, whole weeks and months.

'Is Di your maid, love?'

'My dog, mamma,' said Florence, laughing. 'Susan is my maid.'

'And these are your rooms,' said Edith, looking round. 'I was not shown these rooms the other day. We must have them improved, Florence. They shall be made the prettiest in the house.'

'If I might change them, mamma,' returned Florence; 'there is one upstairs I should like much better.'

'Is this not high enough, dear girl?' asked Edith, smiling.

'The other was my brother's room,' said Florence, 'and I am very fond of it. I would have spoken to papa about it when I came home, and found the workmen here, and everything changing: but—'

Florence dropped her eyes, lest the same look should make her falter again.

'—but I was afraid it might distress him; and as

you said you would be here again soon, mamma, and are the mistress of everything, I determined to take courage and ask you.'

Edith sat looking at her, with her brilliant eyes intent upon her face, until Florence raising her own, she, in her turn, withdrew her gaze, and turned it on the ground. It was then that Florence thought how different this lady's beauty was, from what she had supposed. She had thought it of a proud and lofty kind; yet her manner was so subdued and gentle, that if she had been of Florence's own age and character, it scarcely could have invited confidence more.

Except when a constrained and singular reserve crept over her; and then she seemed (but Florence hardly understood this, though she could not choose but notice it, and think about it) as if she were humbled before Florence, and ill at ease. When she had said that she was not her mamma yet, and when Florence had called her the mistress of everything there, this change in her was quick and startling; and now, while the eyes of Florence rested on her face, she sat as though she would have shrunk and hidden from her, rather than as one about to love and cherish her, in right of such a near connection.

She gave Florence her ready promise, about her new room, and said she would give directions about it herself. She then asked some questions concerning poor Paul; and when they had sat in conversation for some time, told Florence she had come to take her to her own home.

'We have come to London now, my mother and I,' said Edith, 'and you shall stay with us until I am married. I wish that we should know and trust each other, Florence.'

'You are very kind to me,' said Florence, 'dear mamma. How much I thank you!'

'Let me say now, for it may be the best opportunity,' continued Edith, looking round to see that they were quite alone, and speaking in a lower voice, 'that when I am married, and have gone away for some weeks, I shall be easier at heart if you will come home here. No matter who invites you to stay elsewhere, come home here. It is better to be alone than —what I would say is,' she added, checking herself, 'that I know well you are best at home, dear Florence.'

'I will come home on the very day, mamma.'

'Do so. I rely on that promise. Now, prepare to come with me, dear girl. You will find me downstairs when you are ready.'

Slowly and thoughtfully did Edith wander alone through the mansion of which she was so soon to be the lady: and little heed took she of all the elegance and splendour it began to display. The same indomitable haughtiness of soul, the same proud scorn expressed in eye and lip, the same fierce beauty, only tamed by a sense of its own little worth, and of the little worth of everything around it, went through the grand saloons and halls, that had got loose among the shady trees, and raged and rent themselves. The mimic roses on the walls and floors were set round with sharp thorns, that tore her breast; in every scrap of gold so dazzling to the eye, she saw some hateful atom of her purchase-money; the broad high mirrors showed her, at full length, a woman with a noble quality yet dwelling in her nature, who was too false to her better self, and too debased and lost, to save herself. She believed that all this was so plain, more or less, to all eyes, that she had no resource or power of self-assertion but in pride; and with this pride, which tortured her own heart night and day, she fought her fate out, braved it, and defied it.

Was this the woman whom Florence—an innocent girl, strong only in her earnestness and simple truth—could so impress and quell, that by her side she was another creature, with her tempest of passion hushed, and her very pride itself subdued? Was this the woman who now sat beside her in a carriage, with her arms entwined, and who, while she courted and entreated her to love and trust her, drew her fair head to nestle on her breast, and would have laid down life to shield it from wrong or harm?

Oh, Edith! it were well to die, indeed, at such a time! Better and happier far, perhaps, to die so, Edith, than to live on to the end!

The Honourable Mrs. Skewton, who was thinking of anything rather than of such sentiments—for, like many genteel persons who have existed at various times, she set her face against death altogether, and objected to the mention of any such low and levelling upstart—had borrowed a house in Brook Street, Grosvenor Square, from a stately relative (one of the Feenix brood), who was out of town, and who did not object to lending it, in the handsomest manner, for nuptial purposes, as the loan implied his final release and acquittance from all further loans and gifts to Mrs. Skewton and her daughter. It being necessary for the credit of the family to make a handsome appearance at such a time, Mrs. Skewton, with the assistance of an accommodating tradesman resident in the parish of Mary-le-bone, who lent out all sorts of articles to the nobility and gentry, from a service of plate to an army of footmen, clapped into this house a silver-headed butler (who was charged extra on that account, as having the appearance of an ancient family retainer), two very tall young men in livery, and a select staff of kitchen-servants; so that a legend arose, downstairs, that Withers the page, released at once from his numerous household duties, and from the propulsion of the wheeled-chair (inconsistent with the metropolis), had been several times observed to rub his eyes and pinch his limbs, as if he misdoubted his having overslept himself at the Leamington milkman's, and being still in a celestial dream. A variety of requisites in plate and china being also conveyed to the same establishment from the same convenient source, with several miscellaneous articles, including a neat chariot and a pair of bays, Mrs. Skewton cushioned herself on the principal sofa, in the Cleopatra attitude, and held her court in fair state.

'And how,' said Mrs. Skewton, on the entrance of her daughter and her charge, 'is my charming Florence? You must come and kiss me, Florence, if you please, my love.'

Florence was timidly stooping to pick out a place in the white part of Mrs. Skewton's face, when that lady presented her ear, and relieved her of her difficulty.

'Edith, my dear,' said Mrs. Skewton, 'positively, I —stand a little more in the light, my sweetest Florence, for a moment.'

Florence blushingly complied.

'You don't remember, dearest Edith,' said her mother, 'what you were when you were about the same age as our exceedingly precious Florence, or a few years younger?'

'I have long forgotten, mother.'

'For positively, my dear,' said Mrs. Skewton, 'I do think that I see a decided resemblance to what you were then, in our extremely fascinating young friend. And it shows,' said Mrs. Skewton, in a lower voice, which conveyed her opinion that Florence was in a very unfinished state, 'what cultivation will do.'

'It does, indeed,' was Edith's stern reply.

Her mother eyed her sharply for a moment, and feeling herself on unsafe ground, said, as a diversion—

'My charming Florence, you must come and kiss me once more, if you please, my love.'

Florence complied, of course, and again imprinted her lips on Mrs. Skewton's ear.

'And you have heard, no doubt, my darling pet,' said Mrs. Skewton, detaining her hand, 'that your papa, whom we all perfectly adore and dote upon, is to be married to my dearest Edith this day week.'

'I knew it would be very soon,' returned Florence, 'but not exactly when.'

'My darling Edith,' urged her mother, gaily, 'is it possible you have not told Florence?'

'Why should I tell Florence?' she returned, so suddenly and harshly, that Florence could scarcely believe it was the same voice.

Mrs. Skewton then told Florence, as another and safer diversion, that her father was coming to dinner, and that he would no doubt be charmingly surprised to see her; as he had spoken last night of dressing in the City, and had known nothing of Edith's design, the execution of which, according to Mrs. Skewton's expectation, would throw him into a perfect ecstasy. Florence was troubled to hear this; and her distress became so keen, as the dinner-hour approached, that if she had known how to frame an entreaty to be suffered to return home, without involving her father in her explanation, she would have hurried back on foot, bareheaded, breathless, and alone, rather than incur the risk of meeting his displeasure.

As the time drew nearer, she could hardly breathe. She dared not approach a window, lest he should see her from the street. She dared not go upstairs to hide her emotion, lest, in passing out at the door, she should meet him unexpectedly; besides which dread, she felt as though she never could come back again if she were summoned to his presence. In this conflict of her fears, she was sitting by Cleopatra's couch, endeavouring to understand and to reply to the bald discourse of that lady, when she heard his foot upon the stair.

'I hear him now!' cried Florence, starting. 'He is coming!'

Cleopatra, who in her juvenility was always playfully disposed, and who in her self-engrossment did not trouble herself about the nature of this agitation, pushed Florence behind her couch, and dropped a shawl over her, preparatory to giving Mr. Dombey a rapture of surprise. It was so quickly done, that in a moment Florence heard his awful step in the room.

He saluted his intended mother-in-law, and his intended bride. The strange sound of his voice thrilled through the whole frame of his child.

'My dear Dombey,' said Cleopatra, 'come here and tell me how your pretty Florence is.'

'Florence is very well,' said Mr. Dombey, advancing towards the couch.

'At home?'

'At home,' said Mr. Dombey.

'My dear Dombey,' returned Cleopatra, with bewitching vivacity; 'now are you sure you are not deceiving me? I don't know what my dearest Edith will say to me when I make such a declaration, but upon my honour I am afraid you are the falsest of men, my dear Dombey.'

Though he had been; and had been detected on the spot, in the most enormous falsehood that was ever said or done; he could hardly have been more disconcerted than he was, when Mrs. Skewton plucked the shawl away, and Florence, pale and trembling, rose before him like a ghost. He had not yet recovered his presence of mind, when Florence had run up to him, clasped her hands round his neck, kissed his face, and hurried out of the room. He looked round as if to refer the matter to somebody else, but Edith had gone after Florence, instantly.

'Now, confess, my dear Dombey,' said Mrs. Skewton, giving him her hand, 'that you never were more surprised and pleased in your life.'

'I never was more surprised,' said Mr. Dombey.

'Nor pleased, my dearest Dombey?' returned Mrs. Skewton, holding up her fan.

'I—yes, I am exceedingly glad to meet Florence here,' said Mr. Dombey. He appeared to consider gravely about it for a moment, and then said, more decidedly, 'Yes, I really am very glad indeed to meet Florence here.'

'You wonder how she comes here?' said Mrs. Skewton, 'don't you?'

'Edith, perhaps—' suggested Mr. Dombey.

'Ah! wicked guesser!' replied Cleopatra, shaking her head. 'Ah! cunning, cunning man! One shouldn't tell these things; your sex, my dear Dombey, are so vain, and so apt to abuse our weaknesses; but you know my open soul—very well; immediately.'

This was addressed to one of the very tall young men who announced dinner.

'But Edith, my dear Dombey,' she continued in a whisper, 'when she cannot have you near her—and as I tell her, she cannot expect that always—will at least have near her something or somebody belonging to you. Well, how extremely natural that is! And in this spirit, nothing would keep her from riding off to-day to fetch our darling Florence. Well, how excessively charming that is!'

As she waited for an answer, Mr. Dombey answered, 'Eminently so.'

'Bless you, my dear Dombey, for that proof of heart!' cried Cleopatra, squeezing his hand. 'But I am growing too serious! Take me downstairs, like an angel, and let us see what these people intend to give us for dinner. Bless you, dear Dombey!'

Cleopatra skipping off her couch with tolerable briskness, after the last benediction, Mr. Dombey took her arm in his and led her ceremoniously downstairs; one of the very tall young men on hire, whose organ of veneration was imperfectly developed, thrusting his tongue into his cheek, for the entertainment of the other very tall young man on hire, as the couple turned into the dining-room.

Florence and Edith were already there, and sitting side by side. Florence would have risen when her father entered, to resign her chair to him; but Edith openly put her hand upon her arm, and Mr. Dombey took an opposite place at the round table.

The conversation was almost entirely sustained by Mrs. Skewton. Florence hardly dared to raise her eyes, lest they should reveal the traces of tears; far less dared to speak; and Edith never uttered one word, unless in answer to a question. Verily, Cleopatra worked hard, for the establishment that was so nearly clutched; and verily it should have been a rich one to reward her!

'And so your preparations are nearly finished at last, my dear Dombey?' said Cleopatra, when the dessert was put upon the table, and the silver-headed butler had withdrawn. 'Even the lawyers' preparations!'

'Yes, madam,' replied Mr. Dombey; 'the deed of settlement, the professional gentlemen inform me, is now ready, and as I was mentioning to you, Edith has only to do us the favour to suggest her own time for its execution.'

Edith sat like a handsome statue; as cold, as silent, and as still.

'My dearest love,' said Cleopatra, 'do you hear what Mr. Dombey says? Ah, my dear Dombey!' aside to that gentleman, 'How her absence, as the time approaches, reminds me of the days, when that most agreeable of creatures, her papa, was in your situation!'

'I have nothing to suggest. It shall be when you please,' said Edith, scarcely looking over the table at Mr. Dombey.

'To-morrow!' suggested Mr. Dombey.

'If you please.'

'Or would next day,' said Mr. Dombey, 'suit your engagements better?'

'I have no engagements. I am always at your disposal. Let it be when you like.'

'No engagements, my dear Edith!' remonstrated her mother, 'when you are in a most terrible state of flurry all day long, and have a thousand and one appointments with all sorts of tradespeople!'

'They are of your making,' returned Edith, turning on her with a slight contraction of her brow. 'You and Mr. Dombey can arrange between you.'

'Very true indeed, my love, and most considerate of you!' said Cleopatra. 'My darling Florence, you must really come and kiss me once more, if you please, my dear!'

Singular coincidence, that these gushes of interest in Florence hurried Cleopatra away from almost every dialogue in which Edith had a share, however trifling! Florence had certainly never undergone so much embracing, and perhaps had never been, unconsciously, so useful in her life.

Mr. Dombey was far from quarrelling, in his own breast, with the manner of his beautiful betrothed. He had that good reason for sympathy with haughtiness and coldness, which is found in a fellow-feeling. It flattered him to think how these deferred to him, in Edith's case, and seemed to have no will apart from his. It flattered him to picture to himself, this proud and stately woman doing the honours of his house, and chilling his guests after his own manner. The dignity of Dombey and Son would be heightened and maintained, indeed, in such hands.

So thought Mr. Dombey, when he was left alone at the dining-table, and mused upon his past and future fortunes: finding no uncongeniality in an air of scant and gloomy state that pervaded the room, in colour a dark brown, with black hatchments of pictures blotching the walls, and twenty-four black chairs, with almost as many nails in them as so many coffins, waiting like mutes, upon the threshold of the Turkey carpet; and two exhausted negroes holding up two withered branches of candelabra on the sideboard, and a musty smell prevailing as if the ashes of ten thousand dinners were entombed in the sarcophagus below it. The owner of the house lived much abroad; the air of England seldom agreed long with a member of the Feenix family; and the room had gradually put itself into deeper and still deeper mourning for him, until it was become so funereal as to want nothing but a body in it to be quite complete.

No bad representation of the body, for the nonce, in his unbending form, if not in his attitude, Mr. Dombey looked down into the cold depths of the dead sea of mahogany on which the fruit dishes and decanters lay at anchor: as if the subjects of his thoughts were rising towards the surface one by one, and plunging down again. Edith was there in all her majesty of brow and figure; and close to her came Florence, with her timid head turned to him, as it had been, for an instant, when she left the room; and Edith's eyes upon her, and Edith's hand put out protectingly. A little figure in a low arm-chair came springing next into the light, and looked upon him wonderingly, with its bright eyes and its old-young face, gleaming as in the flickering of an evening fire. Again came Florence close upon it, and absorbed his whole attention. Whether as a fore-doomed difficulty and disappointment to him; whether as a rival who had crossed him in his way, and might again; whether as his child, of whom, in his successful wooing, he could stoop to think, as claiming, at such a time, to be no more estranged; or whether as a hint to him that the mere appearance of caring for his own blood should be maintained in his new relations; he best knew. Indifferently well, perhaps, at best; for marriage company and marriage altars, and ambitious scenes—still blotted here and there with Florence—always Florence—turned up so fast, and so confusedly, that he rose, and went upstairs to escape them.

It was quite late at night before candles were brought; for at present they made Mrs. Skewton's head ache, she complained; and in the meantime Florence and Mrs. Skewton talked together (Cleopatra being very anxious to keep her close to herself), or Florence touched the piano softly for Mrs. Skewton's delight; to make no mention of a few occasions in the course of the evening, when that affectionate lady was impelled to solicit another kiss, and which always happened after Edith had said anything. They were not many, however, for Edith sat apart by an open window during the whole time (in spite of her mother's fears that she would take cold), and remained there until Mr. Dombey took leave. He was serenely gracious to Florence when he did so; and Florence went to bed in a room within Edith's, so happy and hopeful, that she thought of her late self as if it were some other poor deserted girl who was to be pitied for her sorrow; and in her pity, sobbed herself to sleep.

The week fled fast. There were drives to milliners, dressmakers, jewellers, lawyers, florists, pastry-cooks; and Florence was always of the party. Florence was to go to the wedding. Florence was to cast off her mourning, and to wear a brilliant dress on the occasion. The milliner's intentions on the subject of this dress—the milliner was a Frenchwoman, and greatly resembled Mrs. Skewton—were so chaste and elegant, that Mrs. Skewton bespoke one like it for herself. The milliner said it would become her to admiration, and that all the world would take her for the young lady's sister.

The week fled faster. Edith looked at nothing and cared for nothing. Her rich dresses came home, and were tried on, and were loudly commended by Mrs. Skewton and the milliners, were put away without a word from her. Mrs. Skewton made their plans for every day, and executed them. Sometimes Edith sat in the carriage when they went to make purchases; sometimes, when it was absolutely necessary, she went into the shops. But Mrs. Skewton conducted the whole business, whatever it happened to be; and Edith looked on as uninterested and with as much apparent indifference as if she had no concern in it. Florence might perhaps have thought she was haughty and listless, but that she was never so to her. So Florence quenched her wonder in her gratitude whenever it broke out, and soon subdued it.

The week fled faster. It had nearly winged its flight away. The last night of the week, the night before the marriage was come. In the dark room—for Mrs. Skewton's head was no better yet, though she expected to recover permanently to-morrow—were that lady, Edith, and Mr. Dombey. Edith was at her open window looking out into the street; Mr. Dombey and Cleopatra were talking softly on the sofa. It was growing late; and Florence being fatigued, had gone to bed.

'My dear Dombey,' said Cleopatra, 'you will leave me Florence to-morrow, when you deprive me of my sweetest Edith.'

Mr. Dombey said he would, with pleasure.

'To have her about me, here, while you are both at Paris, and to think that, at her age, I am assisting in the formation of her mind, my dear Dombey,' said Cleopatra, 'will be a perfect balm to me in the extremely shattered state to which I shall be reduced.'

Edith turned her head suddenly. Her listless manner was exchanged, in a moment, to one of burning interest, and, unseen in the darkness, she attended closely to their conversation.

Mr. Dombey would be delighted to leave Florence in such admirable guardianship.

'My dear Dombey,' returned Cleopatra, 'a thousand thanks for your good opinion. I feared you were going, with malice aforethought, as the dreadful lawyers say—those horrid proses!—to condemn me to utter solitude.'

'Why do me so great an injustice, my dear madam?' said Mr. Dombey.

'Because my charming Florence tells me so positively she must go home to-morrow,' returned Cleopatra, 'that I began to be afraid, my dearest Dombey, you were quite a bashaw.'

'I assure you, madam!' said Mr. Dombey, 'I have laid no commands on Florence; and if I had, there are no commands like your wish.'

'My dear Dombey,' replied Cleopatra, 'what a courtier you are! Though I'll not say so, either; for courtiers have no heart, and yours pervades your charming life and character. And are you really going so early, my dear Dombey?'

Oh, indeed! it was late, and Mr. Dombey feared he must.

'Is this a fact, or is it all a dream?' lisped Cleopatra. 'Can I believe, my dearest Dombey, that you are coming back to-morrow morning to deprive me of my sweet companion; my own Edith?'

Mr. Dombey, who was accustomed to take things literally, reminded Mrs. Skewton that they were to meet first at the church.

'The pang,' said Mrs. Skewton, 'of consigning a child, even to you, my dear Dombey, is one of the most excruciating imaginable; and combined with a naturally delicate constitution, and the extreme stupidity of the pastry-cook who has undertaken the breakfast, is almost too much for my poor strength. But I shall rally, my dear Dombey, in the morning; do not fear for me, or be uneasy on my account. Heaven bless you! My dearest Edith!' she cried archly. 'Somebody is going, pet.'

Edith, who had turned her head again towards the window, and whose interest in their conversation had ceased, rose up in her place, but made no advance towards him, and said nothing. Mr. Dombey, with a lofty gallantry adapted to his dignity and the occasion, betook his creaking boots towards her, put her hand to his lips, said, 'To-morrow morning I shall have the happiness of claiming this hand as Mrs. Dombey's,' and bowed himself solemnly out.

Mrs. Skewton rang for candles as soon as the house-door had closed upon him. With the candles appeared her maid, with the juvenile dress that was to delude the world to-morrow. The dress had savage retribution in it, as such dresses ever have, and made her infinitely older and more hideous than her greasy flannel gown. But Mrs. Skewton tried it on with mincing satisfaction; smirked at her cadaverous self in the glass, as she thought of its killing effect upon the major; and suffering her maid to take it off again, and to prepare her for repose, tumbled into ruins like a house of painted cards.

All this time, Edith remained at the dark window looking out into the street. When she and her mother were at last left alone, she moved from it for the first time that evening, and came opposite to her. The yawning, shaking, peevish figure of the mother, with her eyes raised to confront the proud erect form of the daughter, whose glance of fire was bent downward upon her, had a conscious air upon it, that no levity or temper could conceal.

'I am tired to death,' said she. 'You can't be trusted for a moment. You are worse than a child. Child! No child would be half so obstinate and undutiful.'

'Listen to me, mother,' returned Edith, passing these words by with a scorn that would not descend to trifle with them. 'You must remain alone here until I return.'

'Must remain alone here, Edith, until you return!' repeated her mother.

'Or in that name upon which I shall call to-morrow to witness what I do, so falsely, and so shamefully, I swear I will refuse the hand of this man in the church. If I do not, may I fall dead upon the pavement.'

The mother answered with a look of quick alarm, in no degree diminished by the look she met.

'It is enough,' said Edith, steadily, 'that we are what we are. I will have no youth and truth dragged down to my level. I will have no guileless nature undermined, corrupted, and perverted, to amuse the leisure of a world of mothers. You know my meaning. Florence must go home.'

'You are an idiot, Edith,' cried the angry mother. 'Do you expect there can ever be peace for you in that house, till she is married, and away?'

'Ask me, or ask yourself, if I ever expect peace in that house,' said her daughter, 'and you know the answer.'

'And am I to be told to-night, after all my pains and labour, and when you are going, through me, to be rendered independent,' her mother almost shrieked in her passion, while her palsied head shook like a leaf, 'that there is corruption and contagion in me, and that I am not fit company for a girl! What are you, pray? What are you?'

'I have put the question to myself,' said Edith, ashy pale, and pointing to the window, 'more than once when I have been sitting there, and something in the faded likeness of my sex has wandered past outside; and God knows I have met with my reply. Oh mother, mother, if you had but left me to my natural heart when I too was a girl—a younger girl than Florence—how different I might have been!'

Sensible that any show of anger was useless here, her mother restrained herself, and fell a whimpering, and bewailed that she had lived too long, and that her only child had cast her off, and that duty towards parents was forgotten in these evil days, and that she had heard unnatural taunts, and cared for life no longer.

'If one is to go on living through continual scenes like this,' she whined, 'I am sure it would be much better for me to think of some means of putting an end to my existence. Oh! The idea of your being my daughter, Edith, and addressing me in such a strain!'

'Between us, mother,' returned Edith, mournfully, 'the time for mutual reproaches is past.'

'Then why do you revive it?' whimpered her mother. 'You know that you are lacerating me in the cruellest manner. You know how sensitive I am to unkindness. At such a moment, too, when I have so much to think of, and am naturally anxious to appear to the best advantage! I wonder at you, Edith. To make your mother a fright upon your wedding-day.'

Edith bent the same fixed look upon her, as she sobbed and rubbed her eyes; and said in the same low steady voice, which had neither risen nor fallen since she first addressed her, 'I have said that Florence must go home.'

'Let her go!' cried the afflicted and affrighted parent, hastily. 'I am sure I am willing she should go. What is the girl to me?'

'She is so much to me, that rather than communicate, or suffer to be communicated to her, one grain of the evil that is in my breast, mother, I would renounce you, as I would (if you gave me cause) renounce him in the church to-morrow,' replied Edith. 'Leave her alone. She shall not, while I can interpose, be tampered with and tainted by the lessons I have learned. This is no hard condition on this bitter night.'

'If you had proposed it in a filial manner, Edith,'

whined her mother, 'perhaps not; very likely not. But such extremely cutting words—'

'They are past and at an end between us now,' said Edith. 'Take your own way, mother; share as you please in what you have gained; spend, enjoy, make much of it; and be as happy as you will. The object of our lives is won. Henceforth let us wear it silently. My lips are closed upon the past from this hour. I forgive you your part in to-morrow's wickedness. May God forgive my own!'

Without a tremor in her voice, or frame, and passing onward with a foot that set itself upon the neck of every soft emotion, she bade her mother good-night, and repaired to her own room.

But not to rest; for there was no rest in the tumult of her agitation when alone. To and fro, and to and fro, and to and fro again, five hundred times, among the splendid preparations for her adornment on the morrow; with her dark hair shaken down, her dark eyes flashing with a raging light, her broad white bosom red with the cruel grasp of the relentless hand with which she spurned it from her, pacing up and down with an averted head, as if she would avoid the sight of her own fair person, and divorce herself from its companionship. Thus, in the dead time of the night before her bridal, Edith Granger wrestled with her unquiet spirit, tearless, friendless, silent, proud, and uncomplaining.

At length it happened that she touched the open door which led into the room where Florence lay.

She started, stopped, and looked in.

A light was burning there, and showed her Florence in her bloom of innocence and beauty, fast asleep. Edith held her breath, and felt herself drawn on towards her.

Drawn nearer, nearer, nearer yet; at last, drawn so

near, that stooping down, she pressed her lips to the gentle hand that lay outside the bed, and put it softly to her neck. Its touch was like the prophet's rod of old upon the rock. Her tears sprang forth beneath it, as she sank upon her knees, and laid her aching head and streaming hair upon the pillow by its side.

Thus Edith Granger passed the night before her bridal. Thus the sun found her on her bridal morning.